Blood
and
Treasure

The Douglas Files:
Book Six

Nathan Birr

Beacon Books LLC

Published by BEACON BOOKS, LLC

Cover Images Copyright ©
Boris Diakovsky/Shutterstock.com
Sundraw Photography/Shutterstock.com

ISBN: 978-0-9981813-4-9 (hc)
ISBN: 978-0-9981813-5-6 (sc)

www.nathanbirr.com

Also by Nathan Birr

Overnight Delivery
The Douglas Files: Book One

Three's a Crowd
The Douglas Files: Book Two

All an Illusion
The Douglas Files: Book Three

Shot List
The Douglas Files: Book Four

Chasing the Wind
The Douglas Files: Book Five

Black Male
A Douglas Files Short

WinterKill
A Douglas Files Short

God, Girls, Golf & the Gridiron
(Not Always in That Order) . . . A Love Story

All is Calm?

The Book of Levi

To those who seek the truth,
And to those who safeguard the search . . .
Veritas vos liberabit

Prologue

FLICKERING, DWINDLING CANDLELIGHT reflected off the solemn faces gathered in an undisclosed house in the heart of Jerusalem. They represented the remaining members of the Poor Soldiers of Christ and the Cross of Calvary, known informally as the Knights Calvary. Though other military orders of the day had carried more prestige and bore more power in the Crusader-controlled Kingdom of Jerusalem, recent defeats had weakened them all, and the Knights Calvary found themselves on equal footing with the Knights Templar and Knights Hospitaller. But inter-order rivalries were no longer relevant. Survival—of the order and of all Christendom in the Holy Land—had taken precedence and necessitated this late-night gathering.

Out of hundreds, only five knights of the order remained in Jerusalem. There were other members of the order—squires, burgesses, administrators, a cleric—but many of them had already fled, died as casualties of battle, or succumbed to disease or starvation. The survivors were crowded into the gloomy quarters to see what the leaders of the Knights Calvary would decide.

"We might as well state the facts as they are," Robert of Karmel declared in his booming voice. It easily filled the small house as it emanated from behind a thick beard that covered the knight's face, mouth, and neck. "Jerusalem will fall to Saladin."

There were several exclamations and gasps from those standing behind the knights, and a cry of blasphemy from the lone Knights Calvary cleric remaining in the city. Jacques IV of Aragon, the highest-ranking knight in Jerusalem, silenced everyone by sweeping his piercing brown eyes across the room. He turned them at last to Robert. "That is not certain."

"We will defend it to the death," Leopold II of Acre stated proudly. Several in the crowd echoed him.

"The defense of this city will indeed end in death," Robert growled. "And I will die beside you. But—"

1

"You have no faith in God," the cleric argued, stepping forward to the edge of the table. All five knights turned their attention to him. "Jerusalem, the Holy City, will not fall into the hands of infidels. God, in His sovereignty, will not allow it."

"Was God not sovereign when the Persians captured Jerusalem?" Robert asked. "Or the Muslims after them? Was God not sovereign at Hattin when our ranks were decimated!"

"Blasphemy! God wills—"

"God's will is too often confused with man's desire."

"How dare you speak of things you do not know!" the cleric sputtered. He was about to continue when Jacques called for silence. The room again grew still. Jacques then nodded to the man on his right, the youngest of the remaining knights, Guy Le Fèvre. He was a stark contrast to Robert of Karmel, both with his clean-shaven face and quiet, almost gentle, manner.

He cleared his throat. "Only God knows the ultimate fate of this or any city. But one thing is certain: we face a great opposition in the armies of Saladin. Jerusalem is in grave danger, and whatever our course of action, while hoping and praying for God's deliverance, we must prepare should He withhold His hand."

The cleric again opened his mouth to speak but was silenced by the look of Jacques. He turned to the other three knights, all of whom nodded.

"Agreed," Jacques said. He cut his eyes to the smoldering cleric. "If Jerusalem falls, we must be sure that Saladin does not find it."

"It is clear we must hide it where he will never look," Francis de Jean stated.

"Where in the city will he not look?" Leopold asked.

"Not in the city," Robert said. "We do not know what may happen to the city in the course of battle, nor what Saladin will do once he takes it."

The cleric was nearly beside himself. "This is sacr—"

"Or, for that matter, if we will ever be allowed back to reclaim it."

"Then we must hide it elsewhere," Guy declared.

"Why not return it to France, as originally planned?" Leopold asked.

"Saladin's line is too strong," Robert argued.

"We could take an alternate route."

"And further diminish Jerusalem's already depleted defenses?"

"I thought you said Jerusalem was determined to fall."

"It is, but it will fall with my blood spilt upon its ramparts."

Guy leaned forward. "And what if, God forbid, we were to make an effort to return to France and were captured, and it fell into the hands of Saladin?"

"May it never be," Francis muttered.

A hush fell over the room as the lone candle still burning in the center of the table flickered and threatened to go out.

"Then we're in agreement," Jacques said. "We must hide it, somewhere that will survive any battle, somewhere Saladin will never look, and somewhere from which we can retrieve it when God's favor allows us to do so. And," he said, again turning his eyes to the cleric, "if all our efforts prove unnecessary, we trust God will reward us for our diligence, if not our faith."

"And if we all perish here?" an unrecognized voice piped up. It was youthful, and heads turned to see a young man step out of the darkness. "If our circumstances are as dire as you have all made out—and I do not doubt that they are—we will all meet our death at the hands of the Muslims."

Jacques beckoned the man forward. "Continue."

"If we hide it as you say, will it not just remain hidden throughout the ages?"

"Andre is right," Guy said. "We must take care to ensure that word of our find reaches our High Commander."

"But how?" Francis asked. "We have already said we fear interception by Saladin's forces, and we dare not weaken our numbers here."

"Send me," Andre announced. "I will ride to France with the news."

"As will I," another voice called from the darkness.

Jacques turned from one to the other.

"Send squires?" Guy said. "We could."

"Unless Balian makes them knights," Robert argued.

"Balian of Ibelin can do as he pleases," Jacques said. "I have been entrusted with the oversight of the order in Jerusalem." He looked around. "It is late. Our first priority is deciding upon a suitable place to hide it. Once that is accomplished, we will concern ourselves with how to send word to the High Commander."

Chapter One

JACKSON DOUGLAS'S PHONE rang as Tom Brady began gesturing and barking signals to his offensive line. The ring was a generic chirp, not a ringtone Jackson had assigned to someone he knew and cared about, so he didn't pay it a second thought. It was third-and-eight, and Brady's New England Patriots were driving for a go-ahead score late in the first quarter.

"Aren't you going to get that?" Samantha MacRaney asked from beside him on the loveseat. It had been moved to face directly at her TV, with the coffee table in front of it holding their plates and cups.

"Super Bowl," he said out the side of his mouth, not turning his head or eyes from the screen. Brady took the snap, his eyes surveying the field. As the pocket collapsed around him, he fired a strike into the narrowest of windows, allowing his tight end to make a sliding catch between two defenders and just past the computer-generated yellow line denoting a first down.

Because it kept the defense off balance, and because he could, Brady hurried the offense to the line of scrimmage, ready to run another play. The phone chirped again and was silenced.

"Hello, this is Sam."

Jackson turned to give Sam a "what gives?" look, to which she only smirked. She was not typically a tease but was in one of those moods today. Normally, Jackson didn't mind, but it was a gross invasion of privacy to answer a man's phone during a major sporting event.

Despite the form-fitting comfort of her loveseat, her girl-next-door cuteness, or the fact that they had been sort of dating for the better part of a year, Jackson wouldn't have chosen to watch the Super Bowl with Sam. But Reggie was busy with work, what with owning a popular restaurant on the Santa Monica coastline. Maggie (whom he had also been sort of dating for a year and change), while more likely to be interested in football than Sam, had

4

been consumed with work lately too. And his grandpa, Leroy, hadn't watched a down of NFL football since the Rams moved to St. Louis, leaving Jackson with his fourth choice. What Sam lacked in enthusiasm for the game—she didn't even know who was playing—she made up for with delicious French dip sandwiches, homemade potato skins, fresh fruit with a creamy caramel dip, bruschetta (for the pre-game), and rumors of cherry pie for dessert.

"Just a moment," she said as Jackson turned his eyes back to the TV just in time to see another sliding reception by a Patriot wide receiver, this one in the end zone. As Brady pumped a fist and ran to head butt his receiver, Jackson sighed and turned to Sam with a look that was half sincere exasperation and half for show. Sort of like when she pouted at him with hands on her hips.

He took the phone and stood, pacing around her loveseat while she reached for a few apple slices and settled back into the loveseat.

"This is Jackson."

"Mr. Douglas, my name is Joel Robinson," came the burst of a reply. The voice was slightly high, slightly nasally, but not annoyingly so in either case. And it sounded as if he was standing in the room with Jackson, not on the phone.

"What can I do for you, Joel?" Jackson asked. He had a strict first-name policy with anyone who wasn't proven to be his elder or an elected official.

"I'd like to meet with you to discuss hiring you."

Jackson turned toward the TV as the Patriot kicker booted the extra point through the goalpost, giving New England a 14-7 lead over the Green Bay Packers. Neither team had been stopped yet, and it promised to be a thrilling championship game. Plus, despite her annoying habit of answering other people's phones, he was looking forward to an evening with Sam. Besides that, he'd just wrapped up his last case—one that had him again questioning if he really wanted to be a private investigator for the foreseeable future—two days ago.

"Okay," Jackson said. "I don't charge for an initial conversation, but can you give me a heads up as to what kind of case it is?"

Joel hesitated for just a moment. "Valuables recovery," he said. "I'd rather not go into any more details over the phone."

"That's fair, I suppose."

"I appreciate that your time is precious, but I think you'll agree once you hear what I propose that this will be a highly lucrative deal for you."

Jackson suddenly had that sinking feeling in his gut, the feeling he got when he encountered a used car salesman. Which wasn't that often.

"When would you like to meet?" he asked.

"Time is somewhat of the essence," Joel said. "Are you free this evening?"

Jackson looked at the TV again, showing a slow-motion replay of the Patriots' touchdown. His eyes drifted over to Sam, her blond hair falling onto her shoulders as she hugged her knees in the corner of the loveseat.

"I'm afraid tonight's a no-go," he said, causing her to turn her head with a flutter of blond hair and look at him. "Rest of my week is clear though."

"Tomorrow night?" Joel asked.

"That's fine."

"How about I buy you dinner? For your troubles. Like I said, once you hear what I propose, I think you'll want in. But either way, I'll pick up the check."

There it was again, that feeling that he was getting sold something. Like the time he and Sam had driven to Ventura to hear a timeshare proposition. He'd bought into the idea that he could steal a Caribbean vacation out of the deal, and had persuaded her to come along and pose as his wife so he wouldn't look like a vulture. Two hours later, he had no valid vacation and two sore ears—one from the sales pitch at the timeshare office and one from Sam lecturing him in the car on the way back. He'd commended her for carrying on the nagging wife charade on the ride home, and she had punched his arm into a spasm. But that was off topic.

"That sounds fair," Jackson said.

"Great. Is there any place in particular you prefer?"

"You in the area?"

"Malibu. And I know some great places if you want to make the drive . . . Geoffrey's, Jillian's, Grissini in Agoura Hills has some great Italian. But if there's someplace closer to you, by all means, let me know."

"How about Cameron's in Santa Monica?"

"Cameron's?"

"Right on the beach, about half a mile north of the Pier."

"I can do that," Joel asked. "Is there a dress code?"

Jackson had to smile. "No. No dress code."

"Okay. Does six o'clock work?"

He had nothing on his docket but a virtual Pac-10 Championship and Rose Bowl on his Xbox. "Sure, six works."

"Great. I'll call and make the reservation, and I will see you at six."

"Sounds good."

"Thank you, Mr. Douglas."

"You're welcome," Jackson said, wondering how he was getting thanked for eating a free meal. As the Patriots prepared to kick off, he stuffed the phone into his pocket—and out of Sam's reach—and sat back down on the loveseat. He leaned over and pecked her cheek.

"What was that for?"

"All I had in the fridge for dinner tomorrow was leftover Chinese. Now I get a shrimp-topped steak."

She raised her eyebrows, and he purposely left her wondering. He sat back and watched Aaron Rodgers trot onto the field, unable to shake an unsettling feeling about Joel Robinson. He decided he'd better squeeze some time into his Monday schedule to practice his gentle letdown speech.

*   *   *

Monday, February 4
5:58 p.m.

CAMERON'S WAS actually two restaurants in one. The downstairs was a beachside cantina, with seating inside as well as on the sand under a retractable canopy. The music was lively and the atmosphere festive—especially during warm weather or major sporting events. Upstairs, the music and lighting were softer, the tables and silverware were both swathed in linen, and the wait staff recommended vintage of wine instead of choice of potato.

Jackson seldom ate upstairs. In fact, he ate in the owner's office more than anywhere. Reggie Cameron, the proprietor and occasional head chef, was Jackson's best friend, wingman, and advisor. Once upon a time, six and a half years ago, Jackson had helped Reggie out of a pickle, and it had earned him a lifetime of comped meals. But this time, it felt good not to mooch.

The sun had set, and the air was cool and on the verge of cold as Jackson entered the foyer at Cameron's. It was really more of a landing at street level, with stairs going up to the bistro or down to the beach bar. He climbed to the second story, where the hostess—a pretty blonde named Katie—greeted him with a trademark smile.

"Hi, Jackson."

"Katie. How's it going?"

"It's been a long day."

"I thought you'd be above working nights by now."

"I need the extra cash. You here to see Reggie?"

"No, as a matter of fact, I'm meeting someone."

"A lady someone?" she asked with a teasing grin.

"Would toward that it were."

She frowned, a generation too late to recognize a good Hawkeye-ism.

"What's the name?" she asked.

"Joel Robinson."

She checked a computer screen hidden behind the dais. "Looks like he's already seated. Table ten. Can you find your way?"

"I think I'll manage."

"Enjoy your dinner."

"Enjoy your extra cash."

The modest flirting over, Jackson entered the dining room. A couple dozen tables were situated in a semicircular room and out on the balcony. Table ten was in the middle, near a bank of windows that looked out at the darkened Pacific. During the lunch hour, the view was stunning. At sunset, it could be magical.

Like Jackson had said, there was no official dress code at Cameron's, and he had come in jeans and a button-down shirt. Joel wore a jacket, no tie, and denim pants that looked far too stylish to be called blue jeans. He was sitting, so it was hard to tell, but he looked to be average height and build. Very white skin, short but wispy brown hair, and a pointed nose gave him an academic look. The dinner jacket didn't hurt either.

"Joel? Jackson Douglas," he said, offering his hand.

Joel stood—he *was* average height and build, same as Jackson—and shook it firmly. "It's a pleasure to meet you, Mr. Douglas."

"Please, Jackson."

Joel nodded. "Thank you for agreeing to meet with me."

"Thank you for dinner," Jackson replied as they sat down. Before they could say anything else, a brunette named Amanda brought them water and menus while taking drink orders, announcing the special, and showing every one of her teeth.

"What's good here?" Joel asked when she was gone. He reached for a pair of glasses from the breast pocket of his jacket as he opened his menu.

"Never had anything bad," Jackson said.

"You come here often?" Joel looked up. "Sorry, that sounded like a cheesy pick-up line."

Jackson grinned. "I know the owner."

"Ah. I should have had you pick up the tab," he said, grinning in return and looking back down at his menu.

Jackson quickly picked out his entrée, then studied Joel over his menu. The reading glasses were thin and flimsy, the kind that could be pulled off or on repeatedly—and apparently had been. He wore a class ring on his left hand, gold inlaid with navy and orange, with a white inset V (Virginia?), and cufflinks on a very well-starched peach shirt.

Amanda came and took their orders—Jackson went with shrimp and sirloin, as he'd told Sam—and swept up their menus with a smile. When she was gone, Joel reached for his water. "I have a fascination with new and different kinds of hamburgers," he said, then took a sip. "I've dined at some of the finest restaurants in the world, and what do I get but a hamburger?"

"The Cameron is a good choice," Jackson said.

Joel nodded as he replaced his water. "Well, I'll get right to it. Let me tell you a bit about myself, and then I'll tell you why I want to hire you."

"All right."

"We'll start with what's most important. I'm a born-again, Bible-believing Christian. I know those have become buzzwords—or buzz phrases, I should say—and I don't know that I can prove to you now that I am what I say, but I trust you'll find my actions consistent with that declaration. Anyhow, I did my research before contacting you, and I think we share the same faith. That is one of the primary reasons I sought you out."

Jackson nodded.

"Secondarily, I am a history buff. Always have been. I have a bachelor's from UVA and a Ph.D. from Temple, both in history, which I tell you not to brag but to let you know that I know what I'm talking about, historically speaking. I'm particularly interested in history that affects the world we live in today, but pretty much anything historical gets me going. And I'm afraid I can be a bit nerdy about it at times."

"I'm the same way about the Rams," Jackson said. "I even started a letter-writing campaign to bring them back to L.A."

Joel frowned. "Who would you send such a letter to?"

"Not the governor, apparently. You were saying?"

"Yes. I'm also a one-percenter," Joel said. "My father and grandfather both made big money in Philadelphia real estate. My mother died when I was young, and my father developed brain cancer when I was sixteen. He died my junior year of high school, but not before he put the vast majority of his wealth into a trust that would become mine only when I graduated from college. So I spent my collegiate years waiting tables, delivering pizzas, and manning the college library checkout desk. Three months after graduation, the trust kicked in, and I paid off all my student loans and set aside more than enough to cover three years' tuition at Temple. And I'm still rather flush, as they say."

"I see why you order double fries."

Joel grinned. "That is all preface to say that I don't have a standard job, per se. Rather, I'm a history hunter."

"A history hunter?"

"That's right." Joel tipped his head. "A treasure hunter, only the treasure I hunt isn't always gold and jewels. I work to uncover the past to enlighten the present and future. Schmaltzy, I know, but it looked good on a business card."

Jackson smirked as he took a drink of his tea.

"Now, I won't lie to you. I have recovered some rather valuable pieces of antiquity. I have always turned them over to a museum, but my finder's fees have sustained much of my work and research."

"Do you work alone?"

"No. I have several full-time members of Team Joel, as we call it, and a couple more freelancers with whom I routinely work."

Jackson nodded.

"Anyhow, that's me in a nutshell," Joel said. He reached for his water again. "Unless you have questions, I'll move on to why I want to hire you."

"Go for it."

Joel swallowed and set his cup down. "Now bear with me at the start. I know this is going to sound clichéd."

Jackson nodded again.

Joel glanced around him. Two of the three tables in their immediate vicinity were vacant, and the other was occupied by a middle-aged couple focused on nothing but each other. Still, Joel leaned slightly forward. "How much do you know about the Crusades?"

Somehow, Jackson had known it was coming. The Crusades. The Knights Templar. Solomon's gold, the Holy Grail, wealth untold buried beneath a New York cathedral. It was always the same, and he almost started humming the *Indiana Jones* theme music. But he liked what he knew of Joel so far, so he swallowed any smart-aleck comments and said, "The basics. The Muslims held Jerusalem, the Crusaders took it, Saladin took it back, and the Crusades pretty much petered out after that."

"Not inaccurate. But for the sake of context, let me go through a few more details."

Jackson consented with another nod.

"Pope Urban II called for the First Crusade at the Council of Clermont in 1095, urging European peasants and knights to come to the aid of Christians in the Holy Land who—along with their holy places—were being desecrated by the Islamic Seljuk Turks. Um, his words, not mine."

Yet another nod.

"Nearly a year later, the Crusade was launched, with as many as a hundred thousand knights and peasants and anyone seeking a papal indulgence setting out for the Holy Land. Only a fraction of the original number reached Jerusalem some three years later, where they were resisted by both the Jewish and Muslim inhabitants of the city. The Crusaders—mostly Franks—took the city and established the Kingdom of Jerusalem."

Joel paused to take a drink. "It's somewhat common in the Judeo-Christian world, and perhaps especially so in Christian cultures, to view the Crusaders as 'we' and the Muslims as 'them.' But I have always hesitated to draw such simplistic demarcation lines, simply because I don't know the heart of the individual Crusaders. As far as I'm concerned, a 'Christian' can be just as much an 'infidel' as a Muslim if he is not a true believer in Jesus Christ."

"I agree."

"I try to portray the events of the Crusades objectively and dispassionately, but I'm afraid I sometimes fall into the Western mindset. At any rate, the crusading armies committed great atrocities in Jerusalem, massacring many inhabitants regardless of race or creed. As with so much of history, there are varying viewpoints on how atrocious the Crusaders' actions were, why they were motivated, etcetera. But when all was said and done, the Crusaders had control of Jerusalem, which they held for nearly one hundred years."

"Until Saladin, right?"

Joel nodded. "The Muslims in that part of the world were largely disorganized, fighting amongst themselves, and thus unable to repel the Crusaders. An-Nasir Salah ad-Din Yusuf Ibn Ayyub—or Saladin—became sultan of Syria and Egypt, forming what would be known as the Ayyubid

Dynasty in 1174. With the Muslims united, it was only a matter of time before they set their sights on Jerusalem again.

"Now, depending on who you ask, you'll come up with a number of different reasons for what happened next. But the popular theory is that raids led by Raynald of Châtillon against Muslim caravans prompted Saladin to go on the attack after a dozen years of relatively peaceful coexistence. The Muslims soundly defeated the Crusaders at The Horns of Hattin—near modern-day Tiberias in northern Israel, not far from the Sea of Galilee—on July 4, 1187. Raynald was executed by Saladin himself; Guy of Lusignan, the king of Jerusalem, was captured; and the Crusader army was decimated. Saladin continued to conquer the Kingdom of Jerusalem, and by September, only Tyre and the city of Jerusalem itself remained under Crusader control."

Joel paused to take another drink of water, then resumed. "Jerusalem eventually fell and, whereas the Crusaders a century earlier had killed most of the citizens, Saladin granted the ransomed release of the peasants, refugees, and a few knights remaining in the city."

"Like in *Kingdom of Heaven*."

"Somewhat," Joel said. "But I'd be hesitant in relying on Hollywood for too much historical accuracy."

"Trust me, I spent some time on the fringes of Hollywood. I wouldn't rely on it for anything."

"Saladin's conquest led Pope Gregory VIII to call for the Third Crusade. Led by, among others, Richard the Lionheart of England, the Crusaders made it to the Holy Land. But Richard didn't think he could hold Jerusalem if he captured it and instead negotiated with Saladin for Christian rights to trade with and make pilgrimage to Jerusalem.

"From that point on, the remaining Crusaders were largely unsuccessful. Frederick II, Emperor of the Holy Roman Empire, signed a treaty with Al-Kamil of Egypt in 1228, giving him control over much of Jerusalem and a strip of land from Jerusalem to Acre, on the coast. Sixteen years later, the Muslims razed Jerusalem and expelled the Christians again. By now, we're talking Crusade number six or seven, depending on whom you consult. But for all intents and purposes, the Crusades were over. Jerusalem remained under control of the Mamluks and the Ottomans until quasi-modern times."

Jackson reached for his tea again.

"My apologies if I've bored you," Joel said, "but I wanted to properly set the table."

"I'm not bored." Jackson took a drink and eyed Joel. "Set the table for what?"

"On the phone, I said I wanted your help recovering valuables."

Jackson nodded.

"I assume you've heard of the various monastic and military orders of the day—the Knights Templar, the Knights Hospitaller, and so forth?"

"Yeah."

"Like so much in that period, the merit of these orders is up for debate. While their stated purpose was good, many of their actions and certainly motives were questionable. What isn't up for debate is the existence to this day of numerous legends and rumors of great treasures found or amassed by these knights." Joel looked around him once again before leaning forward. "And this why I seek your help, Jackson. I believe that I am on the threshold of locating one of the greatest Crusader treasures ever."

Chapter Two

6:27 p.m.

AMANDA BROUGHT THEIR dinners while Jackson was still digesting Joel's last statement. A Crusader treasure, really? He'd heard the legends and rumors of course—to a degree. They were usually in the movies or those corny documentaries—the ones with a couple of clips of medieval warfare and a couple more of a guy in a monk's habit sneaking through a tunnel, broken by interviews with professors and authors who looked like they seldom saw the light of the sun (or women), all interspersed with esoteric, dramatic dialogue that ended with no one knowing where the treasure's final resting place was or if it had ever existed to begin with. They made for great late-night, insomnia-fighting TV. But in an upscale Santa Monica bistro while a pretty brunette set a plate of steak and shrimp in front of him, it was hard for Jackson to swallow such a thought.

Or to figure out which question to ask first when Amanda departed.

"Do you, uh, generally pray before meals?" Joel asked.

"A meal of this caliber, I try to give thanks."

"Well, my tab, my blessing."

"That's fair."

Jackson lowered his head, feeling both a little weird for doing so in public and a little ashamed for feeling weird. The feeling was augmented by a long pause before Joel finally spoke. "Our Heavenly Father . . ." He paused again. Jackson opened an eye, sure Amanda was about to return. "We thank You for this evening, for this food, for this opportunity to meet one another and consider what You have before us. Bless this food and our conversation, and all that stems from it. It is in Jesus' name we pray . . . Amen."

"Amen," Jackson said as he opened his eyes. He unfurled his napkin, draping it over his lap, and had his steak knife sawing through perfectly tender sirloin before he remembered Joel had been speaking of Crusader treasure. Jackson nearly asked if he was serious about all this, but one look at

14

the guy confirmed he was. Besides, it would have been an awfully long and pointless con. So he switched to a different query.

"What kind of treasure are we talking? Jack Sparrow's *Isla de Muerta* or some *Da Vinci Code* crap that tries to undermine the gospel?" He finished cutting the first piece of steak, made sure there was also a shrimp on his fork, and gave his taste buds what they had been waiting for since last night. They were not disappointed.

"Certainly not the latter," Joel replied as he lifted the massive, half-pound Cameron Burger to his mouth. "Mmm, that's delicious," he said after swallowing the first bite. He wiped his chin with a napkin. "But to be honest, I'm not entirely sure."

"You don't know what it is?"

"No. I'll explain." He paused to try a few of the sweet potato fries. "Oh, these are really good." He ate another. "As I said, there are lots of legends of Crusader treasure. Some of them are credible; some not so much. I've researched most of them, and I think this one is legit. And as I also said, I think I'm close to locating it."

Jackson swallowed a second bite of steak. "But you don't know what it is?"

"No. Again, bear with me."

"By all means."

"I mentioned the Knights Templar and Knights Hospitaller. They were by far the most famous of the military orders of the day, but they weren't alone. A lesser-known group was The Poor Soldiers of Christ and the Cross of Calvary. Colloquially, they were and are known as the Knights Calvary." He paused for a few more fries. "The order had its origins in France shortly after the Crusaders took Jerusalem. Their intended function was to guard Christian pilgrims in, around, and on the way to Jerusalem or elsewhere in the Holy Land, and to otherwise take up the cross of Christ. Sadly, this often resulted less in Christian service and more in military conquest. But such was the nature of military orders. To this day, to hear Cara tell it."

"Who?"

"One of my team."

"And these Knights Calvary were in Jerusalem until the end?"

"Yes, but barely. Most of them were wiped out at The Horns of Hattin, as was the case for the Crusaders in general. But the survivors returned to Jerusalem to prepare to defend the city against Saladin."

Jackson dug into his garlic mashed potatoes. They weren't bad.

"Saladin laid siege to Jerusalem on September 20, 1187, and Balian of Ibelin surrendered it on October the second."

"Balian. Wasn't that Orlando Bloom in *Kingdom of Heaven?*"

"Yes, but again, that's Hollywood. While the movie is based on a true story, it has a number of historical . . . embellishments."

"But Balian was real?"

"He was. And he was the leader of the defenders of Jerusalem. When he surrendered the city, he and the other inhabitants paid a ransom to Saladin for their freedom. Once it was paid, they were allowed to leave the city. Some of these refugees went to Egypt, others to other cities within Israel, and others back to Europe. All this to say that some years later, a journal was supposedly found, belonging to Jacques IV of Aragon, one of the remaining members of the Knights Calvary who fought and died in Jerusalem."

Jackson couldn't resist. "There's always a journal."

"Well, it was before OneDrive and Dropbox."

Jackson grinned, had another bite of steak, and thus grinned some more.

"The journal was less of a day-by-day recounting of the life of a knight," Joel continued, "and more a last will and testament. I can give you more details later, but the short of it is that several members of the Knights Calvary liberated a Muslim caravan from a raiding party comprised of rogue factions from several other orders. Not entirely altruistic, these knights also liberated some of the caravan's wares, including—according to the journal—a teenage girl's . . . let's call it a hope chest. In this chest, these knights found a treasure, Jacques wrote. He didn't specifically say what it was, but he said it was *'invaluable to our cause.'*"

Jackson watched while Joel had another bite of his burger, savoring every bit of it, so it seemed.

"According to legend, the journal didn't say where the treasure was hidden, but it did give an indication. Jacques quoted a verse from the Gospel of Mark: *'For there is nothing hid, which shall not be made manifest: neither was it made secret, but that it may come abroad.'* That's Mark 4:22, translated from the Latin Vulgate, the Bible Jacques and his fellow knights would have had available to them."

Jackson thought through the verse for a moment. "You think they hid the treasure?"

"Presumably."

"Makes sense if they thought Jerusalem was about to fall, I suppose."

"But that's not all. No one knows where the journal is or even where it has been for centuries, so this is all legend that has been passed down for generations, but the journal apparently references the so-called 'Holy Trinity'—three pieces that will, together, show the way to the Calvary Treasure, as it has become known."

"The 'Holy Trinity'?"

Joel nodded. "The Father, the Son, and the Spirit or Ghost piece."

"Piece. Piece of what?"

"The journal doesn't specify, but it is believed they are three relics or treasures of their own, somehow containing clues that, when jointly assembled, will make that which is hidden *'come abroad.'*"

"Whatever it is," Jackson said.

"Right."

They both ate for a moment, and Amanda came to check on their meals and refill drinks. When she was gone, Joel said, "For centuries, people have been looking for the 'Holy Trinity' while contemplating what the Calvary Treasure itself might be."

"There are no clues?"

"To what the treasure is, no. Not really. People have speculated everything from gold and jewels to various relics and artifacts. But again, Jacques' journal supposedly stated several times how invaluable and priceless the treasure was. So valuable, in fact, that he believed it would enable the Crusaders to finally vanquish the Muslims from the Holy Land."

"According to legend."

"Correct."

"But a legend you believe to be true."

"Also correct."

Jackson sat back, contemplating. Just a hunch, not even worth mentioning, especially since he hadn't read Jacques IV of Aragon's journal. But would a knight refer to gold or jewels as "invaluable" and "priceless"? Didn't that apply to something one couldn't put a price on? Or was he just parsing a dead Frenchman's translated words?

"I first heard about the Calvary Treasure about six years ago from a colleague of mine in France. He believes he has one of the three 'Holy Trinity' pieces."

"He has one?"

Joel nodded and made Jackson wait through another bite of his burger.

"Mmm, that is really good." He wiped his mouth. "He could trace it back through his family to the seventeenth century, but before that, no one knows where it came from."

"What is it?"

"A coffer about the size of a small shoebox, made of cedar, inlaid with gold, and adorned with a . . . figurine, I guess you'd call it, of a leaping lion on one end and an angel waving a sword on the other, both made of gold."

"Sounds like a miniature knock-off of the Ark of the Covenant."

Joel's eyebrows rose. "A number of others have made a similar observation."

"So it's well-known?"

"Moderately, within the right circles, but most only know that it exists or is rumored to exist and a basic description, as I've just given you." He cleared his throat. "What most don't know is that on each of its four sides is a Scripture verse. And the chest itself is locked. Or I should say, it was locked, with a very old—obviously—warded lock. In the late 1100s A.D., it would have been a formidable barrier. Not so much in modern days."

"What's inside the box, anything?"

"Another inscription, this time a rather obscure stanza instead of Scripture verses. It would seem to be describing how to find the treasure from a particular location, but without any mention of the location. Suggesting, of course, the need for the other two pieces."

"How do you know this is part of the 'Holy Trinity'?"

"Three reasons. First, because Philippe—my colleague—says that according to family lore and legend, this box is the Father piece of the 'Holy Trinity.' Not exactly overwhelming proof, I'll grant you. But the lion and angel are also common symbols of the Knights Calvary from its earliest days, representing their protective purpose and also their fierce loyalty and dedication. And lastly, there's a Scripture verse in Latin on the front side of the box."

"Mark 4:22," Jackson said.

Joel smiled. "Very good."

"Any line on the Son and Spirit pieces?"

Joel nodded and took another look around the room. No eavesdroppers. "I believe I know where the other two pieces are."

"You do?"

"Yes. More or less. If you'll excuse my apparent paranoia and mistrust, I'd rather not say more until I know that you're with us."

18

Jackson nodded. "Well, that does bring me to the elephant in the room. What do you want with me?"

"I've done my homework on you, Jackson. As I told you earlier, I believe we share the same faith, which means something to me. I also have spoken to different people who vouch for your character, your cleverness, and your Holmesian powers of deduction."

"Well, now I'm inclined to think you're conning me, Joel, because no one I know would talk about me like that."

"I may have paraphrased their statements," Joel said with a grin.

"Did they also tell you about my baggage?"

"Nevada?"

"For starters."

Joel nodded. "I'm familiar with your career, Jackson. I don't want to give you the impression that I'm passing judgment one way or the other, or that my judgment should matter, but I have no problems with what I've found."

"Fair enough." Jackson speared a shrimp with his fork. "So that's the why me, but why anyone in the first place? Why do you want to hire a P.I.?"

"If the Son and Spirit pieces are anything like the Father piece Philippe owns, merely possessing them will not lead us to the treasure. We'll need to interpret them, decipher the code or crack the riddle or however you prefer to put it. And at least in the case of one of them, some work is left to actually find it, although I have leads. Anyway, from what my research tells me, you're particularly suited for just such a task."

"So you want to hire me to figure out where the treasure is?"

"Simply stated, yes."

Jackson nodded and chewed on a piece of steak.

"My proposal is thus," Joel said. "I'll pay you your daily rate, for however many days our quest lasts. On top of that, I'll pay you five percent of whatever monetary value we recover. That may turn out to be nothing, but it may turn out to be a rather significant finder's fee. And of course, all meals, hotels, flights, and other expenses will be covered."

"That can't be cheap."

"No, not likely. But I am well-funded."

Jackson shook his head. "Why not do all the work, then bring me in? Why pay for me to tag along?"

"It may not be that simple. I prefer to have you in the field, real-time. Being there, I think, will serve you and us quite well."

Jackson took another bite to allow him some more time to think.

"You have another question?" Joel asked.

"I'm wondering what the small print says."

"You think there's a catch?"

"I think I just like to know all the facts up front."

"Certainly fair. All I can tell you, Jackson, is that with any treasure hunt, there is a measure of danger. There might be others pursuing this treasure, although I'm not aware of anyone in particular. There could also be others who don't want the treasure found, although, again, I'm not aware of any such person or group. Other than that, I don't know what else to tell you."

"Isn't this the sort of thing that often takes years of reflection and study before the code is cracked?"

"It can be, yes. My hope is that we can solve it in a timely manner, which is why I want to hire a sleuth like yourself. But if not, then we'll cross that bridge at the appropriate time."

Jackson leaned forward. "Don't get me wrong, but why me again? I mean, surely there are better minds your money could buy—minds that are also sympathetic to your faith."

"Maybe," Joel said. "But I want someone I can trust, and I believe you're that person. I also don't have a lot of time. We'd be looking at starting before the end of the week."

Jackson sat back. "How soon do you need an answer?"

"Whenever you have one," Joel replied. "I don't have a backup plan, Jackson. I did my research, and you're the man I want." He wiped his mouth and set his napkin on the table. "I'll be traveling up and down the coast for the next few days, meeting with donors and wrapping up some details from a previous venture. I'll be back in town Thursday night and wheels up is seven a.m. Friday morning. If I haven't heard from you by then, I'll assume your answer is no."

"Wheels up for where? Can you give me any more?"

Joel hesitated.

"You said you trust me," Jackson said. "I'll shoot straight. I'm intrigued. But I'd prefer to know if wheels are up en route to the Caribbean where you think a ship carrying smuggled Crusader treasure was sunk or to Baghdad to dig through ruins of Saddam's palace."

Joel mulled for a moment. "I suppose that's fair." He took another drink. "I believe one of the pieces is set to go on display at an exhibition in New York City Friday night. And I believe clues to the location of the other can likely be found in or around a Byzantine church in Greece."

"So Greece by way of New York?"

"With a stop in France to see Philippe. And I have an advance team in Greece right now doing some scouting. If that pans out, New York to France to Greece, and from there, wherever the clues lead."

"I appreciate your candor," Jackson said. "If you'll give me just a minute, I have to quickly text TMZ."

It had been a test, to see if Joel was one of those people so intent and obsessed that he couldn't recognize or take a joke. His grin revealed that was not the case.

"Seven a.m. Friday," Jackson said. "Count me in."

Chapter Three

"YOU SURE ABOUT this, J?" Reggie asked from the driver's seat of his black Hummer H3.

Jackson nodded as he looked at his best friend. Reggie was six-three and two-fifty, with faded tats covering much of his dark skin. They represented a past lifetime that didn't fit with the gentle giant Jackson knew. Gentle, yet not always terribly delicate.

"I mean, the last time you went flying around the world, things didn't exactly turn out so peachy."

"They did for the person I went flying around the world for."

"Touché."

Jackson reached to the backseat for his duffel bag.

"Man, you goin' globetrottin' for two weeks and all you got is one duffel bag?"

Two weeks had been Joel's rough estimate when Jackson had called him the previous afternoon to confirm their departure time and location.

"They do have washing machines in Europe," Jackson said. "At least, I assume. I've never been."

"You tell your grandpa you're going?"

"Yeah. Called him last night."

"Sam?"

"Yeah. She's the one who got me into this. Blame her if I end up beheaded in a cave inside a crescent-shaped canyon."

"I'll be sure to do that."

"And before you can ask, I tried calling Maggie too. Had to leave a message." He frowned at the memory, while also checking his duffel's end pocket to make sure he had his passport. His and Maggie's relationship was an unusual one. Excusing their three-month "breakup" the previous fall that hadn't been quite as much of a breakup as he'd thought, they had ebbs and flows. They were currently in an ebb, having hardly seen each other since New Year's. Or did that make it a flow?

"What about Connie?"

Jackson sighed at the mention of his neighbor. "I told her you'd look in on the place."

"I ain't mowin' her lawn for you, man."

"It's February."

Reggie, following Jackson's directions, turned into a parking lot next to a small hangar. "Still no clue what this treasure is?" he asked.

"Sounds like it could be anything from a boatload of gold to one of the apostle's teeth."

"Apostle's teeth?"

Jackson shrugged. "Or a boulder some saint prayed while sitting on or something. They had all sorts of stupid relics back then. What do I care? It's five hundy a day."

"You'd better do some awful good deducin' at that rate, man."

"I just hope I don't run into many French people."

"In France, what are the odds?"

Jackson shook his head. "I really don't like French people."

"Apostle's teeth and disdain for the French. You're sure you're—what did he call it—a Holmesian mind?"

"Holmes was eccentric."

"So are most of the people in asylums, bro."

Reggie coasted to a stop at the end of the parking lot. He craned his neck. "Where exactly do you want me to drop you off?"

"Here's as good a place as any."

Reggie put the gearshift into park. "Seriously, man, be careful. If this treasure is legit, watch your back."

"Only if it's legit?"

"As in real bad dudes might also be after it."

Jackson turned and saw the sincerity in Reggie's dark eyes. He nodded. "I will, Hoss." He reached for his door. "Thanks again for the ride."

"And getting up before the crack of dawn."

"That too."

"You want me to wait in case you get cold feet?"

"Already got 'em."

They slapped hands and Jackson got out of the Hummer. He glanced around for a moment, questioning for the dozenth time since Monday night what he was doing. His recent adventures had merited Reggie's cautious attitude, but it was disconcerting nonetheless.

Shaking off the doubts, Jackson nodded at Reggie through the dark glass of the windshield, hoisted his duffel onto his shoulder, and strode around the corner of the hangar, pretty sure it was the one Joel had indicated. He was convinced when he spotted a Gulfstream parked in front of it. White and sleek—maybe even regal in the pre-dawn light—it was the only jet currently on the apron. That would change. Van Nuys Airport, despite not servicing any commercial airlines, was one of the busiest airports in the world. Celebrities and executives used it for its anonymity and proximity to downtown and other L.A. hotspots.

The jet was parked in front of an open hangar. As Jackson approached, a figure emerged from the shadow of the opening. It only took a moment for Jackson to recognize Joel. He wore khakis and a navy sweater, and his wispy hair was covered by a navy ball cap, emblazoned on the front of which was a thin white V above two crossed orange swords. One of the primary logos for the University of Virginia's sports teams.

"Good morning," Joel called over the idling jet as he offered his hand. It, like the morning air, was cold. "Glad you're along for the journey."

"See the world, solve a riddle," Jackson said with a shrug. "Almost as good as the Navy."

Joel grinned. "Come on, I'll introduce you to my team."

Jackson followed Joel inside the hangar, shaking off unpleasant flashbacks of the last time he'd been inside an airplane hangar. It was empty and massive, with a row of windows and doors lining the far wall. Against the near wall, a small folding table looked minuscule but served its purpose of holding a box of donuts and a drink carrier containing three cups, presumably of coffee. Two people, a man and a woman, stood behind the table.

"Jackson Douglas," Joel said, "I'd like you to meet Cara Tremblay." The woman stood up straight, lifting her eyes from the tablet in her hands. She was short, a touch on the pudgy side, not un-pretty, with thin glasses in front of wide blue eyes. Her blond hair was short and straight, flared at the bottom. She wore jeans and a zipped up hoodie that depicted in contemporary style a red maple leaf.

Cara extended a hand to Jackson, at the same time flicking her head to shake a loose strand of hair from in front of her glasses. "The P.I.?"

"Yeah."

"Cara handles all of our technical and administrative responsibilities," Joel said. "She's a real whiz on a computer, mobile device, or anything technical."

"Nice to meet you," Jackson said.

"You too."

"And this is Rich Hamilton," Joel said, nodding at the man next to her. He too was a little short and pudgy but stood almost at attention compared to Cara's casual posture. Short, gelled brown hair and round, flush cheeks gave him a preppy look. So did his clothes—wrinkle-free khakis and a plaid button-down shirt. Tucked in. His smile revealed perfect teeth, and Jackson noticed manicured fingernails as he shook Rich's hand.

"It's a pleasure to meet you, Jackson."

"You too." He squared him up. "Rich short for Richard?"

A confused frown passed over Rich's light blue eyes. "Yeah, why?"

"Richard 'Rip' Hamilton, Detroit Pistons, 2004. Beat my Lakers."

"I'd offer you my sympathies, but I'm from Grand Rapids."

"Michigan fan?"

"Go Blue."

"Then we're even on account of recent Rose Bowls. Fight on." Jackson winked and pointed at the coffee. "For anybody?"

"Help yourself," Joel said. "Donuts too."

Jackson did, selecting a glazed donut. Breakfast had been rushed cereal to use the last of his milk before leaving.

"Rich helps us with discernment," Joel said.

Jackson frowned, his cup halfway to his mouth. "Discernment. Cultural, linguistic?"

"Not exactly."

"I get visions," Rich said.

Jackson lowered the cup without drinking. "You're a psychic?"

"No," Joel said quickly. "It's not like that. Rich gets visions from God."

Super.

Awesome.

Jackson wondered how far Reggie could have gotten.

"I know that puts some people off," Joel said, "but it's not as crazy as you think. I'll explain more when we're in the air. We should be ready in a few minutes," he said, glancing over his shoulder.

"This is it?" Jackson said. "I thought you said Team Joel would be eight people."

"It is, counting you. We're meeting the rest of the team in New York. And—"

He stopped as a door across the hangar slammed shut. Jackson turned his eyes to see a woman strolling their way. She was tall, fit, and something about her looked familiar. Her gait? The light wasn't great, and she was passing through shadows, but . . .

"Ah," Joel said, "here she is. Our correspondent. Jackson, meet—"

"We've met," Maggie said with a smirk as she stopped beside Joel. "Hiya, Jack."

"Maggie?"

The smirk turned into a grin.

"What . . ." Jackson turned from her to Joel.

"You two know each other?" he asked.

Jackson nodded while Maggie grinned some more.

Joel quickly overcame his surprise. "I hired Maggie to chronicle our search for the Calvary Treasure," he explained. "If this turns out to be the historic discovery I hope it will be, then I want the search recorded for future generations."

"And for legal protection," Cara mumbled.

"I suppose that's true." He looked up. "Everyone ready? Grab a donut, some coffee. Else there's more food and a spacious lavatory onboard."

Joel turned for the plane, followed a pace behind by Cara and then Rich, who first collected the donut box and drink tray, leaving Jackson to stare at Maggie's smirk. Not that he minded looking at Maggie. Her wavy, chestnut hair came to her shoulders, framing a mischievous face. She wore blue jeans and a black, long-sleeve Henley, both of which accentuated her figure. Just physically, she was more than attractive. But it was also her relaxed, playful demeanor and her smart-alecky, witty style that made her almost irresistible.

Maggie winked her eyebrows, Magnum-style. "Let's roll."

She turned and headed for the plane, looking once over her shoulder at him. Jackson sighed, then took a sip of his coffee as he trudged along behind. The Gulfstream looked small from the outside, at least compared to commercial jets, but inside, it was huge. There were half a dozen captain's chairs, a mini-bar, a sofa-sleeper, and a small table and chairs in the back. Upon closer inspection, it wasn't overly plush, maybe a little old, but still far better than riding coach.

Flying did something to Jackson's normally calm stomach, so he chose a window seat to take his mind off his gut. Maggie plopped down in front of him, then promptly turned to look at him around her seat.

"You know the chairs spin, right?" Jackson said.

She ignored him. "Remember the last time we were on a private jet?"

"I do."

"Sorry about that."

"Yeah."

Then just a reporter for the *Los Angeles Times*, Maggie had gotten into trouble while working on an exposé in Mexico. She'd sent a coded message to her colleague Bill, who had talked Jackson into flying down to Acapulco to rescue her. They had succeeded, only to be recaptured aboard the private jet of a supposed ally, Mexican businessman Salvador Delgado. An escape attempt had led to a shootout at thirty-thousand feet, which had left Delgado, his three cronies, and Bill dead. Jackson and Maggie had parachuted into the Mexican desert and wandered back to civilization before ultimately returning to the States so Maggie could write the story that had made her semi-famous in L.A. and earned her a regular column in the *Times*. Not to mention several national accolades. Perhaps the interest in her story from several cable networks and even mention of a movie deal explained why she hadn't been around much lately.

Everyone took their seats—Joel and Rich across the aisle and Cara behind Jackson—and a moment later the pilot introduced himself over the intercom and said they were cleared for departure. Two minutes later, they were airborne. Feeling a little queasy, Jackson watched Greater Los Angeles shrink out his window as Joel's chartered jet ascended over the San Gabriel Mountains and headed over the Mojave Desert. He also nursed his coffee, wondering yet again what he had gotten himself into. That same feeling he'd had in his gut Monday night at Cameron's was back, the feeling that he was getting snowed. Maybe that explained the queasiness.

As soon as the pilot announced that everyone could feel free to move about the cabin, Cara got up and headed to the back of the plane. Rich opened his Bible, somewhere in the middle, and Joel announced that he was going to check a few things with the pilots. Maggie said nothing further, evidently content in her own world. Jackson was itching with questions, but if she wanted to play it cool, he would too.

So he watched the scenery for a while and finished his coffee. By the time Hoover Dam was a speck out his window, his stomach was acclimated to being airborne. Joel was still up front, Rich had his head buried in the Word, and Cara had set up an ops center around the table and chairs. With Maggie still being coy, Jackson decided to try to catch up on some sleep.

"What'd you think of that game Sunday?" Maggie asked as soon as he had closed his eyes.

Jackson slowly opened them. She was kneeling backward in and leaning over her seat, a successful businesswoman of almost thirty still behaving like a girl. It added to her appeal.

"You referring to the Super Bowl or did your Rangers drop the puck on some unheard of satellite channel?"

"My Rangers just happened to blank Philly on Sunday, Mr. Smart-Aleck. A matinee."

"I'm thrilled for you."

Maggie narrowed her right eye. "I meant the Super Bowl."

"I caught it," Jackson answered. Brady had led the Patriots to two touchdowns in the final eight minutes to edge Green Bay 38-35. A real classic. Sam had fallen asleep early in the fourth quarter.

Maggie nodded.

He couldn't hold out any longer. "What are you doing here, Maggie?"

"I'm Team Joel's chronicler," she said with a shrug of her shoulders.

"I know. Why you?"

"Why not?"

Jackson nodded. "I left you a message yesterday."

"I know. I was busy packing."

"You've been busy a lot lately."

"What's that supposed to mean?" she asked, raising one eyebrow.

"Nothing more than what it sounds like."

"Mm-hmm."

Jackson shook his head disarmingly. Rich flipped a page, which was odd because his eyes were closed. Maybe in addition to seeing visions, he could read through his eyelids. Or be edified via osmosis.

"When did Joel call you?" Jackson asked.

"Mmm, about a week ago."

"And you didn't think a 'Hey, Jack, I'm off to find Crusader treasure' call was warranted?"

"I'm sorry, are you my supervisor now?"

"Which reminds me, ol' Walter signed off on another 'story of a lifetime'? Won't your regular readers be disappointed?"

She lowered her chin as she looked at him.

"I'm sorry, Mags. I just get the feeling I'm being sandbagged again."

"Well, if you are, it's not by me. I didn't call because every time I've tried lately, you've been 'working' with some female client. I'm not the only one whose job cramps their social life."

"Yeah, I guess not."

"And I have no idea why Joel picked me. But he's paying well, I had the leave coming, and 'ol' Walter' thought it might be a good story. I had a couple of pre-written fillers for my regular column, so I'm doing this on a semi-freelance basis."

Jackson nodded. "Fair enough."

She turned her head out the window. "Is that the Grand Canyon?"

"Else God just zapped Vegas for its iniquities."

"Cute. You know it's a major chink in the armor of your '*In the beginning, God . . .*' beliefs, don't you?"

"What, the Canyon?"

"Uh-huh."

"Right, because a God who hung the planets and stars in the sky couldn't possibly make a big crack in the ground."

"How do you explain the millions of years' worth of erosion by the Colorado River?"

"How do you explain the hundreds of years' worth of erosion by all the other world's rivers? Is Arizona in an Evolutionary time warp, or is the ground here just really, really hard?" He shook his head. "Does Joel know you're an agnostic?"

"He didn't ask," Maggie said. "Maybe he just wanted an objective mind."

Jackson changed the topic. "So what exactly are you chronicling anyhow? Is this just a diary of our search?"

"Everything," she answered. "I'll journal about the search, summarize the history, authenticate any findings. My first-person recount of Mexico was a big hit, so I figure I'll try the same thing."

"What do you make of it, this Crusader treasure?"

Maggie rested her chin on her arms on the top of her seat. "I don't know. I'm sure all these legends come from something. But whether we'll find it in a couple weeks' time . . ."

"How much do you know?"

"The basics. Knights found an unidentified treasure, hid it, and created three pieces that would lead to it before they died defending Jerusalem. And now Joel knows where those pieces are. You?"

"About the same."

"Well then, the first team briefing should be informative," she said as Joel emerged from the cockpit. "By the way, you should Google carbon dating sometime," she added before slipping back into her seat.

Joel gave Jackson a brief smile on his way back to Cara, and Jackson decided to settle in for a nap again. It took a while, but the drone of the Gulfstream's twin engines eventually lulled him to sleep.

Chapter Four

10:55 a.m. (Central Standard Time)

WHEN JACKSON AWOKE, intermittent clouds partially obscured the Midwestern landscape.

He slowly sat up. Joel was seated across from him, head in a book. Rich and Cara were both eying the same computer screen at the back of the plane. And Maggie sat beside them at the table, staring at her laptop.

Jackson yawned and sat up a little straighter.

"Hey, welcome back to the land of the living," Joel said.

"Where are we?"

"Somewhere over Kansas, I believe. Maybe the Oklahoma panhandle or far eastern New Mexico." He looked at his watch. "We'd better be farther than that."

"We on a tight schedule?"

"The gallery displaying one of the 'Holy Trinity' pieces is set to open tonight at nine. We've got to meet up with the rest of the team, check into our hotel—"

"Eat."

"Right."

"Why tonight?" Jackson asked. "Surely with a treasure this old a day or two won't matter?"

"Likely not, but the piece's presence in this particular collection isn't exactly public news. However, once it's on display, I imagine the clamorers and treasure hunters will come out of the woodwork. I'd rather be ahead of the pack."

Jackson nodded, remembering Reggie's warning to watch his back.

First looking over his shoulder, Jackson leaned a little closer to Joel. "Can I ask you a question?"

Joel folded the page of his book and closed it. "Sure. What's up?"

"Why Maggie?"

"Why not?"

"Funny, that's what she said."

"I did my research on her too, Jackson. She's a very good journalist."

"Yes, she is."

"I didn't know the two of you knew each other though."

"For a couple of years now."

"Small world."

"Can I ask you something else?"

"Anytime."

"You mentioned picking me because we shared the same faith."

"And Maggie doesn't."

Jackson nodded. "Look, I love Maggie. She's great."

"But your private investigator's gut isn't sitting well?"

He grinned. "Something like that."

Joel shifted in his chair, tapping the ends of his fingers against each other. "My father, as I think I mentioned the other night, was a Philadelphia real estate mogul. It can be a nasty business, particularly when you play in the big leagues as Dad did. I remember one year, when I was in junior high, he was accused of some shady bookkeeping. So he called up his chief competitor and asked him if he could borrow his in-house auditor." Joel stopped tapping his fingers and clasped his hands together, resting them in his lap. "I asked him why, and he said he wanted to make sure no one could ever accuse him of cooking the books again."

"So Maggie is here to guard against accusations that you're faking a discovery or something?"

"I want to make sure no one can charge me or my team of being biased. When you're dealing with the Crusades, the Holy Land—the juxtaposition of three major world religions—I don't want anything being tainted by an allegation that we altered history to fit our perspective. And so while I wanted someone who shares my faith to help me solve the Calvary Treasure riddle, I specifically wanted someone who *doesn't* share that faith to record what happens."

Jackson nodded.

"And," Joel said, "Maggie's also here because she is a great investigative reporter."

"You've read her stuff?"

"A small amount. Rich actually did most of the research on her. But I trust him, and what he passed onto me, I liked. She's good. Being as close as you are, I'm sure you know about her Mexi . . . can . . ." His jaw dropped. "Mexico. You're Jack?"

"Guilty."

Joel shook his head. "How did I miss that? Coincidences like that normally ring bells in my head."

"She purposefully kept my full name out of it, and I didn't include my time down there on my résumé either."

"Still, I'm surprised I didn't at least suspect. I guess I had no reason to believe the two of you had a connection." Joel shook his head again.

Once more, Jackson looked over his shoulder before speaking. "Well, for the record, if you want someone who will be hard on a bunch of Christians, you picked the right lady."

Joel returned to his book and Jackson to staring out his window. He watched farm fields and pastures morph into snow-covered farm fields and pastures. Boring, they were also mesmerizing, and slowly gave way to small towns and cities. As they approached what Jackson deemed to be Kansas City, he looked up to see that everyone but Cara was asleep—Rich on the sofa-sleeper, Joel with his reading glasses on top of his head, and Maggie in the seat in front of him. Cara just continued to stare into her computer screen, so Jackson traced the Missouri River out his window. It was his third cross-country flight in the last two months, and the thought that it would be one of their shorter flights on this junket brought back his nausea.

When they crossed another river—it had to be the Mississippi by its size—Jackson could take the boredom no more. He got up to stretch and use the lavatory—Joel was right, it was pretty nice for an airplane. When he returned to his seat, Joel had stirred and was sipping from a glass of orange juice. Jackson leaned over to get his attention before he could return to his book or fall back to sleep and leave Jackson with nothing to do but study farm fields from six miles up.

"Another question for you."

"Of course."

"What do you mean by 'Rich gets visions'? Like, 'dig here' or what?"

Joel turned to where Rich was still asleep on the sofa. "Not exactly." He took a sip of juice and set down his book. "I first met Rich while researching a Lake Erie shipwreck in Detroit. He was leading a Bible study at a church I stopped in; we chatted, had coffee, and a friendship and partnership formed. He shares my interest in history, particularly history as it relates to

Christianity, or any religion for that matter. He's also one of the few people I know who like meticulous research—actually like it."

Jackson raised his eyebrows with the appropriate amount of incredulity.

"Anyhow, Rich explained that since he was very young, he's gotten what he called visions. Sometimes he just gets a vague sense of caution or openness, sometimes the general drift of an upcoming conversation or an opportunity that will come down the pike, and other times a very clear direction regarding an impending decision."

Jackson's gut was at it again, that same general uneasiness he felt when something wasn't quite right. Sixth sense, subconscious, whatever. Imperfect, but nonetheless reliable. But somehow not what Rich claimed to experience, he didn't think.

"How does he get these visions?"

"Like now, when he's napping," Joel said. "He usually takes a couple of naps per day, giving God the opportunity."

"But how does it happen? Is it just a dream or what?"

"I don't know. He says it's sort of like a hazy sense that's suddenly paramount when he awakes."

Jackson pursed his lips.

"I can't explain it," Joel said. "I'm not sure he can either, but you'll have to ask him."

"How does he know they're from God?" Maggie asked.

Jackson leaned slightly forward to confirm she was awake. Because talking wasn't proof enough.

Joel frowned. "As opposed to . . ."

"His subconscious," Maggie answered. "The devil, for that matter."

"Bad chili," Jackson added.

Maggie continued as if he wasn't sitting behind her. "You all believe in the devil, right? Demons. Masquerading as angels of light?"

"I do," Joel answered. He shrugged. "Rich says he can just tell."

"And these visions have helped you find treasures in the past?"

"Not treasures, necessarily. But yes, he's been an instrumental part of our work over the last five years."

"He ever been wrong?" Jackson asked.

"Hard to say. Often times, his visions are pretty vague. We may interpret them to mean something they don't, making them seem wrong. But I can't say for sure."

"Hey, Joel," Cara called.

He turned over his shoulder.

"Ramón has a couple of questions for you."

Jackson frowned. "That the name of her computer, like the Hoff's Kitt?"

"Ramón Estévez, our diplomatic and cultural liaison," Joel said with a grin. "One of the freelancers I mentioned. You'll meet him in New York. Excuse me."

He headed to the back of the plane and Maggie leaned around her seat. "You buy all this vision stuff?"

"Seriously, Mags, the chairs spin."

Biting down on her tongue, she slowly turned the chair to face him, accidentally—or not—kicking him in the shin as she did so. "Happy?"

"It's been so long I'm forgetting what you look like."

This time the kick to his shin was definitely on purpose.

"What was the question?"

"You believe in these visions?" she said with a nod toward Rich.

"I'm skeptical."

Maggie faked a gasp. "Isn't that against being a Bible-believer?"

"We're told to '*test the spirits*.'"

"So what does that mean?"

"Regarding Rich," Jackson said with a glance at the sofa, "I don't know."

"You Christians are sure an odd bunch," Maggie said. "Preaching love and peace and yet going on Crusades to slaughter those who believe differently than you, talking about faith and belief and then doubting someone who says he hears from God. What's up with you?"

"You have an extra side of ornery this morning with your Go-Gurt?"

"Just doing the math."

"Stick to English comp. You're forgetting to carry the one."

With a frown that was either contemplative or angry, Maggie turned her chair back around, leaving Jackson to stare out the window some more. He and Maggie had debated/argued over the merits of the Christian faith a number of times, never really getting anywhere. It always ended with one of them making a smart-aleck comment that made for a good soundbite but didn't really prove anything. And then they agreed to suspend the discussion and enjoy pinball and sliders or something similar.

Joel returned to his seat.

"Everything okay?" Jackson asked.

"Yeah. Just finalizing some details for tonight."

"What exactly is the plan?" Maggie asked, spinning her chair a quarter of the way to face Joel.

"The Mediterranean Exhibition goes on display tonight at Galerie Céleste in Manhattan's West Side. Chelsea, actually. I have it on good authority that one piece of the 'Holy Trinity' is included in the exhibition."

"What's the Mediterranean Exhibition?" Maggie asked.

"A couple months ago, divers discovered a shipwreck off the coast of Cyprus in the Mediterranean Sea. They determined she was a twelfth- or thirteenth-century Italian vessel, and a brass plaque found on her mast identified her as *Ali Della Vittoria*. That is the same name of a ship noted in several ancient mariner records as having departed Acre in 1187, carrying— according to several sources—Crusaders fleeing the Holy Land after defeat at the hand of Saladin." Joel cleared his throat, something Jackson realized he often did. It sounded like a bird preparing to mate or attack, he couldn't tell which.

"It took a while to identify the ship, sort out jurisdiction, and prepare to salvage the ship and recover the cargo," Joel continued. "But three days before Christmas, the first artifact was brought to the surface. In total, almost seventy unique pieces were recovered, along with hundreds of Persian, Egyptian, and Italian coins."

"Quite a discovery," Maggie said.

"Indeed."

"So what's the tie to the 'Holy Trinity' and the Calvary Treasure?" Jackson asked.

"One of the pieces recovered is a lead cross," Joel said, gesturing with his hands to indicate an object about a foot in height and width. "It is engraved with a lion and an angel and with Mark 4:22—same as on Philippe's piece— in addition to several other verses."

"You've seen it?" Maggie asked.

"No. None of this has been released to the public, but an acquaintance of mine works for the museum in Athens that processed the artifacts from the wreck. He knew I had an interest in Crusader-era pieces and alerted me to the find. I probed a little and divulged some specifics. In truth, I know little more than I've just told you, which is enough to make me think the cross is part of the 'Holy Trinity,' most likely the Son piece."

"Which the public will get their first glimpse of tonight," Jackson said.

Joel nodded.

"Who else can put the pieces together? Who else would see this cross and recognize its connection to Philippe's box?"

"I don't know. Philippe told me because he and I are good friends and colleagues, but I'm not the only one to share such a relationship with him. The art world can be very secretive, but also very chatty and prone to gossip. Plus, the presence of my team will no doubt alert anyone else who might suspect the cross's importance that they're likely on the right track."

"Who else knows right now?" Maggie asked.

"I'm not sure if anyone knows for sure what it is."

"Who knows the details of the Mediterranean Exhibition? Who even knows the cross exists?"

"The salvage team, a handful of people at the museum in Athens, select people at the gallery in New York. It's been kept very hush-hush to maximize the appeal when it goes on display."

"Why this gallery?"

"A couple of reasons. For one, Galerie Céleste specializes in historical artwork—not just old art, but art that tells a story. More importantly, the assistant curator of Galerie Céleste has connections throughout the Mediterranean, including Athens, and with the salvage team that recovered the collection. It earned Galerie Céleste the first opportunity to host the exhibit. This collection will travel the world in the next six months, which is why time is somewhat of the essence. Give them an opportunity, and every treasure hunter who's ever dreamed of finding the Calvary Treasure will connect the dots and be looking for it."

"So what do we do?" Maggie asked. "The gallery obviously won't let us take it."

"Oh, good heavens no," Joel said. "But they will let us view it."

"I can memorize pretty good," Jackson said, "but not in Latin."

"I think Cara probably has a digital camera," Maggie said.

"Yes, but photography is often prohibited at these types of exhibitions," Joel said.

"Really?"

He nodded. "It's all about control. If photos of the collection get leaked on the internet, suddenly the exhibition loses its draw."

"Makes sense, I suppose."

"You got a Rosetta Stone on the plane somewhere?" Jackson asked.

"Don't worry about it," Joel answered. "Maggie was on the right track. Cara does have some options for us. I'll explain more when we land."

"Which is when, by the way?"

"We're due in about three local time. In fact, I think I'll check in with our pilots now. Excuse me."

Jackson leaned forward. "Did you see that Templar treasure movie on TV a few years back?"

"I don't think so," Maggie answered.

"Mira Sorvino and that guy who played Cool Breeze on *The Unit?*"

She shook her head and frowned.

"Well, you didn't miss much, but it started with a knight on horseback storming into a New York art gallery."

"Your point?"

"You've heard Joel, worried about everyone else who might be after the treasure."

"You think someone's going to show up on horseback to steal the cross before we can see it?"

"Horseback, no. But I just get that funny feeling we won't be the only ones enjoying the wine and cheese tonight."

"Well, if you're worried, it looks like the visionary is waking up," Maggie said with a nod toward the sofa. "Maybe God revealed the guest list to him."

Chapter Five

3:44 p.m. (Eastern Standard Time)

REMEMBERING HIS LAST trip to the Big Apple, Jackson braced himself for a blast of frigid air as he stepped off the plane at John F. Kennedy International Airport in New York. It didn't come. It might have been a stretch to call the February air balmy, but it was far from cold and bitter. And the sunshine made it feel warmer than the pre-dawn Los Angeles air. Funny, how the sun had just been rising then, and a little over five hours later, it was already low in the southwestern sky.

Joel's chartered jet had not been given a priority landing assignment, and despite making good time across the country, its arrival at JFK had been delayed by half an hour spent in a holding pattern. After landing, the plane had taxied for another fifteen minutes, during which time Cara had checked her watch half a dozen times and mumbled something about M&M's.

"At least we don't have to go through baggage collection," Joel said, holding the door to the terminal for the rest of his team. "The advantage of a private flight."

"That and knees that still flex," Jackson said.

"We do have quite a drive in front of us, especially with traffic," Joel said, turning to face the group. "If anyone has to use the restroom, this would be a good time."

In the span of the next thirty seconds, everyone but Jackson realized their bladders weren't going to hold. He was left guarding a mountain of luggage while they split off to their respective restrooms. Good thing he had had only one cup of coffee.

Maggie was the first one back. "What do you think?" she asked, her hair up in a ponytail. A few strands were still loose, and she tucked them behind her ear.

"About what?"

"This."

"Well, it's certainly better than La Guardia."

"That's not what I meant," she said, rolling her eyes as if dealing with a remedial child.

"'This' is pretty vague, Mags."

"I meant it to be vague. This, as in the entire expedition, the team, the treasure hunt?"

Jackson shrugged. "I don't know. Did you happen to do any background on Joel?"

"I ran his bio. Why?"

Jackson shook his head. "I didn't have a lot of prep time."

"Virtual Rose Bowls getting in the way again?"

"I re-watched both *National Treasures* and all the *Indiana Jones* movies." He winced. "Even *Kingdom of the Crystal Skull*."

"He's clean," she said. "Everything I found checked with what he told me."

Jackson nodded.

"Why, you have reason to doubt him?"

"None whatsoever," Jackson said as Joel stepped out of the bathroom beyond Maggie's shoulder. "That's what concerns me."

"Maybe there's something wrong with your famous gut," she said.

"You not feeling well?" Joel asked.

"I'm fine."

Joel nodded, then pulled out his cell phone. Jackson couldn't hear much of what he said because a departure announcement started blaring through the concourse, but he thought he heard Joel mention M&M's too. It was strange, but more than that, it reminded Jackson that he was getting hungry, despite the sandwiches served on the plane. It may have only been early afternoon back in L.A., but Jackson's stomach was already on Eastern Time.

Rich and Cara returned as Joel ended his conversation. Beckoning everyone to follow him, he led the way through the concourse to the arrivals pick-up area. JFK, as expected, was a mass of people of every race, culture, and style of dress. And every one of them was on a cell phone, either talking or texting. Maybe tweeting. #CityThatNeverSleeps.

Joel got back on his phone as they stepped onto the sidewalk. Almost immediately, a navy Chevy Suburban pulled to the curb. Joel lowered his phone. "This is us."

The driver's door opened, and a tall, well-built, rather handsome man got out. He wore jeans and a plain tee, no jacket. His dark hair was shaggy, his tanned face unshaven in a day or two. Aviator sunglasses hid eyes that Jackson was sure were boring into him as the man circled the front of the Suburban.

He turned his face toward Joel. "Trust you had a good flight, yeah?" he asked in a Scottish accent. Less than a brogue, but more than just an inflection.

"Pretty good, considering," Joel replied. He turned. "Jackson, Maggie, I'd like you to meet Ian Crawford, A.K.A. M&M's."

"M&M's?" Maggie asked.

"Aye," Ian answered. "I'm partial to the brown ones."

"In addition to an affinity for chocolate candy, Ian's also an expert in all things mechanical as well as a munitions specialist," Joel said. "M and M."

"Munitions?" Maggie asked.

"Only as needed, yeah?" Ian said, dropping Jackson's hand and taking Maggie's. "Are you the reporter or the private investigator?"

"Uh, the reporter."

"Aye, lovely." He turned to Joel. "Shall we get going?"

"Absolutely."

Ian nodded a greeting to Rich and Cara, then helped Jackson load the group's bags into the back of the Suburban. Everyone got in, and Ian took the wheel. True to his nickname, as he merged with traffic, Ian reached into a large bag of M&M's on the dashboard and dumped them into his mouth.

"I can't wait to meet the rest of the team," Maggie whispered in Jackson's ear.

"They're not all going to be good-looking Scotsmen," he whispered back, earning an elbow in the ribs.

Traffic was bad just exiting the JFK loop, and Cara consulted her watch again and complained about the time.

"The exhibition doesn't open until nine," Joel said from the front seat. "We have time."

"That reminds me," Ian said. "Ali and Ramón are going to meet us there, instead of at the hotel."

"Everything all right?" Joel asked.

"Aye. Ali's consulting with an old friend, and you know Ramón."

"I do," Joel said. He sat back, and Ian had some more M&M's.

Jackson leaned toward Maggie again. "You pack a dress?"

"No."

"I don't think you can wear blue jeans and a Henley, fetching as the combo may be, to an art gallery in SoHo."

"Chelsea."

"Wherever."

"And 'fetching'?"

"That's a compliment."

She nodded. "You pack a tux?"

"No."

"I don't think you can wear jeans and a USC hoodie either."

"I'm not fetching?"

"You look like you should be playing fetch."

"Cold."

"You don't have to worry," Ian called out. Jackson looked up and made eye contact with him in the rearview mirror. Well, eye-to-sunglasses contact. "Formal wear is on Mr. Moneybags."

Jackson looked to Maggie, then back at Ian. "How . . ."

He flashed a toothy grin. "I can read lips."

"Shouldn't you be watching the road?" Cara asked.

"Aye."

"He reads lips?" Maggie asked.

"Very Ethan Hunt in *M:i:III*. I didn't buy that either, by the way."

"What's to buy? He knew what we were saying."

"Probably means we can stop whispering," Jackson said. He turned forward. "Okay, does anyone else in this vehicle have super powers? Can this Ramón guy shoot webs from his wrist or walk through walls?"

"I can make your bank account disappear," Cara said with a grin over her shoulder.

"That's very comforting."

"Ian is right," Joel said, turning around in his seat. "Once we get settled in at the hotel, we'll make a quick run to rent or purchase whatever apparel everyone needs for tonight."

"Are you serious?"

"He's serious," Cara said. "You don't think we all travel with formal wear everywhere we go, do you?"

"I thought maybe you beamed it through your computer or had a 3-D printer or something," Jackson said.

She grinned again and turned her attention back to her tablet.

Jackson had found the freeways in and around Manhattan to be a tangled mess on his one visit, and he was glad Ian was driving. He navigated like a native New Yorker, and before long, the famous New York City skyline was silhouetted against an orange and blue gradient. The view was impressive, but only temporarily. It disappeared when they submerged beneath the East River via the Queens Midtown Tunnel. When they resurfaced in Manhattan, night had fallen, and high-rises blocked out the sky anyhow.

Traffic was a disaster. Los Angeles was notoriously gridlocked, but that was primarily the freeways. These were city streets. Traffic at one light was backed up to the next, and the traffic at that light to the next. Same was true on the cross streets. From the air, it had to resemble a grid of parking lots. And half of the vehicles were yellow, identifying them as cabs. Jackson could see why. There were no free parking spaces anywhere.

Ian had to circle the block of the hotel twice before he could find a space at the curb. Once he parked, a valet took the vehicle off his hands, and a gregarious bellhop practically whisked them up to their rooms, all on the sixteenth floor. The three women had a small suite, as did Joel, Rich, and Jackson. Ian and Ramón had the third room. Joel gave everyone fifteen minutes to freshen up, then suggested they meet downstairs for an early dinner.

"Your team stays in style," Jackson remarked, checking out their suite. It wasn't overly elegant, but it had all the amenities and a luxurious look and feel.

"We can afford it," Joel said. "And besides, I think that being comfortable enables people to do their best work."

"I won't argue with you."

"Still, don't let this fool you. My teams have been known to camp in the desert and haul rucksacks through the wilderness. We don't always get to enjoy accommodations like this."

Jackson nodded and pulled back the curtain. He was afforded a view of more high-rises, office and apartment lights glowing in the darkness. Down below, traffic still bustled on city streets, everyone coming or going. It may not have been any busier than Los Angeles, but New York just seemed more hectic. Even harried people in L.A. could enjoy the sun and the palms and the beach as they yelled at each other and honked at traffic.

Jackson turned back from the window. Rich was in the bathroom, and Joel was unpacking his suitcase. "I'm starting to sound like my six-year-old self, but can I ask you another question?" Jackson asked.

"Always."

"You said the other night that you were well-funded."

Joel nodded.

"And you mentioned meeting with donors too. So how much of what you do is self-funded and how much of what you do is bankrolled by someone else?"

"Fifty-fifty. Maybe sixty-forty. I've done some guest speaking, fundraising, those sorts of things. And I also have some corporate investors and sponsors—people who believe in the work we're doing or who would profit from our discoveries."

"How so?"

"Remember I said that I'm a history hunter? Sometimes that's treasure; sometimes it's knowledge. In either case, our findings have resulted in financial gains for Team Joel as well as many others."

"You mind if I ask who's bankrolling this venture?"

Joel grinned. "Not at all." He stood. "This one's on me. I do have some typical sponsors who provide some of our gear, communications equipment, discounts on travel, and the like for every expedition. But this one—this one's personal, a quest I've been eager to undertake for years. This one is all out of my pocket."

Jackson nodded.

Joel took a step toward him. "Jackson, I appreciate your inquiries. I would expect nothing less from a private investigator. So please, ask whatever questions you have, without reservation." He shook his head slightly. "I have absolutely nothing to hide."

*   *   *

5:30 p.m.

THE GROUP ate at one of three hotel restaurants, a pub buried in the basement with street access via a narrow stairway, like the bar on *Cheers*. Jackson used the opportunity to pick up a few tidbits on the various members of Team Joel.

Cara was quiet, for the most part, but just when he forgot she was there, she'd make some snarky remark to show that, despite having her head in her phone or tablet half the time, she was indeed paying attention. She did divulge that she was born in Montreal but now lived in the suburbs of

Calgary. Joel was the one to reveal she had a semi-serious boyfriend, and Cara underscored the "semi," then went back to her phone.

Rich was a baseball fan, favoring the Tigers, but loving baseball in general. He and Jackson had a brief discussion about legendary play-by-play radio announcers, from the late Ernie Harwell to Vin Scully. Rich also offered a rather eloquent yet seemingly sincere blessing over their meal and did not appear to have any visions while eating his veal parmesan.

And Ian fulfilled Jackson's Scottish stereotype by being the loud life of the party, regaling everyone with humor and stories from his rather interesting past. He'd worked a fishing boat in the North Sea, drilled with Scotland's version of the Navy SEALs, and spent a winter backpacking in New Zealand. He was gregarious, entertaining, and hard not to like. To that end, he seemed to catch Maggie's eye once or twice. Not that Jackson was looking.

After dinner, the group—sans Rich—headed to a nearby shopping district to procure formal wear for the evening. Rich went back to the room to take a nap, which Jackson concluded was code word for "try to have a vision." Like Joel, Rich had brought black tie formal wear with him, which in itself was kind of weird. But Jackson was quickly learning not to be surprised by anything from this group.

While Jackson and Ian were fitted for rental tuxes, Joel went with Maggie and Cara to buy their evening gowns.

"Crazy, yeah?" Ian asked.

"What's that?"

"All this. You wake up in your own bed and by dinnertime you're across a continent being fitted for a black tie gala."

"Yeah, it's unusual," Jackson said, lifting his head for a measurement. "Is this par for the course?"

"Aye. And it gets better. Tonight you're in a penguin suit, tomorrow you're down to your trunks wading through a snake-infested river, and the next day you've got desert sand blowing in your face."

"Can't wait."

Ian grinned. "It's not all bad. There are perks to being a part of Team Joel. You travel, have adventures, are well compensated. And you wouldn't believe the lovely caliber of women that seem to show up on Joel's expeditions."

The woman measuring Ian cast him a quick glance and then returned to her work.

"How long have you worked with him?" Jackson asked.

"Eight years this June."

"Full-time?"

"Aye. But it's not exactly a nine-to-five."

"I suppose not."

The woman measuring Jackson stepped back. "You can have a seat."

Jackson retired to a sofa that was far more comfortable than his back home. Ian joined him a moment later and pulled out a regular-sized package of M&M's. "So what's your story?" he asked. He extended the bag to Jackson. "Dessert?"

"Thanks. My story?"

Ian nodded. "Joel said he wanted a 'brilliant mind' to help solve the riddle. Never mind my obvious offense at that statement, but you must have some claim to fame, yeah?"

Jackson shrugged, then gave Ian the brief overview of his career as a private investigator. His first "big case" had involved a kidnapped undercover police detective and rival L.A. gangs. It had ended with Jackson playing the hero and taking out five gangsters. A few months later, he had caught a killer, rescued a pregnant woman from her abusive husband, and apprehended a duo bent on breaching national security. Dejected by a client's suicide, Jackson had spun further down a dark hole when a repaid favor for his late brother's fiancée had resulted in the death of twenty-some-odd militia members and crooked CIA operatives in the Nevada desert—all at Jackson's hand. They had been part of a massive paramilitary conspiracy, and the authorities had ultimately ruled Jackson's actions acceptable. But they had left him in an even darker place, contemplating what he thought had been God's calling on his life.

"Sounds like you've had quite a year, yeah?" Ian said.

Jackson nodded. Their tuxes were ready to try on, so he didn't bother recapping his adventures in Mexico with Maggie, tracking down an actress's stalker, the assistance he had provided the FBI in taking down organized crime in upstate New York, or being shot on New Year's Eve. And two weeks ago, he had been embroiled in a crazy chase across Los Angeles and all of Southern California, trying to recover a centuries-old Bible that may or may not have contained CIA secrets. "Quite a year" was an understatement, but maybe Ian had something. As far as a rookie P.I. went, Jackson did have a claim to fame, so to speak.

After trying on their tuxes and having the necessary alterations made on the spot, Jackson and Ian headed down the block to see how Joel, Maggie, and Cara were faring. With the sun long gone, the night was cool, but still incredibly pleasant for early February. New York was susceptible to blizzards and subzero temperatures, so this was a welcome change.

They were just checking out at a swanky boutique when Jackson and Ian wandered in. "Ali just called," Joel said. "She's already at the gallery."

"Already?" Ian glanced at his watch. "It's not even seven-thirty."

"The gallery's open. Just not the exhibition."

Ian nodded. He chugged the rest of the M&M's from his bag and turned to Jackson. He winked. "Wait till you meet her."

A lengthy checkout procedure finally concluded, and the five hurried back to the hotel. "We walking or driving?" Ian asked when they were in the elevator.

"It's only a few blocks to the gallery," Joel said. "But then again, I won't be wearing an evening gown and heels."

"We can walk," Cara said.

All eyes turned to Maggie, and she nodded.

"Call us when you're ready," Joel said as the doors opened on the sixteenth floor.

"In that case, I should have time for a wee nap, yeah?" Ian said with a smirk.

"I heard that," Cara muttered before closing her door. Ian only smirked wider as he ducked into his room across the hall.

Rich was awake when Jackson and Joel entered their room. He sat on the edge of the bed, a glass of water in his hand. His face was white.

Joel stopped. "You have a vision?"

Rich nodded and turned to look at them. He shook his head. "I'm short on details, but I have a strong sense something bad is going to happen."

Joel turned to Jackson, his face serious.

Jackson shrugged. "I get the same feeling every time USC plays in Corvallis."

Chapter Six

8:27 p.m.

GALERIE CÉLESTE WAS located on the ground floor of a ten-story brownstone in Chelsea. Aside from a small black sign with white cursive print hanging under a green awning that covered the front door and two display windows, there was nothing to differentiate it from the shops, restaurants, theaters, wine bars, boutiques, and apartments—not to mention other galleries—that lined the block on both sides of the street in each direction.

The street itself was abuzz with cabs, other cars, and plenty of pedestrians. Jackson was quickly learning that traffic signals were just suggestions in New York City, more to pedestrians than vehicles, although neither obeyed them with terrible stringency. The people themselves were not the diverse bunch Jackson expected from New York's reputation. Most were young, trendy, not overly masculine in appearance. But that was to be expected in such an artsy neighborhood.

Jackson and Ian brought up the rear as Joel's team approached Galerie Céleste, although Jackson speculated they had different motivations for doing so. He hung back because it was just sort of his way, and because he could bum M&M's off Ian, who seemed always to have an endless supply. Too bad his nickname wasn't Pizzeria Pretzel Combos. Ian, on the other hand, appeared to have the primary motive of eying Maggie and Cara in their evening gowns from behind. Jackson did have to admit, they both looked good.

He didn't look too bad in his tux either, he didn't think, but a tux was a tux. If you had a good face, you looked good in a tux; if not, then not. It sure wasn't as comfortable as a pair of jeans and a hoodie, so Jackson hoped this didn't take long.

Joel's plan was simple. Rich had a camera with which to take pictures of the cross, if by some chance the gallery permitted it. If not, it would serve as a good distraction for Cara, who had a small clutch purse with a hidden camera also with which to take pictures. (Jackson had no idea if it was something she had jerry-rigged that afternoon like a techie lady-MacGyver or if it was the sort of gear Team Joel used enough to have special-ordered. Nor did he know, for that matter, if it had been made to match a dress or vice versa, but they complemented each other perfectly.) The rest were there to observe.

Jackson was a little unsure why Joel was spending the money and time for all of them to attend the exhibition reveal, seeing as how he couldn't do anything with Latin inscriptions except possibly make out some Bible references. Maggie was in the same boat, Ian was unlikely to memorize any details unless the cross slipped into a strapless evening gown, and Rich could just stay home and sleep to get a vision of where to go next. But who was Jackson to argue with Joel's money?

Inside, the gallery was far larger than Jackson had expected. The floors were hardwood, buffed until they were practically mirrors. White walls accented by track lighting in the raised ceiling were spotless, save for the occasional piece of artwork hanging on them. Doorways in either side wall opened to additional showrooms, and a wrought-iron staircase led to a loft. It, like the main room, was filled with people. All of them decked to the nines, most holding flutes of champagne or fancy-looking hors d'oeuvres on cocktail napkins.

Ian downed a handful of M&M's.

Joel turned to face the group. "I don't see Ali or Ramón, but we've got a few minutes before the exhibition opens, so feel free to look around. I'm sure they'll have a big announcement before it opens anyhow."

"If I know Ali, she's already in the front of the line, wherever it is," Cara said.

"True," Joel said with a grin.

"If you'll excuse me, this lad is going to introduce himself to a few lasses," Ian said with a wink before he disappeared into the crowd.

Maggie slipped her arm in Jackson's. "Want to take a look around?"

He took just a moment to admire her in her red surplice evening gown before answering. "Might as well."

They shouldered their way through the crowd and into one of the side parlors. It was half the size of the main showroom, with artwork—mostly paintings—hung on the outside walls and a variety of other displays set up in the interior of the room. There was a collection of Civil War-era weapons that had been assembled in some nebulous sculpture, nearly a dozen ships in bottles of various sizes, and a string of pearls belonging to some English queen Jackson had never heard of. The artwork on the walls reflected a number of historical events, from a 9/11 commemorative photo collage to a portrait of some ancient Mayan or Aztec king to an amazingly detailed oil painting of a Revolutionary War battle.

"Here we go," Maggie said, pulling on Jackson's fingers. "This one's right up your alley."

She let go as they stopped in front of a watercolor of Adam and Eve in the Garden of Eden.

"That's pretty good. Whenever I painted with watercolors, everything just ran together."

"You paint with watercolors?" she asked.

"Painted, past tense. When I was six."

"Age six . . . that's about when I stopped believing in fairy tales."

"You think Adam and Eve are a fairy tale?"

"That might be a little strong, but I don't think they're a historical fact like you do."

"Well then, what is a picture of them doing in a gallery that specializes in historical artwork?" Jackson asked.

Maggie grinned. "What can I say to that sort of irrefutable logic?" she asked as she wandered off. Jackson followed a little more slowly, pausing to take some sort of a cracker with cheese spread from a circulating waiter. It was good, and he almost tracked the guy down for another. Instead, he wandered after Maggie.

"What is it you don't buy?" he asked. "Aside from the brown hair."

"What? Brown hair?"

"The painting. They always depict Eve as a brunette."

"And what, your keen insight of Scripture has led you to believe she's not?"

"She listened to a talking snake instead of God. I'm going with a ditzy platinum blonde. 'Like, totally, Ad-am, have some ap-ple.'"

Maggie raised her eyebrows.

"Aside from the artistic license in hair color, yes, what don't you buy?"

"Buy how?" She resumed studying a very realistic, very large painting of a beach just before sunrise or just after sunset.

"The Bible. I know you know it. You quote it to me."

She turned for just a second, half a grin on her face.

"Why do you disregard it?" he asked.

"Because it's old."

50

"So's *The Elements of Style* in this text-and-tweet generation, but you still use it. All of our history books are old. Accounts of D-Day are old," he said with a nod at the plaque beneath the beach picture. It was a "calm before the storm" portrait of Normandy. Upon careful examination, German bunkers were discernable on the beach and Allied amphibious craft on the misty horizon. He frowned. "Wasn't it overcast on D-Day?"

"Can we stick to one conversation at a time?"

"Sure."

"Your examples are different."

"How?"

"History books and *The Elements of Style* aren't claiming to be an authority on the existence of man."

"So that's your beef, something or Someone telling you how to live?"

"When that something is thousands of years old, yeah. I mean, when the Bible was written, there was no electricity, no running water, no computers, no internet."

"Really, so Elijah's lack of a Facebook page is what's holding you back? 'Just killed all the prophets of Baal and getting set to race Ahab. #CloudTheSizeOfAMansHand.'"

She rolled her eyes. "Everything was different back then, Jack. Women were second-class citizens. Slavery was an acceptable practice. People married as teenagers because their parents arranged it for them. The Western world wasn't even recognized. Emerson and Hume and Nietzsche hadn't been born." She shrugged. "The Bible's antiquated. Life has changed."

Jackson paused for a moment, considering his reply. She didn't give him a chance.

"And what about modern science? You can dance around it all you want, but you keep claiming that Adam and Eve were real people and that God created the universe, what, a few thousand years ago? Science has proven you're a few million—if not billion—years off."

"It's been a while since my last science class," Jackson said, "but doesn't the scientific theory involve hypothesizing and testing? How do you test Evolution in a beaker? Or Creation, for that matter?"

"So what, neither's true?"

"No, but it isn't a question of science so much as history."

Maggie shrugged. "Even so, it's still a matter of evidence to support a theory, and I just think it takes a lot of faith to believe that something so old is infallible."

She looked straight at him. They'd been down this road, or at least a parallel one, a dozen times, and it always ended in a standoff. Jackson wasn't sure if he didn't have the words to persuade her or if she just wasn't persuadable, but so far, he'd been unable to sway her opinion.

"It's almost nine," Maggie said. "Should we find the others?"

Jackson nodded.

They strolled back into the main showroom, where Cara was busy on her phone and Rich was sampling an appetizer that looked far too green to be tasty.

Maggie applied ever so little pressure on Jackson's arm. "Are you mad at me?"

"No. I just don't understand—"

Joel appeared through the crowd, a smile on his face. "Maggie, Jackson, I'd like you to meet the rest of Team Joel. Allow me to introduce Dr. Aliana Naceri, our antiquities expert, archaeological consultant, and reference on all things historical and religious."

He stepped to the side, making room for a strikingly beautiful woman. Her skin was dark brown, smooth as silk. Raven black hair caressed her cheeks and hung on her shoulders. One of them was bare, the other covered by the strap of a sparkling green gown that seemed to have been exclusively tailored to fit her graceful figure. Though average in height, Dr. Naceri stood with a poise that also showed in her hazel eyes and radiant smile. The smile was brighter than the diamonds dangling from her ears, around her neck, or sparkling on her wrists and fingers, and that was saying something. Ian was right about the women on Joel's expeditions.

"It is a pleasure to meet you," she said, offering her hand first to Maggie, then to Jackson.

"Likewise," he said, taking a second opportunity to look into her eyes. Sparkling, vivacious eyes were such a cliché, but one that fit in Dr. Naceri's case.

"And this is Ramón Estévez," Joel said. "Among other duties, he serves as our liaison wherever we go."

Ramón was thin and wiry, olive-skinned, with dark green eyes and good hair. Really good, in fact. A pencil-thin goatee and an aloof smile gave him a sophisticated, confident aura. It was augmented by a tuxedo that had a different cut than Jackson's or any of the others worn by the guys on Team Joel. Jackson couldn't place it, not being a haberdasher or gentleman of leisure, but it had a European flair. Terry Benedict meets James Bond, with a little Don Juan thrown in, perhaps. If Jackson was reading Ramón right.

"Nice to meet you," he said, offering Jackson a quick handshake, then turning his eyes to Maggie. "*Señorita*, it is a pleasure." He took her hand, eyed her over it, then kissed the top of it. Yep, Jackson was reading him right.

"I just spoke to the assistant curator," Joel announced, breaking up the swoon-inducing theatrics. "She told me the exhibition will be opening in just a few minutes."

"Where?" Cara asked.

"In the back room," Joel said. "They still have it roped off."

"And they aren't allowing sneak peeks," Dr. Naceri said, her voice tinged with the faintest of accents. "Believe me, I tried." It was a pleasant accent, not the thick, throat-clearing hack of some Middle-Easterners. Jackson knew little of surname derivation, but Naceri sounded more Middle Eastern than Indian or Hispanic.

Ian joined the circle, guzzling more M&M's. "Ali, Ramón."

"Ian, good to see you again," Dr. Naceri said.

Ramón just nodded, then wormed his way over to a waiter serving caviar.

Jackson leaned over to Maggie. "Did he really pull the eye-contact-over-the-top-of-your-hand-before-kissing-it shtick?" he whispered.

"Jealous?" she asked, flitting her eyes to him.

"He didn't roll his R's when he was talking to me."

Maggie grinned in response.

"How was Greece?" Ian asked.

"Cold and rainy," Dr. Naceri said with a cute frown.

"Yeah, well, Joel has no sense of timing, yeah?"

"But it looks very promising," she continued in a soft voice. "I'll fill you in later."

"Ladies and gentlemen," a voice called from the loft. Jackson joined the rest of Team Joel and the entire gallery in turning to view a woman almost as dazzling as her gown. It was dark red, sequined, flowing, and yet somehow perfectly tapered. She was tall, dark-haired, beautiful.

"Welcome to Galerie Céleste and the reveal of the Mediterranean Exhibition."

Everyone applauded lightly, as if the woman had holed a par putt on the golf course.

She responded by gracefully and slowly descending the stairs, continuing to speak. "The artifacts you are about to observe were salvaged from the wreckage of the Italian galley *Ali Della Vittoria* off the coast of Cyprus just weeks ago. They have been dated to the eleventh and twelfth centuries, and their estimated worth is priceless."

The woman alighted to the ground floor, and the crowd parted like the Red Sea. Up close, Jackson realized she wasn't so overly beautiful as she was good-looking and well-accentuated and accessorized. He also saw that she wore a razor-thin headset microphone. The sound system was flawless, because Jackson couldn't tell that her voice was being amplified by anything.

"Rudy and Gerald," the woman said, gesturing at two gorillas in tuxes at the back of the room, "will be monitoring admittance to the exhibition. I assure you, everyone will have ample time to view everything. So please, take your time, enjoy the rest of the artwork on display, and help yourself to as much champagne and hors d'oeuvres as you'd like."

She smiled cordially, and everyone clapped again.

"Let's get in line," Joel said, leading his team toward Rudy and Gerald and the doorway to the back parlor. The two admission assistants/bouncers began forming a line on the far side of a velvet rope divider. Then they admitted a handful of people from the very front of the line. Judging by the size of the group allowed in, Jackson figured Team Joel would be in at least the third viewing group.

Jackson passed the time by giving the other patrons a onceover. He concluded that all of the people he laid eyes on were high-society art snobs and not rival treasure hunters. Then again, Joel didn't look much like a treasure hunter. Even Indiana Jones didn't look like a treasure hunter when in his classroom and without his bullwhip—at least if you didn't know he was Dr. Jones. But nobody in the gallery caught Jackson's private investigator's eye.

Joel broke through Jackson's thoughts. "I think they're going to split us up."

"Seriously?" Cara asked.

Joel nodded as he cast a glance at Rudy and Gerald, who had just let the second wave of patrons into the back parlor. "They're counting exactly," Joel said.

"Yeah," Rich said, "we're twenty-two through twenty-nine."

"Just like the gondola ride in Bolivia," Dr. Naceri said.

"It doesn't really matter," Joel said. "Rich, Cara, just make sure you're in the same group if it does happen."

"Aye, and act like you don't know each other."

They both nodded.

Fifteen minutes passed, during which time Jackson managed to scrounge a shrimp cocktail off a passing waiter, and Maggie and Ramón engaged in some lighthearted banter. Meanwhile, Joel, Dr. Naceri, and Ian were busy reminiscing about some past adventure, and Cara, as usual, had her head buried in her phone. That only left Rich, and Jackson didn't feel like discussing trances and visions or the Tigers' farm system. So he focused on the shrimp. Freshest he'd ever eaten.

When it was time for the next group to enter the parlor, Joel's premonition proved right. He, Dr. Naceri, Ian, and Ramón were admitted with one group, leaving Jackson, Maggie, Rich, and Cara to wait behind. Rich said something about nerves and set out to find something to drink. With Cara still preoccupied and antisocial, Maggie decided to pick on Jackson some more.

"Explain the ark to me," she said. "I've read the dimensions in the Bible. How did two to seven of every animal fit? Do you know how many species of animals there were?"

"Nobody said it was comfortable."

"Or what about bugs? Birds? And the food to feed them all?"

"So what, you think Moses was some mathematically challenged clod who made it up? Don't you think if he was dreaming up a story, he'd be sure to make the ark, say, the size of Manhattan?"

"So your argument is that it's so implausible it must be true?"

"I wouldn't go to that extreme, but sort of. And there aren't that many species. You don't need poodles and beagles and labs and Rottweilers. You just need dogs."

"Then there's my next point," Maggie said. "Where'd all the variations come from?"

"Probably just a cosmic whoopsadaisy."

"What's the Bible's answer for natural selection?"

"Big things eating little things does not prove Evolution."

"And remember carbon dating? How is a two thousand-year-old book supposed to compete with modern science like that?"

Jackson leaned into Cara's line of sight. "We'll be right back. Save our spots."

She looked up, then around. Rich was still gone. "Sure. Whatever."

Jackson took Maggie's arm and led her down a hallway away from the crowd.

"Where exactly are we going?" she asked.

"The evidence locker."

She frowned as he guided her to the door of the men's room. "Wait here."

"You brought me along while you pee?"

Jackson pushed open the door. A steward in a fancy vest greeted him with a, "Good evening, sir."

"Evening," Jackson said, glancing around. The restroom was otherwise empty. He reached into his wallet and pulled out the first bill he came up with. As it was, a ten. Jackson wasn't sure if that was cheap in these circles, but he didn't care. "Can you give me the room for a minute?" he asked.

The steward frowned but took the bill. "I could use a smoke."

"Great."

Jackson followed the steward out and grabbed Maggie by the wrist again.

"Jackson, what—"

He pulled her into the bathroom and waited for the door to swing shut.

"What's going on? Did you—"

"Here," Jackson said, positioning Maggie in front of the mirror over the dual sink. "Look."

"Jack, what are you doing?"

He nodded at the mirror. "Look."

Eyebrows raised, she turned her head to the mirror. He stood over her shoulder.

"What am I looking at?"

"You," he said.

"What is this, the *Cool Runnings* speech?"

"No, but nice old-school reference." He gently nudged her chin back to the mirror. "What I'm looking at," he said, "is an absolutely beautiful woman. Not just because she looks gorgeous in an evening gown—which she does— and not just because she has an arresting figure—which she does," he said, making eye contact with her in the mirror. "I see eyes that transmit a vitality and a spunkiness that are truly unique. I see a mouth that's an outlet for a witty, intelligent mind. I see hands that pen words that reveal a true gift—a knack for writing and ability to craft a story I couldn't dream. I see a budding smile that I've seen hundreds of times before, expressing compassion, love, and a zeal for life. I see all of that, Maggie, every time I look at you. I see a one-of-a-kind woman who never ceases to surprise me." He turned to her. "Do you see that?"

Maggie swallowed hard but said nothing.

"And I find it very, very hard to believe that this beautiful, smart, clever, occasionally feisty girl-at-heart in front of me is the descendent of an ape or a pile of primordial goop—that she is the result of a cosmic mistake. I don't see an evolved animal; I see a brilliantly designed and very nicely fashioned person—a person formed in the image of a Creator. And I think it takes an awful lot of faith, confronted by all the evidence in front of me, to believe anything different."

Maggie slowly turned her head. "You're not too bad with words yourself."

"And I want it on the record that I was making eye contact when I described your figure."

She laughed.

"Anyhow, that's why I don't buy the Evolution argument," Jackson said. "Because all the talk about starlight and Darwin's birds and radio carbon blah-blah-blah—which is all based on a preconceived assumption—can't hold a candle to the evidence I see every day."

She took his hand. "You really mean all that?"

He met her blue-gray eyes. "Every word."

She opened her mouth, but before she could speak, the door swung inward. An old man startled when he saw her, his eyes nearly popping out of his head.

"We were just leaving," Jackson said. He took Maggie by the hand. "Come on."

He pulled her out into the hallway and turned back to the parlor, but she tugged him in the other direction. He looked up as her eyes widened slightly and she began to lead him down the hallway, to a back exit. She pushed open the door to an alley, where they found the restroom steward nursing a cigarette.

Maggie looked at him. "Could you give us a minute?"

He eyed her, then Jackson—who shrugged—and shook his head. He dropped and stomped his cigarette and returned inside.

"Maggie, I don't think this is a great idea. I mean, an alley in New—"

"Shh," she said, gently pushing him against the side of the building. A dim light over the door sparkled in her eyes as they seemed to drink him in. "I'm not going to throw out my entire belief structure and toss science to the wind because you give a good speech, but . . ." She smiled a thin smile. "No one has ever said anything like that to me."

"Well, it's true."

She stared for a moment more, then leaned in and kissed him. It was a short kiss, only a few seconds, but packed with intensity. When Maggie stepped back, her eyes were wide and as vibrant as he'd ever seen them.

Jackson grinned. "Now imagine if I could only roll my R's."

Chapter Seven

9:34 p.m.

"WE SHOULD GET back," Maggie said.

Jackson nodded. "Kissing in an alley is so Abercrombie anyhow," he said, taking her hand.

Rich greeted them with something of a relieved smile when they rejoined the line. Cara glanced up from her phone.

"We miss anything?" Jackson asked.

"A few people came out, but they haven't let anyone else in yet," she said, tapping her screen.

"What are you working on?" Maggie asked.

"Nothing much. It's how I pass time."

"Tetris?" Jackson asked.

"Angry Birds?" Maggie asked.

"Words with Friends."

"Cara would rather play Scrabble than have a conversation," Rich said, smiling to show he was teasing.

"Look at the company I'm left with," Cara said. "Blame me? Besides, we're supposed to act like we don't know each other."

It wasn't long before Joel, Dr. Naceri, and Ramón appeared around the corner and passed through the "exit lane." They were followed by half a dozen others and couldn't stop to talk. But their eyes were all wide with excitement. A few minutes later, the remaining patrons—including Ian, with a beautiful brunette on his arm—exited the back parlor. Rudy and Gerald promptly began admitting the next wave of patrons. Cara tucked her phone into her clutch purse.

"I should have asked," Jackson said as he followed Cara, "are we thinking that anything else in this collection might be relevant?"

"No, but you never know."

The back parlor at Galerie Céleste was cozy. Plush, deep red carpeting, as opposed to the hardwood floors in the rest of the gallery; molding along the stucco walls and ceiling; and soft, warm lighting all mixed with delicate, almost imperceptible background music to provide an ideal environment for the Mediterranean Exhibition.

It wasn't what Jackson had expected for a highfalutin New York art gallery. A U-shaped display table ran around three sides of the room, with a separate display case in the middle. Hundreds of gold, bronze, and brass coins—all in various stages of restoration—lined the displays. They were the bedding for dozens and dozens of other artifacts: gold chalices; rings and necklaces and bracelets; a gold, a silver, and a bronze cross (apparently not part of their own "Holy Trinity") each inlaid with jewels; gold and silver plates, some with jewels and some without; and a handful of other items Jackson couldn't identify. There were also dozens of objects not made of precious metal, from earthenware bowls and cups to a huge brass key to some sort of crude dagger to a series of what looked like petrified wooden idols.

And then, resting innocuously against a small brace near the far corner of the "U," a lead cross. Like the rest of the collection, it was inside a glass case, protected from onlookers, be they wannabe thieves, unscrupulous treasure hunters, or sneezers.

Jackson gave Cara and Rich credit. He would have beelined over to the cross. They acted as if they weren't even aware of it, spending several minutes browsing and looking at the other items with well-feigned interest. They also did a good job of acting as if they weren't together, not that Rudy and Gerald—or half a dozen security cameras—seemed to be paying them the least amount of attention. Jackson figured he and Maggie could be seen together, so he followed her as she perused the objects.

"How much you think all this is worth?" he asked.

"You heard the lady. Priceless."

"I mean is it priceless because it's priceless or because it's ten years older than dirt?"

"What do you think?"

He looked at all the gold. "Yeah. And to think, just sitting there on the seabed for a millennium waiting for Dirk Pitt to find it."

"Too bad you ain't Dirk, huh?"

"In so many ways."

They moved slowly and stopped at the lead cross. By comparison to some of the other items, particularly the three other crosses, the lead cross seemed out of place in the exhibition. Even so, even lacking the shine or pop of the gold and silver pieces, even without any jewels embedded in its surface, there was something impressive about it.

The cross was approximately a foot tall and not quite as wide. The beams were both two inches across, and the cross was maybe an inch and a half thick. It was slightly wider at both ends of the crossbeam, as well as the top and bottom, and was remarkably smooth, lacking any flair or gothic features.

"The cross of a carpenter," Jackson said in his best Harrison Ford.

"What?"

"You have to admit this is a little *Last Crusade*-ish. All this ornate, jewel-encrusted gold, and we're here for a piece of lead."

"Will you just memorize everything about it?" Maggie said, looking over his shoulder.

Engraved on the top of the cross was very small Latin script, barely legible—if Jackson could even read the dead language. On the left arm was an engraving of either an angel with a flaming sword or a dragon, and on the right was a lion growling on its hind feet. Beneath the arms, on the body of the upright beam, were three more inscriptions in similarly small print.

Jackson did his best to memorize as many unfamiliar words as possible, then studied the cross carefully, looking for holes or cracks in the lead. Other than a small imperfection under the middle Scripture reference on the base of the cross, he saw nothing.

"I'm sorry, sir, no photography."

Jackson turned to see one of the gorillas—Rudy or Gerald—pointing out of the exhibition hall. Rich, forlornly, lowered his camera and made some objection Jackson couldn't hear.

"Half a step back," Maggie whispered.

Jackson obeyed, then drifted a little to his right and pretended to study another piece—a gold bowl inlaid with rubies and sapphires—while Cara approached the lead cross. Out the corner of his eye, he observed her very discreetly move her clutch purse around, presumably taking pictures of the cross while Rich kept the attention of the guard and Jackson and Maggie served as screens.

After a minute, Maggie interlaced her fingers with Jackson's and gave him a slight tug. He looked to see that Cara was already moving away from the cross. Rich was nowhere to be seen, having been expelled with his camera. Approximately half of the twenty-one others who had been admitted with the second half of Team Joel were still milling about, and quick glances at Rudy and Gerald convinced Jackson they had no suspicions.

Maggie pulled him a little farther, and he tried to concentrate on some golden utensils in front of him.

"Hard to believe this is real, isn't it?" Maggie asked.

"You mean the quest to find Crusader treasure or Aladdin's cave here?"

"All this," she said, gesturing at the wealth of treasures.

"And there's starving kids in Africa."

"L.A. too. But don't tell me you're suddenly feeling philanthropic."

"It just makes you think about the contrasts in the world. Sort of like every time something good happened on *Lost*, somebody died too."

"Really?"

"Aaron was born, but Boone died; Sawyer and Jin returned to camp, but Ana Lucia shot Shannon; Jack made the call to Fisher Stevens while Charlie drowned in the Looking Glass."

"You are something else."

"Probably happened in the later seasons too, but who the heck knows what was actually going on then?"

"Of all the men in Los Angeles . . ."

Jackson grinned as he turned to look over his shoulder. Cara was studying the three crosses on the other side of the room. He figured that, as the only man on Team Joel still in the back parlor, he should hang around in case she got into trouble—so he could get pummeled by Rudy and Gerald. But he and Maggie had mostly made the rounds, and loitering would likely draw attention. So he put his hand on her back. "Ready?"

"I'd just like to soak this in for a minute . . ."

"You can't get wealth by osmosis, Mags."

She sighed. "Okay. Let's go."

They turned for the exit, arriving by perfect coincidence at the same time as Cara. They walked side-by-side like strangers until they were back into the main showroom, where they quickly sought out the other members of Team Joel. They were huddled around a sculpture in the middle of the room. Ian's lady friend was not with them.

"You get the photos?" Joel asked.

"We'll see," Cara said. "I think so."

"What'd you think?"

"I think we're going to have our work cut out deciphering it. A lot of the words were indistinct."

"I thought the same thing," Dr. Naceri said.

"It looked like it'd been at the bottom of the ocean for a millennium," Maggie said.

"Sea, not ocean," Cara corrected. "But yeah."

"So who's the forensic expert?" Jackson asked. "Who takes Cara's photos and analyzes the way light refracts off a letter to determine its depth in the lead and thus differentiate an O from a D?"

"Me," Cara said. "Or Ali. But we don't have a lab expert, per se."

Joel took a deep breath. "I hate to be paranoid, but maybe you want to find some privacy and e-mail the photos to our account, just in case."

"Already did. I had them default there."

"Good. Smart. Well, then I guess—"

The lights went out.

All of them.

For a few seconds, it was completely black, then a few cell phones and tablet screens provided a dim blue light. They were followed by several flashlight beams. Cries of alarm and murmurings rose in crescendo, eventually being silenced by a shout from the stairway. It was the lady in red.

"Everyone, everyone! Your attention, please! Do not panic. Our generators will initiate in just a few seconds. Please remain where you are and remain calm."

Jackson disobeyed and slipped to the window. He glanced up and down the street and returned to Joel and his team. "Lights are on up and down the block. It's just here."

"This isn't good," Joel said.

"No," Jackson and Ian said at once. In the darkness, their eyes met, and they both turned toward the back parlor. Edging and shoving their way through the still alarmed crowd, they were almost to the entrance to the parlor when emergency lights flashed on, accompanied by a dull hum.

Rudy or Gerald stood at the entrance to the parlor, a walkie-talkie to his mouth. The other, Gerald or Rudy, was absent. Whichever of them it was, he lowered the walkie-talkie and extended a hand to Jackson and Ian. "Sorry, gentlemen, the room is locked down."

"You need to check the exhibit," Ian said.

The man frowned. "Why is that?"

"The outage is just this building," Jackson said. "You think that's a coincidence?"

"Gerald, back now," Rudy said into his walkie-talkie. "Everyone else, remain at your post." He holstered the walkie-talkie. "Wait here."

As he opened the door to the parlor and disappeared inside, Jackson wondered who 'everyone else' entailed. The lady in red? There'd been a uniformed guard on the front door, but none by the back door when he and Maggie had exited. It hadn't struck him at the time, but considering the wealth on display, the security seemed a little lax.

Rudy was gone thirty seconds. When he returned, the walkie-talkie was again at his mouth. "Madam Olivier, we have a situation," he called, looking into the crowd.

Ian flitted his eyes at Jackson, then pushed past Rudy into the parlor just as Gerald returned to the scene, catching Rudy between chasing Ian and restraining Jackson. He succeeded in the latter, and the two guards conferred in person for a moment while Jackson waited anxiously. Around them, the buzz of fearful and inquisitive conversations was growing louder, and out of it marched the resplendent lady in red, Madam Olivier.

Her arrival coincided with Ian's return from the parlor. He nodded quickly at Jackson. "It's gone."

"What's gone?" Olivier asked, the alarm evident in her wide brown eyes.

"Check your collection, yeah?" Ian said. He turned to Jackson. "They didn't come out the front way."

"Back exit," Jackson said, nodding down the hallway. He and Ian took off, leaving Olivier and her two assistants to shout questions after them.

Their wingtips pounding on the hardwood, Jackson and Ian raced past the bathrooms and a maintenance closet and burst through the back door into the alley where minutes before, Jackson and Maggie had shared a kiss. Now the alley was just as dim but completely empty. No casual kissers or smoking stewards.

"Which way do you go?" Ian asked.

Jackson closed his eyes. "Quickest way off the island . . ."

"North to the Lincoln Tunnel," Ian said and took off running.

Jackson followed, not catching up until they were at the end of the alley. "See anything?"

They looked up and down the one-way northbound street.

"Nothing," Ian said. "We couldn't have been more than two minutes behind."

"A lot can happen in two minutes."

"He had a getaway car waiting at the end of the alley," Ian said.

"Unless . . ."

Ian looked at him.

"A thief would have no idea how long it would take the generators to come on."

"So?"

"So, a lead cross is heavy and almost impossible to conceal, and you wouldn't want to tuck it under your arm like a football and make a break for it."

"Backpack, briefcase?"

"You see any of those inside?"

Ian shook his head, and this time Jackson led the way back toward the gallery's rear entrance. They only took a few steps before the door opened and a man burst out into the alley. He was dressed in black, head to toe, and the light over the door only had a second to illuminate a tan face and brown hair before he turned and ran the other way down the alley.

With an indistinguishable yell, Ian chased after him. Jackson was right beside him, and they reached the street at the end of the alley only a dozen paces behind the man. Glancing at oncoming traffic, he darted into the one-way southbound street, drawing the blare of a horn from a cab but making it unscathed to the other side.

Jackson and Ian followed more carefully, then took off down a busy sidewalk, trying to keep their black-clad quarry in sight. But he weaved his way through the crowds like a running back, and by the time he turned right a block and a half south, he had doubled the distance between them.

They chased him west for another block, and just when Jackson was having trouble picking him out of the crowd, the man veered into the street again. Ian swore under his breath, waited for several cars to pass, and entered the street as well. Instead of following, Jackson continued down the sidewalk, trying to stay on a path that was as close to parallel as possible to that of the man they were chasing. He had to stop at the cross street, and from there, watched the man descend the stairs into a subway station.

Jackson motioned to Ian, then *Froggered* his way across the street and followed him down the stairs. By the time they reached the platform, there was no sign of the man. They stood there for several seconds amid the coming and going crowds, scanning them for anyone who resembled their quarry, but it was to no avail. Ian swore again.

Jackson stood beside him for several moments, catching his breath.

"He wasn't carrying anything," Ian panted. "Maybe a harness, yeah?"

Jackson nodded. "He ducks into a bathroom stall, sticks the cross into a harness under his jacket, and then walks out."

"Risky. It wouldn't take them long to find out it was missing and put the place on lockdown."

"Wouldn't take him long to rig it if he knew what he was doing. Or . . ."

Ian turned to him. "Or what?"

"Or had an accomplice. Guy one heads to the can, power goes out, guy two steals the cross and ducks into the bathroom. He slips the cross into guy one's harness and heads back to the party and hangs around for a while, and even if someone spotted him near the parlor while the lights were out, he's got nothing on him."

"Meanwhile guy two slips out the back door, presumably to have a smoke, and walks away," Ian said.

"Yeah."

"So why'd he crash out the door with his tail on fire?"

"Maybe we spooked him by alerting Olivier that the cross was missing and he bumped up the timetable. Or maybe he just wanted to get out. Or maybe it was a one-man job after all."

Ian shrugged. "I suppose we should get back, yeah?"

Jackson nodded, and the duo hurried up the stairs to ground level and backtracked to Galerie Céleste. They re-entered the building via the alley entrance and immediately became aware of a group at the end of the hall. Olivier, Rudy and Gerald, and a uniformed guard were joined by several police officers and a couple in formal wear. They all looked Jackson and Ian's way, and Rudy and Gerald both pointed. "That's them."

They stopped in their tracks, and Ian muttered under his breath what Jackson took for a Scottish curse.

Surprisingly, it wasn't the cops but the nattily attired man and woman who reached them first. He was tall, thin, with a head shaped like an hourglass and thick, high hair. She was short, tanned, with short dark hair and a firm jaw. The guy reached into the breast pocket of his tux and pulled out a badge.

"Agent Duncan John, Interpol. This is Agent Alexandra Fiore."

"Alex," she said, practically cutting the word.

"Charmed," Jackson said.

"We'd like to speak with you about a theft from the Mediterranean Exhibition."

Jackson and Ian exchanged glances.

Agent John nodded. "Please come with us."

Chapter Eight

11:02 p.m.

UPON FURTHER INSPECTION, Interpol Agent Alex Fiore was a pit bull. Jackson and Ian had been promptly separated, and Fiore had been assigned to grill Jackson. Not wanting to parade the duo through the patrons and up to private offices, they had used what was available—in this case, the women's restroom. It made the opulent men's room look like a truck stop, what with its chandeliers, swan faucets, and settee. Jackson had seated himself on it. Fiore had stood.

She was not unattractive, although a blue gown with gold accents made her look more like a Rams cheerleader than an international law enforcement officer. Her eyes matched the dress and had probed Jackson as she asked her questions. She'd left no stone uncovered, going over every second of Jackson and Ian's pursuit, from the time they had suspected the cross had been stolen until they had returned to the gallery. She had spat her questions, very much on the offensive, her eyes daring Jackson to give her an unsatisfactory answer.

Then, when she had exhausted every possible avenue of inquiry, she'd told him to wait and stepped outside. So there he was, alone in the women's restroom at a swanky New York art gallery. And to think, he could have been kicking it with his friend Mouse, slaying virtual baddies. He also couldn't help but wonder what would become of all those elegant, well-dressed women who'd had a glass or two of champagne and were being told very politely to hold it.

Fiore returned and shook her bangs from her eyes. She leaned against the corner of the wall and spent a few moments thumbing through something on her phone. She looked up.

"Jackson Lee Douglas, thirty, born in Honolulu, lifelong resident of California, a private investigator for nearly two years now. So what brings you to Galerie Céleste?"

"I'm a history buff."

Fiore did not appreciate a smart aleck, so said her eyes.

"Like you said, I'm a *private* investigator. Not sure what that means over in Europe, but here, my client has confidentiality."

"Why Europe?" Fiore asked as if her trap had just clanged shut.

Jackson shrugged. "I just associate Interpol with Europe. Besides, you have an accent."

Fiore stared at him for a moment. She blinked. "What's your interest in the Mediterranean Exhibition?"

"I'm not at liberty to say."

"For only being in business less than two years, your file is pretty thick," she said. "Five dead in Los Angeles by your hand, May of last year. A client committed suicide, July of last year. Over twenty more dead in Nevada by your hand, September of last year. Shot, December of last year. One dead in Los Angeles by your hand, January of this year. Are you a private investigator or a paid assassin?"

"Better check your file again, Agent Fiore. I've been legally cleared in all cases. And the suicide is hitting below the belt."

Fiore ignored him and studied her phone for another moment. "Perhaps most intriguing is the fact that you were flagged by the NSA two weeks ago as a person of interest in the theft and subsequent disappearance of a Bible believed to contain national secrets. It makes me wonder what your interest is in a millennium-old lead cross."

Jackson stared at her without speaking.

Fiore didn't let him get to her. "Of almost two hundred people here, when the power went out, only you and Mr. Crawford found it prudent to race to the back parlor and see whether the cross just happened to have been stolen. So I wonder again, Mr. Douglas, what your interest in all this is."

Jackson again said nothing.

"So I'm getting the silent treatment now?"

"Just waiting for you to stop wondering aloud and ask me a question."

Fiore pushed off from the wall and took a few steps toward him. "What are you doing here?"

"I already told you that."

She didn't bat an eyelash. "What's the nature of your relationship with Joel Robinson?"

"Professional."

"Care to elaborate?"

"No."

"You're not fooling me, Mr. Douglas. We know all about Mr. Robinson's treasure-hunting prowess." She glanced at the phone. "Crawford, Estévez, Hamilton, Naceri, Tremblay—we know them all. Your being here with them pretty much explains itself."

"Kind of makes me wonder why you bother asking me then."

For the first time, Fiore expressed her frustration with a small sigh.

"And I can't help wondering what Interpol's interest in a millennium-old lead cross is. Don't you have drug runners and sex traffickers to pursue?"

"I'm the one doing the questioning," Fiore replied.

"Well, a friendly tip, you catch a lot more flies with honey than a big old swatter."

"Is that so?"

"I don't know. I actually like swatting flies. But I've done nothing wrong and have nothing to hide, so the third degree isn't playing well."

"Nothing to hide? Except the details of your relationship with Mr. Robinson and your presence here."

"Which you claim to know already. So why are we sitting in the women's restroom making New York society women squeeze their legs together? The guy you want boarded the subway and is probably halfway to Newark by now. And frankly, I think he might have an accomplice."

"Why is that?"

Jackson explained his harness-rigging theory as he had to Ian a short while ago. Fiore paid close attention, then asked, "I don't suppose you have any idea who the accomplice might be?"

"I don't have any idea who the guy is. The power went out just in this building, which I found odd, and so Ian and I went to check if anything was wrong."

"Yes, and he noticed the cross was missing and a couple of concerned citizens chased after it. You already went over this."

Jackson held out his hands. "So I ask again, why are we here?"

Somebody knocked on the door.

"Occupied," Jackson called in his best falsetto.

Fiore rolled her eyes as she went to the door and talked in undertones for a moment. When she returned, she extended a business card to Jackson. "Call me if—"

"I'm already seeing someone."

She huffed. "If you think of anything that might be helpful."

"So I'm free to go?"

"Yes."

He stood. "I might be able to think of something helpful if you tell me what Interpol's after."

"Let's just say you weren't the only ones who had reason to think something might be wrong when the power went out."

"You were here for the cross?"

Fiore made no response.

"Is Interpol treasure hunting now?"

Still nothing.

"Or are you tracking someone who is?"

Fiore still didn't say anything, didn't even blink. But there was a slight readjusting of her posture—almost imperceptible—that indicated Jackson had hit the mark.

"You know what, it's not my business," Jackson said. "I'm good to go?"

Fiore nodded, then stopped him as he reached the doorway. "Mr. Douglas."

He turned.

"If you think of anything . . ."

He nodded and exited the restroom. Joel was waiting for him at the end of the hallway. Behind him, the gallery was still bustling, although slightly more subdued than it had been earlier. The Mediterranean Exhibition appeared to still be open, with Rudy and Gerald running the show as before. All police presence had vanished. Wouldn't want to ruin an exhibition opening with a little thing like a crime scene investigation.

"I'm terribly sorry about that," Joel said, welcoming Jackson with an arm around the back. He steered him through the crowd.

"You knew?"

"Not at first. But when you and Ian didn't return, and we saw the police and Interpol agents, we put the pieces together."

"Speaking of Mr. Chocolate Candy, where is he?"

"They released him a few minutes before you."

"Thanks to you?"

Joel stopped. "What makes you say that?"

"Just a hunch. She was giving me the third degree, then somebody knocked on the door, and suddenly it was a business card and 'call me if you think of anything else.'"

Joel grinned. "I have built up a small network of friends and confidants, but I don't have control over Interpol interrogations."

Jackson nodded.

"I did, however, vouch for you and Ian to the Agent-in-Charge. I also explained who I was and what we were doing here, which may have impacted their decision."

"And I was sticking to name, rank, and serial number," Jackson said.

"Well, I appreciate the loyalty. And I'm sorry you had to go through that."

"All part of the small print, right?"

Joel smiled as he led Jackson to the corner of the gallery, where Ian was waiting with Maggie. He had a sulky face, and his bow tie hung loose beside the lapels of his jacket. Maggie, fingering but not drinking from a flute of champagne, sighed with relief when Jackson appeared.

He gave her a smile in return and nodded at Ian. "They let you out alive too, huh?"

"Aye. Just shows no good deed goes unpunished."

"What exactly happened?" Maggie asked.

"Let's talk elsewhere," Joel said with a couple of quick glances over his shoulder. "I think our business here is done."

"I'll drink to that, yeah?" Ian said. He nodded at Maggie. "You going to finish that?"

She looked down at her champagne, then shook her head. He took the flute, drained the contents, and placed the empty glass on a display case. "Let's get out of here."

Joel led them out the front exit and onto the street. The air had cooled considerably since they had arrived, and maybe since Jackson and Ian's chase of the thief. At the time, Jackson hadn't been paying attention to atmospheric conditions. The crowds on the sidewalks were also thinning, but not drastically. It was, after all, still shy of midnight.

"I sent everyone else back to the hotel," Joel said as they walked. "Cara should have the photos she took for us to look at when we get there."

"You might also want to form a short list of quote-unquote 'known associates' who could also be after the Calvary Treasure," Jackson said. "Agent Fiore as much as admitted to me they're watching someone."

"What'd she say?"

"Nothing, but her body language implied I'd struck a nerve when I asked the question."

"Makes sense, yeah?" Ian said. "Why else would they be at the opening?"

"I don't suppose you have an in with Interpol, do you?" Maggie asked.

"I don't," Joel answered, "but Ramón may know someone. His list of friends and sources never ceases to amaze me."

"Well, look on the bright side," Jackson said. "Whoever they are, they've tipped their hand. Now we know we're not the only ones hunting the treasure."

"And they have a leg up," Ian said. "They have the cross."

"Maybe, maybe not. If Interpol's after them, there's no way they can get it out of the country by any typical methods. Even if they could, I doubt they'd risk it. If they want to fly to France or Greece or wherever, they'll have to leave it behind and will be working on photos and memory just like us."

"Aye, assuming Cara's aren't half blurry and half of the inside of her purse."

"What's gotten into you?" Maggie asked.

"Half hour of Interpol interrogation not enough?"

"Jack's practically chipper."

"Aye, and he got the bonnie female Interpol agent, and I got cantankerous Agent Duncan John."

"Fiore was no picnic," Jackson said. "Believe me."

Rich, Cara, Dr. Naceri, and Ramón were all waiting in Joel, Jackson, and Rich's suite when the group returned. They had all changed into more casual clothes, and Jackson couldn't help but notice that Dr. Naceri was as stunning in jeans and a long-sleeved blouse and with her hair clipped back as she was in a shimmering evening gown.

She was the first to greet the returning foursome. "You are both all right?" she asked.

"Brilliant," Ian muttered while Jackson nodded.

"I've got the photos up," Cara said, nodding at the flat screen monitor that had been her obsession on the plane. The group of eight huddled around the table to look at a series of nine photos—the best of the bunch, she'd said—of the lead cross.

"I can't make out the writing," Ian said.

"It's in Latin."

"Aye, but I can't even make out the letters."

"Well, I couldn't exactly zoom and focus. I took thirty-six pictures in six seconds, through glass."

"How'd the thief penetrate the glass?" Maggie asked.

"Adroitly," Jackson said.

"Aye, and fast."

"Can you enhance these?" Joel asked.

"I'm working on it."

"Probability?"

"High," she said. "It'll just take some time. I was trying not to pay obvious attention to the cross while whipping my camera purse around."

Nobody moved.

"Maybe give me some room here?" Cara said. "This is going to take more than five seconds."

They slowly stepped back, and Ramón was the first to ask, "So what'd you guys do anyhow?"

Jackson and Ian took turns recounting their escapade and the ensuing questions asked by the respective Interpol agents. Rich and Dr. Naceri peppered them with questions about the theft, chase, and interrogation while Ramón seemed more interested in a description of Agent Fiore.

"Jackson's theory that Interpol is tracking another treasure hunter is valid," Joel said when they were finished. "Ali, can you make some calls and see if you can get any heads up on who it might be?"

"My contacts will wonder why I am asking," she said. "They will assume we are after it too."

"Be as discreet as possible, but it's a chance we'll have to take. Ramón, do you know anyone who might be able to give us a clue on what Interpol has so far?"

"I can make a call."

"What do you want from me, oh fearless leader?" Ian asked.

"Background on Fiore and John. You don't need to do a deep dive, but just see if there's anything obviously relevant. Particularly where they're from, if they have any discernible connection to the Calvary Treasure, that sort of thing."

"Lovely," Ian said, downing a handful of M&M's.

"Rich, I want you to make travel arrangements."

"Where and when?"

"Considering recent developments, as soon as possible," Joel said. "As for where, Ali, Maggie, Jackson, you and I will head to France."

"Marseille?"

"Yeah. We can rent a car from there, so you might want to arrange that as well."

"And where are we headed?" Ian asked. "Greece?"

"Yeah. You, Cara, and Ramón can get us set up there. Cara can handle logistics on site, and Ramón can smooth anything out with the locals to make sure we're ready to roll when we arrive."

"And I'll become acquainted with the local indigenous population."

Joel ignored him. "We'll meet with Philippe and be a day behind you."

Ian nodded and announced that he just wanted to change before getting busy. Jackson followed suit, then sought out Joel. "What can I do?"

"Help Rich. I'd have you work on the cross, but until Cara can get a clear image that we can translate, we're at a standstill."

Maggie and Dr. Naceri had returned to their suite for the evening. Ian and Ramón were likewise working from their room, so Joel, Jackson, and Rich were alone in their suite. Except for Cara, who still sat at the table by the window, dead to the world around her, only mumbling occasionally. Jackson sat down beside Rich, and they spent the next twenty minutes parsing flights. There was nothing direct from New York to Marseille, forcing them to route through either London or Paris. There was also a red-eye to Moscow that backtracked through Istanbul, but that didn't get them to Marseille any sooner than flights leaving the following afternoon, which didn't arrive until late morning on Sunday.

"That's the soonest?" Joel asked, having overheard their conversation.

"Afraid so," Rich said.

"Not atypical," Cara said without looking up.

"Do what you think is best," Joel said as he ducked into the bathroom.

"Paris or London?" Rich asked.

"What about chartering another jet?" Jackson asked.

Rich shook his head. "Joel got a discount on that from a buddy who owed him a favor. Don't expect that to be the norm."

"In that case, London. I disdain all things French."

"It's a little longer flight . . ."

"London," Jackson said again.

Rich reserved five tickets and began plugging in information. Jackson helped him select the best seats on the two flights, wondering if Rich noticed that he tried to place himself between Maggie and Dr. Naceri. He was, after all, only human, and if he were going to spend half a day cramped in a flying tube, he'd rather look across a lovely archaeologist at cloud tufts than share a *SkyMall* with an alleged psychic.

Ian entered the room while Rich took a confirmation phone call on the car rental in Marseille. "John and Fiore are dead ends," he announced. "Not much to find and what's there is trivial."

"It was worth a try," Joel said. He'd since changed into khakis and a long-sleeved University of Virginia tee.

"Also met Ali in the hallway. She said she crapped out trying to find out who else is after the treasure. Asked me to pass it on to you."

"I'm guessing she didn't use the words 'crapped out' though," Joel said.

"Aye."

"Thanks, Ian."

"No problem," he said, popping a few M&M's. "If that's all, I'm sacking out, yeah?"

"See you tomorrow."

"Aye. Not too early," he said with a glance at Rich.

"Not a problem."

"I'm leaving too," Cara said, standing up. "I'll pack up the computer tomorrow."

"How'd you do?" Joel asked.

"I've still got a few things to try. In the morning? I'm bushed."

"That's fine. Get a good night's sleep."

Jackson offered a smile at Cara as she passed, and then the three guys were alone in their suite. Rich was checking flights to Greece, and Jackson didn't have much interest in the other half of Team Joel's flying arrangements, so he crashed in a chair with a view of the city that, true to its reputation, didn't sleep.

"So what do you think, now having a day's experience?" Joel asked. He sat in a chair opposite Jackson.

"It feels like three days' experience," Jackson replied. "But I have to say, I had a feeling something might go down tonight."

"Oh?"

Jackson shrugged. "Call it a hunch. If there are other guys out there like you who spend their life hunting old Crusader treasures, it only stands to reason your guy at the Athens museum isn't the only insider in the bunch. Or you aren't his only contact."

Joel nodded.

"I didn't necessarily expect a smash-and-grab, but again, I can't say I'm surprised somebody else made a play."

"You're not alone."

"You suspected?"

Joel shook his head, then nodded at Rich, who was back on the phone. "His vision, remember? That something bad would happen."

Jackson sighed.

"Hey, I don't know what to make of it either," Joel said, "but you can't deny what happened."

"What happened, no," Jackson said. His second sigh turned into a yawn. "You know, one thing's curious."

"What's that?"

"Why'd they take the cross? Why not just sneak a few photos like we did?"

"You see the trouble Cara's having cleaning up harried snapshots?"

"Yeah, but it sure lowers the risk factor."

"This also keeps anyone else from getting a look at it."

Jackson cut his eyes to Joel and slowly nodded. "That . . ." He shook his finger. "That makes sense." He leaned forward. "It's one thing to have clues, but another if nobody else has what you have."

"And they don't know we do."

"So they think we're out of it."

Joel smiled.

"Hey, that reminds me. This friend of yours."

"Philippe."

"He's got the so-called Father piece, right?"

"Right."

"And it's not public knowledge?"

"Very few people know he has it, and even if they did, it wouldn't do them much good. Philippe's security is second to none."

"But he's going to let us look at it?"

Joel nodded.

"So no matter what everybody else has, we have a leg up on them?"

"As long as we get the piece in Greece first."

"So why not all of us go to Greece right away?"

Joel steepled his fingers. "The legend of the journal sort of implied that the pieces were necessary, not only to find the Calvary Treasure but also to reveal information about each other. I don't know what that means, but I want as much information up front as possible."

Rich set his phone down and stood. "Cara, Ian, and Ramón are all set. They leave JFK a couple hours after we do."

"Good work, Rich."

"Just don't check the credit card statement."

Joel grinned as a knock sounded on the door. Rich was closest and went to open it. Disregarding him, Ramón pushed through, wearing a white ribbed tank top, boxers, and black socks. A nice look.

"I called a friend in Barcelona who owed me a favor," Ramón said. "His brother works with the *Centro Nacional de Inteligencia* and can't say what Interpol is or isn't doing. But he suspects that the group they're after is called the *Chevaliers Calvaire*. And get this," Ramón added with a smirk. "The *Chevaliers Calvaire* is thought to be—"

"The remnants and or descendants of the Knights Calvary," Joel said.

Ramón frowned. "You know them?"

"No. I just translated."

"You don't speak French, man."

"No, but I know that *chevalier* is French for knight, and *calvaire* is fairly obvious."

"Why'd your friend's brother think they were the ones Interpol was after?" Jackson asked.

"He said the exhibition comes to Spain in a couple months and they're already on the alert that the CC might be after this particular cross."

Joel sighed. "Well, if someone else is after the Calvary Treasure, the *Chevaliers Calvaire* would make as much sense as anyone else."

Jackson frowned.

"You disagree?" Joel asked.

"No. But we thought the cross was stolen so that whoever took it wouldn't have to worry about anyone else beating them to the treasure. Maybe their concern isn't being beaten to the treasure but having anyone find it at all."

"You mean they're protecting the treasure?" Joel said.

"It's a theory."

"What difference does it make, man?" Ramón asked.

"Because about the only thing more dangerous than greedy treasure hunters—no inference implied," Jackson said with a glance at Joel, "are zealots motivated by ideology—in this case, to keep a millennium-old treasure secret."

Chapter Nine

Saturday, February 9
2:06 p.m.

JACKSON HAD SLEPT until ten a.m., which he determined at the group's brunch put him somewhere in the middle of the waking order. Team Joel had dined at an upscale café on Manhattan's East Side on their way back to JFK, where, shortly after two, they passed through security in the International Concourse. Their gates were less than a hundred yards apart, and Ian, Cara, and Ramón's flight to Athens via Rome didn't leave until five. So they waited with the rest of the team until it was time for them to board their 747 to London Heathrow International Airport.

"Anything good?" Jackson asked Rich as he thumbed through the sports section of *The New York Times*.

"Pitchers and catchers report this week."

"Baseball, already? Hard to believe," Jackson said as he stared out the window at a cold, gray sky. The mild weather of the day and night before had been swept out to sea by an overnight cold front, and February in New York now looked and felt like February in New York. Jackson hoped the south of France would be warmer.

"Can I ask you something?" he said. He and Rich were seated in a different row, slightly set off from the rest of Team Joel. It was going to be a crowded flight, and they had been the only seats left after Jackson returned from the bathroom.

"Of course."

"Joel said he has several permanent members on his team and the rest are freelancers."

"You want to know who's who?"

Jackson nodded.

"Cara, Ian, and I are the full-timers," Rich answered. "Ali and Ramón are quote-unquote freelancers, although I can't remember the last major excursion they didn't join us on."

"So how long have you been with Joel?"

"Coming up on five years."

"That's a long time."

"Ian's almost eight. Cara's the newbie," he said, flipping the page of his paper. "Joel hired her two and a half years ago."

"How about Ramón and the doc?"

"They were both working with him before I started. Ramón was a little more infrequent back then. But Aliana's as loyal as they come."

"How do you mean?"

"Well, they aren't technically on the payroll, but she's as much of the team as anyone."

"And Ramón isn't?"

"I shouldn't say that," Rich said. He folded the paper. "Ramón's just a little more . . . aloof."

Jackson nodded, then dipped his head at the newspaper. "You done?"

"Be my guest."

The Super Bowl had been a week ago, which was as good as the twelfth-century in modern news cycles. Jackson skimmed headlines about the NBA and NHL regular seasons, not holding out much hope for the Lakers. He scanned a story about a Phil Mickelson charge at Pebble Beach, then returned the paper to Rich.

"Keep it. It was on the seat when I sat down."

Jackson shrugged, figuring it might be good for a crossword puzzle somewhere over Newfoundland.

A few minutes later, the first boarding calls were made for the group's flight. Joel stood, and the rest of his team followed suit, locating their tickets and IDs and making sure they had their carry-on luggage. Joel took a deep breath. "I guess we're off then."

"I'll send you my translation as soon as I have it finished," Cara said after a round of handshakes and well wishes. She had finished enhancing the photos on the ride to the airport. One inscription was identifiable as Mark 4:22, the verse Joel had quoted to Jackson back at Cameron's and that also, according to him, was engraved on Philippe's Father piece.

The other three weren't quite so clear, and Cara hadn't had a chance to translate the Latin to English. The plan was for her and Dr. Naceri both to take a crack at translating, Cara via her computer software and Dr. Naceri through her knowledge of Latin. It wasn't as simple as plunking the verses into Google, Cara had explained, because a lot of the Latin was partially indecipherable and needed to be analyzed. Plus she wanted maximum accuracy, not a thirty-second search engine result. And Dr. Naceri, while she was familiar enough with Latin and had translated from it before, wasn't fluent enough to translate on the fly and thus would also need to take her time for accuracy's sake. Once they were done, they would compare their translations to each other's and to English translations of the Latin Vulgate— assuming the rest of the inscriptions on the cross were indeed Scripture verses. With any luck, all the translations would match and make some sort of sense.

"Sounds like a plan," Joel said. He gave Cara a brother-to-sister side hug. "Keep these two in line."

"Yeah right."

"We'll see you in a day or two," Joel said. Then he, Jackson, Maggie, Rich, and Dr. Naceri joined the line of people slowly shuffling toward the Jetway.

"Give my best to Philippe, yeah?" Ian called after them with what sounded like a trace of sarcasm.

"That's two L's, one P," Jackson said as if Maggie should be taking notes.

"Actually it's one L, two P's and an E," Rich corrected.

"Ah, yes, the French spelling," Jackson muttered.

The 747 was massive, but sadly not a double-decker. At any rate, bigger was better, Jackson figured, as far as avoiding turbulence and the other side effects of flight. Rich had booked coach seats, meaning rows of three on the left side of the airplane. Jackson's ticket had him between Maggie and Dr. Naceri and he saw no reason to switch with Joel, Rich, or the stranger in the window seat beside them two rows ahead.

They sat on the apron for a while, and both Maggie and Dr. Naceri busied themselves on their phones. So Jackson made a production of unfolding and refolding the newspaper to try his hand at the crossword puzzle. Bad, he knew, blowing his only distraction before they even started moving. But sitting idling on the apron drove him nuts if he thought about it.

When they finally lifted off, it was as smooth of an ascent as Jackson had ever experienced. They took off to the southwest and then promptly banked over the ocean until they were heading just north of east. Long Island passed out the window, and by the time it was just dark blue beneath them, Maggie was dozing, and Dr. Naceri was haphazardly flipping through her magazine.

So Jackson ran all the facts of the "case" through his head. There weren't many of them, and he wasn't sure what they might mean in the future. But his brain liked to ruminate on the back burner, and he felt obliged to stir the pot now and again. So he spent some time recalling conversations with and about the various members of Team Joel, the events that had transpired at the gallery and the presence of Interpol there, and Joel's historical accounts of the Crusaders and the Calvary Treasure. That brought to mind the research Joel and Rich had conducted that morning (they had been early risers) on the CC, or *Chevaliers Calvaire*.

The CC didn't exactly have a website with an "About Us" page, so much of their research had been secondhand or hearsay. But over brunch and on the way to the airport, Joel had expressed his belief that the facts were genuine. According to legend and lore, the majority of the Knights Calvary had perished at The Horns of Hattin or in the Siege of Jerusalem or else had been scattered after Saladin's conquest. But a few had remained, taking up residence in the Middle East or returning to Europe. The small core maintained their identity and continued to be a part of subsequent Crusades.

When the Crusades petered out in the thirteenth century, the Knights Calvary-turned-CC resolved to rid the earth of Islam. But lacking the numbers to do anything of consequence, their focus turned to finding relics and other religious treasures, both to empower them in battle and as a means of amassing wealth. As a result, although their number had remained small over the years, they had become a prosperous, powerful group. And their ideology had morphed from ridding the world of Islam to something of an "us against the world" mentality that opposed not only Islam but also anyone who sympathized with Islam or who wasn't as passionately anti-Isalm as the CC was. While they professed opposition to violence, their lack of tolerance for anyone not fully aligned with them was growing.

Jackson agreed with Joel's assessment that such a group could indeed be dangerous, but with this new knowledge, he wasn't so sure they were interested in protecting Crusader treasure. If the research was valid, and Joel believed it was, the CC was more likely seeking it for their own purposes. Whatever the reason, their involvement could only complicate things.

A flight attendant offering drinks interrupted Jackson's thoughts. He opted for a ginger ale and ordered one for snoozing Maggie as well. Outside, the sky had grown dark, and what little of Canada's rugged eastern coast might have been visible was lost in the blackness.

So Jackson decided to make conversation with Dr. Naceri. She was slowly sipping her tea and staring blankly out the window at the night sky, and Jackson had to remind himself to be a gentleman and not stare. He cleared his throat softly. "So, Dr. Naceri, how long have you been working with Joel?"

She smiled. "Aliana, please. Or Ali if you prefer." Her accent was very thin, almost untraceable to Jackson's ears, and took nothing away from her perfect diction. "Dr. Naceri sounds so formal."

Jackson returned the smile. "Okay, Aliana. Rich said you were working with Joel before he joined the team?"

She nodded. "I have been with him for just over six years now. I first met Joel when he was working on a dig in Egypt with Philippe. By chance, I happened to be quite familiar with the particular piece they were seeking. I provided meager assistance, but more importantly, Joel and I formed a trust with one another. He brought me in on consultations a couple more times. Before I knew it, I was practically a regular."

"Where's the doctorate from, if I may ask?"

"Cairo University," she replied as she took a sip of tea.

"Archaeology?"

"Yes. I also studied religion and history at the University of Paris before that."

"Wow."

"It is not as impressive as you may think. I have always had a passion for the past, for the people, their culture, their beliefs. Studying is easy when you care about the subject."

"I suppose."

"How about yourself?" she asked. "What is your passion?"

"Good question," Jackson said, pausing for a moment to consider his response. "I've bounced around my whole life, trying to find my place, my calling, if you will. I became a private investigator because I thought it was the way God could use me. I thought I could help people," he said with a shrug. "I guess you could call that a passion."

"How long have you been a private investigator?"

"Going on two years this May."

"I think that is a very noble choice."

"Perhaps."

"Well, Joel speaks very highly of you."

"Truth be told, I'm feeling a little under the gun. The 'brilliant' P.I. who comes in to solve the riddle?"

"Well, 'brilliant' might be overstating it a little," Aliana said, then laughed softly to show she was teasing. "In truth, I feel the same way. Every piece that is found, every old coin or tablet or page of a journal, I am expected to be able to identify. They presume that I will know who wrote it, when, and what they were having for lunch at the time."

"Why do I have the feeling you can do exactly that, though?"

Aliana looked down as she took another drink of her tea. While the plane continued to cut through the night sky and Maggie continued to slumber beside him, Jackson got to know Dr. Aliana Naceri better. Born in Toulouse, France, she had spent her childhood mostly in Paris and Cairo, depending on where her father's work took the family. An archaeologist, professor, lecturer, and renowned man of knowledge, he had instilled in Aliana her passion for antiquities. She now lived in Paris, but her apartment there served as more of a base camp than a permanent home. When it wasn't Joel, it was someone else seeking her expertise. The constant travel kept her from marrying and having a family of her own, she shared, surprising Jackson with the vulnerability offered to a relative stranger.

But it was a two-way street with Aliana. She asked Jackson about his family, his childhood, and his bare ring finger. After nearly an hour of conversation, he concluded the openness was just Aliana's style. And in a world of guarded, closed people, he found her refreshing.

During the course of their conversation, Aliana also revealed that she was a semi-devout Sunni Muslim. She confessed to Jackson that it wasn't something she was overly open about, in large part because so many people associated the word "Muslim" with terrorism. Whether it was 9/11 jihadists or Saladin's armies of the twelfth century, Muslims were generally labeled as the enemy, and she insisted that wasn't true.

"I do not disagree that there are fanatics and zealots in Islam," she said. "Even many of them. But almost one-quarter of the world is Muslim, and the vast majority of us are not terrorists."

"I have to admit," Jackson said, "I'm probably guilty of falling prey to that perception at times."

"I think most in America were after the horrible images of September 11, 2001," Aliana said. "Unfortunately, the rotten apple spoils the barrel, to use a phrase."

Jackson wanted to ask her about jihad and how she explained the fact that the Quran seemed to promote so many of the fanatical actions that gave Islam its reputation. But he didn't know enough about the religion to argue the fine points with her and he didn't want to upset her with what would just sound like ugly American attitudes. He also didn't think it particularly wise to have a long conversation about jihad on an airplane.

He was given a reprieve when dinner was served and when Maggie finally woke up.

"Where are we?" she asked.

"Five minutes outside of London."

"Really?"

"No," Aliana said. "A couple of hours out from New York. It is only five-thirty, Eastern Time."

Maggie sighed. "Super."

"Look on the bright side," Jackson said as the flight attendant set steaming plates of chicken, rice, and vegetables in front of them.

"What's that?"

"They aren't serving British food."

The chicken wasn't bad, perhaps a little tough, and the mixed vegetables resembled the plastic toy food made for little kids. Tasted about the same too, if Jackson remembered correctly after three decades. And the rice was, well, rice.

When he had finished eating the edible parts of dinner, Jackson turned again to Aliana. "So can I ask you a question . . . about being a Muslim?"

She glanced at him for a moment before nodding.

"How does it affect your view of the Crusades? Joel rightly said that Americans, particularly Christians—however you interpret the word—tend to have a 'we' and 'them' mentality. I was just wondering if you view it the other way around."

"Not so much," she replied, placing her silverware on top of her cleaned off plate. "I think, for one thing, it was a very long time ago. Being a Christian or a Muslim a thousand years ago is different from being one now."

"Aren't the core beliefs still the same?" Jackson asked.

"Theoretically, yes. But that does not mean they have always been adhered to with the same intensity or accuracy. I think that saying two people, centuries apart, have the same theology because they are both Christian or Muslim is an assumption."

Jackson nodded, mulling her words.

"But to answer your question, I think both the Christian and the Muslim sides had valid claims to Jerusalem and the Holy Land, and I think they both acted regrettably during the Crusades . . . and ever since. I also think they had factions in their group that acted contrary to their particular beliefs—as they were then and as they are now—who again, like the 9/11 terrorists, cast a negative light over an entire faith."

"So both sides shoulder the blame," Maggie said.

"Yes," Aliana said. "As is the case with almost any war or conflict, I would imagine. Very seldom is it a clear case of good versus evil."

"See, that is an open, objective viewpoint," Maggie said. "Jackson defends his Christian faith as if it is the great white hope and all other views will be damned for all eternity."

"Mine wouldn't be much of a viewpoint if it held yours to be equally valid, would it?" Jackson asked.

"Of course. Reasonable people can disagree."

"Sure. But that doesn't mean they're both right."

Maggie shook her head. "Why do you have to be that way? Only you're right. That isn't a fact, you know?"

"No, that only I'm right is my belief. What's fact is that you and I can't disagree and both be right—not about something like this."

"Why not? Why can't different religions both be valid?"

"Because they make contrasting claims. Christians believe in an omnipotent God. Atheists believe there is no God. So can God both exist and not exist at the same time? Either He is, or He isn't. Either the Christian is right, and the atheist is wrong, or the other way around."

"So you're saying Ali's Muslim beliefs are incorrect?" Maggie asked.

"I wouldn't be adhering to my beliefs if I said otherwise. Christians believe in a triune God—Father, Son, and Holy Spirit. Muslims—correct me if I'm wrong—acknowledge Jesus as a prophet, but not as God."

Aliana nodded. "That is correct."

"They also believe that Muhammad was the final prophet, whereas Christians don't recognize his claims. Again, correct me if I'm wrong, Aliana, but Muslims believe a person gets to heaven or Paradise if their good works outweigh their bad; Christians believe a person gets to heaven because Christ's blood paid the penalty for their sins. How can two belief systems who disagree on who God is, disagree on the authority and identity of the central person in their religion, and disagree on how one obtains eternal life—the ultimate purpose of any faith or religion—How can they be equally valid? Either one or the other or neither is correct, but they cannot both be."

"He is right," Aliana said. "Though many people would argue otherwise, and though they do share some similar beliefs, the claims of Christianity and the claims of Islam are, at their core, mutually exclusive."

"Isn't that what's led to wars over the years?" Maggie asked. "Dogmatic disagreements?"

"I would argue it is less the disagreements and more the handling of those disagreements," Aliana stated. "Like Jackson said, the two of us have opposing views, but we have been talking civilly for several hours."

"Yeah, Maggie," Jackson said. "If you could just learn to be more intellectual and highbrow, perhaps we could agree to disagree without so much tension."

"I'll show you tension," she said. Then she leaned forward to look at Aliana. "This from a guy who ends every argument with a smart-aleck comment or an '80s TV reference."

Aliana grinned.

Jackson turned to Maggie, staring at her until she finally asked, "What?"

"I'm going through the Rolodex," he said, "and I can't think of a single applicable line from *Magnum*, *MacGyver*, *The A-Team* . . . *Rockford*, anything." With that, he excused himself to use the restroom and stretch his legs.

Chapter Ten

Sunday, February 10
5:21 a.m. (British Standard Time)

THE REST OF the flight had passed peacefully, with Jackson even catching some meaningful sleep. It had been a seven-hour flight, plus a five-hour time change, putting them in London just after three a.m. on Sunday. Or ten p.m. Saturday, New York time. Or seven p.m. Saturday, L.A. time. It was the second short day in a row, and Jackson found himself wide awake and wandering London's massive Heathrow Airport while the other members of Team Joel slept or read or counted minutes until their eight a.m. departure for Marseille.

Starving, he found a Krispy Kreme and was suddenly overcome with the decency to buy donuts for everyone. He brought them back to the waiting area where Maggie was currently the only one awake. He set the donuts on her lap.

"Peace offering?"

"Wasn't aware we were at war."

"You enjoy our verbal sparring?"

"And you don't?"

She fought a sly grin as she opened the donut box. The movement or the smell woke Joel beside her, and she passed him the box. He nudged Rich awake, deeming it was time for him to have breakfast, then pulled out his phone as he started on a jelly-filled.

"It's Cara," he said, reading a text. "They just arrived in Rome, and she finished the translations."

"That's great," Rich said.

"Ip a mab?" Jackson asked through a mouthful of donut. Maggie kicked his shin. Beside him, Aliana stirred, awoke slowly, and was passed the news that Cara had translated the other three verses found on the cross.

"She come up with the same thing as me?" Aliana asked, having translated the verses from Latin to English on the flight. "No thanks," she said to the donut box.

"She's e-mailing an encrypted version now," Joel said. "I'll pull it up when we get to the hotel. It'll be easier to view them side by side on a laptop."

Aliana nodded. She'd had to guess at a few words, she'd informed Jackson as they'd begun their descent into London, but had concluded the four engravings were quotations of Psalm 103:4, Mark 4:22, John 1:14, and John 15:26, albeit without the chapter and verse references. Aside from the Mark allusion to finding hidden things and a mention of the Holy Spirit in John 15, she hadn't detected any obvious relevance to their search.

"So I never asked," Jackson said while Joel returned Cara's text and Rich closed his eyes to get more sleep/another vision, "as our antiquities expert, do you have any hunch or take on what the Calvary Treasure is?"

"It could be anything," Aliana said. "Crusaders were known for their love of gold and jewels and other valuables, like we saw last night, wh—"

"Two nights ago," Rich said, his eyes still closed.

"Was it?"

He nodded.

"I suppose so. But that does not separate them from most anyone else. But Crusaders were also very intent on finding objects of religious significance."

"The Holy Grail and the Ark of the Covenant," Jackson said, taking another bite of his donut.

"Yes."

He swallowed. "So we could be hunting for millions of dollars' worth of gold or Saint Peter's long-lost belt buckle?"

Joel grinned as he set down his phone. "I doubt it's quite that wide of a discrepancy, but I told you I was a history hunter, not necessarily a treasure hunter."

"You did."

"I know we're mostly working off legend and this long-lost journal," Maggie said, "but is there anything from the history of the Knights Calvary or their time in Jerusalem that would give us a clue?"

"If there is, I haven't been able to find it," Joel replied. "There are a number of legends of treasure linked to the Knights Calvary, but they all pale in comparison to the so-called Calvary Treasure."

"And none of them appear to have any link to it," Aliana added.

"What about from the Muslim side?" Maggie asked. "We're looking at this from a perspective of what the Crusaders found. Maybe we should also look at what the Muslims lost. Didn't you say something, Joel, about the treasure originating with a Muslim caravan being robbed?"

Joel nodded. "In the hope chest of a young—likely teenage—girl traveling with the caravan, yes."

"Does that open any possibilities?" Maggie asked.

"Not from the research I have done," Aliana said. "But that does not mean no."

"I'm just thinking, don't Christianity and Islam have the same starting point? Don't they both trace things back to Abraham?"

"Yes," Joel said.

"So couldn't this be something that wouldn't be of significance only to Christians but also to Muslims? Something that unites their two faiths?"

Joel shook his head.

"Why not?"

"Two reasons. First—and this is according to legend so take it with a grain of salt—the treasure supposedly was something that would help the Crusaders defeat Islam, not unite them. Second, although both religions trace human ancestry back to Abraham and his two sons, Isaac and Ishmael, they have drastically different beliefs."

"But you both believe in the same God, right? You just use different terminology."

"No," three voices said at once.

Maggie frowned. "I've always heard that Allah is just another name for God."

"Muslims believe in an all-powerful, sovereign God," Joel said.

"'*There is no god but Allah*,'" Aliana stated.

"But ask her if she believes Jesus was and is also God."

Maggie looked at Aliana, who shook her head.

"It's like I told you on the plane," Jackson said. "Christians believe that Jesus Christ was and is God in the flesh. He's as much God as God the Father or God the Spirit."

"Which to Muslims is blasphemy," Aliana said.

"Jesus is the central figure of all history," Joel said. "He claimed to be God and then He did things to back it up. No one else, not even Muhammad, ever claimed deity."

Maggie looked at Aliana. "What do you say to that?"

"He is right that Muhammad never made claims of deity because Muhammad knew that he was only a prophet of Allah."

"What about Jesus?"

"He too was a prophet. According to the Quran, on the Day of Resurrection, Jesus will deny before Allah that he is deserving of worship. *'Worship Allah, my Lord and your Lord.'*"

"The coexist bumper stickers and messages of tolerance the media pushes sound great and make everyone feel warm and fuzzy," Joel said, "and I don't deny that we need to be tolerant and allow others to have their own beliefs. But either Jesus was who He said He was or He wasn't. If He was, there are very real implications that each of us needs to deal with. If not, then there are other implications that other religions are left to meet."

"But if your beliefs are so diametrically opposed to one another, how do you work together?" Maggie asked.

"Just because I disagree with someone," Aliana said, "does not mean that I cannot respect them, particularly in matters other than that which we disagree about."

"Right, but your purpose on this team is to find history—to find the truth about history. How does that work when you disagree about what truth is?"

"We have different starting points," Joel said. "And we disagree because of them, at times. But while we both believe that our potential finds add credence to our beliefs, we're not likely to find the smoking gun that unilaterally proves or disproves Christianity or Islam. We're seeking historical truth, which can be viewed through a lens of Christian faith or Muslim faith. Regardless of the lens, it doesn't change our find—at least, not in any instance thus far. And, as far as working with someone with whom I disagree, Jesus said we are to love everyone. He didn't exclude those who don't share our faith; in fact, it is those people we are especially called to be light to."

"So you basically admit you're trying to convert each other?" Maggie asked.

"Some would suggest the Quran promotes hostility toward anyone who does not share my beliefs," Aliana said. "I think a better interpretation is that I am called to share the truth with them in the hope that they will one day embrace it as I do."

"Aliana knows where I stand," Joel said, "and she is very familiar with the claims of Christ. The choice of what to do with those claims is up to her. Either way, I am called to love her with the love of Christ."

"Well, I have to hand it to you all. That can't be easy."

"Sharing a common goal certainly helps," Joel said. "To that end, I have a phone call I must make. Will you excuse me?"

Jackson frowned. Who was Joel calling at five-thirty-something in the morning? Then again, they had been all over the world in the last few days. It could be lunchtime the following day or dinnertime the day before wherever Joel was calling. And Jackson was too interested in a second donut to worry about it.

* * *

8:03 a.m.

THE JET that took them from London to Marseille was smaller than the 747 that had borne them to London but was still plenty roomy. Jackson sat beside Aliana again, this time with Rich beside him (Joel wanted to discuss some things with Maggie). Rich split his time between reading the Bible, scouting a *Sporting News*, and sleeping. No visions were reported. Aliana, meanwhile, briefed Jackson on the city of Marseille.

Situated on the rugged southern coast of France, Marseille was the second largest city in the country, behind only Paris. It was also the country's oldest, having been settled over twenty-five hundred years prior by the Greeks. From under Greek to Roman to Visigoth to French rule, the city had continued to grow and had been introduced to Christianity. It became a major center of commerce and culture, which Aliana claimed it still was to the present day. In addition to its many first-rate restaurants, clubs, and theaters, the city boasted several fine art galleries and museums, as well as an opera house. She didn't comment on its sports teams.

As expected, Marseille had a Mediterranean climate, which meant even in the winter, the weather was usually mild and humid. But she did warn of the mistral, a strong wind that swept through the Rhone Valley at speeds up to ninety kilometers per hour. While it often brought with it clear weather, it could make the temperatures quite cold. Suddenly Jackson became anxious to check the forecast.

Out the window, it was clear and sunny as they flew over the English Channel and northern France. But as the landscape changed to more rugged, mountainous terrain, clouds began to obscure the view. Jackson hoped they weren't accompanied by strong winds. He'd experienced the Santa Anas back in L.A. and preferred gentle breezes or perfect calm.

Marseille Provence Airport was located some fifteen miles northwest of the city center just over Lake Berre, which Aliana explained was actually connected to the Mediterranean by a small canal. The flight touched down just before eleven a.m. local time, but it was noon by the time the group passed through customs. They grabbed a quick lunch at the airport's food court (Jackson found a McDonald's and felt right at home) before taking a shuttle to the rental car lot. With all of Joel's money at his disposal, Rich had suddenly gone cheap and reserved a cramped, five-passenger Renault. Ever the gentleman, Jackson had volunteered to sit in back, crammed between Maggie and Aliana.

Shortly before one o'clock Central European Time (nine hours ahead of Pacific Standard Time) the group, with Joel at the wheel, departed the airport and headed to their hotel a few miles away. It was still several miles from the sea, with a view of a commercial park that looked very American. Aside from a check-in clerk who came off as something of a milquetoast, Jackson had to admit that so far France wasn't too bad.

Joel gave the team a few minutes to freshen up, during which time he tried calling Ian. The other members of Team Joel were in Athens, waiting for a flight to the coastal city of Kavala. It had the closest airport to the Byzantine church that would provide clues, presumably, to the third piece of the "Holy Trinity," and would serve as the team's home base during their time in Greece.

While at the hotel, Joel also booted up his laptop and pulled up Cara and Aliana's translations of the verses found on the lead cross. They were almost a word-for-word match, and he next opened an online version of the Latin Vulgate (with an English translation) and compared each of the three translated verses to it. Another almost perfect match.

Joel had already made repeated mention of Mark 4:22, and Jackson just glanced at the words once to refresh his memory:

For there is nothing hid, which shall not be made manifest: neither was it made secret, but that it may come abroad.

The other three he studied more carefully, committing them to memory while trying to figure out what they were doing engraved on a lead cross that had found its way to the bottom of the Mediterranean:

Who makest thy angels spirits: and thy ministers a burning fire. – Psalm 103:4?

And the Word was made flesh and dwelt among us (and we saw his glory, the glory as it were of the only begotten of the Father), full of grace and truth. – John 1:14

But when the Paraclete cometh, whom I will send you from the Father, the Spirit of truth, who proceedeth from the Father, he shall give testimony of me. - John 15:26

"Why no references in the Latin?" Maggie asked over Jackson's shoulder. There had been no references on the cross, just the verses, and Cara or Aliana had added them to their translations.

"The Bible wasn't written with chapters and verses," Joel said. "They were added much later, well after the time of the Crusades."

"Why the question mark after Psalm 103:4?"

"Cara said some of the references don't match exactly with what is in our modern translations. I think she said this verse is actually Psalm 104:4 in her Bible." He shrugged. Maggie raised a skeptical eyebrow at Jackson. He too shrugged.

Joel looked at Jackson, ready to close his laptop. "Good?"

"Yeah. Shut her down."

"Got it solved already?" Maggie asked.

"Very nearly," he said, tongue-in-cheek.

None of the group was excited about more travel, but time was of the essence. So shortly before two, they loaded back into the Renault and set out for the town of Trois Ruisseaux some hundred miles north and east of Marseille. This time Aliana sat in front, giving her a little more room to use Joel's laptop to research the three verses to see if there were any ties to the Crusades, the Knights Calvary, or anything else connected to the hunt for the treasure. That left Jackson in back with Maggie and Rich. He opted for a window seat and watched the blur of Marseille blend into the blur of Aix-en-Provence. As they left the cities behind and followed the Durance River into the foothills of the Alps, a blustery gray sky began to spit flurries. Jackson missed Southern California.

Tired of looking out the window, he turned to Rich. "You happen to have a vision today?"

Rich turned an inquisitive eye to Jackson. "No."

"Why do you ask?" Maggie asked.

"Just curious."

"You're never just curious, Jack."

"I'm always curious."

"Yes, and you always have a reason to be curious."

He sighed. "I thought I saw somebody at the airport."

Joel glanced at him in the rearview mirror. "Who?"

"I don't know. Guy, six-foot, a little bulky. He was wearing too-tight jeans and a plain brown shirt, very nondescript, always looking at his phone."

"Isn't that everybody?" Rich asked.

"I saw him when we passed through customs, saw him when we were buying food, and caught a glimpse of him when we were getting on the shuttle."

"You think he was following us?" Joel asked.

"I don't know. He could have just been a guy, hungry and looking for transportation after an international flight. But I sort of had a feeling there was something off about him." He shrugged. "Then again, it's France. There's something off about most of the guys."

"I haven't had any visions since New York," Rich said.

"How often do you usually get them?" Maggie asked.

"It varies. There's no set schedule or frequency." He looked to Jackson. "Who do you think is following us?"

"Other treasure hunters, the *Chevaliers Calvaire*, Interpol."

"Well, we have that mystery to look forward to solving too," Maggie said.

The hills around them began to rise, still far from being anything Matterhorn-like, but the scenery was good enough to warrant Jackson's attention. The flurries turned into actual snow showers, and before long, the flakes were beginning to accumulate on grassy areas and the shoulder of the road.

"I hope this Trois Ruisseaux has a hotel," Jackson said.

"I'm sure if the weather turns, Philippe will put us up," Joel said.

"I should have brought my toothbrush."

"You said Philippe was a colleague of yours?" Maggie asked.

Joel nodded.

"How so?"

"We were partners, actually."

"Partners?"

"For over six years. I was still working on my Ph.D. from Temple when I met Philippe," Joel said. "We both had similar interests and bank books, and, whereas Philippe had experience and contacts from years of traveling the world looking for historical finds, I had an exuberance and fortitude that he liked—his words, by the way. We determined that we could accomplish more working together than if we were constantly straining against each other."

"Makes sense," Jackson said. "As long as you agreed on how to split the booty."

"Is that what caused you to split?" Maggie asked. "You spoke of your partnership in the past tense."

"No. Our interests simply began to change. Philippe was always a spiritual man, but instead of faith, he operated on superstition and sensationalism. Philippe believes the world can be redeemed through history, that understanding past cultures and beliefs is vital to the survival of the human race."

"Isn't that sort of what all historians believe?"

"Yes and no. I believe that history provides us excellent insights that can shed light on our present and future, but it isn't something mystical or redeeming. It fundamentally transforms what, why, and how you look for truth."

"And that's why you split?"

"It had also been six years, and we thought perhaps a fresh start was best. We could have continued to work together, just like Ali and I do despite our contradictory beliefs, but we agreed to go our separate ways."

"We?"

Joel nodded. "It was a joint decision, and the dissolution of our partnership was amicable. We've remained close friends to this day."

"But if you're not working together, why is Philippe letting you see his piece of the 'Holy Trinity'?" Jackson asked. "Isn't he after the Calvary Treasure too?"

"Not anymore," Joel said. "In recent years, Philippe has turned his pursuits from hunting to studying what has already been found. I've assured him that if we are successful, he'll have plenty of opportunity to pore over what we find."

"Sounds like a partnership to me," Maggie said.

"What's Ian's beef with him?" Jackson asked.

"You picked up on that, did you?" Joel chuckled. "Mostly personality. The two have never rubbed each other quite the right way."

"Is that why he's in Greece?" Maggie asked.

"Among other reasons."

When the questions ceased, Joel turned to Aliana. "You finding anything?"

"Nothing of note. Sorry."

"Is there anything else we need to know about this guy?" Jackson asked.

Joel met his eyes in the rearview mirror. "Philippe?"

Jackson nodded.

"I would say not. Just don't disagree with the man unless you know what you're talking about. Philippe is an expert at many subjects—history, religion, food, wine, music. And he has a narrow view of those who disagree."

"Sounds pleasant."

"I'm probably making him out to be worse than he is. Philippe's just like many very intelligent people in that he has trouble relating to those who aren't as intelligent—or rather, who he doesn't deem as intelligent—as he is."

"Or perceives himself to be," Aliana said.

"You don't care for him either?" Maggie asked.

"It is not that. I just have disagreed with Philippe enough times to indicate that either I am very foolish or he is not quite as intelligent as he thinks."

Joel smiled. "I will admit, Philippe can be a bit of a snob. And that has influenced his opinions and the intransigence of them."

Maggie nudged Jackson. "You need me to translate some of these big words?" she asked quietly.

"Thanks, but I'm following the general flow."

They continued to climb and soon arrived in the small village of Trois Ruisseaux. Situated on the slopes of a small valley almost four thousand feet above sea level, it was definitely quaint. The main drive was lined with shops, restaurants, and a small country inn ideal for honeymooning couples. Around the commercial center of town were a bunch of one-family houses that would have all had smoke curling from their identical chimneys in a Dickens novel or on a Christmas card. Jackson leaned toward the latter, seeing as how a couple inches of snow now blanketed the roofs, sidewalks, and city streets. All that was missing was the smoke-stained brownstone factory on the edge of town. The people of Trois Ruisseaux must have all been bookstore owners and baristas.

"Philippe lives in this town?" Jackson asked.

"No. He lives in Château LeCavalier, a castle twenty-five miles and a couple thousand feet up into the mountains," Joel replied.

"A castle?"

Joel nodded.

"Philippe lives in a castle in the Alps?"

He nodded again.

"Oh this just keeps getting better and better."

Chapter Eleven

4:25 p.m. (Central European Time)

GIANT SNOWFLAKES WERE gently but steadily fluttering to the ground as Joel pulled the team's Renault up to a wrought-iron gate in the middle of the woods. The gate was anchored in two ornate stone columns, on the left of which was mounted a small intercom device. As Joel lowered his window, a light blinked beneath the intercom, turning red and then green. A moment later, an austere, possibly feminine voice spoke through the intercom. "State your business please."

"Joel Robinson to see Mr. LeCavalier."

"One moment please, Mr. Robinson."

Seconds later, the gate split and swung inward. Joel pushed the car forward, its tires crunching on the new-fallen snow as he rolled up his window.

The group had left Trois Ruisseaux forty-five minutes earlier, climbing winding roads along sheer drop-offs higher and higher into the Alps. They had leveled off into a small forest of magnificent conifers, all coated with several inches of snow. Judging by the color of the overcast sky, sunset was still an hour or two away, but as the car wound through the trees, it felt like blackest night. When they emerged after several minutes, a spectacular view stretched before them.

To the right, the forest seemed to drop off the side of a gorge that extended straight ahead of them as far as the eye could see and that was lined by snow-capped mountains on either side. To the left, on the near side of the gorge, the same mountains seemed to scrape the sky, jagged peaks of purple and granite knifing through a blanket of pure white snow. It was nature at its most spectacular, a panorama that was jaw-dropping.

And yet, it wasn't the mountains or gorge that dominated the view, but rather a giant castle perched on the slope of the nearest mountain. Overall size was impossible to tell, seeing as how it rambled along the edge of the precipice on myriad levels and stories. Jackson counted at least a dozen circular turrets, all adorned with dark cone roofs. The slate-gray walls were smooth and pristine as if it had been built in the twenty-first century instead of centuries ago. There had to be a hundred windows, each nothing more than a dark slit in the granite from this distance. Cast in the gloom of late afternoon, shrouded by snowflakes, Château LeCavalier resembled something from a dream or a Disney fairy tale more than it did a medieval fortress.

The castle was not alone in the clearing. Maybe fifty yards from the entrance stood a small (only by comparison) outbuilding. Resembling a stable in design, it was actually a multi-car garage. No doubt housing a Rolls Royce and an Allard coupe or something else out of Clive Cussler's collection. But with the doors closed and no sign of any motor vehicles, it was not hard for Jackson to imagine he had been transported back to the Middle Ages and it housed snorting steeds, raring for battle.

Joel circled around in front of the garage and parked in front of the entrance to the castle. Or rather, the bridge to the entrance. A wide, stone walkway spanned some thirty feet of ravine, a small crevice that funneled runoff from the mountains to the main gorge. The walkway was flanked by a stone battlement and stopped at two massive wooden doors, the outside of each rounded to form a circular top. They were each at least ten feet tall, and as Jackson got out of the car, he realized he had underestimated the height of the castle's walls and towers.

"I take it your boy Philippe does pretty well," he said.

"He does," Joel said with a nod. "But he didn't buy the castle. He inherited it."

"Inherited?"

"Philippe can trace his lineage back to the fourth century after Christ. The castle has been in his family since it was built in the middle 1400s."

Jackson whistled.

"Do you want your laptop with you?" Aliana asked, looking at Joel across the Renault's roof.

"I have my tablet." He looked at the group as she closed her door. "Shall we?"

The walkway to the front doors had recently been shoveled, although Jackson didn't see any piles of snow. The group proceeded tenuously on the slick stones as the snow continued to fall around them.

"No drawbridge," Jackson observed.

"Probably not a lot of invading armies climbed to the timberline," Maggie said.

The left of the two massive wooden doors had a brass plaque inset in it, welcoming them to Château LeCavalier. A brass knocker was built into the right door, and Joel pounded it several times. Jackson strained his ears but couldn't hear the resounding footfalls of an approaching servant. In fact, he was amazed at how incredibly quiet the mountains were under the falling snow.

Then the door groaned as it was slowly pulled inward by a woman in a navy pantsuit, the jacket worn over a lighter blue shirt and ornamented with an ascot. She was young, nondescript except for dark eyes. Short light-brown hair rested on her shoulders, lacking any styling. When she spoke again, without the interference of an aged intercom system, her voice was a cross between Cate Blanchett and a French Judi Dench. "Mr. Robinson, I presume."

Joel nodded.

"Welcome, sir, to Château LeCavalier. Please come in."

Joel stepped inside, followed by Aliana, Maggie, Rich, and Jackson last of all. Each was greeted with a pleasant "Good evening, madam" or "Good evening, sir."

The woman introduced herself as Dufort and then declared that "Master LeCavalier" was waiting for them in the den. "Please follow me," she said and led them through an archway into a long, high-ceilinged hall. The entryway had been more spacious than Jackson's house; the hall was positively cavernous. The ribbed vault ceiling was at least thirty feet high. Red carpet ran down the middle of a gold and tan marble floor all the way to a wide spiral staircase at the far end of the hall. Arcades lined the left and right walls, sheltering doorways to other rooms and small seating alcoves, and housing various works of art. Above them, more arches partially concealed a mezzanine that circled the great hall. It was dark and shadowy compared to the brightly lit lower level.

Halfway to the staircase, Dufort turned and led the group through another archway and into a short hallway. It ended in a pair of double doors, which Dufort opened and pushed inward. She stepped into the room and spoke as if introducing the president at the State of the Union. "Mr. Joel Robinson and guests, sir."

Joel again led the group, this time into a wide room with a Palladian window overlooking the gorge and the mountains beyond it. In front of the window, a pair of armchairs flanked a table and a lamp. The left half of the room contained more plush furniture arranged around a crackling fireplace. A bookshelf ran the entire length of the right wall, with a large desk—complete with a green-shaded banker's lamp—in front of it. Soft recessed lighting above accompanied the fire and bathed the den in a warm, cozy glow.

At first, the room appeared empty. Then a shadow emerged from one of the chairs facing the window. The shadow turned into a man as he stepped around the chair and was lit by the fire and the overhead lamps. He was big, more than stocky, but not fat. His shoulders were bulky and his head big and round, and he stood with the posture befitting a man well over six-feet, not several inches under, as he was. Short, somewhat curly grayish-white hair was thinning on top. It was matched in color by a full but well-trimmed beard. His eyes were set deep above pudgy cheekbones and shaded by bushy eyebrows (also white).

He pulled a pipe from his rather large mouth and grinned. "Joel," he said in a rumbling baritone. He pronounced it with two syllables—Jo-El as if it rhymed with Noel. "I thought perhaps this snow shower might keep you away." There was a slight French accent, but his English was clear and crisp. "Thank you, Dufort."

She bowed and backed out, closing the doors behind her.

The man set down his pipe and shook Joel's hand voraciously, then the two exchanged a quick hug. Joel turned to face the rest of the team. "Philippe, you, of course, know Aliana."

"The beautiful Dr. Naceri, of course," Philippe said, taking her hand and offering it a gracious kiss. "It is a pleasure to see you again, Doctor."

"Philippe. I trust you have been well."

"I am surviving."

"And I believe you've met Rich Hamilton as well," Joel said.

"Of course."

Philippe and Rich shook hands and exchanged pleasantries.

Joel gestured at Maggie. "Allow me to introduce our intrepid reporter, along to chronicle the journey, from the *Los Angeles Times*—"

"Maggie," she said before Joel could wax eloquent any longer. "It's nice to meet you."

Philippe only shook her hand, but his eyes twinkled. "The pleasure is mine."

"And this is Jackson Douglas," Joel said. "Jackson's a top-rate detective here to assist with interpretations, deductions, and the like."

"Mr. Douglas," Philippe said, his massive hand enveloping Jackson's in a viselike grip.

"Phillipe. Nice little place you have here."

"Would you care to take a tour?" Philippe asked, looking across the group. "Or perhaps you'd rather get on with business, no?"

"It is a long trip back to Marseille," Joel said. "I think we'd better get on with it."

"Well, can I offer anyone something to drink? Tea, coffee, juice, water?" Everyone declined.

"Something stronger?" Philippe asked with a grin. Then he laughed. "We'll have time for all that later. Come with me."

Philippe led them back into the main hall and strolled ahead of them to the spiral staircase. As he walked, he leisurely pointed out various paintings and works of art, describing their significance and history or relating the story of how he came to own them. Rich caught an eyebrow raise Jackson had intended for Maggie and whispered, "I'm the same way with my baseball card collection."

"Bear with me," Philippe said as they started to climb the stairs. "My knees aren't what they once were."

The staircase was a marvel, a dozen feet wide and spiraling in a circle with a diameter of at least forty feet. It climbed several stories, with access to the mezzanine level, ultimately winding around until it was back on top of itself. In the center, a massive chandelier hung halfway down from the ceiling. Jackson did a quick survey and guessed it contained at least a thousand individual bulbs.

"You know anything about fifteenth-century castles?" Philippe asked as they slowly climbed the stairs.

"I know they're no match for a well-aimed trebuchet," Jackson said.

"A trebuchet," Philippe said. "I thought most of you Yanks called them catapults."

"What can I say?" Jackson said. He leaned toward Maggie. "Played a lot of *Age of Empires* in the day."

"We are headed for the keep," their host explained as they climbed, and Jackson tried to picture the outside of the castle and estimate where within it they were. "From the Old French *donjon*, a keep was the final sanctuary in the event of an attack. If the main castle was stormed, the king or nobles could take refuge in the keep to make their final defense. The keep was the most secure, most impenetrable part of the castle."

"Do you find it ironic that a Frenchman is lecturing us on military defense strategy?" Jackson whispered.

Maggie elbowed him in the ribs.

Following Philippe, the group crested the stairway and turned into a narrow, dark hallway. It was lit only by sconces on the stone walls. Substitute torches for the sconces and remove the ever-present red carpet, and it actually felt like the interior of a castle.

They stopped where an archway opened into a turret extending from the side of the castle. Built into the circular wall was a six-foot-high bay window. "This is the best view in the castle," Philippe said, sweeping his hand at the panorama of the gorge and mountains. "On spring mornings when the sun rises over the canyon . . . My, my, it is positively sacred."

"I can imagine," Aliana said.

"Well, come along."

They curved around the outside of the castle in the narrow hallway until it opened into a wide, circular vestibule. A much smaller chandelier bathed the room in light, not an easy task considering its walls and high ceiling were all stone. An unlit fireplace was built into the wall on the left, spaced equally between the entrance they had come through and a similar doorway leading to parts unknown.

Philippe reached into his pocket and withdrew a brass key. He inserted it into the lock of a sturdy wooden door across from the fireplace. It opened with a click, and he reached for a light switch. Soft yellow light flooded a landing maybe four feet across, with a window on the far wall providing more views of the mountains.

"Please watch your step," Philippe said. "These stairs are a might steep."

Jackson was again last as the five members of Team Joel followed Philippe up a stone staircase that wrapped around the keep. It also, Jackson confirmed with a quick glance, led down in the other direction. They made half a revolution around the keep, if Jackson's internal compass was correct, before stopping at another landing, this one a dead end. Faced with another oak door, Philippe produced another key.

"How much you want to bet there's a sleeping long-haired blonde behind this door?" Jackson asked Maggie.

"You're mixing your fairy tales."

"Welcome to my private collection," Philippe said grandly. "Only the rarest and most valuable artifacts are here," he said.

"Here where?" Rich asked as the group stared at blackness.

Philippe moved to a small console on the wall and punched in a key code. When he did so, a bevy of lights came on above them, illuminating what was, in fact, a very spacious room, at least forty feet in diameter. Evident now with the lights was a wall of glass, splitting the circular room in half. Philippe pressed another button on the console and glass panels parted with a whoosh.

"This was at one time the lord's private residence," Philippe said, gesturing with his hands. "Here they lived in luxury, at least relative to the day." He stepped through the opening in the panels. "Now, it's home to these," he said with a flourish.

Set against the semicircular stone wall opposite the glass were a dozen or more display cases, each with its own spotlight in the ceiling above. Philippe described several of the artifacts—a sword belonging to Charlemagne, a crown worn by Philippe II, Duke of Orléans, and a letter written from Napoleon to his first wife, Joséphine de Beauharnais, preserved in excellent condition inside the air-locked case.

"But here is the object that has brought you all here," he said, drawing their eyes to a display case in the middle of the semicircle. "'The Father' of the 'Holy Trinity.'"

Jackson took several steps forward on the red carpet that covered this half of the semicircle. From the back of the group, he admired the piece over Maggie's shoulder and around Rich's arm. It was, as Joel had described, about the size of a shoebox, its lid rounded like a pirate's treasure chest. The entire surface was gold, including two small figurines on either end of the box. Despite only standing three inches tall, they were so intricate that they were easy to recognize as the same sword-bearing angel and leaping lion as were engraved on the lead cross. A small keyhole was just below a seam on the box's front side and just above an engraving in Latin. Jackson recognized the now familiar—and much more distinct than on the cross—verse from the fourth chapter of Mark:

non enim est aliquid absconditum quod non manifestetur nec factum est occultum sed ut in palam veniat.

"Where did you ever acquire this?" Maggie asked at length, the first words spoken in several minutes.

"It has been in my family for generations," Philippe answered. "It was first discovered during the Renaissance and was passed down and bequeathed for centuries. I've owned it now for almost thirty years."

"Any idea who possessed it before your family?" she asked.

Philippe stroked his beard, then shook his head. "Unfortunately, no. According to legend, a squire by the name of Rene Dumelle brought it back to France after the Fall of Jerusalem and delivered it to the High Commander of the Knights Calvary, Leon of Toulon."

"Just this one piece?" Rich asked. He, like Joel, was crouched down to study the chest more closely.

Philippe nodded. "Presumably the other two were earmarked for Leon as well, but they never made it. Now, with the discovery off Cyprus, we know why—at least for one of them."

"What did Leon of Toulon do with it?" Maggie asked.

"No one knows," Philippe said. "He died in 1194, just seven years after Jerusalem fell to Saladin. And the legend, for what it's worth, is over eight hundred years old. There aren't many details left, and that is where the trail goes cold."

"It's not uncommon," Joel said. "After World War II, hundreds and hundreds of paintings and works of art that had been lost for centuries were found in Nazi possession or in private collections, and no one knew how they had gotten there."

"So where did the legend of the squire come from?" Maggie asked as Jackson shuffled past Rich to get a closer look at "the Father."

"The same place they all come from," Philippe answered.

"Where's that?" Rich asked.

"No one knows. The legend . . . appeared."

Jackson studied the piece in silence for a few seconds. In addition to the verse etched on the front, three more were engraved, one each on the two sides and one on the back:

dicebant ergo ei ubi est Pater tuus respondit Iesus neque me scitis neque Patrem meum si me sciretis forsitan et Patrem meum sciretis

dicit ei Iesus ego sum via et veritas et vita nemo venit ad Patrem nisi per me

omnia mihi tradita sunt a Patre meo et nemo novit Filium nisi Pater neque Patrem quis novit nisi Filius et cui voluerit Filius revelare

"Can we see inside it?" Jackson asked.

"But of course," Philippe said, stepping forward. He reached into a small box built into the wall on the left and withdrew a pair of white gloves. Then he excused himself past Jackson and stooped down to remove a small panel from the back of the base supporting the box. He punched in a code, which was followed by a small whirring sound. Philippe stood and gently lifted off what appeared to be a very heavy glass case.

"Let me help you," Rich said.

"Careful," Philippe warned as they lifted it over the chest. They set it down next to another display case, then all five members of Team Joel stood back as Philippe ever so delicately lifted the lid off the chest, revealing hidden hinges built on the inside of the lid.

"In the twelfth century, this lock would have barred anyone without a key from opening the box. However, in more modern times, it did not prove so challenging."

"So you don't have the key?" Maggie asked.

"No."

"Any idea where it is?"

"None." He stepped back with a flourish, and Team Joel again swarmed the chest. The inside too was inlaid with gold, pure and smooth except for an inscription that wrapped around the inside of the box.

"We couldn't be hunting a treasure hidden by English-speaking Crusaders," Jackson mumbled.

"That's not Latin," Maggie said.

"French," Joel said.

"'*As darkness begets dawn,*' Aliana said as she peered into the box, "'*thou wilt findeth the light whence thou liftest thine eyes at the arrow's mark.*'"

"That was my translation as well," Philippe said.

"Is that another Bible verse?" Maggie asked.

"If it is, it's from deep in the Old Testament," Jackson said.

"That or the Apocrypha," Rich said, earning him a wink from Jackson.

"'*As darkness begets dawn, thou wilt findeth the light whence thou liftest thine eyes at the arrow's mark,*'" Joel said.

"Pretty straightforward," Jackson said. "Don't know why you'd need me."

Joel gave him a small grin in reply.

"May we take photographs?" Aliana asked.

"I assume strictly for your personal use?" Philippe said with a twinkle in his eyes.

"Of course. No one but the members of Team Joel will ever see them."

"In that case, take all the photos you wish."

"Thank you, Philippe."

"But of course."

Rich withdrew a small but fancy digital camera from a shoulder bag, and while he began taking dozens of pictures, Jackson asked, "Jacques of Aragon's journal said there were three pieces, right?"

"Essentially, yes," Philippe said.

"Essentially?" Maggie asked.

"It never specifically described them as objects. It said, rather, *'when you find the Father, the Son, and the Spirit, you will find that which you seek.'*"

"Then how did that come to be interpreted as three artifacts?"

"Well, Jacques' journal does make several references that do indicate that the 'Father,' 'Son,' and 'Spirit' are individual artifacts or relics. But I suppose much of it could be attributed to legend, were you not looking at this particular piece."

"Have you seen the journal?" Maggie asked.

Philippe chuckled. "*Mademoiselle*, I have it in my possession."

"You have Jacques of Aragon's journal?" Joel asked. Jackson and Maggie looked at the two former partners. Aliana's eyes were wide with surprise, and Rich nearly dropped the camera.

"How do you think I learned all that I know?" Philippe asked with a wink.

"You never said anything."

"I must be permitted some secrets, Joel."

Joel gasped in disbelief for a moment. Then composure washed over him again. "May we see it?"

"But of course. In fact, I've even taken the liberty of making you photocopies of each of the pages. I thought they might aid in your search. The original, I'm afraid, is in no condition to travel."

"This is great news," Aliana said.

"I hate to temper your enthusiasm," Philippe said, "but I've been over it dozens of times, and it doesn't reveal anything about where the treasure is located. At least, nothing I could deduce."

"Don't worry, we have a deductive expert along," Maggie said, nodding at Jackson.

"Easy on the sarcasm, would ya?"

"I keep the journal in my library," Philippe said. "Downstairs. If you're through here?"

"Almost," Rich said.

"How do you know this is the Father piece?" Maggie asked.

"There are several references in the journal to a vessel or chest," Phillipe answered. "Also, it bears at least a minor resemblance to the Ark of the Covenant, which the Hebrew Scriptures claim contained Jehovah's Ten Commandments."

"But the Jews don't believe in a triune God, do they?" Maggie asked. "They deny the deity of Jesus, same as Muslims, correct?"

"Not the same," Aliana said, "but that is true."

"So the Christian Crusaders wouldn't make a reference to the Hebrews' beliefs regarding the Holy Trinity, would they?"

"Many Christians also view the God of the Old Testament—Jehovah—as God the Father," Philippe said with a trace of offense. "Indeed, Jesus does not appear until the New Testament."

"That's sort of debatable," Jackson said.

"I beg your pardon?"

"There are several Old Testament references believed by many scholars to refer to the Trinity."

"Such as?" Maggie asked.

"Abraham's three visitors are often considered to be the three Persons of the Trinity. The fourth man in the furnace with Shadrach, Meshach, and Abednego was one who looked like '*a son of the gods.*' Some say Melchizedek was actually Jesus, and that He appeared to Jacob, Joshua, and Isaiah."

Maggie looked at him skeptically.

"Christophanies," Joel said. "Pre-incarnate appearances of Christ."

"Plus there are hundreds of prophecies that don't use the name Jesus, but clearly refer to him," Jackson said. "But Philippe is correct in that, at least in the circles I run, we typically think of God in the Old Testament as God the Father."

"You learn something new every day," Maggie said.

"Finished?" Philippe said as Rich returned the camera to his bag.

"I think so," Joel said. "Thank you so much, Philippe."

"For you, Joel, a pleasure."

This time Jackson helped Philippe with the case, lowering it back over the gold chest. Philippe then punched in a code in the panel, causing another whirring sound as the case locked itself down. He then ushered the group out of the room, pausing to close the panels and dim the lights before locking the door behind them.

"I hope this doesn't sound suspicious or accusatory," Maggie said when they reached the turret with the magnificent view, "but isn't an oak door and a brass key rather thin security for such magnificent artifacts?"

Philippe smiled. "It would be, if not for the lasers and heat sensors I turned off when I turned on the lights. The glass walls are bulletproof, and the outer wall of the keep is over two feet thick, solid rock. It's secure, my dear girl."

"Good to know."

Philippe grinned, wiping away the briefest of frowns. "Now, about that journal."

Chapter Twelve

PHILIPPE LED THE group back downstairs and to a new wing of the castle, where his library was set in what had once been the small cathedral of the great structure. He boasted of owning over ten thousand volumes, including first editions of Shakespeare, Faulkner, and Austen. Jackson drifted in and out of the shelves that surrounded a central studying desk. Soft yellow candles—real or fake, Jackson couldn't tell—dimly lit the old, gothic cathedral, the vaulted ceiling of which disappeared into a haze of darkness that created the perfect ambiance for the moment. The candles did provide just enough light, however, for Jackson to make out titles on some of the dusty spines: *War and Peace*, *The Odyssey*, *Where the Wild Things Are*, and more than a few French titles he couldn't make out. This was more impressive than a real library, and Jackson concluded the candles were fake. No sense in risking burning such a collection. Besides, the light wasn't flickering.

Jackson rejoined the group as Philippe withdrew a small book-shaped box from a shelf against the head wall of the room. It appeared to contain the oldest and rarest of tomes, all stored under a portrait of a gray-haired, grim woman. Philippe's mother? A former queen? Or the current queen, for that matter? Jackson knew nothing of France's government, other than its weak knees.

Philippe set the box on the table in the middle of the room and pulled the chain on a green-shaded lamp, similar to the one in his den. His large fingers gently lifted the lid off the box. As he stepped back, Jackson leaned over Aliana's shoulder to see a worn, brown book inside of a small glass case.

"May I?" Rich inquired, lifting the camera.

"Of course," Philippe said. He stepped around to the side of the desk-like table, opened a drawer, and pulled out a thin binder. When the fascination with the cover of the journal had ceased, he handed the binder to

Joel. "I'd rather not open the original again," he said. "I went to great pains to preserve it while I made this. Even so, I'm afraid it suffered additional wear."

Joel took the binder from Philippe as if possessing a sacred text. "Of course. Thank you, Philippe." He opened the binder, which contained actual-size photographs of the interior of the journal, each in a three-ring sheet protector.

"Every page," Philippe said. "Unfortunately, some of them were no longer legible."

"Looks like I have my work cut out translating," Aliana said.

"I figured you would want to do the work yourself, rather than take the translation of an old man."

"With age comes wisdom," she replied, and he bowed slightly at the compliment.

"This is quite a collection," Maggie said, her eyes wandering around the cathedral-turned-library. "It must have taken years to acquire everything here."

"Indeed," Philippe said. He began listing off more exotic sounding titles and the story of how he came to possess said titles, leading Maggie around the library. She hung on every word, Jackson assumed so she'd have filler for whatever story she ended up writing. She certainly wasn't fascinated by a dusty old book collection.

"This is spectacular," Joel said, clapping the binder shut. "Definitely gives us a leg up on any competition. Thank you again, Philippe," he added when he reemerged with Maggie from the stacks.

"Think nothing of it. Now, how about some dinner? My chef has prepared canard à l'orange that is exquisite."

"That sounds wonderful," Aliana said.

"Please, follow me."

Philippe led them back to the main hallway and from there into a high-ceilinged dining room that was large enough to seat an army. A magnificent chandelier hung from the center of the room, and the walls were graced with swords, shields, suits of armor, crests, and banners. Philippe gave them a brief lecture on some of the various shields and crests before directing them to seats at the table. It was long and narrow, rich mahogany so polished that it almost glowed. The place settings were sterling crystal, fine china, and actual silver. Jackson's seat was next to Maggie, and he marveled as they sat down. He nodded at the silverware around his plate. "I don't even own this many forks," he said.

"Or if you do, they're made of plastic."

A door on the other end of the dining room opened, and Dufort walked through. "Are you ready for dinner, sir?" she asked.

"Yes indeed, Dufort. Tell Sébastien we're all set for the first course."

"Of course, sir. But if I may, you have a telephone call."

Philippe looked to Joel, then the rest of the group. "Will you excuse me for just one moment?"

"Of course," Joel said, and Philippe stood and exited. He was followed out of the room by Dufort.

"What do you think?" Joel asked.

"I think I am as anxious as you are to start working on that journal," Aliana said.

"I know. I can't believe it," Joel said. "He never mentioned owning it."

"We'll still need the three pieces, right?" Maggie asked.

"If everything about the legend is true, yes." Joel glanced to her left. "What are your thoughts, Jackson?"

"I think there's an old maxim about a silver platter."

"You don't trust Philippe?"

"No offense, but I don't know him."

"But Joel does," Rich said, "and he trusts him."

"That's fair. But I wouldn't be doing my job if I didn't keep an open mind and a wary eye."

"Jackson's right," Joel said. He appeared to bite off more words as he reached into his pocket.

"Something up?" Aliana asked.

"It's Cara," he said. He returned the phone to his pocket. "She just texted to say they arrived in Kavala. They're headed out for dinner now."

"Cell service here?" Jackson asked.

"You think this guy can't find a way to make that happen?" Maggie asked.

"Fair point."

Philippe returned a moment later and apologized for the interruption, explaining it was a casual call from a colleague and he had put him off until another time. Promising no more interruptions, he took his seat, and almost immediately the door to the kitchen opened, and a young woman entered pushing a silver cart. She poured glasses of water for everyone, then offered wine. Everyone but Jackson and Joel partook.

The woman disappeared and returned with another cart a few minutes later. As she set several dishes on the table, she announced their contents: duck liver pâté, brie, smoked apples, and crackers. She departed without another word, leaving Philippe and his five guests. The Frenchman raised his wine glass. "To a successful venture."

"To success," several of the group echoed, also raising their glasses, then following Philippe in drinking. Aliana complimented Philippe on the wine. Joel praised the pâté. Rich admired more of the art on the walls, leading to more stories from Philippe. Jackson marveled at the fact that he was dining on fine French cuisine in a castle in the Alps, whereas earlier that week he'd been deciding between a frozen pizza or a turkey pot pie in his hovel of a kitchen back in L.A.

Over the second course—mushroom soup—talk turned to the Calvary Treasure. "Tell me more about this location in Greece," Philippe said.

Joel deferred to Aliana, who dabbed her mouth with a napkin before speaking. "It is a seventh-century Byzantine church, built on the leeward cliffs on the island of Thasos, off the Macedonian Coast. Last year, during a planned restoration, one of the caretakers discovered some ancient etchings beside the iconostasis."

"The what?" Maggie asked.

"In Eastern Christian churches, the iconostasis is a barrier that separates the nave from the sanctuary," Aliana replied. "The iconostasis is covered by icons and religious paintings, commemorating feasts, apostles and prophets, and Christ Himself."

"And there were etchings beside the iconostasis?" Jackson asked.

"Yes. The iconostasis replaced the templon, a similar, albeit simpler version of the iconostasis, that would have been in place back when the church was built."

"Potato, po-tah-to," Jackson said.

"But at any rate, the caretaker called in an expert and had the etchings analyzed, and several sources concluded they formed, among other things, a medieval coat of arms matching that of the Knights Calvary."

Philippe's deep blue eyes widened slightly as he reached for his wine. Aliana had a quick sip of hers before continuing. "Ramón and I were just in Greece last week to scout the church, and we authenticated the coat of arms. It is indeed that of the Knights Calvary."

"But did you find the third piece of the 'Holy Trinity'?" Philippe asked.

"No."

"But you assume it's there?" he asked, turning to Joel.

"We do. Or else something that would indicate where it is."

"Many of the Crusaders journeyed through the Greek Isles," Aliana said, "but Thasos is somewhat off the path, and there is no record of any members of the Knights Calvary ever being present in or around the area, and nothing like this has ever been found to suggest any of them were."

"But clearly someone familiar with the order inscribed the coat of arms beside the iconostasis."

"Yes. The Knights Calvary were formed in the middle of the twelfth century, and the coat of arms was hidden by the early thirteenth century."

"Hidden?"

Aliana nodded. "An earthquake shook the island in 1205, and a section of the southern wall had to be rebuilt. The inscription was hidden behind this second wall and remained there until recently when the restoration cleared away some of the crumbling second wall."

"So the etching had to have been made before 1205," Philippe mused.

"That is the assumption we are working on," Aliana said.

"It's still a stretch to assume the third piece is there, isn't it?" Maggie asked.

"I wouldn't call it a stretch," Joel said. "It's far from conclusive either, but the legend refers to the 'Father,' 'Son,' and 'Spirit.' One piece—'the Father'—made its way back to France and is upstairs in the keep now. A second piece—'the Son,' presumably—was on display in New York after being found shipwrecked off the coast of Cyprus, in a common passageway between the Holy Land and Europe. If the third piece—'the Spirit'—never made it back to Europe, this is the general region of the world in which I'd expect to find it."

"The region, yes," Maggie said. "But why on an island?"

"Any number of reasons," Joel said. "If the person transporting it was traveling by boat, he could have shipwrecked there. He could have sought refuge if he was being pursued, or could have merely used the island as an out-of-the-way resting place. Like I said, it's far from conclusive, but it's worth further inspection."

"And you have people there now?" Philippe asked.

"Yes. Ian, Ramón, and Cara. I'm not sure you've met her."

"I've never had the pleasure, no." Philippe had a spoonful of soup. "So you will all join them when you are through here?"

"That's the plan," Joel said.

"And then?"

"We go wherever the clues lead."

Philippe nodded. "I only wish I could be of more help. I've been over the Father piece and the journal dozens of times, and I cannot make heads or tails of them. The verses from the Christian Bible, the stanza on the inside, even the journal itself—as far as I can tell—reveal nothing concrete about *where* the treasure is."

He let the unspoken "but" hang in the air while the second course was cleared away. Their server, who Philippe identified as Christelle, then brought out the main course, canard a l'orange, served with rice pilaf and steamed asparagus. After bragging on his personal chef for a few moments, Philippe sat back and watched his guests sample their dinner. They all nodded their approval. Even Jackson, who preferred a good steak to just about anything, had to admit that a French duck was delightful.

Finally, Joel addressed Philippe's previous comment. "You said the journal reveals nothing about the treasure's location?"

"Nothing specific, no."

"What about the treasure itself? The legend is very ambiguous as to what the treasure is. Does the journal say anything more?"

"Not more, per se," Philippe said, wiping his mouth with his napkin. "I will, of course, acquiesce to Dr. Naceri on the matter, as she is the expert, but the legend goes that the treasure is something invaluable or priceless. As I read the journal, Jacques of Aragon seems to be speaking of a treasure that has a specific and particular value, or even a purpose."

"Defeating Islam?" Joel asked.

"That has been the legend," Philippe said.

"And that's wrong?" Maggie asked.

"Not so much. But the consensus, if I may speak for those who have pursued and studied the treasure, is that the Crusaders found something of great worth that would help them fund more Crusaders, more weapons, and so forth. However, after reading the journal—and again, Dr. Naceri, please correct me if you find me to be wrong—I believe the entire tone of the journal suggests that this is not just another cache of gold or jewels. This treasure had a specific value to the Knights Calvary, not because it was a treasure, but because of what the treasure was."

"What are you not saying, Philippe?" Joel asked.

"I hesitate to say too much. I don't want to influence the good doctor."

"Please, I would like to hear your thoughts," she said. "I will still be objective in my translation."

"Very well." He took a deep breath. "We have to remember the context. In the late twelfth century, the Knights Calvary—along with the other military orders—had one thing and one thing prominently on their mind: ridding the Holy Land of the infidels—the Muslims. Who, by the way, had the same goal. Both fought for control of Jerusalem and the rest of the Holy Land. But the Knights Calvary in particular, by the late 1100s, had in mind not only to drive Muslims from the Holy Land but also to wipe out the religion entirely. It was their express desire to rid the world of Islam. And to read the journal in its native French, I think the author—Jacques of Aragon—had reason to believe the Calvary Treasure would be paramount in that effort."

Joel sat back.

"How?" Maggie asked.

"A relic?" Rich asked.

"Perhaps."

"Or did the Knights Calvary not only discover gunpowder before the Chinese but nuclear technology as well?" Jackson asked.

"Nothing so absurd," Philippe said. "Mr. Hamilton is likely closer to the truth. The Crusaders had a number of relics that they felt gave them victory in battle. Until they were captured, that is. But I'm guessing the Calvary Treasure, at least in the mind of Jacques of Aragon, was something even greater."

"Like what?" Jackson asked. If Philippe said the Ark of the Covenant or the Holy Grail, he was grabbing Marion—er, Maggie—by the hand and booking the first flight back to the U.S. of A.

"I have no idea," Philippe said. "But whatever it was—whatever it is—if it has the specific value I believe Jacques of Aragon felt it had, then nothing like it has ever been found before."

His words hung ominously in the air for a moment, the silence filled with the clanking of silver on fine china.

"That explains why the Knights Calvary were so desperate not to have it found by Saladin," Joel said. "Hiding it, creating clues, attempting to smuggle them back to Europe."

"What is the theory on that?" Maggie asked. "Why create three treasures in their own right to mysteriously reveal the location of the treasure? Why not dispatch a courier to report the finding to this Leon of Toulon or whoever was in charge of the order?"

"According to the journal," Philippe said, "the few members of the Knights Calvary who knew the identity and location of the treasure all remained behind to contend for Jerusalem, and all likely perished. Thus they sent squires to bear the pieces back to Europe separately, fearing they might all fall into the hands of Saladin if they were all carried together."

"It also would explain why they didn't just tell the squires the location," Jackson said.

"If they were captured, they could be forced to reveal what they knew," Maggie said.

Philippe nodded. "As it was, if Saladin captured one of the squires, he would gain possession of one of three pieces of the 'Holy Trinity,' in and of itself useless to him."

"Clever," Joel said.

"If the treasure is what Jacques of Aragon believed it to be, their efforts to protect it were well justified."

"I guess that also explains the presence of the CC in New York," Maggie said.

Philippe startled. "The CC?"

"We suspect they were the ones who stole the cross from the gallery exhibition in Manhattan," Joel said, filling in the details of the theft—at least those that were known—to Philippe. The Frenchman listened with rapt attention and chased the story with a drink of wine. He sat back.

"And you have reasons to suspect them?"

"Not particularly," Joel said. "But if you're right and the journal hints that the treasure isn't purely monetary in value but something that would have aided the Crusaders in their fight against Islam, a group with similar or even more aggressive goals jumps to the top of the list of those wishing to find it and protect it from falling into the 'wrong' hands."

"I suppose you're right," Philippe said. "I just haven't heard of the *Chevaliers Calvaire* spoken of in quite some time."

"What do you know about them?" Jackson asked.

"Oh, no more than anyone else. They're the remnants of the surviving members of the Knights Calvary. They've endured for centuries primarily on their hatred of Muslims or anyone who doesn't share their particular beliefs, but they've always been too small in number to do more than cause a nuisance."

"Unless they find the treasure," Maggie said.

"Quite true. And if your hunch that they are behind the gallery theft is correct, they now possess one-third of the 'Holy Trinity.'"

"We as good as have it too," Joel said. "Ali and Cara were both able to translate photos we took at the exhibition before it was stolen. And we have a line on the third piece in Greece."

"Which they might as well," Philippe said.

"True. But we have what they don't have—the journal and access to the third piece."

"He is right, isn't he?" Maggie asked. She leaned slightly forward. "No one else has seen the Father piece?"

"My dear girl, it has remained locked in the tower for decades and hidden among my family's things for decades prior to that. Joel saw the chest a number of years ago, and until today, he was the last person other than myself to view it. Whatever the *Chevaliers Calvaire* may find elsewhere, I assure you, they haven't—nor will they—see 'the Father.'"

Chapter Thirteen

8:04 p.m.

PHILIPPE'S HOSPITALITY EXTENDED through coffee and dessert consumed amidst countless tales of adventures he and Joel, he and other partners, or he by himself had experienced while hunting down and examining various treasures and historical artifacts. Finally, as eight o'clock chimed on the grandfather clock in the den where they had settled after dinner, Joel insisted that he and his team head back. It was a two-and-a-half hour drive to Marseille, at least, and it was still snowing.

Everyone thanked Philippe for his hospitality and help, then loaded into the Renault for the trip back. Aliana was exhausted and said she would take a backseat to try to sleep. Maggie felt similarly, and when Joel said he was up for driving, Jackson magnanimously let Rich sit in front and wedged himself between the two women.

"Well, that was informative," Maggie said as they wound through the trees and back to the main road. Several inches of snow had fallen through the evening, but the trees kept the driveway mostly clear.

"I can't believe he had the journal all along," Joel said.

"Where'd you think it was?"

"I had no idea," he answered. "It was just part of the legend. For all I knew, it was lost forever."

"What do you make of his comment about the treasure not being silver or gold but something to aid the Crusaders in their war against Islam?" she asked.

"I don't know. I guess we'll have to study the journal more thoroughly."

"You mean Cara and I will have to study it," Aliana said playfully, her eyes closed. "First thing in the morning. Right now, I just want to sleep."

"No more questions," Maggie said. "I promise."

"I can sleep through them. Just do not be offended if I do not participate in the conversation."

"What are your thoughts, Jackson?" Joel snuck a quick peek in the rearview mirror as he asked the question. Then he focused on the road in front of him. They had just turned out of Philippe's driveway and onto the mountain road leading down to Trois Ruisseaux.

"Thoughts on . . . ?"

"The topic at hand."

"You mean do I believe the Knights Calvary stumbled upon a supernatural weapon that if properly harnessed would wipe out all the Muslims in the world—present company excluded? No. Do I think they might have thought they stumbled upon it? Possibly." He sighed. "In which case, my percentage of the finder's fee ought to come out to about a dollar and a quarter."

"Not necessarily," Joel said. "Not all valuable treasure is bright and shiny."

"But, I will reserve judgment until Ali can take a crack at the translation," Jackson said, noting that he'd referred to her as Ali for the first time. So did everyone else. Nothing to it.

"We'll send these images to Cara too," Joel said. "Let them translate separately and see if they agree on the meaning."

Silence followed, in which Jackson wanted to ask Aliana what her thoughts were about searching for an item—treasure or otherwise—that had been prized and possessed for the purpose of eliminating her religion. Knowing her the little that he did, he surmised she would still be all in on the search.

The snow had stopped, but the roads were still caked in two to three inches of white. Even though the conditions weren't treacherous, there were plenty of valleys and ravines to carelessly slide into, and Joel drove slowly and cautiously.

"How early do you think we'll leave tomorrow?" Maggie asked.

"It depends," Joel said. "We haven't even checked into flights yet."

"I didn't think of it," Rich said. "I should have booked them right away."

Joel shrugged. "I wasn't absolutely positive this would be a one-day stop. You never know with Philippe. But to answer your question, Maggie, as soon as possible given the fact that the CC might be after the treasure as well."

"Not to mention who knows who else," Rich said.

"Right."

"Do you think we can at least sleep in a little?" Maggie asked. "I'm suddenly bushed."

"Me too," Rich said. "Do you mind if I sleep?" he asked Joel.

"Go ahead."

Maggie lifted Jackson's arm, adjusted it slightly, and used his shoulder for a pillow. On his left, Aliana's slow, rhythmic breathing indicated she was already asleep. In moments, the same was true of Maggie, and by all appearances, Rich was on his way to dream/vision-land. Joel made a hairpin turn, and the road leveled off for a moment. He accelerated marginally and glanced in the rearview mirror. He scanned the road ahead, then smiled as he met Jackson's eyes in the mirror. "Guess they can't hold their wine."

"I'm just glad the driver didn't imbibe."

"On these roads, in these conditions, it would be suicidal."

Joel glanced in the mirror again, this time the smile gone.

"Something wrong?" Jackson asked, realizing before Joel could answer what the issue was. Joel's face had suddenly gotten brighter, illuminated by headlights behind them. Jackson turned to look over his shoulder and saw a pair of high headlights bearing down on them. He blinked against their blinding glare as Joel slowed down, approaching another curve.

"He's not slowing," Joel said, his voice tense but firm. He gripped the wheel with both hands, his jaw tight.

Maggie stirred and lifted her head. "What's going on?" she asked as Jackson turned around again.

"We've got company," he answered. The headlights were almost upon them, and suddenly the vehicle behind them veered over into the opposite lane.

"What a crazy dr—"

Joel didn't finish the sentence. Instead of passing them, the vehicle pulled two-thirds of the way into the other lane and accelerated. A second later, it nudged the back of the Renault, sending it careening toward a guardrail on the right side of the road. Joel fought to regain control of the vehicle, but the snowy conditions made it impossible. He did manage to steer so that the car hit the guardrail sideways instead of head on, but the collision spun them around.

Maggie grabbed Jackson's arm, Aliana woke with a scream, and Joel pawed the steering wheel in a mad effort to keep the car from going off the side of the road. He failed. It spun ninety-plus degrees as it slid across the road and over the shoulder. In that instant, Jackson tried to remember the drive up to Philippe's castle. Had the turn before the hairpin contained a vertigo-inducing drop-off? He couldn't remember, but time was up.

With a sickening thud, the back of the Renault crashed into a snowbank, or a bush covered in snow, or maybe just into the ground. Jackson didn't know, because the headlights had swept past them and the other vehicle was barreling down the road, leaving them in total blackness. But the Renault had stopped and wasn't plummeting down a slope. So the news wasn't all bad.

Joel released his death grip on the steering wheel and turned around. "Is everyone okay?"

Maggie muttered an, "I think so."

Rich nodded.

Aliana gasped for breath.

"I think maybe we should have let one of the wine drinkers drive," Jackson said.

"What happened?" Aliana said.

"We were run off the road," Jackson said. "Seriously, nice driving, Jo-El."

"Are they gone?" Maggie asked.

"Yeah, they didn't stop to survey their handiwork," Joel said. "They're long gone."

Maggie turned to Jackson. "Did you get a look at them?"

"A van," he said. "That's all I could tell."

"Mr. Crack Detective."

"Don't blame me." Jackson nodded at Rich. "He should have foreseen this."

"It doesn't w—"

"Work that way, I know. I'm just messing with you, dude."

"I hate to break up the frivolity, but I think we're stuck," Joel said.

"Awesome."

"Can we push?" Aliana asked.

"I don't know. I'll have to check," Joel said, opening his door.

Jackson nodded at Maggie, and she opened her door and got out, allowing him to do likewise. "Wait inside," he said to her.

"I can help."

"Not until we know what we're up against."

"Jack, if this is some macho—"

"Keep an eye out. Just because they're gone, doesn't mean they won't come back."

"If they do?"

Jackson glanced around, trying to make out the terrain through the darkness. One of the Renault's taillights had cracked and gone out on impact, and the other was mashed up against the snow bank, while the headlights pointed over the road and into the sky. Even so, there was enough ambient light for him to tell they were in a small meadow, maybe fifty yards wide as it separated the road from the pines. It was vaguely familiar. "I don't know. Make a dash for the trees. In the meantime, stay warm."

She didn't fight him but got back in. Jackson and Rich joined Joel at the back of the car. "How's it look, boss?"

"We're angled pretty steeply uphill," Joel answered. "If four of us push, one of the girls might be able to drive us over the lip."

"There a flashlight in the glove or somewhere?" Jackson asked.

"My phone," Rich said, handing him his smartphone after activating the flashlight app.

"Thanks," Jackson said. He dropped to all fours and peeked under the rear fender.

"What do you see?" Joel asked after a minute.

"I'm not a candy-swilling Scottish mechanic, but I'm pretty sure this car isn't going anywhere." He stood and handed Rich his phone. "Rear axle's cracked. Must have hit a rock or something coming over the edge of the road."

"So we're stuck?" Rich said.

"But good."

Joel exhaled. "I'd say we're about seven or eight miles from Trois Ruisseaux. Maybe ten."

"How far from Philippe's?" Rich asked.

"Maybe twice that."

Jackson nodded.

"We can call him," Rich said. "Surely he'd come get us."

"We may have to consider the fact that he already did," Jackson said.

"What?"

"Joel, I don't mean to insult your old friend and colleague, but unless we were followed up here, the only person who knew we'd be on this road now was Philippe or one of his staff."

"Why would Philippe want to run us off the road?" Rich asked.

"I don't know. He wants the treasure for himself?"

"Then why show us anything?" Joel asked. "Why divulge the journal?"

"I don't know. I agree it doesn't make sense. But the facts are what they are."

"Let's bring the girls into this," Joel said, and the three guys got back into the car.

"What's up?" Maggie asked as she scooted over to make room for Jackson in the backseat.

"Broken axle," he said.

"So we're stranded?" Aliana said.

"Afraid so."

"Anybody have cell service?" Joel asked.

None of them did.

"Told you to get that sat phone at the auction in Zurich," Aliana said.

"I know, I know."

"How much gas you have, Joel?" Jackson asked.

"We were just under half a tank."

"Okay. Run the heat off and on as long as you need to stay warm."

"You act as if you're leaving."

"We wait for a passing motorist, we could be here until the spring thaw. You guessed less than ten miles down to town. I can make that in several hours, come back with help."

"Are we closer to town than Philippe's?" Maggie asked.

"That and Jackson thinks Philippe is responsible," Rich said.

"What?" both ladies asked.

"I didn't say exactly that, but unless this was just an accident—and I think that's unlikely—someone had to tip those guys off. The what and why can wait. But none of us is getting warmer, so the sooner I set out, the better."

"You don't speak French, Jack," Maggie said. "How are you going to get help, hand gestures?"

"Surely somebody's phone has Google Translate," he said.

"I will go with him," Aliana said.

"It's a long walk," Jackson said. "And cold."

"I have been through worse."

"Okay. We should get going."

"Are you sure about this?" Maggie asked.

"Yeah."

"You don't have to go," Joel said. "It's my team, my responsibility."

Jackson met his eyes in the mirror and nodded out the window. They both got out, closing the doors behind them.

"Those guys could come back," Jackson said. "My money says no, but you can't be too careful. If they do, and if they spot me and Aliana on the road, I'm the best bet to defend her. Unless you or Rich are holding out some serious MMA skills?"

"No."

Jackson nodded.

"What about defending Maggie?"

"There's two of you. And personal experience, I know Maggie's a fighter."

"So's Ali, but I see your point."

"If you see lights coming from down the mountain, get into the trees and hide. If it's me or somebody else, I'll signal somehow. You'll know it's me or I sent them."

Joel nodded.

"Keep checking your cells too, in case you get a signal."

"Will do."

"But don't call anyone you know. Whether it was Philippe or not, we don't want word getting out that we're okay. Let them think our status is unknown at best."

Joel nodded again.

"Couple miles an hour, we should be back before you run out of gas."

Joel extended his hand. "Be safe, brother."

"You too."

Jackson opened the back door and leaned in. "You ready, Doc?"

"I am."

"Be careful, Jack," Maggie said.

"You have my word."

He closed the door and nodded at Aliana, and the two of them trudged through the snow and up the bank onto the side of the road.

"Excuse my indelicacy," Jackson said, "but you look like you keep in decent shape."

"I do."

"High altitude, in the cold, we don't want to over-exert, but we'll push the pace as fast as you can go."

She nodded.

"Or as fast I can go. Forgive the machismo."

"Nothing to forgive," she said.

"Let's go."

Failing to check the forecast, none of the team had dressed for cold weather. Jackson was decked in only a long-sleeved shirt over an undershirt, jeans, and standard tennis shoes. Aliana had changed at the hotel, into a blouse with sleeves flared at the wrist. She already looked frozen.

"Not to be indelicate again, but what are you wearing under the blouse?"

She looked at him.

"Do you have another shirt or just that?"

"A camisole."

He nodded, then peeled off his outer shirt. Immediately the chill cut through his thin T-shirt and assaulted his bare arms.

"No," Aliana said.

"You have less body weight, and I'm pretty warm-blooded." He handed the shirt to her, and she reluctantly pulled it on.

"Thank you."

"You owe me a coffee when we get to civilization."

"A deal."

The first mile or so went fine, the adrenaline still pumping. Jackson was cold, but at least the mountain air wasn't frigid—low thirties, he guessed. His feet, however, as he traipsed through snow, were like ice cubes. They wound around several curves and found themselves thoroughly in the middle of nowhere, a low mountain range separating them from Trois Ruisseaux, if he remembered his geography properly.

"How you doin'?" he asked.

"Fine."

"Pace good? Too fast, too slow?"

"Just right."

He nodded. They walked for a few minutes. His phone indicated it was a quarter after nine. "You know, I saw this made for TV movie once," he said. "It was about this couple and their baby trying to get home for Christmas, and they got stranded in a mountain snowstorm." He looked down at Aliana, whose eyes were focused on him. "They stayed in their truck as long as they could, until they ran out of gas and food. Then they set out, hiking through the mountains. He finally hid his wife and baby in a cave and set out alone. He found help and brought a rescue party back just before a snowstorm wiped out his tracks back to her."

Aliana shook her head. "Why would you tell me that?"

He shrugged. "It's on my mind. And this isn't as bad as that."

"You are worried," she said.

"Why do you say that?"

"You use your witty personality to deflect tension."

He shrugged again. "I suppose. I wouldn't say worried so much as concerned."

"Do you really distrust Philippe?"

"I don't know. Joel raised the question of why he would invite us to his castle, show us 'the Father,' and give us the journal if he was going to run us off the road."

"That is a fair argument."

"And yet, I didn't see a tracking device under the back of the car. I checked. And nobody followed us that I could see. So where did the truck come from, and why?"

"That is also a fair argument."

They trudged in silence.

"You warm enough?" Jackson asked.

"Are you going to give me more clothes if not?"

"No, but I would deflect more concern with obscure movie references."

She chuckled. "I am warm enough."

"Good."

They walked for another mile, the breeze perhaps strengthening a little. Jackson had his head down, methodically putting one foot in front of the next, when Aliana grabbed his arm. He looked up as she said, "Headlights."

He followed her outstretched arm down the road, around a sweeping curve, maybe half a mile to where a vehicle was slowly coming their way.

He stopped and quickly looked around. "Hide in the trees," he said, pointing to a grove of pines fifty feet off the road, up a slight embankment. "I'll call for you by name if all's clear. If something else happens, wait till it's clear and hurry to town without me."

Aliana didn't argue but hurriedly scrambled up the slope. Jackson watched her until she disappeared into the trees, realizing his brilliant plan for her to hide didn't take into account her leaving rather obvious footprints in the snow. Oh well, at least she was out of sight. Hoping his paranoia was just that, he positioned himself in the middle of the road, planted his feet, and began waving his arms as soon as the headlights turned his way.

A vehicle began to take shape, not a van. It was a dark coupe, and going slowly enough in the snow that it had no problem stopping before running

Jackson down. He dropped his arms and hurried around to the driver's window as it was lowered. A man in a suit jacket, no tie, sat alone in the front of what Jackson realized was a high-performance sports car.

"*Qu'est-ce qu'il y a?*" the man asked.

"Do you speak English?"

"Yes."

"Our vehicle was run off the road. Can you give us a lift into town to get help?"

The man frowned at him, and Jackson feared the man understood only enough English to say that he understood English. Then he shook his head. "I'm . . . late for an appointment."

"Seriously?"

The man frowned but said nothing.

"It'll take you fifteen minutes to run us down to town and back." That was cutting it short, given the road conditions, but Jackson was desperate.

"I am sorry, sir. Now if you will please get out of the way. I will send for help when I get to—"

Jackson leaned his head in the window, quickly appraising the build of the man and the look on his face. He wasn't intimidated.

"Sir, please re—"

"What if I drag your wimpy French butt out of your nice warm sports car and let you shiver here on the road while I drive back to town?"

"How dare—"

"I am freezing. I'm wearing nothing but a T-shirt because I gave my other shirt to a woman who weighs a hundred pounds soaking wet, which she is by now from climbing through the snow and hiding in the trees for fear that you were the people who ran us off the road and had come back to finish the job. So I can either carjack you here on the side of the road and force you to drink some milk of human kindness, or you can be a guy, drive us to Trois Ruisseaux, and tell whoever you're meeting that you're a little late because you were saving some stranded motorists. Or blame it on the roads. Now, which is it gonna be?"

The man's eyes were wide, either in fear or shock. But he nodded slowly.

"Good. Turn off the car and give me the keys."

"What?"

"I'm not having you drive off and run over my foot while I wait for my friend to get here. Keys."

The stunned driver complied. "Aliana," Jackson shouted, his voice echoing in the night. "Ali, it's clear. Come on down."

A moment later, she appeared from the woods. A quick glance down at the driver indicated that seeing her had perhaps softened him. "Unlock the doors," Jackson said, then circled around the front of the car to get in the backseat and let Aliana sit up front, closer to the heaters. As he opened the door, however, he realized this particular sports car had no backseat. He'd figured as soon as he saw it that it would be too small to hold the entire team and that the best plan would be to head to town and get help. Now, he realized it wasn't even big enough to hold both he and Aliana. Unless . . .

"Hey," he said.

"Hey," she greeted, relief evident on her face.

"I have to impose on you with one more indelicacy."

"Okay?"

"You'll have to sit on my lap."

"One does what one has to."

He nodded and got in, pushing the seat back as far as he could. Even so, and despite her small size, Aliana barely fit on his lap and under the roof, her knees bent in front of the dash. Jackson passed the keys to the driver, whose face was still a mix of shock, anger, and disdain.

"Trois Ruisseaux, driver, and step on it."

Chapter Fourteen

11:39 p.m.

"YOU CARJACKED HIM?" Maggie asked.

"I appealed to his better angels," Jackson said. "While grabbing his jacket lapels and threatening to drag him from the car."

"And you wonder why there's an ugly American stereotype."

"You're safe and warm, aren't you?"

"Half right," she said, pulling a blanket around her. The only inn in Trois Ruisseaux did not have any vacancies, but a bed and breakfast half a mile outside of town, overlooking a small alpine lake, did. Sort of. It had one room, which the proprietor was preparing for Team Joel—or some of its members. In the meantime, Jackson, Maggie, and Rich huddled in front of the fireplace in the living room, trying to regain their warmth.

Joel and Aliana, his translator, were paying the brother-in-law of the attendant of the town's sole gas station, a man who had a van that seated six passengers. Their reluctant rescuer had dropped Jackson and Aliana off at the gas station just as it was closing, and her persuasive smile and a few shivers had convinced the attendant to rouse his brother-in-law (the town apparently went to bed quite early), who had then driven them back up the mountain to rescue Joel, Rich, and Maggie. But not for free.

"You really think Philippe's responsible?" Maggie asked.

"I don't know."

"Joel's known him for a long time," Rich said.

"I know. But Joel and I aren't yet to the 'any former partner of his is a friend of mine' stage. Maybe he knows him better because he's known him for years, or maybe he's too close and can't see Philippe's betrayal." He shrugged. "But I'm not saying it was Philippe. We could have been followed, and I just didn't spot the tail. Or maybe French baddies don't place their tracking devices under the rear bumper like in the movies. Or maybe one of us . . . is the mole," he said in his best Anderson Cooper.

"They could have hacked our phones or Joel's laptop, right?" Rich asked.

"Sure, but why make an attempt now, here? It seems it's tied to what we saw at Philippe's."

"So it is back to him," Maggie said.

Jackson shrugged again. "Not necessarily. It could have been Philippe, could have been Dufort, could have been the cute server lady who tipped off the guys in the truck. I'm not saying he's guilty. I'm saying we can't rule it out, so we need to be cautious."

She sighed. "I could be sleeping snug in one of Château LeCavalier's umpteen guest bedchambers right now."

"Or better yet, raiding leftover duck from the fridge," Jackson said.

Joel and Aliana returned, her now wearing the bed and breakfast proprietor's wife's sweater. Joel sighed. "I called my travel insurance company, and they are going to coordinate with the car rental company, but it will likely be morning before we know what's up. The town has no towing service, so it's more than likely we'll be getting a replacement vehicle instead of having this one fixed."

"Does European Enterprise pick you up even in a small town in the Alps?" Jackson asked.

"I guess we'll find out. In the meantime, we should try to get some rest. Any word on rooms?"

"Room, singular," Rich said.

Joel sighed. "Standard room, suite?"

"Two doubles."

Another sigh.

"The girls can have the room," Jackson said. "There's a couch here, a chair. We'll manage."

"We've certainly done with worse," Joel said.

"Plus there's a fireplace."

"So your true motives come out," Maggie said.

"Would you like to be back on the side of the mountain?"

"Did you really force that guy to take you back to town?" Joel asked.

"I was just getting to that when he suddenly had a streak of compliance."

The proprietor appeared in the doorway, waiting hesitantly until they stopped speaking. Then he shuffled toward them and announced in what sounded to Jackson like a mixture of English, French, and I-forgot-to-put-in-my-dentures that the room was ready. He also said, according to Aliana's translation, that Mrs. Proprietor had put out some snacks for them in the dining room.

Neither Maggie nor Aliana was hungry, but each of the three guys—with nothing to do but camp out in the living room all night—were. So they said their goodnights, Maggie and Aliana splitting for the stairs and the three guys following the proprietor.

"Uh, Jackson."

He turned to Aliana.

"Might I have a brief word with you?"

"Yeah," he said, and they hung back. She shivered again, and he motioned toward the fireplace. "What's on your mind?" he said when they stood in front of it, the warmth welcome to both of them.

"I wanted to thank you for your heroics this evening."

"Hardly."

"Perhaps not a death-defying feat, but still. And I want to apologize for what I said, before getting into the car."

He frowned.

"I believe my words were 'One does what one has to.' I did not mean it like that. I . . . You are smiling."

"Aliana, don't think anything of it. I know what you meant."

"You were not offended?"

"Not at all."

She nodded. "Okay." Now she smiled. "Good night, then."

"Good night."

He watched her walk to the stairs, then headed for the dining room and, with any luck, some meat.

*   *   *

Monday, February 11
12:12 p.m.

IT WAS noon by the time Joel and Rich, both working with Aliana as their translator, made all of Team Joel's arrangements. Joel's insurance company had agreed to pay for another rental car for them while the original was repaired. But getting the car had proven to be a problem since the nearest rental station was back in Marseille, and once they got back to Marseille, there would be no need for a rental car, as they could just as easily take a taxi back to the airport.

The bed and breakfast proprietor had informed them that a bus ran from Trois Ruisseaux to Marseille once a day, departing at one. So they had eschewed another rental car and bought bus tickets using the internet at the town's administrative/police building. While there, they had also checked into flights from Marseille to Kavala. Given the duration of the bus ride, they would be forced to spend another night in Marseille. So, having called to update the other half of the team already in Greece, they resigned to their fate and filed into a small café to have a quick lunch before the bus arrived.

"What if we've been thinking about this wrong?" Rich asked as they ate sandwiches and wraps.

"You want to drive to Kavala?" Jackson asked. They'd nearly booked and canceled half a dozen flights before finally settling on an option that routed them from Marseille to Rome to Athens to Kavala.

"I mean the treasure. Ever since Philippe mentioned his belief that it was something that would help the Crusaders defeat Islam, we've been thinking of it as a weapon of sorts that would kill Muslims. Maybe it wasn't something to defeat Muslims so much as defeat Islam."

Jackson washed down a bite of his sandwich with a gulp of coffee. He was still cold from the night before. "Discredit the religion instead of killing its people, you mean?"

"Something like that."

Maggie shook her head. "Haven't people been trying to discredit various religions for centuries? Do you really think there's something out there that could cause an entire religion to abandon its faith?"

"It's not a matter of whether it exists or not," Joel said. "It matters if the Knights Calvary thought it existed. That is, if this object—whatever it was— was something they thought could discredit Islam."

"What would that be?" Maggie asked.

Jackson turned to Aliana, who seemed more intrigued by her panini than the conversation thus far. "I can't speak for Islam," he said, "but the Apostle Paul outlined the method of destroying Christianity."

"What?"

"First Corinthians 15. '*If Christ has not been raised, our preaching is useless and so is your faith.*'" He shrugged. "Disprove the resurrection and you destroy the Christian faith."

"What's the equivalent in Islam?" Maggie asked.

"To the resurrection? Nothing."

"I mean what's the lynchpin that would cause even a devout Muslim to abandon Islam?"

Aliana looked up. "I do not know of any similar comparison. I guess the closest thing would be someone discrediting Allah or the prophet Muhammad. But opponents of Islam have been trying that for centuries, and they have all been unsuccessful."

"Maybe that's what the knights thought they had," Rich said. "Whatever it would be."

"*Les gens, votre autobus est ici,*" the owner of the small café announced from behind the counter.

"What?" Jackson asked.

"He said our bus is here," Aliana said.

"It's twenty after twelve."

"Maybe public transportation actually runs on time in Europe," Maggie said.

They quickly scrambled to their feet, taking what of their food they could and digging around to come up with enough money to pay on the spot. Then they hurried outside, reaching the bus just in time.

The snow of the night before had quickly melted, leaving a beautiful day in its wake. Jackson settled back with half a sandwich and the unspilled portion of his coffee. Having not packed for an overnight trip, no one had any personal items or changes of clothes. Joel, Rich, and Aliana seemed used to roughing it, and neither Jackson nor Maggie complained. Still, the urge to get back was almost palpable as the bus descended toward the coast. Beside Jackson, Maggie dozed. A seat ahead of him, Rich and Aliana did the same. Only Joel, across the aisle, and Jackson stayed awake the entire duration of the two-hour trip.

When they returned to Marseille, they still had to take two taxis back to their hotel. They took turns showering and changing, and Joel called Cara and updated her while learning that all of their "prep" work in Greece had gone smoothly. (They had not been run off the road by any angry Greeks.) Then, with everyone feeling refreshed, Joel took the group to dinner.

They had hashed out all they could about who had run them off the road and why, and Joel had filed a police report that morning in Trois Ruisseaux. Plus no one wanted to talk about it anymore. Naturally, the conversation turned to the "Holy Trinity" and the Calvary Treasure. Aliana had done some looking at the journal photographs from Philippe but would wait to do a thorough translation while en route to Greece the next day. So they focused on the gold chest of Philippe's, the piece believed to be 'the Father.'

While waiting around that morning and in between making reservations, Aliana had carefully studied Rich's photographs of the verses on the outside of the box. She had translated the engravings, and Jackson had committed the three verses (in addition to Mark 4:22) to memory, then spent much of the bus ride mulling them.

The familiar Mark verse about hidden things being disclosed had been on the front of the box. Inscribed on the back was Matthew 11:27: *All things are delivered to me by my Father. And no one knoweth the Son but the Father: neither doth any one know the Father, but the Son, and he to whom it shall please the Son to reveal him.* On the left side was John 8:19: *They said therefore to him: Where is thy Father? Jesus answered: Neither me do you know, nor my Father. If you did know me, perhaps you would know my Father also.* And on the right, John 14:6: *Jesus saith to him: I am the way, and the truth, and the life. No man cometh to the Father, but by me.* Great theology, but what did it mean in terms of finding a Crusader treasure?

"Not a theologian," Maggie said, "but they seem to be linking the pieces together."

"You think the references to not knowing the Father without knowing the Son mean you need all pieces to find the treasure?" Rich asked. They were in a corner table, relatively secluded at a fine-dining place near the coast.

"And didn't one of the verses on the cross mention the Spirit too?" she asked.

"John 15:26," Joel said, sawing into his steak. (The restaurant hadn't offered a hamburger.) "'*But when the Paraclete cometh, whom I will send you from the Father, the Spirit of truth, who proceedeth from the Father, he shall give testimony of me.*'"

"Do all Christians have the Bible memorized?"

"Just the really good ones," Jackson said with a wink.

"What is the Paraclete?"

"It comes from the Greek word *parakletos,*" Joel said, "and means advocate or comforter. John uses it several times in reference to the Holy Spirit."

"So based upon that theory, the Spirit piece would have some verses linking to 'the Father' and 'Son,'" Aliana said.

"Yeah," Maggie said.

"Jackson?" Joel asked.

"Mmm. Yeah, I think Maggie's onto something. But . . ."

"What is it?"

"The wheels are spinning," Maggie said.

"'*No one knoweth the Son but the Father.*' '*No man cometh to the Father, but by me.*' '*If you did know me, perhaps you would know my Father also.*'"

"What are you getting at, Jackson?"

"What if the message isn't just that all three pieces are needed to find the treasure, but actually hold keys to each other? As in, you won't be able to fully understand or know the Father piece without the Son piece."

"Keys of what kind?" Maggie asked.

"There was a keyhole in the chest," Jackson said, stabbing at a piece of shrimp. "Inside of which seem to be directions for finding the treasure." He ingested the shrimp.

"You think the Son piece might have been the key to 'the Father'?" Rich asked.

Jackson reached for his drink. "It's possible."

"How? It was smooth and way too big; it wouldn't fit into the lock."

"Unless the Father piece isn't the only one that needs to be unlocked."

"It was solid lead," Maggie said.

He shrugged.

"It could need to be unlocked in a different way," Aliana said. "More like interpreted."

"It's a theory," Jackson said. "Nothing more."

The theories died out, and the conversation turned to past adventures. Team Joel, it seemed, had been just about everywhere, but Jackson's tales as a P.I. rivaled those Joel, Rich, and Aliana told.

Their flight to Rome was due to leave at ten the following morning, and hopping from peninsula to peninsula, traveling east, would again take them most of the day. So the team retired to their hotel early, their bodies all thrown off by repeated trips across multiple time zones. Jackson fell asleep quickly and dreamed that he donned a suit of armor and defended a castle against Turks and Saracens with nothing more than snowballs.

Chapter Fifteen

Tuesday, February 12
10:05 a.m.

AIR FRANCE FLIGHT 5598 left Marseille on time, at ten. Some morning clouds had cleared and a crystal clear blue sky reflected off the Mediterranean. Jackson sat next to Rich (having not been present during the reservation process to choose his seat), and they discussed the upcoming baseball season. Rich felt the pieces had fallen into place and the Tigers were finally going to win the World Series. Jackson was pleased with some of the Dodgers' offseason moves but wasn't convinced they were headed for the postseason. Eventually, the conversation died, and Rich settled back for a nap while Jackson watched the coast of Italy appear out his window.

They touched down at Rome's Leonardo da Vinci-Fiumicino Airport a little before eleven local time, having circled over the ancient city to land into the wind. Jackson found it strange to be looking down on a place he'd only read about in history books or the Bible. He was surprised to see modern buildings instead of first-century stone and brick structures. Probably a safe bet, too, that the people weren't wearing togas and that the guards at the airport wouldn't be dressed like Tommy Trojan.

Their flight to Athens didn't leave until two, so Team Joel had several hours to kill. Their terminal had numerous lunch options, and Jackson decided to sample authentic Italian pizza. It was thick and gooey, and he preferred Domino's. But it satisfied his hunger.

Maggie joined Jackson by the window. "Not what I expected," she said, nodding in the general direction of the city, some ten or fifteen miles from the airport.

"Yeah, me either. I expected chariots instead of taxicabs."

"Did the Romans even have chariots?"

"They did in *Gladiator*."

"Then it must be true."

"And *Ben-Hur*."

"Point made."

"Good, because I'm out of Roman movies." He glanced over his shoulder. Rich and Joel were chatting over last bites of lasagna and Aliana had momentarily disappeared. "So," Jackson said, "you got enough for a story yet?"

"A story's about right."

"What's that mean?"

"We're dealing in nothing but myths and legends," she said. "An old knight's journal, rumors of this and that, engraving on lead crosses and gold boxes. It's a little far-fetched."

"Let me guess, because it's old? Tell me, do you believe anything written before the turn of the century?"

"Come on, Jack," she said, turning to face him. "You have to admit it's a long shot. Even if all this stuff is true, us actually finding it . . ."

"So why'd you come along?"

Maggie grinned. "Because Joel isn't paying me on commission. And I've already been to France, now Rome, Greece next. It's a girl's dream."

"I thought your dream was to be first row for a Rangers-Bruins bench-clearer."

"Well, there are dreams, then there are *dreams*."

After staring out toward the city for a few more minutes, Jackson and Maggie returned to the others. They still had well over an hour until they needed to board the flight to Athens, so they wandered around the airport, watched Italian TV, or made small talk about anything and everything. Shortly after one-thirty, they boarded an Airbus A319, this time with Jackson, Maggie, and Joel sharing a row and Rich and Aliana—both wanting to take a catnap on the flight—sitting two rows ahead and on the other side of the aircraft.

The scenery was spectacular as they flew along the length of Italy and over the Apennine Mountains. But as they moved over the Adriatic Sea, clouds drifted in and obscured the brilliant Greece coastline. So instead of marveling at the view, Jackson, Joel, and Maggie drifted into a conversation about the Middle Ages, with Joel recapping some of the major events that transpired during the two hundred years that made up "The Crusades."

"I still don't get it," Maggie said. "All these religions—Christianity, Islam, Judaism, Eastern religions—they all talk about wanting peace and love, and all we've had for centuries are wars instigated and fueled by religion."

"That isn't all we've had," Joel said. "There have been hundreds upon thousands of cases of charity and benevolence performed in the name of religion—whichever you name. And I think it would be inaccurate to compress an entire religion down to peace and love."

"Yeah," Jackson said. "Ever heard of *jihad*?"

"I thought *jihad* was the personal struggle against sin," Maggie said.

"That's one component of it," Joel said. "It can also mean a battle against all who oppose Islam."

"But Christians are no better," Maggie said to Jackson. "You launched the Crusades, the Spanish Inquisition."

"Be careful labeling all Christians as Christians," Jackson said.

"Huh?"

"You have to define what you mean by 'Christian,'" he answered. "Do you mean someone who simply uses the label, as in 'I'm a Christian, as opposed to being Muslim, Hindu, atheist, etcetera'? Because if you do, a lot of people get lumped in as Christians, and I don't think that's fair."

"So what makes a person a Christian?"

"Simple answer: faith in Jesus Christ. You can't just believe there's a God or even believe there was a person named Jesus. You have to put your faith in Him and in His death upon the cross for your sins. There's a personal component to it."

"So what are all these other people?"

Jackson hesitated. He knew Maggie knew these answers, or most of them. Was she just trying to get him to admit something she could come back and attack later? Whatever the case, he pressed on. "I call them lowercase Christians. They use the name, but they aren't true, saved, born-again Christians."

"How do you know?"

"I don't," Jackson said. "Not for sure. But there's usually pretty good evidence to indicate if a person is one or the other."

"Such as?"

"According to the Bible, a true 'uppercase' Christian is going to have the Holy Spirit inside of them. A person can quench the Spirit, but the Bible also says *'by their fruit you will recognize them.'*"

"Another good test," Joel said, "is to ask them if they agree with Jackson's statement a moment ago. A person who acknowledges they need to personally place faith in Christ for salvation probably is a person who has done so. And anyone who would disagree—well, I can't imagine why a true Christian would."

"And that is what separates true Christianity from any other world religion," Jackson said. "Every other religion or belief system I have ever encountered or heard of has a person needing to do works, perform deeds, or meet some sort of standard to 'get saved.' Ask Aliana about Islam; it requires works. Buddhists and Hindus both require a person to 'achieve' nirvana or karma. Cosmic humanists and New Agers believe in an ultimate perfection of the human race. Even many quote-unquote Christian 'faiths' believe in salvation through works. Biblical Christianity is different in that the work has been done by Christ on the cross. All that is required of us is a response to that. Faith, not religion."

Maggie nodded. "So why do you do good works then? Insurance?"

Joel shook his head. "Because it is our purpose. Ephesians tells us that we were created to do good works. Ideally out of love and gratitude, but admittedly sometimes out of duty. But it's all in response to the original love of Jesus."

Maggie sat back for a moment. "So you're telling me that the Crusades and inquisitions and wars weren't the result of your 'true' Christians, the ones who actually had faith like you described?"

"Not necessarily," Jackson said. "I'm walking proof that having faith doesn't make you perfect. Not this side of heaven. We're still sinners, and that doesn't change—not completely. I'm just saying, don't lump everyone who claims to be a Christian together." He nodded. "Take bloggers. Any bozo with a few minutes and basic computer skills can launch his opinion to the world. Doesn't make them an accredited, legitimate reporter like yourself. They could be, but it'd be unfair to categorize you and your colleagues at the *Times* with anyone and everyone who's ever blogged or tweeted."

"Fair. But don't you have to apply that same standard to Muslims? Christians are always blaming Islam for 9/11 and this or that terrorist attack. But maybe they're not true Muslims either."

"That's a valid argument," Joel said. "I've heard and know of many peaceful Muslims, like Aliana, who say that the terrorists and jihadists have hijacked—no pun intended—the Muslim religion. Conversely, the jihadists will tell you that they are truly following Islam and the peaceful Muslims are weak and lack commitment."

"So who's right? What's the true Islam?"

"You have to go back to Islam's source of authority."

"The Quran?"

Joel nodded.

"And what does it say?"

"Depends who you ask."

"Suppose I ask you?"

"I was afraid you would," he said with a thin smile. "I am far from an expert. But from what I've read of it, from what I've studied about it, from what I've heard from people with far more authority on the subject than me, I believe it is both. If you look at the life of Muhammad, in his early years, he spoke peacefully, and many of the verses in the Quran reflect that. But once he and his followers fled to Medina, Muhammad, along with some of the more recent verses of the Quran, began to take on a much more hostile tone. Islam also makes use of abrogation—that is, the principle that when verses or teachings are in conflict with each other, the latter overrides the former. Based on all that, I would say the jihadists actually hold more closely to the true nature of Islam."

Maggie nodded. "Okay, what about Christianity? If Christians—true Christians—can still sin and act like everybody else, how do I know if someone who does something awful like slaughter innocent bystanders in Jerusalem is a true Christian who did something horrible or a lowercase Christian who really isn't one?"

"Good question," Jackson said. "Probably why we all get lumped together."

"Kind of puts the onus on us not to miss the mark, so to speak," Joel said.

"What if I ask Aliana about this? Will she say the same thing about true Christianity and true Islam?"

Jackson shrugged. "Ask her."

"We have nothing to hide," Joel said. "The claims of Christianity are exclusive, as are the claims made by Christ, and people take offense to that. Particularly, in this day and age where we're all told to coexist and tolerate. But all I ever ask anyone is to look into it. Read what Jesus said. Read what the Bible says. Check it out. Then check out the other religions of the world. Check out what their leaders say. Put them both to the test and decide."

Maggie appeared ready to reply when the engines suddenly cut power. She sat up and looked out the window. Jackson leaned over too, hoping to catch a glimpse of the Parthenon or the Acropolis or the Areopagus or something famous and easily recognizable. All he saw was more clouds until a runway jumped up from the gray. Seconds later, wheels touched down and the Airbus slowed and taxied to the terminal at Athens International Airport.

"How were your naps?" Joel asked Rich and Aliana when they joined up in the terminal.

"Refreshing," Aliana said. "I am ready to finish working on the journal on the flight to Kavala."

Rich didn't answer, and Joel looked to him. "Rich?"

"I had another vision."

"Of what?"

"It was vague. The closest thing I can equate it to is calmness and peace."

"No more details?" Joel asked.

"No," Rich said. "Sorry."

"Well, what are you going to do?" Joel said with a shrug. "Come on."

They had just missed a connecting flight to Kavala by minutes, so they had a two-hour wait until the next one. After finding their departure gate and using the restrooms, they sought out snacks or an early dinner.

"Ask you one more question?" Maggie said as she and Jackson stood in line for gyros.

"Mm, what's that?"

"Where do vague, unspecific visions of bad things happening or of calmness and peace fit on the spectrum of lowercase and uppercase Christians?"

Jackson looked at her. "I have no idea."

*   *   *

Wednesday, February 13
9:24 a.m. (Eastern European Time)

JACKSON, MAGGIE, Joel, Rich, and Aliana had been detained in Athens for an extra two hours because of mechanical issues with the plane that was to carry them to Kavala. For a while, it had looked as if they might have to wait until morning, and once Jackson had seen the small propeller plane, he kind of wished they had. But the flight, once it took off, had been uneventful, putting them down on the Macedonian Coast of Greece just after ten-thirty p.m. It had been closer to eleven-thirty by the time they gathered their belongings and found a taxi to take them to their hotel west of the city.

A good night's sleep had rejuvenated Jackson, and judging by the rest of his traveling companions' faces at breakfast Wednesday morning, the same was true for each of them. They were joined by Ian, Cara, and Ramón, who had spent Monday and Tuesday doing some preliminary scouting and acquiring. After listening to mostly Joel recount the visit to Château LeCavalier, being run off the road, and passing an extra day in Trois Ruisseaux, they brought the rest of the group up to speed.

Cara, working off Rich's photos, had compiled translations of the verses inscribed on the outside of Philippe's gold chest and the verse on the inside of it. She'd done the same with photos of each of Philippe's photos of the journal. All her translations matched Aliana's almost verbatim, giving the team accuracy assurances. Regarding the journal, Philippe was right. It did not provide much in the way of direction, but the team did concur with Philippe's analysis that the Calvary Treasure seemed, in the eyes of Jacques IV of Aragon at least, to be something that would help the Crusaders defeat Islam. The group planned to study it further, but at the moment, it didn't seem to aid in their search.

Ramón had greased the wheels with the local authorities and made sure Team Joel had the necessary permits and consent for their search and hopeful recovery of 'the Spirit.' The church was a historic landmark, but one that was still occasionally used for festivals or religious celebrations. To that end, it would be inaccessible from late afternoon through the following day for a wedding. That news had been met with frowns until Ramón reminded them the following day, Thursday, was Valentine's Day.

Ian, with the knowledge that there were other players in the game, had scouted for any signs of pursuit. A friend of a contact of a friend who worked at Kavala International Airport reported nothing that set off Ian's suspicions, nor had his surveillance detected any signs that Team Joel wasn't alone in Greece. At least for the time being.

After finishing a tasty breakfast of pastries and quiches, the group boarded a city bus that took them to the port. Built on the side of a hill so that the entire city sloped down toward the Thracian Sea, Kavala was a blend of the new and the old. Condominiums and high-rises along the bay gave way to stucco houses with clay shingles on the next block. It wasn't exactly the stereotypical Greek Isle postcard, but it was something to behold.

The weather helped. It was unseasonably warm off the Macedonian Coast, with mid-morning temperatures in the seventies. The winds were light and pleasant, and the sky and the sea were battling to present the prettiest shade of blue. Occasional tufts of cloud and whitecaps on the water added distinction to the beautiful scene, and for the first time since leaving L.A., Jackson didn't feel like he was a world away from home.

The next ferry to Thasos wasn't until ten. After buying tickets, Team Joel filled each other in on remaining details of the last few days. Aliana, having been to Thasos recently, also briefed the others on the island. Covering almost one hundred fifty square miles, Thasos was the twelfth-largest of the Greek Isles and the farthest north. The ferry would take them across the Gulf of Kavala to Limenas, the capital of Thasos, on the northeast side of the island. From there, they would take taxis or a bus south to the church.

The eastern half of the island was filled with steep ravines and hills, some over half a mile high. The slopes were mostly covered in pines, but on the southeastern corner, a series of magnificent white cliffs broke out, forming several sheltered coves and private beaches. It was atop one of these cliffs that seventh-century Greeks had constructed a place of worship.

"It is really very beautiful," Aliana said. "When you are standing on the side of the cliff, overlooking the sea, it seems a million miles away from everything. Not to mention a few centuries."

"How densely is the island populated?" Joel asked.

"Not very. The people are mostly farmers unless, of course, they work in the tourism industry."

"Is it a tourist trap?" Cara asked.

"Tourism is the main industry, but the island is not overcrowded."

"So eight treasure hunters will stand out," Jackson said.

"Perhaps."

"And the ferry's the only way on or off the island," Ian said, "unless you charter a boat or a chopper, yeah? But there's no heliport on which to set it down."

Joel clapped his hands. "Okay, we have until . . . when?"

"Six, seven," Ramón said, flipping his hand back and forth.

"When's sunset around here?"

"Six-oh-two," Ian reported.

"Okay, that works well then. Normally, I'd say we'd take it easy today, just do some recon. But since we know there are others after the 'Holy Trinity,' and since we can't get back again until Friday, and since you three have already done recon, I think we should get as much work done as we can today. The last ferry back is at seven, so we shouldn't have a problem with that."

"What's our plan of attack?" Maggie asked.

"First thing, we look around, get the lay of the land," Joel said. "From there, we try to escalate the lay of the land eight hundred years ago. The original southern wall of the nave was largely destroyed by an earthquake, and the new wall, built circa 1205, is in a state of disrepair currently. Or at least it was until the restoration project last year. At any rate, we essentially have three churches—as it was before the earthquake in 1205, as it was after, and as it is now. We need to identify what it was like before 1205 when a squire of the Knights Calvary presumably visited it."

"Can't we just look at the etchings?" Jackson asked.

"Of course. But remember, we're not after etchings. We're after 'the Spirit.'"

"So we have to search through ruins?"

"No," Aliana said. "The etching of the Knights Calvary coat of arms is not alone. There is more on the wall, and it is likely a clue that will lead us to 'the Spirit.'"

"And you saw all this last week?"

Aliana nodded. "I know what you are thinking—where are the photos? Photography is strictly prohibited on the church grounds."

"It was also confusing," Ramón said.

"It's why we are all here, to investigate," Joel said.

"How well preserved is the church?" Maggie asked.

"Moderately well," Aliana said. "It stopped being regularly used over two hundred years ago, and so the preservation efforts waned. It wears its years, but it wears them well."

"What I mean is, is this going to be more like scouring a modern church or an archaeological dig?"

Aliana smiled. "A little of both."

Chapter Sixteen

10:44 a.m.

THE FERRY WAS almost fifteen minutes late and appeared to be attempting to make up time as it surged through the waves toward the island of Thasos. Jackson rode on the top deck, bumming M&M's off Ian and prodding Aliana for more details on Byzantine architecture and the Eastern Orthodox Church. He felt a little silly asking a self-proclaimed Muslim about the Christian religion, but swallowed his pride for the sake of finding the treasure.

As the ferry approached Limenas, Jackson was reminded of his most recent case. He'd spent the better part of a day on Santa Catalina Island off the coast of Los Angeles, and at first glance, Limenas greatly resembled Avalon, the major city and ferry dock on Catalina. It was situated in the middle of a crescent-shaped piece of land around an azure bay. The buildings gleamed white under a bright sun, their clay shingles varying shades of red and orange. Beyond the town, the tree-covered hills of Thasos rose toward white peaks in the center of the island. At first, Jackson thought he saw snowcaps, but as they drew closer, he realized it was just the color of the terrain at the top of the mountains. It was still a beautiful sight.

The ferry docked, and Team Joel found each other and made their way onto dry land. They had no trouble finding cabs, but it took a little dickering to select two that would drive them to the other side of the island, then pick them up again around six. While Joel, Aliana, and Ramón handled the negotiations, Ian briefed Jackson on some of the logistics of the island.

The main highway wrapped around the edge of Thasos so that, in theory, one could drive in laps around it. The interior of the island was accessible but by a series of winding and meandering dirt roads that often traversed the side of the mountain. Although it was far from fast, the highway was the quickest route to the church on the southeast side of the island.

With the cab issue finally settled, Jackson found himself lumped in one cab with Maggie, Rich, and Cara while "the brain trust"—as Cara referred to them—rode in another. The driver of Jackson's vehicle was chatty, covering everything from the weather to the history of Thasos to the best place to find a good meal or bottle of ouzo on the island. He spoke English, mostly, with a strong Greek accent. Once or twice a sentence he slurred into his native tongue as if he'd had a minor stroke, making it almost impossible to follow him. Mentally weary, Jackson eventually gave up and focused on the scenery out his window. Vibrant blue water sparkled in the afternoon sunlight to his left. Forested hills, occasionally broken by valleys that were home to small towns, resorts, or farm fields, stretched inland on his right.

Two-thirds of the way to the church, the driver suddenly decided to step on the gas, racing past the other half of Team Joel's cab, and ultimately beating them to the church by several minutes. It gave Jackson, Maggie, Rich, and Cara—all newcomers to the island—a chance to gawk.

Protruding from the island was a short, stubby peninsula. Although it only extended a few hundred feet into the Thracian Sea, it rose sharply to probably a hundred feet above sea level. Contrary to much of the surrounding hillsides, the slopes of the peninsula were jagged and barren, with only a few cypress trees clinging to the sides of them. With the backdrop of hundreds of square miles of blue, broken only by the outline of distant islands, the view would have been spectacular in and of itself.

But for all the natural beauty, what caught Jackson's eye was the small yet impressive structure atop the rounded hilltop. From the road, the white stones that made up the walls appeared flawless, a patchwork of perfectly interlacing natural building blocks. Archways that cast distinct shadows on the pure white walls covered regressed door and window openings, a few of which still housed their original stained glass panes. The clay shingles on the cupola were faded, cracked, and in some places, flat out missing. And the bell tower on the western end of the church seemed canted slightly away from the rest of the building. But when viewed as part of one panorama, the defects seemed to fade into a perfect representation of the church as it had been over eight centuries before.

The foursome was still staring when the other cab pulled into the dirt turn off that served as a parking lot. It was a few hundred feet from the church, which was accessible via a narrow dirt pathway that looked a little precarious as it hugged the edge of the cliffs on the east side. Joel paid both cab drivers and gave them a word of instruction about when to return. They sped off, and Team Joel was alone. In the whole world, it seemed.

"Beautiful, isn't it?" Joel said.

"It doesn't look eight hundred years old," Cara said.

"More like fourteen hundred," Aliana said. "The etchings are eight hundred years old, but the church itself has been here since the seventh century."

"Even more so then."

"Wait until you get up close," Ian said.

Joel nodded. "Daylight's wasting. Let's go."

He led the way, single file, down toward the church. The path continued to hug the cliffs all the way on their left, with a pair of small ridges creating a valley halfway along on the right—a valley that contained an ancient cemetery. Beyond the second ridge, the drop was much more gradual down to the sea but still perilous. There was ample room to walk safely, but it was worth paying attention.

"Bet the old ladies in dresses loved this walk on blustery Easter mornings, yeah?" Ian said.

Ramón chuckled.

Ian was indeed right; up close, the church showed its age. Cracks and crumbles began to appear, and instances of thirteenth-century reconstruction were evident. Still, the ancient church was impressive.

There was no landscaping around the building. The dirt path slowly petered out into a mixture of dirt and grass and bare rock, which was characteristic of the entire peninsula, save for a little more green in the valley that contained the cemetery. The grass was kept short, or else just didn't grow, which added to the appearance. No trees, no bushes or shrubs. The only thing growing was a series of vines in one corner on the northeast side of the building.

Aliana served as a guide, leading the group around the outside of the church. On the east side, she warned them to watch their step, as the distance between the outer wall of the church and the drop off to the water below was only half a dozen feet. On the south side, there was room for them all to congregate, and she approached the wall.

"You can see a line," she said, extending her hand almost as high as she could, and tracing along the length of the wall. "This was the top of the original south wall."

"Before the earthquake?" Rich asked.

"Right." She gestured at the length of the line, which angled up the farther west it ran, eventually disappearing. "They built on top of the old wall, but then found they had to reinforce their work because it was leaning to the north, in danger of falling in on itself. So they built a second wall on the inside that essentially became the load-bearing south wall."

"How do you know all this?" Cara asked.

"She became very friendly with a local cleric," Ramón said.

Aliana ignored him. "Unlike some people, I worked the first time I was here."

Ramón just chuckled under his breath.

"Didn't you say they found the etching behind the new south wall during a restoration?" Jackson asked.

Aliana nodded.

"So doesn't that mean the new south wall isn't there anymore?"

"Part of it."

"Should have brought hard hats, yeah?" Ian said.

"According to the gentleman I spoke to," she answered, "the new south wall was not holding well, and had actually crumbled away in places. The restoration last year reinforced both the old and new south walls to make sure they continue to support the roof. On the west end," she said, pointing with an outstretched arm, "they had to insert some steel support columns and girders, which you will see from the inside. On the far east end, they found that the old south wall was actually fully supportive."

"Ladies first," Jackson said.

"I'm sure it's safe," Joel said, "or they wouldn't be allowing a wedding here tomorrow. To wit, let's get moving."

Aliana again led the way, around to the entrance on the west side of the church. A small colonnade ran the entire length of the western wall, but all attention was drawn to two large, ornate doors in the center, leading into the church. Cara commented that she was surprised the church was left unlocked, a point Aliana had brought up on her first visit. But vandalism wasn't a concern in Thasos, apparently, and the church was open to anyone at any time.

Jackson expected Aliana to produce a torch or an oil lantern like they always did in the movies. Instead, she and Joel both clicked on LED flashlights as they entered the dark church. "Just give me a moment," Aliana said. "There are oil lamps somewhere over here."

While she searched, Joel played his beam around the interior. It was tiny, with almost no furnishings, and looked the part of a church in ruins. Directly ahead stood two doors, rounded at the top to fit under an archway, although none existed. They came to eye level and were magnificently sculpted, depicting the Virgin Mary on the right and an unknown angel—Gabriel?—on the left. They did not appear to be anywhere near eight hundred years old.

"Ah, that is better," Aliana said as she lit a pair of lanterns. They flooded the small room with more than ample light. She handed them to Rich and Ramón, the two people closest to her. "This is the narthex," she explained. "It was where the non-orthodox worshippers congregated."

"Was it empty then too?" Maggie asked.

"Somewhat. There would have been no pews, as sitting down during a service is only practiced in the West. But along the outer walls, there would have been *stacidia*—high-armed chairs for worshippers to lean on as they stood."

"For the quasi-devout," Jackson said.

"There would have been also been brass candle stands, called *manoualia*, which represented the pillar of fire that went before the Hebrews after the Exodus from Egypt, as well as a baptismal font."

"And the doors?" Maggie asked.

"Royal doors, and yes, these are replicas," Aliana said. "But they are probably based on the originals as much as possible."

"Do they differ from church to church?"

"Yes and no. Most have the Annunciation depicted on them, but there is no exact form that it follows."

"Annunciation?" Maggie asked.

"When the angel Gabriel announced to Mary that she would give birth to Jesus," Joel said. "As recorded in the Gospel of Luke."

The group proceeded through the Royal Doors and into the nave, the main body of the church. It was shaped like a stubby crucifix, and Aliana lit two more fixed lamps that, along with the two carried by Rich and Ramón, provided more than enough light to fill the room, which Jackson estimated was three times larger than the narthex.

Aliana again gave a visual tour. "Originally, the side walls would have been covered floor to ceiling with icons and paintings of saints, biblical characters, and events. As you can see, some of the originals remain, which is probably why no replicas were ever created."

"And these date to the twelfth century?" Ian asked.

"Or older. Remember, the church was built in the 600s C.E. The exception is those on the new south wall." Aliana paused to illuminate a crack that separated the old and new wall, and to point out the restorative work done recently to reinforce the structure. "As in the narthex, there were no pews in the nave, but more *stacidia*. Men traditionally stood on the right side and women on the left, equidistant from the altar. There would have been a cathedra, or bishop's throne, on the right side, and choir stalls in either arm of the crucifix."

Joel played his flashlight up toward a chandelier hanging from a beautiful dome. Painted on the dome was a portrait of Christ, holding a book in his left hand, with his right hand raised. "Christ *Pantokrator*," he said. "The Ruler of All."

Aliana directed her gaze upward as well and nodded. "It is a feature of the Orthodox Church. The chandelier is called the *horos*, and portrays various saints."

"Are you getting this all down?" Jackson asked Maggie.

"I was counting on you to remember it all."

"Aha."

Aliana continued to talk about various features in the nave, and Jackson let his eyes wander over the walls. The images painted on them were faded at best. In many places, half of a particular painting had worn mostly or entirely away. In other places, the wall itself had crumbled or disintegrated or had been replaced by a more modern wall, sans paintings.

Jackson had expected the images to reflect the Renaissance style so prevalent in old churches: half-naked people, all with alabaster skin, generally with downcast faces. Instead, they were more primitive, less authentic, very angular. Half were of saints or persons Jackson couldn't identify, but he did recognize a few familiar scenes—Christ breaking bread for the thousands, Peter being awakened in the Roman jail, David slaying a lion with his bare hands. A few others weren't so obvious. Jesus—presumably—sitting down to what looked like a Thanksgiving feast, minus the Native Americans or pilgrims in cockle hats, and three men with fingers in the air, Plato-like, as they debated something.

"And this is the iconostasis," Aliana said, approaching and gesturing at the wall on the eastern end of the nave. It stood at least two stories tall but failed to reach the ceiling. Made of wood, it was covered in more icons, depicting saints, feasts, prophets, and apostles. Set in the middle of the iconostasis was another set of doors, the "Beautiful Gates," she explained.

There were two more sets of doors on either side of the Beautiful Gates, the Deacons' Doors—or simply, the North and South Doors—all leading to the sanctuary at the head of the cross-shaped church. As with the barrier between the narthex and the nave, Aliana admitted the iconostasis was also a replica and not the original.

After a few minutes of studying the icons on the iconostasis, the group moved into the sanctuary. Like the rest of the church, it bore a fading resemblance to its former glory, and again Aliana highlighted the sanctuary's various features—from the half-domed apse that still displayed its original artwork to the modern altar, table of preparation, and various other worship instruments.

"I don't get it," Maggie said. "I thought this was largely unused. Why are all these implements here?"

"The church is not used for regular worship, but they do still have special services and observances," Aliana said.

"I assume they're all pretty exact replicas?" Joel said.

"Yes, I believe so."

"It certainly adds to the aura," Rich said.

"Aye, the aura's lovely," Ian said. "How about you show us the etchings?"

Joel agreed, and the team returned to the nave. Aliana took them to the southeast corner, where the iconostasis butted against the southern wall. "Here you can see where the new south wall was," she said, pointing to a line on the floor about a foot from the current wall. The stone slab floor was a different color where the wall had been, and Aliana again summed up how the construction had played out, with the new wall built after the earthquake in 1205, crumbling over the centuries, and being removed in spots where modern surveyors deemed it no longer necessary for support purposes.

"The etchings are down here," she said, dropping to a knee a few feet from the iconostasis and directly underneath a paned, arched window. She brushed her hand over the stone wall, then took a lamp from Ramón and set it on the floor. She stood back to let the others study the etchings.

"Where?" Cara asked.

"Here," Joel said, crouching at Aliana's side. "They're faint."

"They're eight centuries old," Aliana reminded.

"I can see why they were missed," Cara said.

Jackson viewed them from the back of the group. What he saw was hardly a work of art, but more accurately, crude carvings in the wall. Rough as they were, Jackson was able to distinguish a shield with a cross in the middle, and what appeared to be an animal on its hind feet on the right and a knight or soldier on the left. Beneath the shield was a banner or scroll, and Jackson couldn't tell if words were actually scratched into the stone on the banner/scroll or if they were just representations of words.

"It's crude, but it's the Knights Calvary coat of arms," Joel said.

"You want to tell us what we're looking at?" Jackson asked.

"The shield in the center, which was also the actual shield carried by many of the knights, would have been blue with a white cross. The blue signified truth and loyalty, and the white purity. The cross was originally at an angle and covered the entire span of the shield, but it was reoriented to be upright and widened slightly at each end."

"Same as the lead cross," Maggie said.

"Reoriented when?" Ian asked.

"Middle of the twelfth century, well before the Fall of Jerusalem or any of the events in question."

"So this would be accurate?" Maggie asked.

Joel nodded.

"Why the switch?" Jackson asked.

"I'm not sure. The original version with the cross at an angle was meant to symbolize each member of the order's taking up the cross of Christ, so it depicted a cross as it would be while being carried or borne on the shoulder. Anyhow, the animal on the right is a leaping lion, symbolizing bravery and nobility. On the left is an angel with a sword, representing guardianship and protection."

"Same as was engraved on the cross and fashioned atop the chest," Rich said.

Joel nodded again.

"What's the chicken scratch at the bottom?" Jackson asked.

"It's hard to make out, but I assume it's the Knights Calvary motto, '*ut protegantur sanctos*'—'To safeguard the saints.'"

"What's that beneath it?" Cara asked.

"More Latin," Joel said. "And French."

"Great, more bilingual translation."

"Didn't Ali already translate these?" Maggie asked.

"Yes, but I was not able to make anything out of them."

"I'm sorry, I don't mean to whine, but couldn't we have been working on this for the last several days?"

"We could have," Joel said. "But I wanted Cara to translate them unprejudiced by Ali's translation. And I thought it best if we tackled this puzzle all together, with it having our sole focus."

"Fair enough."

Cara sighed. "Okay, let me take a look." She dropped to her knees, then adjusted her glasses: "Forgive me for butchering this: *'det tibi Deus de rore caeli et de pinguedine terrae abundantiam frumenti et vini.'*" She looked up. "'Deus' is God, but apart from that . . ."

"'Vini' is wine, yeah?"

Cara whipped out her tablet and began pecking the Latin phrases into it.

"What about the French?" Rich asked.

"Uh . . . it doesn't make any sense. A-J-A-C-Q-U-E-M-A-I-N, space, A-V-R, something I can't read, 1-8-8."

"His hand was much steadier at the top," Joel noted. "Either he was more diligent at first, or his strength was failing."

"Awesome," Cara muttered. "He probably left off the last half of what he wanted to tell us."

Joel took a deep breath. "Do either of you make anything from the part in French?"

"The very last part I think is the date," Aliana said. "The French word for April is *Avril*—A-V-R-I-L. April, unknown date, 1188."

"That would make sense," Joel said, tilting his head in an effort to make out the undecipherable markings between the A-V-R and the 1-8-8.

"So what's A-J-A-C-Q-U-E-M-A-I-N?" Rich asked.

"I was—and am—stumped," Aliana said.

"A name?" Maggie said. "Jacquemain sounds French."

"Could be," Joel said. "There's a clear separation between those letters and the A-V-R we're assuming is April."

"There are no similar words in French, so that theory is sound," Aliana said with a nod.

"Okay, I've got a Latin translation here," Cara said.

"That was fast."

"It's the first online translator I found, so don't chart our course on this."

"What do you have?" Joel asked.

"*'God give thee of the dew of heaven, and of the fatness of the earth, abundance of corn and wine.'*"

"Is that Scripture?" Rich asked.

"Let's find out," Joel said, reaching for his tablet. Cara beat him to the draw.

"Genesis 27:28. Almost an exact match to the King James," she said.

"Which is typically quite close to the Latin Vulgate."

"Almost and quite close," Ian said. "Sounds like a sure thing, yeah?"

"We'll verify later, but for now, let's see if that leads us anywhere," Joel said. "Can you repeat it, Cara?"

"*God give thee of the dew of heaven, and of the fatness of the earth, abundance of corn and wine.*"

"Isn't corn a New World crop?" Ramón asked.

"If we are talking about corn as we typically think of it—maize—then yes," Aliana answered. "But corn in the Bible typically refers to some sort of grain—wheat, rye, barley."

He nodded.

"Would they have kept bread and wine in the church somewhere?" Jackson asked.

"Yes, in the tabernacle."

"Where's the tabernacle?" Ramón asked.

"It is a small box or container kept in the sanctuary," Aliana said.

"Might be worth checking," Joel said. He led them there, and they spent ten minutes scouring the replica of a seventh-century tabernacle, but it contained no discernible clues.

"Why would he write some in Latin and some in French?" Maggie asked as they stood together in the sanctuary.

"There was no French Bible at the time, so he was likely quoting the verse as he knew it."

"Or had been told it and memorized it," Jackson said.

"Are we sure it's all one drawing?" Ian asked. "Maybe a different person etched the coat of arms and Scripture as the initials and date, yeah?"

"It's possible," Joel said, "but it sure looked like they're all from the same hand."

"I agree," Aliana said.

"Well, you're the expert."

"So now what?" Jackson asked.

"Now," Joel said with a grin, "you earn your money."

Chapter Seventeen

1:59 p.m.

TEAM JOEL SPENT several hours looking over every inch of the church, searching for any other etchings or signs to where the third piece of the "Holy Trinity" was located. They studied every icon, every painting, every instrument and utensil—whether an original or a replica. They paid particularly close attention to the painting of the Ascension in the apse above the altar and to the stained glass windows—some of which Aliana believed to be original, at least to the time of the Knights Calvary, and some of which had been replaced in the centuries since. They found nothing—no further etchings, no key by which to decipher what they'd found, and no clue as to where the Spirit piece was. So they took a break to eat some dried fruit, veggies, cheese, and crackers Cara had packed in. It was at least nourishment.

"I've been thinking," Joel said after several minutes of silent eating. The group had taken seats in the grass west of the church, in an area about the size of a basketball half court. The day was warm and beautiful, especially from such a vantage point. "The Genesis reference. Maybe we're getting too specific. It's from the passage where Isaac blesses Jacob. Maybe that's our clue."

"How so?" Rich asked.

"There are a lot of biblical scenes depicted in there on the iconostasis and murals. I can't recall all of them, but maybe there's one showing that scene, and also showing us something else of significance."

"It is worth checking out," Aliana said.

"It's vague, I know, but worth a shot."

Excited by the prospects, the group hurriedly finished eating and headed back inside the ancient church, where they split up to scour the various icons and paintings, looking for anything reminiscent of Isaac blessing Jacob. They met up after fifteen minutes, all reporting a lack of success.

"It was a good thought," Aliana said.

"Aye."

"So now what?" Cara asked.

"Is it just me," Ian asked with a shake of his head, "or is this a lot of hoops to jump through? Wasn't the whole point of this to help someone actually find the treasure?"

"Yes," Aliana said, "but keep in mind, those 'hoops' would have been designed so that someone who did not share the Knights Calvary's beliefs would not be prone to jump through them."

"Well, I guess we keep looking and thinking," Joel said. "We have several hours yet before the wedding party, so let's make use of it."

They split and wandered again, with Jackson heading for the inscription. He studied it carefully, paying close attention to the angel and lion, same as on the lead cross, same as on Philippe's chest. Even when looking at photos of the other items on Cara's tablet, he was unable to pick up any discrepancies that might provide a clue. Gradually, the group joined around them, a sense of hopelessness and purposelessness washing over them.

"Any thoughts, detective?" Cara asked, nudging Jackson.

"Yeah. What'd Hebrews eat for dinner?"

"What?"

"Typical meal. Say Jesus and His disciples sat down to eat. What were they having?"

Aliana answered with a furrowed brow. "Lots of breads and grains, unleavened if they were observing the Mosaic Law during Passover; fruits such as figs, dates, and pomegranates; and wine or water."

"You said before that corn in the Bible didn't mean corn on the cob like we think of it," Jackson said, "but grain or wheat, right?"

She nodded. "That is right."

"Which in and of themselves weren't Jewish dinner staples."

"No, not unprepared."

"But the Bible does talk about Jesus' disciples walking through the fields on the Sabbath and eating the heads of grain."

"What are you getting at?" Joel asked.

"I think we're barking up the wrong tree with Isaac and Jacob here. I think the inscription is talking about Genesis 27:28 specifically, and the key word is corn—or translated in today's vernacular, grain." He turned and looked over at one of the murals painted on the inside of the north wing of the church. Portrayed were Jesus and several other people sitting around a table, laden with various foods. "Look what's laying across the table," Jackson said.

"Stalks of grain," Joel said, wandering toward the mural.

"Although edible, out of place in that particular setting, wouldn't you say?"

"I would."

"Hold on," Maggie said. "Because the Bible verse that may or may not be etched into the wall mentions corn, in the English version of the old Latin Vulgate, which when translated into modern Bibles is grain, you think we're supposed to look at this mural and . . . what?"

"I don't know. What is this? Last supper?"

"No," Aliana said, following after Joel. The rest of the team migrated more slowly. "Look at where they are seated. Jesus is to the right of center, at the place of honor. He is the guest. And the man in the middle—the host—is not a disciple or a commoner. He is a Pharisee."

"You can tell by his appearance, yeah?" Ian asked.

"Aye," Aliana said with a twinkle in her eye and a half smile. "The style of his clothes, the long tassels, a well-trimmed beard, and a seal on his ring finger. He is most definitely a Pharisee."

"Okay, when did Jesus eat in the home of Pharisees?" Cara asked.

"Several times in Luke," Joel said. "He was having dinner with a Pharisee named Simon when the so-called 'sinful woman' came and anointed Him with oil. He also performed healing while dining at a Pharisee's house on the Sabbath."

"What about when they accused His disciples of not washing their hands before they ate?" Rich asked.

"I don't know if that specifies that Pharisees were present at the meal," Joel said. "At any rate, multiple times."

"There is more, though," Aliana said. "Look at what Jesus is holding."

"A cup or a bowl?" Ramón asked.

"And he is pointing at it. It is the focus of the discussion."

"Lighting a lamp and putting it under a bowl?" Rich asked.

"That was the Sermon on the Mount," Joel answered.

"Yes, of course, that's right."

"What's this say down here?" Jackson asked, pointing to a phrase inscribed beneath the mural. A caption of sorts.

"It is in Latin," Aliana said. "*vae vobis Pharisaeis.*"

"What's tha—"

"'*Woe to you, Pharisees*,'" Joel said.

Aliana nodded.

"When did Jesus give woes to the Pharisees in the Bible?" Jackson asked.

"Matthew 23 has the list of seven woes," Rich said.

"It's also in Luke, I believe," Joel said, again activating his tablet. The group waited for a few minutes, Aliana carefully studying the mural for further clues. "In Matthew," Joel reported, "the woes are listed . . . but it doesn't give the setting. In Luke," he said, pausing for a few moments. "Aha. Luke 11:37: '*And as he was speaking, a certain Pharisee prayed him that he would dine with him. And he going in, sat down to eat.*' Verse 38: '*And the Pharisee began to say, thinking within himself, why he was not washed before dinner.*'" Joel looked up. "From there, he went on to list various woes."

"Seven?" Maggie asked.

"No. Three to Pharisees, and it looks like . . . two to lawyers and one general woe."

"Six," Maggie said.

"The missing woe?" Cara asked.

"What's that, a Dickens novel?" Jackson said.

"Which three are to Pharisees?" Ian asked.

Joel read again. "'*But woe to you, Pharisees, because you tithe mint and rue and every herb and pass over judgment and the charity of God. Now these things you ought to have done, and not to leave the other undone. Woe to you, Pharisees, because you love the uppermost seats in the synagogues and salutations in the marketplace. Woe to you, because you are as sepulchers that appear not: and men that walk over are not aware.*'"

"So we either need to dig up a Byzantine garden, tear apart the chairs in here, or become grave robbers," Jackson said.

"The Genesis verse talked about abundance of corn and wine, didn't it?" Maggie said. "Sounds like a garden."

"Would there have been a garden by the church?" Ian asked.

"Maybe," Aliana said. "But no guarantee."

"Anybody see any signs of a garden outside?" Joel asked.

"After eight hundred years?" Ramón said.

"Let's at least look."

They spent thirty minutes examining every piece of flora on the peninsula or the surrounding area, looking for anything that didn't appear native. There was little but grass and weeds growing.

"I suppose finding a grapevine with depressed and sunken ground in front of it would have been too much to ask for," Jackson said.

"In the mural, Jesus is pointing to a cup," Ian said. "Anything in that passage about cups?"

"A few verses above," Joel answered, back on his tablet. "'*And the Lord said to him: Now you, Pharisees, make clean the outside of the cup and of the platter: but your inside is full of rapine and iniquity. Ye fools, did not he that made that which is without make also that which is within?*'"

"Not sure what that tells us," Rich said.

"Little."

"What are the other woes, the ones to lawyers?" Cara asked. "Since we're being thorough."

"Let's see. Picking it up after the last woe to scribes and Pharisees . . . '*And one of the lawyers answering, saith to him: Master, in saying these things, thou reproachest us also. But he said: Woe to you lawyers also, because you load men with burdens which they cannot bear and you yourselves touch not the packs with one of your fingers. Woe to you who build the monuments of the prophets: and your fathers killed them.*' And then all the way down in verse 52, '*Woe to you lawyers, for you have taken away the key of knowledge. You yourselves have not entered in: and those that were entering in, you have hindered.*'"

"Well, that helps."

After another ten minutes of hashing out possibilities, Joel suggested they not assume or disregard anything. Instead, Team Joel scoured the church again, looking for anything that might tie in with the mural. Any ideas were valid ideas, Joel said. They were gathering information, taking in as much as possible, since they'd have a full day to ruminate. They spent the better part of two hours looking over every mural, icon, stained glass window, and crack or scuff that could possibly be another etching. A few possibilities temporarily piqued their interest, but nothing panned out by giving credence to any plausible theory linking back to the actual etchings or the "Woe unto you, Pharisees" mural.

"Found something, yeah?"

The remaining seven members of Team Joel hurried through the Deacons' Doors to join Ian in the northeast corner of the sanctuary, where he was crouched down. "This slab," he said, pointing to a section of the floor, "it's different, yeah?"

"How so?" Rich asked.

"The texture or grain or whatever. I'm not a geologist. And look here. There's a crack."

"A crack?"

"Aye. And it's loose. Do we have a pry bar or something?"

"I have a knife," Ramón said, unsheathing a jackknife from somewhere on his waist. Ian also had opened a knife, and the two of them knelt down and pried them into the crack. The blades bent, but the slab didn't move.

"We need something heavier," Ian said.

"One of the utensils," Ramón said, standing and walking toward the table of preparation.

"Please be careful," Aliana said. "Those are valuable."

"I thought they were just replicas," Cara said.

"Even so."

"What we really need is a stanchion," Jackson said.

"What?" Cara asked.

"Remember, Indy in the library and that old guy who thought his stamper was echoing through the whole building?"

"Forgive him," Maggie says. "He lives in a fantasy world."

"It's getting late," Joel said. "Maybe we should call it a day. We don't want to unearth some secret chamber right before a bunch of wedding guests are here. We also don't want to get careless in a rush. Let's come back Friday with proper tools."

Ian stood and wiped his hands on his pants. "Aye, he's right. The mysterious crypt will have to wait."

Chapter Eighteen

5:54 p.m.

THE SUN WAS hanging low over the southwestern horizon as Team Joel left the church behind and walked back past the two ridges and the small graveyard to the dirt turnout where the dual taxis had dropped them late that morning. Their words were a mixture of disappointment at finding no obvious clue to the whereabouts of the last piece of the "Holy Trinity" and anticipation at what might be beneath the slab Ian had discovered. A very unscientific and unprecise test—stomping on it and adjacent sections of the floor (there had been no available stanchions)—had led to the conclusion a hollow compartment existed beneath it. Time would tell.

"Where's the wedding party anyhow?" Ian asked, checking his watch. "We were supposed to vacate so they could prepare for the ceremony, yeah?"

"They said six or seven," Ramón answered. "It's only six."

"In that case, where are our taxis?" Rich asked.

"Drinking ouzo," Cara mumbled, checking her watch as if it would be different than Ian's. Jackson was content to wait and watch the sun dip into the Thracian Sea. The colors—the blue of the sea, the green of the surrounding hills, the white of the cliffs, and the brown of the dirt, along with the oranges, reds, pinks, and purples of the sky and clouds at sunset—were even more breathtaking than the vista had been earlier that afternoon. It was as if Jackson had gone from watching TV via rabbit ears and tinfoil to HD on a plasma screen. With any luck, they'd have lamb chops for dinner and the evening would be complete.

"What time'd you say that last ferry was?" Cara asked.

"Seven," Ramón said.

"We are on island time, yeah?" Ian asked.

"Did you pay them ahead of time?" Cara asked.

Joel shook his head.

"Then they'll be here. They won't pass up the fare."

"I hope you're right."

Jackson continued to watch the sunset, wondering what it would look like half a day later to his grandpa or to Reggie or Mouse or Sam. He grinned, realizing Sam would probably be up to her elbows in somebody else's blood in ER, Mouse would be busy gaming with no knowledge of the outside world, and Reggie would be putting in extra time in the kitchen or glad-handing customers, leaving just his grandpa to enjoy the sunset. That is if Leroy Douglas hadn't put on some Pavarotti and fallen asleep.

As six came and went, Joel pulled out his cell to try to call the cab company. But he had no service.

"Not to worry, yeah?" Ian said. "We passed a lovely looking resort just a wee part up the road. If we have to spend the night here, we can."

"If it isn't booked with wedding guests," Cara said.

"Does anybody have cell service?" Joel asked.

"You really need to get that satellite phone," Aliana said.

No one had service, and they waited as the sun dipped below the horizon, momentarily splashing both the sky and the sea in magnificent shades of orange. Cara used her phone to snap several photos, which Jackson sadly realized would never compare to the real thing. He glanced at Maggie, seeing a smile on her face as she enjoyed the view as well. It drew him back to several months ago on the California coast near Big Sur. Like then, he wished he could press pause on the world so the moment would last. He couldn't, of course, and it didn't.

Finally, at ten after six, one taxi careened around a curve and skidded to a stop in front of them. The usually reserved Joel was adamant as he scolded the driver. "You're late."

"Sorry. I make up time."

"Uh, we can't all fit," Cara said.

"Other taxi coming."

"Soon?" Joel asked.

"Five minutes."

They spent less than a minute splitting into two groups, based on who "needed" to get back and who was "adventurous" enough to stay behind and possibly spend a night on the island if they missed the ferry. Joel, Rich, Cara, and Aliana got into the taxi after Joel made sure the others had enough money. Assuring him they did, Jackson, Maggie, Ian, and Ramón waved them off and watched as their taxi disappeared around the hills.

"Ten says there is no other cab," Ian said.

Ramón grinned.

Maggie sighed. "All I can say is this resort of yours better have a restaurant that serves cold beer."

"Aye, I'm sure it does," Ian said. "First round is on me."

"Do they eat seafood in the Greek Isles?" she asked.

Ramón nodded. "It's universal."

"Good deal."

"You guys want to bother waiting around?" Jackson asked sarcastically.

Ian grinned. "Just for that, you get no holdover." He pulled out a small bag of M&M's, offered some to Maggie and Ramón, and then downed the rest of the bag with a smirk at Jackson.

The breeze freshened a little as darkness started to stretch over Thasos, and, in all seriousness, Jackson was about to suggest they start walking toward the resort before it got too dark to see. But before he could say anything, headlights swept around the curve in the road and a second taxi appeared. It pulled into the small parking area, causing the gold crucifix that was undoubtedly hanging from the rearview mirror to swing back and forth.

"You owe me ten dollars," Ramón said.

"You never took the bet," Ian replied.

They quickly got in, and Ramón delivered a quick line in pigeon Greek to let the driver know they were in a hurry to make the ferry. Jackson buckled his seatbelt just in time. The driver punched the accelerator to the floor and never let up as they raced around the curves on Thasos' main highway at breakneck speed. Two or three times, Jackson thought his life was over and they would hurtle off the side of the road and over a cliff into the sea. But it never happened, and their driver delivered them to the ferry dock four minutes before seven.

"Friday," Joel said as he shook hands and welcomed the group aboard the ferry, "we pay extra to bring our own vehicles."

*   *   *

9:39 p.m.

AFTER STOPPING by the hotel to freshen up, Team Joel headed out to a very late, very much appreciated seafood dinner. While they were finishing up, Joel announced that since they couldn't return to the church on Thursday, everyone had the next day off to do as they pleased in Kavala.

"Shouldn't we still be working tomorrow?" Rich asked.

Cara shot him an evil look and Ramón told him to go have a vision.

"I did," he answered.

"What?" Joel asked.

"On the ferry ride back. I found a bench and dozed off."

"What did you see?" Aliana asked.

"That we need to look up."

"Look up?" Ramón asked.

Rich nodded.

"That's it?"

Another nod.

"Well, that would contradict looking down at the etchings or a subterranean cavern, yeah?"

"I don't know what it means," Rich said. "I only know what I saw."

"We'll worry about it when the time comes," Joel said. "But in answer to your question, I talked to Ali and Jackson on the ferry. We all agreed the best thing we can do right now is ruminate on what we have. We're going to examine the passage in Luke more carefully, comparing the Latin Vulgate and English translations with the commonly used French of the day, in case the author of the etchings was thinking in French. And Ali and I both plan to consult experts regarding a couple of potential interpretations in the journal."

"What about asking about the church and whether it was known to have a crypt or cellar?"

"Nothing in my preliminary research turned up any evidence that it did," Aliana said, "although it would not be abnormal."

"I don't think we want to do anything to raise a high profile," Joel said. "Asking more details about the church and a hidden cellar is the sort of thing that could attract attention. We'll check it out on Friday. Until then, I'm certainly not telling any of you that you can't spend your day studying the journals or Luke's Gospel or doing whatever clandestine research you want. But I don't think it would be productive to force everyone to sit contemplatively in the hotel all day. It's like Jackson said, sometimes the best way to approach a problem is to let it rest a little and not go full speed after a solution."

"You're the boss," Rich said without any hint of offense.

"Amen to that," Ramón said.

Joel clapped his hands. "Dessert, anyone?"

They enjoyed *galaktoboureko* (custard inside a series of paper-thin sheets of dough) while discussing plans for the following day. Aside from their visit a week ago, Aliana and Ramón had both been to Kavala previously and recommended various destinations. Aliana's were historical and artistic whereas Ramón's leaned to a more sensual bent.

It was close to ten-thirty when the eight finally left the restaurant. As they were crossing the street to their vehicles, Ian bumped Jackson's shoulder. "Don't look now, but we have a tail."

Willing his head not to turn, Jackson asked, "Where?"

"Your five o'clock. White male, tall, thin, European."

Jackson nodded as he stepped onto the curb. "Hey, Maggie."

She turned around.

"I'm sending you a text."

She frowned. "You don't tex—"

"Play along," he said quietly.

"Huh?"

"Lift your phone like I just sent you an image. Chuckle, give me a dirty eye, and while you're at it, see if you can snap a few photos of the guy at my five o'clock. Discreetly of course."

Still frowning, she reached into her pocket and pulled out her phone. She studied it for a minute, then smiled. "Cute," she said a little louder than normal. "Just for that, I'm going with Ian tomorrow."

Ian winked at Jackson. "Works for me, yeah?"

"If you're all done text-flirting, I'm tired," Cara said. "Can we get home?"

"Aye."

Jackson got into the backseat of one of their two waiting taxis. Maggie squeezed in beside him. "What was that all about?"

"Ian spotted a shadow," Jackson answered. "Else conned you into a date. Let me see what you got."

She handed over the phone. Taken on the dark street, the images weren't ideal, but she had at least gotten a partial shot of the man's face.

"What do you mean by shadow?" Maggie asked Ian. "He left the restaurant the same time as us?"

"Aye. He also entered the same time we did and took a long time to eat for a gent sitting by himself. He also seemed to show a particular interest in us from across the room." He shrugged. "Maybe it's nothing, but there's a third taxi behind us right now."

"Can we do anything with a photo?"

"Cara might be able to run his face."

"You have access to criminal databases or something?"

"Not me personally, no."

Jackson spent a few minutes studying the taxi behind them. When it followed them off the main highway, he leaned forward. "Change of plans," he said to the driver. "Can you take us to the Esperia Hotel instead?"

"Whatever you say," the driver replied.

"The Esperia Hotel?" Rich asked from the front seat.

"I saw a sign for it on the way in. We'll give the guy behind us a choice."

"It'll clue him in we're onto him," Ian said.

"True, but it might throw him. And at least he'll know that he can't read us so easily."

"I'll call Joel and let him know what's going on."

The driver obeyed Jackson's directions, and soon after he veered onto a separate path, the trailing taxi whooshed past them and disappeared into Kavala traffic.

"I guess that's a possible outcome too," Jackson said. "Driver, never mind. Back to the Marriott."

"Your euro."

They returned to their hotel, arriving at the front entrance just as Joel, Cara, Aliana, and Ramón's taxi was leaving. The other three headed inside while Joel waited for Jackson and his group to get out.

"What was that all about?"

"Just playing a little *I Spy*," Jackson answered. He explained in more detail as the group headed up to their rooms. Before they all turned in for the night, Maggie sent the photos to Cara and Ramón. Cara picked the best image and checked the face against a bank of photos Team Joel had compiled over the years. Ramón sent it to his friend's brother with Spain's *Centro Nacional de Inteligencia*. Cara generated no hits and Ramón said it would be morning before they heard anything, so with nothing further to do, they called it a night.

Jackson's body wasn't adjusting well to jet lag, and instead of being tired, he was wide awake. So he read the translation of Jacques IV of Aragon's journal for a while. It didn't give him any brilliant deductions, but it did help put him to sleep.

Team Joel only had two rooms, and Jackson had opted for the hard floor instead of sharing a bed. As a result, he slept fitfully, dreaming that he was vacationing in Greece with the entire cast of *Full House*. The only person missing was John Stamos' character, Uncle Jesse, who continued to stalk them from the shadows, all while shoveling in Greek yogurt hand over fist. Whatever the cure, Jackson resolved during one of the many times when he woke up and glanced at the clock to see if morning was ever going to arrive, he had to find a way to stop dreaming.

Chapter Nineteen

Thursday, February 14
9:32 a.m.

THURSDAY DAWNED BRIGHT and warm. Or so Jackson assumed. After a mostly restless night, he'd finally fallen into deep sleep, and it had been well after dawn when he awoke. As was becoming tradition, Team Joel met for breakfast in their hotel before splitting up for the day. The first ferry left for Thasos at eight the following morning, and Joel wanted to be on it. To that end, he asked everyone to be back Thursday night at an hour that would have them ready to leave the hotel by seven-fifteen. Then he wished them a good day.

Ian and Ramón's chosen venues wouldn't be opening until much later, but Kavala F.C. or Real Kavala or some such soccer team had a home game at noon. They convinced Rich to tag along, telling him that if he could sit and watch three hours of baseball, he could sit through a soccer match. They also promised not to stop off at any place that he wouldn't approve of, and he ultimately agreed.

Joel excused himself away from any morning session, stating he had some personal things to take care of, and Cara said she was going to head to the beach. Joel wasn't wild about her going alone, but she said she could handle ogling Greek men just fine. Besides, she wasn't going there to model but to read.

That left Jackson the choice of attending a *futbol* match in which he didn't have even the remotest rooting interest or going wherever Maggie and Aliana chose to go. Ever the antiquities expert, Aliana wanted to tour some of the historical sites and landmarks in and around Kavala—the ones she hadn't hit on her previous visit. Ever the reporter, Maggie figured getting some contextual background wouldn't hurt, and it beat soccer or reading at the beach. Ever the guy, Jackson liked the way Maggie looked in her jeans and form-fitting royal blue New York Rangers tee and the way Aliana looked in a long, flowing black tank top and with her hair in a loose ponytail, and figured some museums and ruins couldn't be all that bad, right?

Joel said he might join up with the trio for a late lunch, as did Cara. They promised to all stay in touch, and after a few minutes plotting their route, Jackson, Maggie, and Aliana took a taxi to the Archaeological Museum of Kavala. The museum contained artifacts dating back as far as the fifth century B.C., from marble busts to gold rings to coins to figurines to sarcophagi. Jackson wasn't big on random antiquities, but even he had to admit seeing items that were twenty-five hundred years old was somewhat surreal and a little cool.

Aliana felt slightly stronger than that, gushing over almost every piece. She talked on and on, apologizing for boring Jackson and Maggie. But Aliana was far from boring, and Jackson liked to think it had as much to do with her passion, knowledge, and method of conveying both as it did with her long, slender arms and silky black hair. Maggie also found Aliana's lectures intriguing, peppering her with questions that would no doubt serve as a foundation for the epic she would write about the search for the Calvary Treasure. What a bust of the Roman Empress Agrippina had to do with Crusader treasure, Jackson didn't know, but he couldn't wait to read Maggie's column to find out.

He also mulled what he'd read in the journal the night before and the last portion of Luke 11. Jackson had always been good at memorizing, and his parents had tried to get him involved in his church's Bible quizzing program when he was a teenager, but he'd found it a little dorky. Talent wasted, Hannah Douglas had said, but he'd made good use of his talent that morning while waiting for everybody to get ready, committing to memory a dozen verses covering Jesus' woes to the Pharisees. Now, as he trailed the two women through the museum, he pondered what clue they might contain—how they might point to the location of the third and final piece of the "Holy Trinity." He got nowhere.

Leaving the museum, the trio's next stops were the Castle of Kavala and The Imaret. The castle traced its modern origins to the fifteenth century, displaying the reconstructive efforts of the Byzantines, Venetians, and Turks. The Imaret had been built during the Ottoman period by Mehmet Ali, the founder of modern Egypt. The massive and lavish Islamic structure had functioned as a Muslim seminary, a home for refugees, an abandoned edifice, and, most recently, as a luxury hotel.

"The founder of modern Egypt?" Maggie asked as they left the Imaret.

Aliana nodded. "Muhammad Ali Pasha al-Mas'ud ibn Agha."

"Muhammad and Mehmet, that's the same name, right?" Maggie asked.

"Mehmet is the modern Turkish translation."

"So this guy was essentially Muhammad Ali?" Jackson asked.

"Yes. It is actually a very common name in Islam."

"Sort of like that UCLA running back named Kareem Abdul-Jabbar, just spelled differently?"

Both women looked at him.

"Never mind."

Aliana continued. "Ali was an Ottoman army commander who became *vali*—that is, governor—and then declared himself to be the *khedive*, or viceroy, of Egypt and Sudan."

"So why is The Imaret in Kavala?" Maggie asked.

"Kavala was Ali's hometown," Aliana replied, "so he wanted to grace them with it."

"What became of him?"

"Unfortunately, he succumbed to mental illness and died in 1849. He is buried in the mosque named for him in Cairo."

By now it was early afternoon, and after touching base with Joel and Cara, the trio picked up a snack of *tiropita* and dined in the shadow of the *Kamares*, also known as the Kavala aqueduct. Almost a thousand feet long and over eighty feet high, the aqueduct had been preserved for over five hundred years. As recently as the early 1900s, it had carried drinking water from the mountains north of town.

"Suddenly the Coliseum back in L.A. isn't so impressive, huh?" Maggie said as she took a bite of her fried pastry.

"Bite your tongue," Jackson said. "I'll bet Reggie Bush never graced these ruins."

Aliana smiled. "Americans are always amazed when they travel to other countries and see buildings, structures, and relics far older than their country."

"It is fascinating to think that much of what we're seeing was here before the western hemisphere was even discovered by the Europeans."

"Well, then, what's the point?" Jackson asked. "I mean, it's all so antiquated. Life has changed."

"You are not a fan of history?" Aliana asked.

"He's digging at me," Maggie said.

"She's sort of a 'what have you done for me lately?' type of girl."

"I didn't say that. I just have trouble putting any faith in a book that was written thousands of years ago."

"Why is that?" Aliana asked.

"Because life was different. Just look at what we're seeing around us. Look how they got drinking water and how we get it now. And that was a hundred years ago, not two thousand."

"So stealing and killing should suddenly be okay since we have modern plumbing?" Jackson asked.

"That's not what I'm saying."

"Do you not believe there are some values that transcend time?" Aliana asked.

Maggie shrugged. "Maybe. But if they do, then they stand on their own. They don't need to come from the Bible or the Quran to give them validity."

"Then where do they get validity?" Aliana asked.

"Practicality."

"So if the Bible or Quran makes a claim that is practical or legitimate as it concerns your life today, it is valid?"

"Essentially."

"Isn't that kind of short-sighted?" Jackson asked.

She shrugged again. "Maybe. But given the span of history, so is a human life."

"Forget practicality," Jackson said. "The question is, is the Bible true?"

"Define true."

"There's only one definition. Right as opposed to wrong. Accurate as opposed to inaccurate. True as opposed to false."

"That's three definitions," she said.

"Don't get cute."

She winked.

"I know you, Maggie. You're not a postmodern relativist. You know there are truths and falsehoods. Truth can't be what each person says it is. I say the Bible is true. Aliana says the Quran is true. When they disagree, one or the other or neither is true. By the definition of the word, they can't both be."

"Okay."

"So is the Bible true?"

"Which part?"

"All."

"No, I don't think all of it is."

"Then none of it?"

"I didn't say that either."

"The Bible isn't a collection of short stories," Jackson said. "It's one Book, one message. It's either true, or it's false."

"That's your opinion."

"No, it's the Bible's opinion. Paul wrote that '*All Scripture is God-breathed.*' Jesus repeatedly quoted the Old Testament and referred to Old Testament events like the flood, Jonah, and the destruction of Sodom and Gomorrah as real events. Peter confirmed Paul, and Paul confirmed numerous other authors. You start picking and choosing, you invalidate it all."

"Okay, you say it's true. Prove it."

"Do you mind if we continue walking?" Aliana asked. "Our next stop is only a few blocks away."

They agreed and started.

"Okay, first proof," Jackson said. "Disprove it."

"Huh? You can't put the onus back on me."

"Hear me out. The Bible makes a lot of claims and, more than that, declares an awful lot of facts. My first proof is that you can't disprove any of them."

"How about Genesis 1:1?"

"You can't disprove that."

"Science has."

"No, it actually hasn't. 'Science' cannot prove or disprove Creation or Evolution because you can't put either in a beaker and test them. Science hasn't found any of Evolution's missing links, hasn't explained fossils inside of fossils, and hasn't produced a whole lot of mutations and adaptions that would have to exist. If anything, science supports Genesis 1:1. But try again."

"Don't get smart with me."

"Sorry, habit."

"I don't know, Jack. Not off the top of my head."

"Ask the lady with the Ph.D. She'll tell you of all the archaeological discoveries they've found that support the Bible. Or just look around you. Suddenly a two-thousand-year-old book doesn't seem so old, does it?"

They turned onto a side street, and for some reason, Jackson was suddenly nervous. Maybe because they were off the main avenue and away from the crowds. Maybe because his subconscious had observed something. Or maybe just because he was having déjà vu. Not the real thing, of course. But he had seen so many spy TV shows and action movies that there was something familiar about everything. At any rate, he kept his eyes peeled for a few moments while Aliana spoke.

"Both Christianity and Islam have their basis in historical facts," she said. "No scholar can dispute the existence of Jesus or Muhammad."

"Nor am I," Maggie said. "I'm just saying that men who lived hundreds and thousands of years ago didn't necessarily have all the facts."

Jackson, seeing nothing to substantiate his sudden wariness, jumped back in. "Jesus wasn't just a man. He was, and is, God in the flesh."

"Can you prove that?"

"Prove? I don't know if I can prove it. But there's a lot more evidence for it than against. Start with the resurrection. Jesus claimed He would rise again, then He did." Jackson saw the look on Maggie's face and spoke before she could challenge him. "Remember what I told you before, if you can disprove the resurrection, you take down the Christian faith? But no one ever has. The tomb was empty, to the befuddlement of the most elite and thorough soldiers of the day, and no other reason for why makes sense. Jesus appeared to hundreds of people in multiple places and multiple times. Plus you have a bunch of cowardly disciples suddenly transformed into men who traveled the world with the message of the risen Christ, even to their deaths. They must have been convinced it was true, else were complete lunatics. As for the evidence against . . . it's nothing more than what ifs and maybes and theories, none of which have any backing."

They turned a corner, back onto a more main street.

"Beyond that, Jesus made outstanding claims," Jackson continued. "Claims no other person has ever made. Not even Muhammad. Those claims led Him to a cross, so either He was nuts, or He was telling the truth. Read the Gospels and study credible external sources about Jesus. He wasn't nuts. Throw in fulfilled prophecies against staggering odds . . ."

"So how do you counter what he says?" Maggie asked Aliana.

"Christians have their sacred text. Muslims have ours as well. On many points, they agree. But where they differ, one must carefully examine the differences and decide for themselves which is true."

"So do you believe any of the Bible is true?"

"Yes, some of it. But it has also been corrupted over the years, leading to much misinformation."

"Jack?" Maggie asked.

"Rebuttal?"

"Do you think any of the Quran is true?"

"I haven't read it, so I can't say."

"So it might be valid?"

"I didn't say that. You asked if any of it was true. I'm sure somewhere in there you could find something that is a fact, but as a Christian, I don't believe the book as a whole is true."

"Okay, so why can't I take that same view with the Bible?"

"I think you two are getting caught up in semantics," Aliana said. "There is a difference between objective truth, as Jackson claims the Bible represents, and a simple true statement. For example, I could write a story that was entirely fictional and include one accurate statement in it. My story would contain truth, technically, but it would not be a true story."

Maggie nodded. "That makes sense. Why can't you just say it like that, Jack?"

"Because I dropped out of college after two years."

That drew a grin.

"But that's my point. The Bible reveals God's objective truth. If you reject part of that truth, you as good as reject it all. I don't believe the Quran reveals any objective truth, but it may state some things that are true."

Maggie thought some more, and it appeared she wanted to reply. But she didn't get a chance.

"We are here," Aliana said.

"Where's here exactly?" Jackson asked.

"The Kavala International Library."

"Business or pleasure?" Maggie asked.

"A little of each, hopefully," Aliana said. "If any place in town has records of the church as it was eight hundred years ago, this is it. The library is home to some of the oldest and rarest texts from the Mediterranean and the Middle East."

"You know," Jackson said, nudging Maggie, "nonsense that's antiquated."

"You win a lot of people to Christianity by mocking?" she asked.

"It's a beta method," he said. "The Apostle Paul became all things to all men, so I'm appealing to you as a bantering smart aleck."

"That I'll agree with."

Chapter Twenty

"DID YOU SAY library or greasy spoon offering four-for-ten-dollars gyros?" Jackson asked as they stood in front of the Kavala International Library. It was located on a one-way street in sight of the aqueduct, situated between an apothecary and a clothier of some kind. A large window spanned most of the storefront, leaving room for a glass door beside it. The second story balcony hung over both, creating a canopy. That wasn't atypical for the street, which appeared to be commercial on the ground level and residential on the second and occasionally third stories.

"Another American perspective," Aliana chided without chiding. "Newer, bigger, and glitzier is not always better."

A bell over the door tinkled as they walked in. Directly in front of them was a high, L-shaped counter, behind which stood a thin man with salt-and-pepper hair and wire-rim glasses high on his long nose. The rest of the library, save for a small seating area immediately beyond the desk, was filled with rows of shelves extending farther back into the building. It was maybe twenty feet wide and fifty deep, but the shelves went floor to ceiling and were packed.

Aliana greeted the man behind the desk with a Greek, "Hello," and he reciprocated with a curt nod, then turned his attention back to a book open on the desk.

"Seriously, this is a world-renowned library?" Jackson whispered as he followed Aliana back into "the stacks."

"No. It is a diamond in the rough. A friend told me about it, and I had to check it out. But I promise not to stay too long."

Jackson shrugged and strolled around, reading a few spines—or rather, trying to; they were in Greek. Even so, it didn't take a genius to realize the books were old and somewhat unique. No best sellers or steamy paperbacks. Books made him think of Cara reading at the beach, which made him think of the beach and the beautiful views, which—the company not withstanding—he'd rather be taking in than a dusty old "diamond in the rough."

Aliana bumped him in the arm.

"What's up?"

"Help me out over here," she said, leading him through several rows of books.

"You find something?"

"Maybe. I found a few books I want to check out briefly."

"I don't read Greek."

"No, but they're heavy."

"Aha."

The first tome she found was a roach-killer that looked as if it hadn't been touched in years. "Check this out," she said. A single Greek word was etched into the surface: Θάσος

"What's that?"

"Thasos," she said, continuing down the aisle. "It is a historical guide to the island."

She found three more books, which she piled into Jackson's arms, and they took them to the seating area next to the front desk. Maggie materialized from somewhere and joined them.

"This seems dangerously close to work," Jackson said as Aliana opened the first book.

"Yes, but only a little," she said as she appeared to skim a table of contents.

"You can read Greek?" Maggie said.

"Better than I can speak it. Enough to get around."

"What can we do?"

"I have been thinking," Aliana answered. "The etchings were directly underneath a window, one that clearly is much more modern than most of the church. However, back in the late twelfth-century . . ."

"It could have been a stained glass window," Maggie said.

"Yes. Maybe the etchings were placed where they were at random, or maybe, just as we detected a connection to one of the murals, there is also a connection to the window above them."

"It's worth checking into, at least," Jackson said.

"You want us to look for pictures?" Maggie asked.

"It is a long shot, but yes."

Jackson slid Maggie a book and grabbed one for himself. They took seats, and for the next half hour, the trio flipped pages. Jackson found plenty of pictures of various architectural features in and around Thasos and Kavala, but nothing his eyes identified as belonging to the church.

"Here," Aliana said as he was about to give up. "The church."

Jackson and Maggie both scooted closer to peer at the book with her.

"Near as I can tell, this book is about a hundred years old," Aliana said. "These drawings are copies of drawings from several centuries earlier."

Jackson peered over her shoulder. "Is that the iconostasis?"

"Yes. The image on top is of the original templon."

"The iconostasis looks like the one that's there now if memory serves," Maggie said.

"That one was probably created from this book and based off the original." Aliana turned the page.

"So what are these?" Maggie asked.

"Probably more of the paintings on the walls or on the Royal Doors. Here is the Virgin Mary and the angel Gabriel."

"What about over here?" Jackson said, pointing at several drawings on the opposite page. Like the rest, they were incredibly vivid and detailed.

"I saw that," Maggie said.

"At the church?"

She nodded. "One of the stained glass windows."

Aliana read for a moment. "It looks like that is what all of these are," she said, flipping the page to look at the backside. "Yes, and here and . . ." She turned another page. "Here are the paintings on the dome and apse."

"Does it say where any of the windows are from?"

"I will have to read what it says here," she said, referring to the Greek text on the bottom half of the page.

"Read especially about this one," Jackson said, jabbing a finger at an image of one particular window.

"Why that one?"

"Because," he said, lowering his voice in case the man at the front desk spoke English and was listening, "the engravings on a lead cross told us we needed to find a third clue, and here is a stained glass window featuring a cross."

*　　　　　　*　　　　　　*

3:14 p.m.

"AND YOU think this has something to do with the etchings?" Joel asked. He and Cara had joined Jackson, Maggie, and Aliana at a beachside cabana for an afternoon snack. Aliana had eagerly shown them her drawing of the stained glass window, a very good black-and-white replica of the illustration in the book. Jackson characterized Joel's response as cautiously optimistic. Very cautiously.

"We think it is possible," Aliana said.

"Why?" Cara asked.

"According to the book, this window is believed to date back to the early twelfth century, meaning it would have been part of the church in 1188 when we believe the etchings were made. The book also said it was between the sanctuary and the south transept, where the etchings are."

"And right where there is currently a regular old everyday window," Jackson said.

"The original was damaged in the earthquake in 1205 and replaced along the way?" Joel asked.

"That's the theory."

"So what does it mean?" Cara asked. "I mean, a cross and a sun or a moon or something." She shrugged. "How does that help?"

Aliana looked at Jackson, who looked back at her.

"One of you tell us."

"It was your idea, Jackson."

"Buoyed by your knowledge."

Maggie sighed. "There were words on the cross. Not actual words, but scribble to imitate words."

"Like on the lead cross?" Cara asked.

"Like a grave marker," Maggie replied.

"The cemetery?" Joel asked.

Jackson nodded. "There's a verse at the bottom of the window, from I Corinthians 15:22."

"Which says?" Cara asked.

"'*For as in Adam all die, even so in Christ shall all be made alive.*'"

Joel nodded, thinking.

"So was he telling us to go to the window or the mural?" Cara asked.

"Both," Jackson said. "Aliana, tell her about the stained glass."

"According to the book—and this was the belief of the person who wrote the particular section about the church and also, according to him, the common belief of the time—that window was inaccurate."

"How so?" Joel asked.

"It depicted an east-facing headstone. In the Greek Orthodox Church, parishioners are buried facing east, in anticipation of the resurrection, and the grave marker is also placed so that those who face it will be facing east, meaning the grave marker itself would be facing west."

"How do you know this one's not?" Cara asked.

"Two reasons. One, the stained glass portrayed the hills beyond the cross. Now, granted, this is a drawing of a drawing of a stained glass window, but the hills on the window look much more like those looking north of west from the church, not north of east. You see this little depression here, between the two peaks?"

Cara frowned, but Joel nodded. "Yeah, I remember that feature."

"The second reason is because of the verse inscribed on the window, from I Corinthians. It references the resurrection. Now, while neither Jackson nor I are aware of any biblical verses promising the resurrection of the dead will occur in the morning, that was and is a common belief, particularly when the resurrection is depicted in various works of art."

"That would make sense," Joel said. "Jesus was raised early on the first day of the week."

"If the image in the window is to be interpreted precisely, it inaccurately shows the headstone cross facing the wrong direction."

"Why would they do that?" Cara asked. "As a clue?"

"No," Aliana said. "Remember, this window was in all likelihood made decades if not centuries before any member of the Knights Calvary visited the area."

Cara shook her head.

"It was likely artistic license, or just a simple error."

Joel leaned forward. "We're basing a lot on this book. What kind did you say it was?"

"General history of the island," Aliana replied.

"Did you check it out?"

She shook her head. "The Kavala International Library is a resource library only. No check-outs."

"Distrustful souls," Jackson muttered.

"That's not all," Maggie said.

"You found something else?"

"More like someone else. Jack spotted a tail as we were leaving the library and coming here."

"Again?" Cara asked.

"I saw him as we were going into the museum but didn't think anything of it until I saw him again as we were leaving the library. Could be coincidence, I suppose."

"Snap any pictures this time?" Cara asked.

"Tried," Maggie said. "Missed."

"Did you get a good look at him?" Joel asked. "Was it the guy from last night?"

"No. This guy was short, very dark hair, hawk-like nose."

"He could have been the other guy's partner."

Jackson nodded. "Could have been."

"And he followed you from the library?"

"Until we got in the taxi."

"So he could have gone back to the library," Joel said. "Any chance he saw what you were looking at?"

"I don't think so."

"He could have asked the librarian," Maggie said. "He wasn't far away; he maybe could have identified it."

"Maybe, but not likely," Aliana said. "But in any case, it is a good thing Jackson hid the book behind others on a completely different shelf."

"The Dewey Decimal System has always confused me."

"This Mr. Magoo spy craft is fascinating," Cara said, "but you said the etchings pointed to the window and the mural. What's the connection?"

Aliana looked back to Jackson.

"The mural was entitled 'Woe to you, Pharisees,' right?"

Joel and Cara both nodded.

"Luke's Gospel lists three woes that mention the Pharisees by name: tithing but not loving, loving the best seats in the synagogues and markets, and for being, and I quote, '*sepulchers that appear not: and men that walk over are not aware.*'"

Cara's eyes widened. "It's buried in one of the tombs."

Jackson smiled. "Maybe. But here's another theory. What if whoever wrote this message, A. Jacquemain if that is his signature, took advantage of the window depicting a backwards tombstone and a mural that mentions walking over graves but not knowing it, and buried the Spirit piece of the 'Holy Trinity' on the east side of a tombstone, and not the west?"

"Okay, but which tombstone?"

"There's the question," Maggie said.

Joel closed his eyes. "I'm trying to picture the cemetery. About fifty or sixty markers?"

"Roughly," Jackson said.

"No way we can dig them all up, or dig up the east side of all of them. I don't even know if we can dig there at all."

"Call Ramón," Cara said. "Get him greasing the wheels."

"With any luck, the markers will have names on them, or at least dates," Aliana said. "Otherwise, we are left to guess."

"I'm going to call the guys," Joel said. "See what their plans are for the rest of the day."

"You call them back in to work, they won't be happy."

"They'll get over it," Joel said.

"Liberty granted is liberty that can be recalled," Jackson said.

"And which founding father said something roughly equivalent to that?" Maggie asked.

"Um, I just made it up, but it sounded rather Madisonian."

She shook her head.

Jackson exhaled. "I'm getting another batch of whatever these are," he said, nodding at their empty pastry plates. "Get you ladies anything?"

They all declined, and Jackson wished he knew enough Greek to flirt with the pretty girl at the service counter. All he could do was smile, and he returned to the table munching on one of his *loukoumades*.

"They're headed back," Joel said.

"To the hotel?"

"A little siesta before an evening of partying, according to Ramón."

"Wonderful," Aliana said.

"I asked him to make time to very discreetly check into what right we have, if any, to dig around the cemetery."

"Maybe Rich can divine which grave to disturb," Maggie said.

"He said look up," Jackson said.

"Yes, but it was just a catnap."

"Mock if you want," Joel said, "but he's provided some serious assistance over the years."

"Not questioning that," Jackson said, "but I rate his visions just above a Magic 8 Ball at this point."

"Ramón also heard back from his friend's brother at the *Centro Nacional de Inteligencia*," Joel said. "The tail you spotted last night was a man named Nigel Moyers. He's a British national who works for Interpol."

"Interpol?" Aliana asked.

"What are they doing here?" Maggie asked.

"I guess we're not off their radar yet," Jackson said.

"We know they had an interest in the cross at Galerie Céleste," Joel said. "Whether they're after the Calvary Treasure and 'Holy Trinity' or someone else who's after them, we don't know. But they clearly are monitoring our activity."

"Maybe the guy at the library was Interpol too," Maggie said. "After we blew Moyers' cover."

"Possible," Joel said. "Whatever the case, we know we're not alone here. We'll just have to be extra careful as we go forward."

Chapter Twenty-One

Friday, February 15
8:12 a.m.

THE MORNING AIR was cool and damp as the ferry cut through the somewhat choppy waters between Kavala and the island of Thasos. Team Joel was all present and accounted for, although some were more present than others. Cara and Ramón were both bleary-eyed from long nights. Hers had been at the computer, his at the Kavala party scene. Ian had been with him, but appeared none the worse for wear, chugging M&M's and flirting with Maggie and seemingly enjoying the brisk morning.

The team had dined separately last night, with Jackson enjoying a delicious meal of *keftedakia* (fried meatballs) with Maggie, Joel, Rich, Cara, and Aliana. The women had then stopped at a local hotspot for drinks before returning to the hotel. The three guys had retired early and analyzed their evidence and theories, looking for something to substantiate Jackson's notion that a member of the Knights Calvary had buried the final piece of the "Holy Trinity" in the cemetery outside the church. Cara had joined the discussion upon her return, prompting her late night spent running a variety of cross-reference searches on the clues and partial clues the team had thus far uncovered. She, like the guys, had crapped out. So had Ramón, who before partying, had made some calls and attempted to prime some pumps in the hopes of getting authorization to disinter potential remains of a Crusader. But as of their departure from the hotel that morning, the group did not have permission to exhume any graves, and it wasn't likely they'd ever get permission—at least not without slicing through a lot of red tape.

If, however, Jackson's specific theory was right—that the Spirit piece was buried east of a grave marker instead of west, as was Orthodox practice for the deceased—they wouldn't actually be disinterring any remains or disturbing actual graves. In that case, Ramón assured them they had the appropriate clearance. He would have been more convincing if he'd been able to keep his eyes open. And hadn't carried with him the scent of women's perfume.

Ian, before joining Ramón for a night out, had rented a seven-passenger van that could fit eight in a crunch. He'd also picked up a couple shovels, a crowbar, and a few other "archaeological" tools. They weren't allowed to damage or deconstruct the church in any way, but Joel had reasoned that opening what amounted to a trap-door panel didn't fall under that prohibition. Plus, he'd said on the drive to the ferry dock, there was no way Aliana would let them desecrate the church in any way.

As they crossed to the island, Jackson and Ian kept a sharp eye out for Nigel Moyers or the man Jackson had spotted tailing him, Aliana, and Maggie around Kavala the afternoon before. If either man was on the ferry, he was doing a good job of hiding himself.

It took a while after the ferry docked to get the van ashore, and then they had to drive all the way to the south side of the island again. By the time they arrived at the church just before ten a.m., the dampness in the air had turned into a steady drizzle, with low clouds obscuring the tops of the island's mountains. Fortunately, Cara's weather forecast had been spot on, and they were dressed for the task at hand.

Joel split the group in two. He, Cara, Rich, and Ramón planned to study the cemetery in the hopes of detecting which of the headstones signified the potential location of the buried Spirit piece. The cemetery was clearly ancient, with grave markers ranging from simple crosses to more traditional rounded headstones to plain old rocks. They were angled, fallen, sunken, and shrouded by grass that was seldom trimmed.

"Have fun with that, yeah?" Ian said as he, Jackson, Maggie, and Aliana headed back inside the church to dislodge the stone slab they believed covered some sort of crypt or cellar. Using a crowbar, Jackson and Ian were able—after several minutes—to lift the end of the slab. Ian wedged the crowbar into the opening, then dropped to hands and knees. He extended a hand. "Flashlight?"

Maggie handed it to him, and he shined it into the crevice.

"Catacombs?" Jackson asked. "Old choir books? Rats?"

"Steps."

"Really?" Aliana asked.

"Aye." He turned and aimed the light the other way.

"How do we get in?" Maggie asked.

Ian stood. "I think we can slide it over to the side, yeah?"

"With our hands?" Jackson asked.

"Where are the shovels?"

"In the van for now," Maggie said. "You want them?"

"Aye," Ian said, turning for the door.

"I'll get them."

"Thank you," he said with a grin, then spent the next few minutes plotting with Jackson where and how to place the various implements to move the slab. When Maggie returned with a pair of shovels, he had Jackson and Maggie—who was slightly more muscular than Aliana—pry under the slab with the shovels. He then removed the crowbar and took it to the opposite side of the slab, against the wall.

"Be careful," Aliana said as he grunted, trying to get the crowbar into a crack between the slab and the wall.

"Aye."

It took several minutes, including chipping away at some mortar with his knife while Aliana winced and bit down on her lip, but he managed to wedge the crowbar into a narrow opening. Arms bulging, his face red, he grunted to lift the slab. "Extend your shovels," he said, and Jackson and Maggie pushed them into the crevice on their end, at the same time pushing down on the handles. While they "pulled" with the shovels, Ian used the crowbar's leverage to pry the slab a few inches in their direction.

"Again," he said.

They repeated the procedure, moving the slab another few inches.

"Again?" Maggie asked.

"I'm out of leverage," he said. "Flashlight."

Aliana gave it to him. He shined it down on the edge of the opening. "Look here. The slab's resting on a ledge. And on this side."

"Meaning it is a trapdoor," Maggie said.

"Aye, so to speak. At any rate, it was meant to be opened." He came around to their side and looked at where the slab rested on the shovels. "We're over the edge here. Here," he said, giving the light back to Aliana. "Jackson and I will lift. Maggie, take your shovel and pull it out, then slide the handle under it this way." He pointed east, horizontal to the way the shovel was laying presently. "Right about here."

She nodded.

"On three," he said, then counted down. Using the crowbar, he lifted while Jackson used his shovel. Maggie pulled out her shovel and quickly inserted it as Ian had directed. "Down," he said, and he and Jackson let the slab down.

"Now what?" Aliana asked.

"Now I go all he-man, yeah, and Jackson does the same with his shovel."

"You got it?" Jackson asked.

"We'll find out, yeah? Stick the handle in right here," he said, pointing to the narrowest place where he could jam the wooden shovel handle into the crevice. On three again, he grunted the slab up, and Jackson quickly moved his shovel. When Ian let the slab down, they had two shovel handles under the far end of it, forming very rudimentary rollers on which to slide it back.

Unfortunately, Ian still didn't have any way to get leverage with his crowbar on the other end, and the slab was too heavy to slide by hand.

"We need at least another foot before I can wriggle through," Aliana said.

"Aye, and the stairs are at this end. We'd have to lower you down."

"Rope," Maggie said. "Did we bring any rope?"

"No."

"Nothing to rig it to anyhow," Jackson said.

"Not to lower her down," Maggie said. "To pull the slab, on the shovel handles."

"Aye, like they did with the pyramids."

She nodded.

"But we have no rope."

"They must sell it somewhere on the island."

"I've got another idea," Jackson said. "Maybe."

"Let's hear it, yeah?"

"Give me a few minutes."

They all looked at him as he hurried out of the sanctuary and out the front of the church. The other half of Team Joel was still in the cemetery, hoods up and hats on as the rain continued falling. Jackson trekked back to the van, digging around in the back until he found what he was looking for.

"Jumper cables?" Ian asked when Jackson returned to the sanctuary.

"They're long. We loop them under the slab and pull."

"Will they hold?" Aliana asked.

"We'll find out."

It took some work to get the slab lifted enough to thread jumper cables under it in a place that would enable them to pull it in the same direction as the shovels, but with Ian imitating a lasso-throwing cowboy and Aliana laying off the end of the slab to catch the metal clamps, they managed. The cables were just long enough, and Ian and Jackson each took one end and pulled. The slab edged forward an inch.

They adjusted the shovel handles and tried again. A few inches.

After another adjustment, the third pull brought the slab almost a foot, and then the last pull slid it over the shovels and onto the floor of the church with a loud groan. But the chamber was open.

"Very MacGyver," Maggie said as Jackson stood with hands on knees, catching his breath.

"Not hardly. MacGyver would have hooked them to the van battery or rigged some sort of hydraulics to lift it. But thanks."

Ian reached for a flashlight from Aliana. "I'd say ladies first, but in this case . . ."

"Go for it."

Ian, then Jackson, Aliana, and Maggie carefully made their way down the stone steps, which proved more than sturdy. They found themselves in a dank, obviously dark chamber no more than a dozen feet in either direction and just taller than Jackson's head. Stone and mortar shelves had been built into the walls and contained old jars and dishes, utensils, wood crates, and disintegrating cardboard boxes of miscellaneous junk.

"When do you suppose was the last time anybody was down here?" Maggie asked.

"I'd say about 1944," Ian said, nodding at one of the crates as his light played over it. Stenciled diagonally on the box was a single word in all caps: STIELHANDGRANATE.

"German," Aliana said.

"Aye, and I wouldn't touch it. Seventy-year-old hand grenades can be a wee bit unstable."

"Should we get out of here?" Maggie asked.

"They won't blow just because we're here," Ian said.

"But don't light a match."

"Aye."

"What were the Germans doing here?" Maggie asked.

"Greece was actually occupied by Nazi Germany from 1941 to 1944," Aliana said. "I did not uncover any record of them using this church, but they easily could have occupied it and stashed weapons here."

"You think they left these here too?" Maggie asked, looking at a jar of rotten pickles on the shelf.

"Grenadiers had to eat, yeah?" Ian said with a chuckle.

Jackson found a wood shelf spanning what looked like a crumbled portion of a stone shelf. The wood plank was old and rotting, but still supported a pair of thick books. One was an old Bible, the pages practically flaking as he set it aside to examine the other. It resembled a journal but, when he opened it, looked more like a guestbook with a list of names.

"What'd you find?" Maggie asked.

"I don't know. List of parishioners, maybe?" He shrugged. "It's all Greek to me."

"Cute."

He turned a few more pages while Maggie examined the Bible. It too was in Greek, she said, dating it to sometime in the last few centuries.

"Hey, Mags . . ."

"Yeah?"

"Check this out."

"What?"

He opened the book wide, causing it to crack. He ignored the sound and showed her a "drawing" that spanned both pages.

"What is it?"

"If I had to guess, it's a plot."

"A plot?"

"Of what?" Aliana asked, joining them. Ian too wandered over, shining his light on the book.

"You're the one who reads Greek," Jackson said, "but judging by the way it's laid out, names and dates, I'm thinking it's a map of who's buried where in the cemetery."

Three sets of eyes looked up at him.

"It is roughly the right number of graves," Aliana said. "We would have to compare it to the real thing to be sure."

"Any of these names stand out?"

She began scanning the Greek, but Maggie beat her to it. "Here. *Jacquemain*. That's not Greek."

"Aye," Ian said.

"And look at the date," Maggie said. "1188." Her eyes met Jackson's. Even in the dim light, he could see the excitement.

"Alec or Andres or Albert Jacquemain," he said, "the late French Crusader, member of the Knights Calvary, and master treasure-hider."

"Maybe," Aliana said.

"Let's take it up and find out, yeah?"

"It looks very fragile," she replied. "We definitely do not want to subject it to the elements."

"Your phone has a camera, Maggie. Snap some photos."

"No photography in the church, remember?"

"This isn't in the church. It's under."

"Your situational ethics are so convenient, aren't they?"

"I can memorize the layout too, but this will save time. It's not like I'm going to sell the photos online or something."

"Right, 'cause there'd be a big market for that."

"Meanwhile . . ." Ian said.

"Sorry," Maggie said, digging into her pocket for her smartphone. She took several pictures of the two pages. Aliana studied the book briefly for a few more minutes while the other three scoured the rest of the chamber for any additional clues. They found nothing obvious and climbed back up into the sanctuary. They were just in time to see Joel, Cara, Rich, and Ramón entering the church.

"Any luck?" Joel asked.

"You could say that," Ian replied. "You?"

"Nothing," Cara muttered. "Most of the graves were blank. They didn't seem to be in any order. And my Greek to English software blows."

"What'd you find?" Joel asked.

"We gained access to the chamber," Aliana said, "and Jackson found an old book that contains what we believe is a plot of the cemetery, including names."

Maggie extended her phone to show Joel the pictures.

"You took photos?"

"He said I could."

"I did," Jackson said. "Most of the names are in Greek, but check out this one," he said, pointing to the phone. "Jacquemain sounds French, and the date is 1188."

"It was a signature," Rich said.

Jackson nodded.

"Cara," Joel said.

"Bringing it up."

"Cara plotted the cemetery, putting in the few names we found, listing the type of marker, and so forth."

"Can you e-mail me this?" she asked Maggie. She took back her phone and did so, and in the time it took Ian to relate the other findings in the chamber, particularly the German grenades, Cara had overlaid the two plots. She spun her rain-dappled tablet around. "Nothing there but a plain, white—well, gray now from wear—cross that's about to fall over."

Joel placed his hands together as if praying and touched his fingertips to his nose. "Let's think about this for a minute. We have the book Ali found at the library showing the stained glass window that was above the etchings, in all likelihood, in 1188, and it shows a cross believed to be a grave marker but facing the wrong direction, if we're to believe the topography was accurately re-created and if the verse from I Corinthians below it hints at resurrection and if we go with the popular belief that resurrection takes place at dawn, not sunset."

"That's a lot of ifs already, yeah?"

"Below the window are the etchings of the Knights Calvary coat of arms, Genesis 27:28, likely a date in April of 1188, and—apparently—the signature of an A. Jacquemain. Genesis 27:28 mentions, among other things, corn—or grain—which is depicted in the mural over here, where stalks of grain are seemingly out of place in said mural, which is titled 'Woe to You, Pharisees' and seems to be portraying the scene from Luke 11 where Jesus said, among other things, that the Pharisees were like sepulchers—or graves—that men walk over without knowing they're there."

"I'm getting a headache," Cara said.

"And, lastly, we have a book buried in a secret chamber that also houses German grenades and pickles that tells us that a Frenchman named Jacquemain was interred in the cemetery in 1188 and shows us where he is buried. Does that sum it up?"

"Wait a second," Maggie said. "Jack, the other day you said the stalks of grain were out of place in the mural, right?"

"They would seem to be, based on what the Jews typically ate."

"So why are they there? I mean, is the thought that Jacquemain painted or commissioned this mural?"

"Not likely," Joel said.

"So he just happened to find a painting that depicted a scene he could tie into his clue trail and that, for some reason, had stalks of grain randomly lying there."

"The lady's got a fair point, yeah?"

"It's a thousand-year-old painting," Jackson said. "Aren't they kind of known for being a little quirky?"

191

"Yes, but Ali also pointed out the details that clue us in to which meal this is of all that Jesus ate in the Bible and what He was talking about at the time—right down to pointing at the cup. You really think they went to that amount of detail and then painted in some stalks of grain for kicks?"

"Bummer," Cara said.

"Maybe it's not grain," Rich said. "The passage talks about '*mint and rue and every herb.*' Maybe those stalks are there to add a clue to the scene."

"How so?" Aliana asked.

"Just like Jesus is pointing to a cup to tell us that this is the passage where He gave the woe regarding the cups and platters, maybe there's an herb on the table to tell us that it's also the passage where He talked about '*mint and rue and every herb.*'"

"That would fit," Joel said, "if that can be interpreted as some kind of mint, rue, or herb."

"Still doesn't explain a reference about corn or grain etched into the wall," Maggie said.

"So maybe it's about Isaac and Jacob after all?" Rich said.

"Or maybe corn is the wrong word to clue in on," Ramón said.

"Or maybe," Jackson said, "a dumb Crusader couldn't tell the difference between an herb and corn or between rue—what's rue by the way?—and corn."

"He thought it was grain and figured it was a good way to make the connection?" Joel said.

"As good as any," Jackson said. "The whole thing is convoluted, but these Knights Calvary boys didn't seem to be big on straightforward directness."

"Everybody buy that?" Joel asked.

"Depends on the price," Ian said.

"Anybody think we're completely off?" Joel asked.

Jackson raised a hand, and Maggie backhanded him in the arm.

"Okay," Joel said. "We'll make this our working theory. So then, is Jacquemain telling us to dig where his grave is or to the east of it?"

"How is he telling us either?" Cara asked. "He'd have been dead."

"He must have had some connection with the church here," Aliana said. "He is the only non-Greek listed in the cemetery plot. Presumably, he was granted the right to be buried in the cemetery and knew that ahead of time."

"So the question really is," Joel said, "did he bury 'the Spirit' east of his grave, in his plot in place of himself, or was he buried with it?"

They all looked at each other.

"My money's on east," Jackson said.

"Why?" Joel asked.

"If you add up the grave facing the wrong way in the window and the reference in Luke about *'sepulchers that appear not'* and men walking over them but not being aware of them, that seems to point to the burial site being not where you'd expect it."

"But is that him or the piece?" Cara asked. "How do we know he didn't bury himself on the east side, not being a Greek, and put this piece in his spot?"

"Well, first because he'd have been dead and couldn't have buried himself."

She stuck out her tongue. Maggie whapped him again.

"Ouch. And because none of this seems to be about him and his burial but about the Spirit piece."

"I'd buy that," Ian said.

"For a decent price," Jackson said with a wink.

"Aye."

"And," he added, "because we aren't forbidden from digging east of a grave."

"Right, because that factored into Jacquemain's thinking," Maggie said.

Jackson shrugged. "We might as well rule that location out before we illegally dig up a grave and get in Dutch with the Greeks."

Joel clapped his hands. "That settles it for me. Everybody?"

No one dissented.

"Then let's get digging."

Chapter Twenty-Two

11:29 a.m.

BEING IN A valley between two ridges, the cemetery was invisible from the road. Not that the road was exactly the PCH, but still, inconspicuousness worked for Team Joel. After doing a more thorough check of the chamber, they had rolled the slab back into place, freeing the shovels for digging.

The first shift fell to Rich and Ramón, who carefully unearthed an approximately four-foot square directly to the east of the cross identified as having belonged to a Frenchman named Jacquemain. It was in the north middle portion of the cemetery, surrounded by several other similar crosses and a few unmarked graves. On the east, it was bordered by a small projection of the ridge that cut into the cemetery, meaning no one was buried directly east of the cross. It also meant the ground was a little harder, despite the rain that fell steadily.

Even so, none of Team Joel sought refuge in the church or the van. They stood with hoods and hats, or in Cara's case, scowling up at the sky in defiance. But the anticipation of possibly finding the final piece of the "Holy Trinity" was worth getting soaked.

When Rich and Ramón had dislodged the sod, Jackson and Ian took over, shoveling dirt to rival John Henry. They'd excavated a foot-deep hole when Joel volunteered to take a shift, followed by Maggie. Her third jab into the earth produced a clank.

"That did not sound like a rock," Aliana said.

Maggie removed her shovel and Joel dropped to his knees. "Do we have a hand trowel or something?"

"Aye, in the van," Ian said, already on his way. While he was gone, Joel directed Maggie to make a few more careful excavations by the side, then brushed clumps of dirt and mud with his fingers.

"What do you see?" Rich asked.

"It looks metallic."

194

"Preciously so?" Jackson asked.

"It's hard to tell."

Ian returned and handed Joel both a small gardener's trowel and a stiff brush. Aliana dropped into the hole to help, and in minutes, they had unearthed a dark-colored metallic block, not quite square, a couple inches by maybe an inch and a half. It stuck up out of the dirt at least two inches.

"What is that?" Ramón asked.

"I don't know," Joel said. "Let's keep digging."

His trowel hit metal a minute later, uncovering a similar substance. They continued working, unearthing more metal on the other side. By then, it was becoming apparent that they were excavating a very familiar object.

"A lead cross," Cara said as they reached the bottom and it fell into Aliana's hands.

"At first glance, it looks awfully similar to the one on display at Galerie Céleste," Joel said.

"So is it not the third piece?" Rich asked.

"A cross doesn't represent the Holy Spirit very well," Cara said.

"Does a box represent God?" Ramón asked.

"When you put it like that . . ."

"Is it possible neither cross is part of the 'Holy Trinity'?" Rich asked.

"Let's hold on a little," Joel said, climbing out of the hole. He extended a hand to Aliana to help her up as well. "Let's get this cleaned up, see if it's inscribed, and wait on making any haphazard deductions."

Using her fingers, Aliana brushed more of the dirt off the cross, but it was caked on heavily.

"We should fill in the hole, yeah?"

"I don't think there's anything else buried here," Joel said.

"Might not hurt to dig a little bit," Jackson said.

"We do have the time."

They excavated for another half hour, finding nothing, then spent as long replacing the dirt in the hole. Meanwhile, Aliana meticulously worked to clean the cross as best she could without any specialized tools. She reported there were definitely carvings in it, like on the other cross, but she wouldn't be able to make them out until she could examine it more carefully.

"We won't be able to hide the fact that we dug here," Ian said.

"You think somebody will track us here?" Rich asked.

"Even if they do," Joel said, "they won't know what we found. Or that we found anything."

"Or that we were the ones to do the digging," Jackson said.

"Right," Cara said. "We've got Interpol watching us everywhere, we've booked passage on a ferry twice, hired two taxis to bring us here, rented a van, rented shovels, Ramón's been greasing wheels, but somebody else made this hole?"

"I didn't say they wouldn't have well-founded suspicions."

"So what's next?" Maggie asked.

"When's the next ferry back?" Joel asked.

"One, but we'll never make it," Ian said, consulting his watch. "So three."

"I think we've done all we can here," Joel said. "Let's grab some lunch and be ready to go at three. We'll get back to the hotel and let Aliana and Cara do their stuff. Hopefully, that will give us some answers."

Having cleaned up their presence as best as possible, the eight returned to the van, where Aliana wrapped the cross in a blanket for protection and safety—they hoped—in transit. It wouldn't fit in any of their backpacks, and those were subject to searching anyhow. Eventually, Ramón would have to clear things with the Greek government, but not until they left Greece with it. So for now, they wanted to keep the discovery secret, which meant hiding it under the seat for the ferry ride back.

As they headed in search of an island restaurant that wouldn't frown on a bunch of wet, muddy patrons, Aliana turned around to face Jackson in the rear seat. "You did very good work these last couple days."

"Just had a few hunches," he answered.

"Do not be modest. Your deductions were spot on. Without them, we would never have found the cross."

"Don't forget Rich's vision," Ramón teased.

"You had another vision?" Aliana asked, facing forward to question Rich in the front seat.

She had to pass on Ramón's remark to him, and he shook his head. "The last vision I had was to 'look up.'"

"We looked up at the window," Maggie said. "Or would have, had it been there."

"And the book was on the top shelf in the library," Aliana said.

"Aye, and the book with the cemetery map was on a high shelf in the church cellar."

Ramón chuckled, and Jackson found himself grinning.

"What are you smirking at?" Maggie asked.

"Nothing. You all are just working awfully hard to 'fulfill' these visions."

"They were true."

"So's the fortune cookie that says you'll meet a handsome stranger this week and then your waiter at dinner's better looking than Tom Brady, and suddenly you find yourself quoting Confucius. Besides, when did you go from skeptic to blind leaper?"

"First, I've never had a waiter who was better looking than Tom Brady."

"Touché."

"And I'm not a blind leaper. I'm just reporting on what I see."

"Well, don't forget to report on what Aliana just said about my incredible contribution."

"Those weren't her words."

"Use creative interpretation."

"I'd get sued for libel. Besides, don't pat yourself on the back too much. We found a third piece, but unless it has a lot better clues than the first two, we have no idea where the Calvary Treasure is."

"She is right," Aliana said. "The work is just beginning."

*   *   *

5:14 p.m.

TO EVERYONE'S relief, the cross was still wrapped in the blanket under the backseat of the van when the ferry docked in Kavala. Team Joel drove back to their hotel, cleaned up, and met in the guys' room to analyze the cross. Using a combination of water, some special anti-corrosive solution, and some very special brushes, Aliana—changed from wet clothes into jeans and, oddly, an Auburn Tigers T-shirt, her hair down and smelling quite nice—carefully cleaned up the cross, revealing it to be an exact replica of the one found at the bottom of the Mediterranean and displayed in New York City at Galerie Céleste. Well, almost exact. It was the same size and shape, also made of lead, and also engraved, most notably with a leaping lion on the right side of the crossbar and an angel with a flaming sword on the left. Mark 4:22 was also etched into the top of the cross, same as on the other one. Or at least, it looked the same to Jackson, but he would defer to the experts as to whether the Latin wording was indeed a quotation from Mark's Gospel.

"Okay, so what are the other verses?" Ramón asked when Aliana had revealed her initial analysis.

"Let's not rush them," Joel said. "We can order something to eat while they get working. What sounds good?"

Lunch had been at a roadside stand selling fruit, fresh vegetables, and bread. So while Cara and Aliana worked on translating the Latin inscriptions, the rest of the team debated dinner options. They settled on a Greek-Italian pizza place and ordered delivery. By the time several varieties of pizza arrived, Cara and Aliana had finished and produced matching translations.

"Three verses again," Aliana reported. "Each matching accurately with English translations of the Latin Vulgate."

"Which verses?" Rich asked.

"First is Matthew 3:11, which reads: '*I indeed baptize you in water unto penance, but he that shall come after me, is mightier than I, whose shoes I am not worthy to bear: he shall baptize you in the Holy Ghost and fire.*'"

"The Holy Spirit again," Rich said.

"The second is I Corinthians 2:10: '*But to us God hath revealed them by his Spirit. For the Spirit searcheth all things, yea, the deep things of God.*'"

"Again," Maggie said.

"Lastly, Colossians 2:9: '*For in him dwelleth all the fulness of the Godhead corporeally.*'"

Jackson clapped his hands and rubbed them together. "All right then, that settles that."

They resumed eating, kicking around ideas, mulling and pondering, and, in short, getting nowhere. Needing some fresh air, Jackson stepped outside, onto the small balcony of the third-floor room. The rain had abated, but the dampness in the air was still heavy. It was appropriate.

An elbow bumped his, and he looked to see that Maggie had joined him on the balcony.

"Hey," she said.

"Hey."

"Brain fried yet?"

"Almost."

"Aliana was right, you know. You did really well figuring things out."

"I can't exactly control it," Jackson said. "Things click, make sense." He shrugged.

"She was right about your being modest too."

Jackson said nothing, staring out into the darkness.

Maggie nudged him again. "Is it me, or do I sense a little something between the two of you?"

Jackson turned. "Something?"

"You know. Chemistry."

"What makes you say that?"

Maggie shrugged. "Different things. Your sudden interest in museums, for once not being bored by long stories, the mutual admiration society in the van earlier. Or your tag-team effort to convert me," she added.

"To two contradictory points of view," he said. "You're reaching."

She shrugged indifferently.

"Look," Jackson said, "Aliana's smart. She's a bank of historical knowledge . . ."

"Attractive."

"Yeah, she's attractive."

"But she's a Muslim, and you're not supposed to be unequally yoked."

"We're not even to the stage where that matters," Jackson said. "We're colleagues. At the most, there's a professional appreciation between us."

"Professional appreciation? If The Edge can professionally appreciate the drummer in a garage band, maybe."

"That's cold, Mags."

She shrugged again, smiling.

"Besides, how would you notice, what with your fending off overtures from Ian and Ramón all the time?"

"Overtures?"

"Whatever. So it's harmless flirting and banter," Jackson said. "Even so, they're horning in on my territory."

"Don't worry, Jack. You can flirt and banter with me any time you want."

"Well, if Ali's busy . . ."

Maggie punched him in the shoulder, hard enough to sting. "You'd better get back in there, what with your being the brains of the operation and all."

"I suppose," he said. "Come on, you can work on your rough outline."

They returned to the room, and Jackson concentrated on Jacques IV of Aragon's journal. He'd read through it a number of times, but hoped it contained some sort of key to the cipher. Then again, he was assuming Philippe hadn't doctored it somehow. He didn't know why he'd bother, as opposed to not giving them the journal at all, but he wasn't getting paid to figure out old, reclusive French billionaires.

Working on the premise that the journal was trustworthy, Jackson took particular notice of two things. First, as Philippe had mentioned, it didn't specifically say there were three or only three artifacts constituting the "Holy Trinity." Rather, as Philippe had quoted, Jacques wrote, "*when you find the Father, the Son, and the Spirit, you will find that which you seek.*" Second, in that same section, Jacques wrote of being stirred by "*our Lord emptying himself*" and "*making the ultimate of sacrifices.*" He hoped The Poor Soldiers of Christ and the Cross of Calvary could emulate Christ, citing several Scripture verses. One passage especially, due to its familiarity, stuck out to Jackson:

For let this mind be in you, which was also in Christ Jesus: Who being in the form of God, thought it not robbery to be equal with God: But emptied himself, taking the form of a servant, being made in the likeness of men, and in habit found as a man. He humbled himself, becoming obedient unto death, even to the death of the cross.

It was from Philippians 2, one of the best-known passages in Christianity, and it fit with the supposed mission of the Knights Calvary. But was that the only reason it was included in the journal, or had Jacques been hinting at something more?

"You onto something, yeah?" Ian said as Jackson stroked his chin.

"Maybe."

"What's that?" Joel asked.

"Still formulating an idea."

"I'm sick of thinking," Cara said. "If you've got something, spill."

"I'll just be thinking out loud . . ."

"It worked yesterday," Aliana said.

He shrugged.

"Okay." He stood. "Okay, I've just been reading the journal, and I remind you that Philippe said that the journal never comes out and says there are three pieces or artifacts, but that you'll need to find the 'Father,' 'Son,' and 'Spirit' to find '*that which you seek.*' A little bit after that, Jacques wrote that he hoped the knights would emulate Christ's emptying Himself and His sacrifice. He cited Philippians 2:5-8, which in part says, '*Christ Jesus: Who being in the form of God*' and then a little later, '*being made in the likeness of men, and in habit found as a man.*' The passage speaks to Jesus being both divine and human. Now, stick with me."

He picked up a photo of the first lead cross off the dresser. "In the middle of the cross was John 1:14: '*And the Word was made flesh,*' another reference to Jesus' divine and human natures."

"The hypostatic union," Rich said.

"Now move to the cross we found today," Jackson said with a nod at Rich. "On it we find Colossians 2:9, which speaks of Jesus saying, '*in him dwelleth all the fulness of the Godhead corporeally.*' In other words, the dual nature of Christ."

"You think the Son piece is dual," Cara said.

"Yes, thank you, thunder-stealer." He looked at Joel. "One Person of the Trinity, but two natures—human and divine. One 'piece'—if you will—of the 'Holy Trinity,' but two crosses."

Joel exhaled.

"Am I crazy?" Jackson asked.

"Aye, but that's not relevant," Ian said with a grin. He'd opened a bag of M&M's a while back and now popped a couple into his mouth.

"No, no you're not crazy," Joel said. "It's a viable theory. I'm just letting it sink in."

"I think it makes perfect sense," Aliana said. "But it leaves us with a huge question."

Jackson nodded. "Where and what is the Spirit piece?"

Chapter Twenty-Three

10:38 p.m.

TEAM JOEL STAYED together for a few more hours, continuing to mull and ponder. If Jackson's theory was right, that both crosses were Son pieces—representing the dual nature of Christ—why had the Knights Calvary gone to such trouble and a complex method of leaving clues to their treasure? Added security, to make it even harder for Saladin and his army to intercept the "code" and find the Calvary Treasure?

Or was it possible Team Joel had the identity of the pieces confused? There were multiple references to various Persons of the Trinity on the crosses and the gold-lined chest Philippe owned. The team had been working on the assumption that the crosses represented the Son, and Philippe's family lore was that his chest was 'the Father.' But what if those assumptions were wrong? What if they had the Father, Son, and Spirit pieces already, only two of them were crosses? After all, how did one depict the Holy Spirit in artifact form? But if that was the case, the "Holy Trinity" was more than lacking in clues to find the Calvary Treasure.

Had they misinterpreted some of the verses? Or improperly translated them? Had they missed a clue in the journal? Was there a secret component to the crosses as with the chest? Given their lack of direction, did it make sense to go on? Before making any decisions, Joel suggested his team sleep on it, and no one argued. The girls headed back to their room, and the guys divvied up sleeping arrangements. Jackson opted for the floor again.

His mind was racing with ideas, second- and triple-guesses, and something akin to fear that he and Team Joel had failed. Eventually, the steady drumming of rain lulled him to sleep.

He awoke sometime later with a start and immediately had the sense that something wasn't right. Still foggy, he wasn't sure if he was just coming out of a dream, was disoriented from a REM cycle, or if something was indeed amiss. Not moving, he shifted his eyes around the room. Everything was as it should be until he spotted a shadow that looked a little too dark by the table.

Then the shadow moved, morphing into a human silhouette.

Jackson deftly turned his head. Ramón was snoring, and Jackson observed a lump behind him. Ian. The shadow, which Jackson's eyes were discerning better, was too muscular to be Joel or Rich, and their bed didn't look disturbed as if one of them had gotten out.

Jackson weighed his options and decided against creeping. There were too many ways and too much time in which he could alert the intruder if he did that. Carefully positioning his hands to use them as springboards, Jackson pushed himself up. In one motion, he rose to his feet and charged, yelling just before he crashed into the body perched over the table.

It was a pretty good tackle—Ray Lewis quality. Jackson drove the intruder away from the table, and they fell to the floor, landing in a heap. Jackson's senses had come around quickly after waking, but the intruder's had been on high alert, and he recovered immediately. Finding his mark in the darkness, he blasted Jackson with his elbow. The blow rattled Jackson's jaw as it knocked him backward, and he momentarily saw stars.

They were replaced by a fist, and he ducked his head just in time. The blow grazed his head and hit the wall instead, creating an opportunity for Jackson to flail a punch and a kick that rebuffed the attack. Jackson started to get to his feet, but the intruder came back before he could. Fortunately, Jackson's yell and the ensuing fracas had awakened the other guys, and before the intruder could hit Jackson again, Ian plowed into him. He drove the man into the wall and drilled him in the stomach and chest with a series of quick blows.

Jackson stood, ready to aid in the fray, but things happened too quickly. Somehow recovering, the intruder hit Ian, knocking him backward and creating separation. Seeing he was outnumbered, the intruder ran for the balcony, reaching for the lead cross on the dresser as he did so. Jackson responded just in time, checking the man against the dresser, dislodging his grip on the cross and knocking him into the TV. It and he fell to the floor, with Jackson's momentum carrying him onto the dresser, on top of the cross.

Again, the man got up quickly, and instead of retreating to make another grab at the cross, he ran straight for the balcony, past a startled Joel and Rich. Jackson noticed for the first time that the balcony doors were open as the man darted onto the balcony, climbed over the railing, and began descending via a rope already attached to the railing.

Ian wasted no time. Whipping out a knife, he ran to the railing and sliced the rope. Jackson reached the railing just in time to see the intruder fall the final five or six feet to the ground. His growl was louder than the thud, but he got to his feet and quickly limped into the darkness.

"Where did you get that knife?" Jackson asked.

"My pocket."

"You sleep with a knife in your pocket?"

"Aye."

"What just happened?" Joel asked, still trying to make sense of what he'd seen.

"I guess we didn't keep our discovery a secret," Jackson said.

"We should check on the girls," Ian said.

"Was he in their room?" Rich asked.

Jackson shook his head. "I don't think so."

"We should check anyhow," Joel said. "And someone should contact the police."

"Somebody want to turn on a light, yeah?" Ian asked.

Rich quickly found the bedside lamp, and the light that momentarily blinded everyone finally stirred Ramón, who up until that time had remained snoring quietly. He groaned. "What's going on?"

"Your lip's bleeding," Rich said, and Ian touched his mouth.

"Aye." He uttered something under his breath that Jackson assumed was a Scottish curse. "That guy was built like a bag of rocks."

"Tell me about it," Jackson said, rubbing his suddenly sore jaw.

"Was he after the cross?" Joel asked, nodding to where it sat askew on the dresser.

"Aye, he was trying to grab it when Jackson hip-checked him into the boards. And by boards, I mean that lovely flat screen TV, yeah?"

"It doesn't look like he took anything," Joel said, eyeing the photos, papers with various doodles and ideas, and electronic equipment at the other end of the dresser or now on the floor, thanks to the scuffle.

"I didn't see a flashlight," Jackson said. "He was operating in the dark."

"You two want to check on the girls?" Joel said. "Rich and I will go speak to the front desk and work with them to contact the authorities. I'm sure they'll be interested in knowing their hotel was breached."

"Maybe you can get a discount on the room," Jackson said.

"What about me?" Ramón asked, working all the way up to a sitting position.

Ian nodded. "Just sleep it off, princess."

*   *   *

Saturday, February 16
4:13 a.m.

NO ONE slept much the rest of the night. Joel sincerely doubted the intruder or his comrades would come back, but he insisted on keeping a guard awake. Jackson and Ian both volunteered, and Joel assigned Jackson to keep watch in the women's room. They didn't protest much, a combination of fear, trusting Jackson to behave himself, and general sleepiness. Maggie and Aliana dozed briefly, but Cara was too wide awake and spent the final few hours of darkness working on her computer.

Quietly, Jackson padded across the room and joined her at the table. The women's suite was the same as the guys, only in reverse, and he pulled up a chair. "What are you working on?" he whispered.

"When do you think all those Facebook cat memes get created?"

He slowly shook his head. "You know what, I'd never known."

Her eyes went back to her laptop screen, and he studied her. Somehow, he doubted she was making cat memes. But he let it go.

"Can I ask you something?" he said.

"Yeah."

"Is there any chance something from the journal got lost in translation?"

Cara's eyebrows shot up. "Why?"

"We're missing something. I'm grasping at straws."

"Yeah, you are. Especially with Ali. There's no way she—You know what, with me too."

He held up a hand. "Just a thought. I withdraw the question. I don't want to get beat up again tonight."

Cara stared at him. "What, you fishing for sympathy now?"

He shook his head.

"Good. I hate guys who act tough just so girls swoon and kiss them on their jaw."

"Preferably not the jaw," Jackson said with a wince.

She went back to work, and he ran through all the verses on the three pieces again, along with the poem or whatever it was inside the chest. Maybe the leaping lion and angel held some clue. Or did they just confirm the pieces had each been formed by the Knights Calvary? And what about Mark 4:22 being engraved on each? Jackson mulled the verse: *For there is nothing hid, which shall not be made manifest: neither was it made secret, but that it may come abroad.* Was that telling them there was a treasure to be discovered, or that there was a deeper meaning to be found in each piece—i.e., the clue on the inside of the chest? But if so, how did they "get inside" a lead cross?

Cara closed her laptop and stood.

"Do you mind?" Jackson asked, pointing at it.

"What?"

"I want to look at cat memes."

That actually drew a smile.

"I'm sorting all these clues in my head, and I could use some visuals. I assume you have them all saved on here somewhere."

Still smiling, she opened the laptop and quickly logged in and brought up a folder containing photos, translations, and what amounted to the minutes of their earlier brainstorming. "Knock yourself out," she said.

"Thanks."

She took her tablet out onto the balcony to do some reading, and Jackson examined all the evidence again, even though he was intimately familiar with it. He could do in his head what most people needed pen and paper or mouse and keyboard to do, but every once in a while, the pot could use some stirring. An idea was starting to take shape when he was distracted by Maggie getting up. She brewed some coffee while she took a shower, then joined Jackson at the table, bringing him a cup.

"Thanks."

"Any breakthroughs?"

"Maybe."

"Oh?"

"Still kicking it around."

"How's the jaw?" she asked, seeing him wince as he sipped his coffee.

"Like Ali's after the first fight with Frazier."

"That good?"

"We'll find out the next time I order steak."

"You should put some ice on it."

"You smell nice."

"Shampoo. You're clearly tired."

"Nope. Just getting my flirts in first."

Maggie took a drink before leaning in to look at the laptop screen. "So what are you kicking around?"

"I'm working on a few assumptions here, so don't butt in and point that out to me."

She raised an eyebrow.

"Cara's rubbing off on me," he said. "Okay, start with the Father piece, Philippe's chest. In addition to the Mark 4 verse that's on all three pieces, the three verses on the outside of the chest are Matthew 11:27, John 8:19, and John 14:6. Now look at these key phrases," he said, pointing to the verses on the screen. "'*Neither doth any one know the Father, but the Son, and he to whom it shall please the Son to reveal him.*' '*Neither me do you know, nor my Father. If you did know me, perhaps you would know my Father also.*' '*No man cometh to the Father, but by me.*' I think they're saying that in order to understand the Father piece, you need the Son piece."

"How so?"

"I'm getting to that. Now look at these verses on the two crosses: '*But when the Paraclete cometh, whom I will send you from the Father, the Spirit of truth, who proceedeth from the Father, he shall give testimony of me.*' That's John 15:26, from the New York cross. And from the Greek cross, I Corinthians 2:10, which says, '*But to us God hath revealed them by his Spirit. For the Spirit searcheth all things, yea, the deep things of God.*'"

Maggie shook her head.

"'The Spirit,' also known as the Paraclete, will testify or reveal 'the Son.'"

"Okay, I guess I can buy that."

"It's not exactly 'dig here,' but plausible."

"Agreed."

"Now, understanding or knowing the Father piece seems to mean opening the lock and finding the message inside. After hundreds of years, a simple lock in a gold box wasn't all that hard to crack, but back in the late 1100s, it would have required a key."

"Okay, so how are these lead crosses—the Son pieces—the key?"

"Check out the other verses on the crosses. One on each of them refers to the Spirit's revelation. One on each—John 1:14 and Colossians 2:9—seem to speak of the dual nature of Christ, suggesting there are two crosses."

"If your theory is right."

"One of those assumptions."

She nodded for him to continue.

"That leaves two verses, Psalm 103:4 and Matthew 3:11." He pointed to the screen, where Maggie read the verses.

"'*Who makest thy angels spirits: and thy ministers a burning fire.*' '*I indeed baptize you in water unto penance, but he that shall come after me, is mightier than I, whose shoes I am not worthy to bear: he shall baptize you in the Holy Ghost and fire.*'" She looked up. "Okay, what am I missing?"

"This," he said, clicking on a photo of the New York cross. Under the middle verse was a small depression, barely noticeable, but there nonetheless.

"What's that?"

"A key."

"What?"

"I think there's a slight depression because it's hollow under that point."

She squinted.

"Maggie, why are the crosses made of lead?"

"I don't know."

"The chest is gold. All the treasures aboard the *Ali Della Vittoria* were gold and priceless metals. So who would make a couple of lead crosses?"

"Someone who didn't want them possessed as a treasure but used as a map?"

"Maybe. Or maybe someone who was hiding something."

She frowned.

"Were you much of a chemist in high school?"

"Can't say I was."

"Me either. Bored the tears out of me. MH this and PH that and nickel cadmium that. But I did some Googling while you were in the shower. Lead, compared to other metals like gold or silver, has an incredibly low melting point. Six hundred twenty degrees or something. Meaning you could stick these crosses in a very hot fire, melt off the lead, and not damage the metal underneath if it was, say, gold like the chest."

Maggie stared at him. He wasn't sure if she thought he was a genius or a crackpot.

"'*Who makest . . . thy ministers a burning fire,*'" Jackson quoted. "'*He shall baptize you in . . . fire.*'"

"You think we're supposed to stick these crosses in a fire to melt off the lead?"

"Maybe."

"Revealing what, a key to a lock that's already opened?"

"That's only on one cross, which we don't have."

"And what do we find on the one we do have?"

"I don't know."

"Another key?"

"Maybe."

"To what?"

He shrugged.

She exhaled and sat back.

"It's a theory," Jackson said. "It may be off the wall, and it's certainly risky."

"You can say that again."

He stroked his chin. "You think I should tell Joel?"

"Why not? He's the boss. Let him make the call."

"Can I count on you to have my back when I pitch it?"

"I don't know, Jack."

"How about not to snicker aloud when I pitch it?"

"I might be able to manage that."

"Good."

"But I am going to need some more coffee."

Jackson slid his mug to her. "You and me both, sister."

Chapter Twenty-Four

8:16 a.m.

JOEL RETURNED FROM the police department at quarter after eight, having been there less than half an hour. He reported there wasn't much they could do without a description of the intruder, seeing as how Ian had reported he'd been wearing gloves. While he was gone, Cara made sure she had digital copies of everything saved on her hard drive, in the cloud, and on Team Joel's servers at his home outside Philadelphia. When Joel got back, the team checked out of their hotel and headed toward the harbor and new digs.

The Lucy Hotel was a five-star luxury hotel, eight stories tall, with views of Kavala, the mountains to the north, and the Thracian Sea. Joel checked them into a pair of adjoining executive suites on the top floor. The rooms were bright and airy, and plenty spacious. The roominess would enhance their productivity, the views of the bay and Thasos in the distance would inspire them, and the eight stories and five-star brand would insulate them from further intrusions. Or so Joel hoped as he outlined his plan for the day to the other members of the team over room service brunch. None of them felt ready to pull up stakes just yet, but at the same time, they were clueless as to where the journey led next.

"All right, folks," Joel said. "Let's start clean. I'm open to any ideas. No theories are off the table."

"Jackson actually figured it out," Maggie said.

"What?"

"I have a theory," Jackson said. "It's a little out there, though."

"Let's hear it."

He recapped, around mouthfuls of scrambled eggs with ham and feta cheese with hash browns, his belief that the two lead crosses contained "hidden" clues that could be found by melting down the lead. The verses inscribed on them seemed to suggest that only with the addition of "the Spirit" could they be interpreted, similar to how verses on the gold chest implied the Son piece(s) were needed to interpret the clues on it.

"We've been working all along on the theory that each 'piece' of the 'Holy Trinity' was a physical object," he concluded. "But just as the actual Holy Spirit isn't a physical object, maybe the Spirit 'piece' isn't either."

"Rather it's fire that will reveal 'the Son'?" Joel asked.

"So goes the theory."

Joel exhaled. "It's risky, melting down the cross."

"It is, and it isn't. We know what it says, we have pictures, translations. If we're wrong and we just melt away the engravings on the lead, what have we really lost?"

"Besides an ancient, priceless artifact?" Aliana asked.

"Well, right, besides that."

"We also eliminate any chance of it falling into the wrong hands and being interpreted, yeah?" Ian asked. He was interspersing M&M's with his eggs and hash browns.

"A depression in the surface of the New York cross doesn't necessarily mean a key's hidden under it," Cara said. "These things are ancient. It could just be an imperfection."

"It could," Jackson agreed. "Or it could be that some pertinent clue is engraved in silver or gold underneath the lead, and we'll never see what's on the other cross and so melting this one down will do us no good. Like I said, it's a theory."

"And it does make all the verses fit," Maggie said.

"You think it's the right play?" Joel asked.

"I think the theory's growing on me."

Joel stood and paced. "I'm very hesitant to take such a drastic action, so let's table the idea and see if we can brainstorm any other possibilities. I'd rather play out a few, less destructive strings first."

"Fair enough," Jackson said.

For the next two hours, they kicked around ideas, debated alternate meanings of verses, analyzed journal entries, and otherwise brainstormed. They got nowhere. If "the Spirit" was an actual physical object, they had absolutely no clue what it was or where it was located. If the chest and the two crosses were the complete "Holy Trinity" and if there was no hidden component to the two crosses, meaning Team Joel thus possessed all clues to the Calvary Treasure, they were thoroughly stymied. If, however, Jackson was right and the "instructions" on the crosses were to melt them down to reveal something—keys, a gold cross with engravings, or anybody's guess what else—there really was nothing to lose from a pure investigative perspective.

And according to the deals negotiated with the Greek government by Ramón, the lead cross was property of Team Joel. The only consideration was with respect to antiquity and the potential destruction of such an artifact.

"Okay," Joel said. "Openness and honesty time. Show of hands, who thinks Jackson's theory is credible?"

Eight hands went up.

"Who thinks it is the most credible theory we have?"

"We have other theories?" Ian asked as eight hands again went up.

Joel nodded. "Who thinks—and if it isn't unanimous, we don't go forward—that we should proceed with attempting to melt the cross?"

Seven hands went up, Aliana being the sole objector.

"Okay," Joel said. "Then we work on other theories."

"I am not saying no," Aliana said. "But I do not want to rush into such a decision."

"That's fair," Joel said. He clapped his hands. "Let's take a break for a little while. Stretch, get some air, clear our heads."

To that end, Jackson filled up his coffee and headed out onto the balcony. Low morning clouds were burning off, and vivid blue sky was peeking out over the sea and the island of Thasos. Aliana joined him a moment later. She leaned on the railing beside him.

"Is this the scene where you reveal yourself to be a double agent working for the CC and throw me off the balcony?" he asked.

She grinned at him.

"I watch too many spy movies."

"I see. I am not working for the CC, and I doubt I could throw you off the balcony if I wanted to . . . which I do not."

"Good to know."

"But I do want to talk to you."

"Okay."

"How strongly do you believe in your theory?"

He took a drink of coffee and studied her eyes as they studied his. "I guess it depends how you're asking."

"Please do not take this the wrong way, but you can be aloof and glib. And it has its charms, but . . ."

"You want to know if I'm serious or just throwing out wacky ideas before you consent to destroying an eight-hundred-year-old artifact."

Aliana grinned. "I suspect it is the former, but I would not be fulfilling my obligation to Joel and the team if I did not ask."

"I agree. And you're right, I'm a terrible smart aleck, and I would and have thrown out some crazy ideas. But trust me, with all that's at stake, I'd never let you all actually take action on something if I didn't believe it was legit."

She smiled wider and gently touched his arm. "That is what I hoped to hear. I am going to go tell Joel he has his eighth vote."

$$*\qquad\qquad*\qquad\qquad*$$

3:47 p.m.

THE EFFICIENCY of Team Joel was almost as impressive as the process that had melted the lead off the cross, revealing a solid gold cross inside it.

Joel, Ramón, and Aliana had worked the phones like pollsters on election night, finding a local blacksmith with the capabilities they needed and the integrity to keep silent, persuading him to come in on a Saturday afternoon, and arranging payment. Then Jackson, Joel, Ian, and Aliana had transported the cross to the blacksmith's shop on the outskirts of Kavala, where he had heated the cross in a crucible until the lead liquefied and dripped off into the fire. He'd then dunked the cross in water to cool it, and ten minutes later, Team Joel had departed with the gold cross in tow.

Now, it was laid out on a bed in the guys' suite, already thoroughly photographed and documented. Smaller, it was similar in shape to its leaden exterior, with the same lion and angel engravings on the arms of the cross. Four separate verses or bodies of text were engraved on it as well, all in Latin except for the bottom one that was in French.

Cara and Aliana had both translated the Latin and French separately, again agreeing on the meanings. Cara had then entered all the translations into her tablet and rigged a miniature projector to display the translations on the wall above one of the suite's beds. She'd also, after some brief research, matched and typed in references for the two passages of Scripture and noted the language of origin. Now, Team Joel gathered around to read everything in one place:

For victory over the infidels, declare the words of the great deceiver. (from Latin)

And David swore to Saul. So Saul went home: and David and his men went up into safer places. – I Samuel 24:23 (from Latin)

And the Philistines heard that they had anointed David to be king over Israel: and they all came to seek David: and when David heard of it, he went down to a strong hold. — II Samuel 5:17 (from Latin)

Ascend to the place from which thou canst look upon the bloody sea of death and the way of the serpent, and from whence true understanding of the Father will serve as thy guide. (from French)

"Okay," Joel said once everyone had had a few minutes to read, "what do we have here?"

"Safe places and strong holds," Maggie said. "A fortress or a castle?"

"Or it could be a cave, a typical place of refuge," Aliana said.

"That makes sense, I suppose," Rich said.

"But where?" Ramón asked.

"Maybe the verses give us the clue," Jackson said. "Any way we can figure out which 'safer places' and 'strong hold' David went and hid in?"

"It's certainly worth a try," Joel said. "There are also a lot of unique phrases that could hold a clue—'bloody sea of death,' 'way of the serpent' . . . If we're talking about an actual place."

"Why is the top line in Latin?" Aliana asked.

"It's not anywhere from Scripture?" Ian asked.

"I searched half a dozen translations," Cara said. "Nothing even close."

"It doesn't sound familiar either," Rich said.

"Wasn't there something written above Jesus' head in Latin?" Cara asked.

"*'Jesus of Nazareth the King of the Jews,*'" Rich said. "No obvious connection."

"This part's different," Jackson said, pointing at the top line. "So far, the Scripture inscriptions have been in Latin, because it was the only Bible they had at the time, whereas everything else has been French because it was the language Jacques and the knights spoke. And so far, everything else on all the pieces seems to be telling us how to find something, where to find something, how to interpret the other pieces. This," he said, pointing at the Latin inscription, "seems to be telling us what to do with what we find."

"You think we're finding words?" Cara asked.

"Maybe a book, a journal," Jackson said. "Maybe words inscribed on some other piece of immense value."

"*'For victory over the infidels, declare the words of the great deceiver,*'" Joel read. "Infidels clearly means Muslims in the context of the journal, right? No offense, Ali."

"No, you are correct. And Jacques said the purpose of the Calvary Treasure was to defeat Islam, so that would be consistent."

"Who's the '*great deceiver*'?"

"The devil," Cara said.

"According to I John, it's anyone who denies that Jesus has come in the flesh," Rich said. "'*I say this because many deceivers, who do not acknowledge Jesus Christ as coming in the flesh, have gone out into the world. Any such person is the deceiver and the antichrist.*'"

"The devil is also called the serpent, yeah?" Ian said.

"So we're supposed to declare the words and look upon the way of the devil?" Cara asked.

"Count me out," Ramón said.

"I don't think it's as simple as that," Joel said. "And '*the words of the deceiver*' may not be the entirety of the treasure. It could be a cover letter, if you will, or an introduction that explains how to use whatever it is we're looking for."

"Or it could just be a letter," Ramón said. "So much for a finder's fee."

Aliana shook her head. "Not necessarily. It depends obviously on how well it is preserved, but letters from Thomas Jefferson and Sir Francis Drake have recently sold for hundreds of thousands of dollars. Philippe also had a letter from Napoleon preserved in his keep vault. And remember, we are talking about something far older than any of those letters. That in and of itself will give it value, in addition to any generated by the identity of the author or the recipient."

"I'm no theologian," Ian said, "but do the Scriptures record the devil ever writing a letter?"

"*The Screwtape Letters*," Cara said.

"That wasn't Scripture or the devil," Rich replied.

"I know it wasn't Scripture."

"No, Ian, it doesn't," Joel said.

"Writing anything?" Ian asked.

"Not that I can recall."

"Then who could it have been?"

"That's kind of the question," Cara said.

"I mean, in the context, who would Crusaders view as the great deceiver?"

Jackson groaned softly.

"What?" Maggie asked.

"The context," he said. "The Calvary Treasure was lifted off a Muslim caravan and hidden by the Knights Calvary, and the 'Holy Trinity' clues were created by the Knights Calvary, whose single goal in life was to defeat Islam."

"Saladin, yeah?"

Jackson shook his head. "Older than that. Remember, they believed this 'treasure' would enable them to destroy Islam, not just one army. There's only one hand I can think of that could pen a letter or a journal or a book to destroy the entire religion."

Everyone looked at Jackson, waiting for him to give the answer. But it was Aliana who breathed the name.

"Muhammad."

Chapter Twenty-Five

4:01 p.m.

"IT'S JUST A theory," Jackson said after several seconds of stunned silence.

"It does make sense," Aliana said. "As the final prophet, Muhammad's words are the final revelation from Allah, and as such, fulfill all the other prophets. Most scholars hold to the opinion that he was illiterate and did not write the Quran but dictated it to scribes. Thus, he could not have written a letter. However, if he spoke something—theoretically of course—that dismissed his previous words or countermanded them in some way . . ."

She didn't need to finish the sentence. The gravity of Jackson's theory as to the meaning of the Latin phrase inscribed on the gold cross hung in the room until Joel spoke.

"Look, everybody, until we find the Calvary Treasure—whatever it is— all we're going to have are hypotheses and conjecture. To that end, I suggest we focus our efforts on finding it, and when we do, we can analyze what we find."

Several heads nodded.

"Okay, with that in mind, Rich will you head up the study of the two verses to see if they give us any clue as to what stronghold or fortress is being referred to?"

"Sure."

"Cara, can you use your web skills to see if you can uncover any hits on the various phrases in the message? Maybe they refer to a somewhat commonly known place none of us is aware of."

"You got it."

"I'm going to call a few people who may be able to clue us in toward that end as well."

"I will research with contacts I know to see if the phrase *'great deceiver'* means anything," Aliana said, "particularly in the context of the Crusades. It is possible the Latin inscription is also telling us where to look."

Joel nodded.

"I know a guy who's a Latin professor in Seville," Ramón said. "I can see if he has any insights too."

"Good idea."

"I'm going to turn over my laundry," Jackson said.

"Is that some sort of American euphemism?" Ramón asked.

"Washer to dryer. I'm out of drawers."

Jackson made quick work in the hotel's laundry room, then rejoined the team in the guys' suite. Aliana and Ramón had left to make calls in private, and Maggie and Ian were already "helping Cara." So Jackson sat down beside Rich. "Solved the riddle yet?"

"Hardly. Here, check this out." He handed Jackson his Bible, open to I Samuel 24. "Start at the beginning."

Jackson read:

After Saul returned from pursuing the Philistines, he was told, "David is in the Desert of En Gedi." So Saul took three thousand able young men from all Israel and set out to look for David and his men near the Crags of the Wild Goats.

"En Gedi," Jackson said. "Where is that?"

"Now known as Ein Gedi, it's a nature reserve in Israel."

Immediately, Jackson equated bloody with red and wondered if the inscription about a "*bloody sea of Death*" was referring to the Red Sea—bloody from the destruction of the Egyptian army, maybe, or else just because it was the Red Sea? He left that one for Cara.

"Any idea what the Crags of the Wild Goats are?"

"No. I read through it once, and I'm going to start researching a couple geographic features," Rich said, opening his laptop. "You want to read it and see if you find anything I missed?"

"Might as well."

Three minutes later, Jackson looked up. He'd read about sheep pens, a cave, and the final verse of the chapter, where David and his men went, according to the NIV, to a "stronghold." But the closest reference to a known place was Ein Gedi, which the maps at the back of Rich's Bible located twenty miles south of Jerusalem.

"Looks like the Crags of the Wild Goats are in that same area," Rich said after several minutes of internet searching. "Not a big surprise."

"No."

They repeated their search with II Samuel 5, and, although it contained a number of names of places and locations in the Holy Land, none of them seemed to pertain directly to the location of the fortress, other than that the NIV stated that David went "down" to the stronghold. But down on a map, meaning south, or down in elevation?

Jackson stood to stretch. "You ladies find anything?" he asked Cara and Maggie. Ian too had taken a break and was no longer sitting with them.

"Plenty," Cara said, heavily sarcastic. "*Bloody Sea* is the name of an album by a Japanese band called Merzbow. Looks like it protests the slaughter of whales. It's also the name of a Mexican movie from the '60s."

"We're close, I can feel it," Ramón muttered, having returned a minute ago. He'd crapped out with his professor friend, he said.

"What's this one?" Maggie said, pointing to a link about a Russian body of water that had turned blood red. Cara clicked on a link and began reading the article aloud.

"'*Scientists were as confused as the citizens of the nearby village of Berdyansk when the Sea of Azov turned blood red last July. While most believe the condition is related to an abundant blossoming of brown algae which, due to high temperatures and southwest winds, was directed toward shore, others attributed the phenomenon to chemicals released by a nearby pharmaceutical plant. Some, citing a higher—or perhaps lower—cause, believe the condition is a sign of things to come.*'"

"Algae?" Ian asked.

"Just like in *Sahara*," Jackson said. "I'll be Al because I'm funny and a smart aleck, you can be Dirk because you have the wavy hair and unshaved look, and Aliana can play Dr. Eva Rojas because she has the dark hair and exotic accent."

"We should tell Joel," Maggie said. "This could be something."

He was still on the phone, and Cara took charge. "Ian, you still close with that Swedish botanist?"

"Not as close as I'd like to be."

"Give her a call. I'll see what else I can find out about this."

Ian nodded.

Joel ended his call a moment later, and Cara briefed him. He turned to Jackson and Rich. "You guys find anything?"

"Not yet."

Joel turned back to Cara. "All right, see if you can find out where and when something like this algae phenomenon might have happened, particularly in proximity to the Holy Land."

She nodded.

"Ramón, I know you know people in Israel and throughout the Middle East. Can you check with any of them to see if these names of places trigger anything?"

He too nodded.

"Just be careful not to give any one person too much of the puzzle."

"Of course."

"I've got one more call to make," Joel said, excusing himself.

"That leaves you and me," Jackson said to Maggie.

"You can go fold your underwear."

"What? Are you jealous because I made Aliana Eva?"

Maggie rolled her eyes.

His phone to his jaw, Joel said, "Jackson, Maggie, I have a list on my computer of all Middle Age fortresses in the Holy Land. Maybe the two of you could do a little digging on them, see which are located by seas."

Jackson nodded, and Joel, while bantering with an old colleague, set up his computer for them. He opened a file containing the list of medieval fortresses. It was lengthy.

"Who built these all?" Jackson asked. Joel was apparently holding.

He shrugged. "Depends. Crusaders in some cases. The Muslims other times. Some were around centuries before the Crusades were launched."

"What if it isn't a real sea we're looking for?" Maggie asked.

"How so?"

"A *bloody sea of death*," she said. "Sounds figurative, for a valley filled with the blood of battle or something like that."

"That's positively biblical," Joel said. "We can't overlook anything— Yeah, I'm here, Carlo," he said, holding up a hand as means of apology while he continued on the phone.

Jackson turned to Maggie. "Mags, don't be bummed. It's just that Aliana looks more like Penélope Cruz, and certainly sounds like her."

"She sounds nothing like her."

"Well, they both have accents."

"What is it with men and accents?"

"I don't know."

Maggie made some sort of a groan. "Penélope Cruz isn't even that good-looking."

"Agree to disagree, although maybe that's the accent talking—pun intended. But seriously, Maggie, if we were doing one of the *Jurassic Parks* or

Deep Impact or something you'd be my first thought for Téa Leoni. I mean, she is blond, but—"

"What are you even talking about? We're not 'doing' anything? Ugh, what is with you?"

"Nothing. It's just . . . Forget it."

She looked at him under raised eyebrows.

"We'll get to work," he added.

"Good."

"And for the record, I didn't leave you out. There just really aren't any women in *Sahara*. Unless you want to be one of the Tuaregs."

"Are you about done?"

He held out his hands in resignation, then clicked open an internet browser.

"Téa Leoni. You really think I sound like Téa Leoni?"

"She's a little whinier sounding than you, although right now that's—"

Her glare stopped him cold.

"Fine," he said. "Just work."

She shook her head, and for several minutes, they plugged various Middle Age Middle East fortresses from Joel's list into Google, looking for any tidbit of information that might be relevant.

"You sound more like Jessica Biel anyhow."

"You're going to sound like a falsetto if you don't shut up."

They managed to get some serious work done, although none of it was productive. When the group reconvened thirty minutes later, no one had much to report. Joel and Aliana's phone calls had largely proved fruitless, as had Aliana's investigation into less literal meanings of "bloody sea of death," which she had undertaken while Jackson and Maggie analyzed real fortresses. They'd gotten nowhere. There were some by water, which they had noted, but none by water that had any reference to being bloody. Ian had struck out with his lady botanist friend, and Ramón's contacts in and around Israel had found nothing, although one was still making inquiries. That left only Cara and Rich, who had taken a phone call out onto the balcony.

"This algae condition isn't unheard of," Cara said, providing a few more details from the original article for those who hadn't heard them previously. "I found a number of instances like this, the most interesting being in the Dead Sea in 1980."

"The Dead Sea?" Joel asked, noticeably perking up.

"That's close to Ein Gedi," Jackson said.

"What's at Ein Gedi?" Ian asked.

"Wild goats. The I Samuel passage on the cross starts in Ein Gedi."

Cara nodded. "In 1980, an excessively rainy winter caused a form of algae called *Dunaliella* to blossom. This algae was filled with pigmented bacteria that turned the waters red. The typical dry weather has kept it from recurring since."

"Do we know when previously this has happened?" Joel asked.

"Say in 1187?" Jackson said.

"Not that I could find," Cara said, "but I'm still looking."

"Would that constitute a bloody sea?" Aliana asked.

"If they were speaking figuratively," Joel said with a glance at Maggie.

"Or if they thought it was really blood, yeah?" Ian said. "We aren't talking about the world's foremost scientists here."

"Superstition was pretty high in that day and age too," Ramón said.

"It's certainly a possibility," Joel said.

"If we can find a fortress by the Dead Sea, we'll really be in business," Cara said. "Especially since it's also known as the Sea of Death."

"That's right, it is," Joel said.

"We found several fortresses in the general vicinity," Maggie said, "most notably Kerak Castle."

Joel shook his head. "It was already under Muslim control by the time of the Siege of Jerusalem. The Knights wouldn't have hidden anything there."

"I may have another lead," Jackson said.

They all looked at him.

"What is it?" Joel asked.

"It's not a Crusader fortress, and I'm pretty sure it wasn't in any sort of use then, but I know a fortress overlooking the Dead Sea."

Cara frowned. "You do?"

Jackson nodded. "Masada."

"What's Masada?" Maggie asked.

All eyes again focused on Jackson. "I'll defer to the historian," he said.

"Cop out," Cara muttered.

"Actually, Ali can probably describe it better than I can," Joel said.

She stood. "Well, Masada was—and is—a fortress built atop a rock plateau in the Judean Desert, just west of the southern end of the Dead Sea. I do not recall when it was first constructed, but I know Herod the Great fortified it and built a very impressive palace on the northern end, carved out of and into the rock. In its day, it would have been magnificent."

"So what kind of fortress are we talking?" Ian asked.

"To begin with, the rock plateau had cliffs in excess of four hundred meters on some sides, and the only access was by narrow, winding paths. Then Herod had a twelve-foot-high casemate wall built around the perimeter. And in addition to his palace, there was a barracks, an armory, a storehouse, and cisterns that were filled by rainwater. It was very nearly impenetrable."

"But it was penetrated?" Maggie asked.

Aliana nodded and looked at Joel, who took over the narrative. "Herod had fortified Masada, like Ali said, as a safe haven in case of revolt. But in 66 A.D., a group of Jewish rebels called the Sicarii overpowered the Roman garrison and occupied Masada. When the Roman army under Emperor Titus sacked Jerusalem and destroyed the temple in 70 A.D., a number of Jews fled to Masada and took refuge in the fortress."

He cleared his throat. "The Romans eventually laid siege to Masada, ultimately using Jewish slaves to build an earthen ramp up the western slope as means of entry. When they stormed the gates, they found the storehouses on fire and almost all the 960 men, women, and children inside the fortress dead. They had committed mass suicide."

"How awful," Cara said.

"They preferred it to being enslaved and mistreated by the Romans," Joel said. "But yes, I cannot disagree with you."

"How do you know about this place?" Maggie asked, looking at Jackson.

"I was an inquisitive kid who read a lot."

"Most of what Aliana and I told you has been discovered and confirmed by archeologists in recent years or else recorded by the great Jewish historian Josephus."

"So what about in 1187?" Ian asked. "Was Masada used during the Crusades?"

Joel shook his head. "Not to my knowledge. It's quite a ways from anything strategic."

"What about now?" Maggie asked.

"For the better part of two millennia, due largely to its location, Masada has remained abandoned. It's just recently become a tourist attraction."

"Tourists?" Cara asked. "At a place like that?"

"It is in close proximity to the Dead Sea, as mentioned," Joel said. "And the Dead Sea, because of its salt content, has become a tourist hotspot as well."

"So the big question is," Ian said, "is it the right place?"

As if cued by someone offstage, Rich burst in through the balcony door.

"You look as if you've just had a vision, yeah?" Ian said, noting Rich's wide eyes and flushed cheeks.

"Not exactly. But I did just get off the phone with an old pastor of mine, an expert in the Old Testament, and in particular Old Testament geography. He believes he knows what the specific 'safer places' and 'strong hold' the two Samuel passages refer to, and that is in fact mentioned four different times in the Psalms as well."

"Where?" Joel asked.

Rich took a breath. "A place called Masada."

Chapter Twenty-Six

5:42 p.m.

RICH'S FORMER PASTOR'S intel had seemed solid: The Hebrew word *"metsada,"* from which Masada was derived, translated as fortress or stronghold and was the same word used in the I and II Samuel passages on the cross, as well as several other times in the Psalms. He'd traced David's movements and various geographical points of reference to further make his case, and Rich had relayed them to the rest of the team. Combined with Jackson's theory on Masada, they had come to the conclusion that it was indeed the location the "Holy Trinity" was pointing to. A little more research had confirmed that one of the ways to reach the summit of Masada—some thirteen hundred feet above the desert floor—was a narrow, winding path known as the Snake Path. A.K.A. "the way of the serpent."

Joel had clapped his hands and smiled. "I think we're headed to Masada."

"Okay, that's brilliant work, yeah, but then what?" Ian asked.

"We follow the directions on the cross," Aliana said. "'Ascend to the place from which thou canst look upon the bloody sea of death and the way of the serpent.' That would put us on the east side of the fortress," she said, pointing to a somewhat grainy satellite view of the region.

"Aye, and then what?"

"'*And from whence true understanding of the Father will serve as thy guide,*'" Jackson quoted.

"The inside of the Father piece," Aliana said, beaming.

"'*As darkness begets dawn, thou wilt findeth the light whence thou liftest thine eyes at the arrow's mark.*'"

"So we get up at dawn and look for an arrow, yeah?"

"Something like that."

"I am guessing we will not be able to interpret these directions fully until we are on site," Aliana said.

"Also, it's been eight hundred years," Cara said. "And didn't that Ziggy guy pretty much excavate everything?"

"Yigael Yadin," Aliana corrected. "Yes, his team did excavate Masada extensively in the 1960s, but that does not mean we will not be able to find this 'arrow's mark.'"

"We may find ourselves at a dead end, or we may have to reexamine some of our evidence and conclusions," Joel said. "But for now, unless there are any objections, I think our next step is clearly to check out Masada."

There had been no objections, and with plans underway for travel to Israel, the guys' suite was chaotic. Flights, rental vehicles, hotels, weather patterns, the history of the Dead Sea, the layout of Masada—all became a blur of conversations and debates and phone calls. With no role to play and about to lose his mind, Jackson stepped out onto the balcony to clear his head and watch the sunset.

Ian was already there, texting. He looked up, grinned, and slipped his phone into his pocket. From the other, he pulled out a now familiar brown wrapper, unfolded it, and extended it to Jackson. "M&M's?"

"Aye," Jackson said as he returned the grin.

Ian turned and leaned on the railing. "Lovely night."

"That it is."

They studied the sunset for a few minutes, two guys, and just before it would have gotten awkward, Ian turned his head. "You ever been to Israel?"

"No. Not even close. You?"

He shook his head. "Can't say as that I've had the pleasure."

Another minute of silence passed.

"I have to say, I had my doubts about you," Ian said.

"That a fact?" Jackson asked, extending his hand for some more M&M's. Ian delivered.

"Aye. First Joel brings in a psychic—or whatever they call it—then a private detective. It's like one of your American television dramas, yeah?"

Jackson grinned. "Yeah, sort of."

Ian turned his head toward the west. A brilliant orange fireball peeked out from beneath a thin bank of purple clouds, turning the Thracian Sea a combination of the two colors.

"And now?" Jackson asked.

"That depends on whether we find a buried treasure or a fistful of sand."

Jackson grinned again as the door slid open and Aliana peeked out onto the balcony. "Are you both all right with an early flight?"

"How early?" Jackson asked.

"Seven a.m."

"Do we get a choice?" Ian asked.

Aliana smiled. "Not really."

"Seven would be great," Jackson said.

Aliana turned over her shoulder and called out a response to someone inside. Then she slipped onto the balcony, shutting the door behind her.

"You just missed a great sunset," Jackson said, noting the sun had dipped under the horizon. "And a discussion of my worth to the team."

"Is he giving you a hard time?" Aliana asked.

"On the contrary," Ian said. "I gave him a ringing vote of confidence, yeah?"

"Well, I agree," she said. "Without you, we would be nowhere."

"That might be an overstatement."

"Hardly. You figured out where the cross was at the church. You practically interpreted every clue on the crosses and the chest. You deduced Masada as the location."

"All I've done is guess and theorize. It's people like you and Joel who know enough to tell me if I'm off base or not who really get the credit."

"Not to mention Rich's former pastor, yeah?" Ian said as his phone chirped, an indication of a text or voicemail or something. He glanced at it. "If you'll excuse me, I'll leave you to your compliments."

He returned inside, and as Jackson and Aliana remained on the deck, he couldn't help but think of Maggie's words from the night before. Denying that he felt an attraction to Aliana was pointless, but he also didn't attribute much to it. Aliana was naturally beautiful, and he felt an attraction to lots of naturally beautiful women. It didn't mean anything had to come out of it. Especially when that woman held spiritual beliefs that were drastically opposed to his.

And yet, he couldn't deny there was something there, a certain intensity that seemed to be in the air when he was around her. Call it chemistry. Call it harmony. Call it a figment of his and Maggie's imagination. Call it trivial, because that's what it was in light of all that was going on.

Beyond any romantic attraction, Jackson was intrigued by Aliana the person. She continued to work with a detached calmness. If Team Joel were looking for an artifact that supposedly would destroy the Christian faith, Jackson wouldn't be participating in the search, let alone pleasantly.

"Can I ask you something?" he said.

"Of course."

"Have you considered what it might mean if we find this treasure?"

"You mean to the Muslim faith?"

Jackson nodded.

"That depends on what we find," she said. "We are dealing largely on speculation."

"True."

She shrugged. "Even if we do find some letter or diary allegedly dictated by Muhammad, there would have to be a lot of tests done to prove its authenticity. You, of course, know how people attempt to contradict and prove false our religions. As there are defenders of your faith, there are many in Islam who would fight to make sure any such document was not deceptively or incorrectly validated. And not to mention, this is allegedly a letter that twelfth-century Christian Crusaders thought would give them victory over Islam. Muslim scholars might interpret it differently."

"All good points."

"Let me ask you this: if the situation were reversed, how would you handle it?"

"Probably not as calmly as you."

"Is that because deep down inside you fear the result?"

"No. No fear."

"Why not?"

"Because of faith," he answered. "Not that I'm some great hero of the faith or anything, but I don't care what they find, or purport to find or think they find. I believe Scripture to be true, period."

"But what if the thing was something that could disprove the Bible?"

"Such a thing doesn't exist," Jackson said.

"But what if it did?"

"Then it would be a fake."

Aliana nodded. "So it comes down to blind faith? No matter what, you will believe the Bible."

"I don't see it like that. I think the Bible is incredibly well documented and substantiated. It would take more than a letter or a journal or an artifact to disprove it. Might an object call into question the Christian faith? Sure, I suppose so. But it would be stacking one piece of evidence against hundreds. I'm going to discount the former in light of the latter, should such a piece of evidence ever come to light."

"What if I told you the same thing, but substituted the Quran for the Bible?"

"I guess it would lead to a debate over the legitimacy of the two books, and I doubt I can hold my own in a debate with someone of your caliber."

"I did not mean to suggest anything of the sort. But as you are convinced of your faith, to the point that no one artifact or piece of evidence will shake it—because it pales in comparison to the evidence you believe supports your point of view—so I am equally convinced of my faith."

"I understand that. I just don't think if it were Christianity under the gun I'd be going about it as stoically as you. I'd be all up in arms. I don't know, maybe that's just our demeanors."

"My father told me something once," Aliana said. "He said there are plenty of things in life worth worrying about, so there is no sense worrying about the hypothetical."

Jackson nodded.

"Trust me, if and when Islam comes 'under the gun,' I will not be quite so stoic."

"Well, I have to commend you. Most people would have become defensive during some of our talks in recent days. You haven't."

Aliana shrugged. "Getting defensive usually only implies that you have been wounded or insulted in some way. I prefer a rational discussion."

She shrugged again, and it dawned on Jackson that it was actually a shiver. With the sun down, the sea breeze was getting chilly.

"We should head in," he said.

"I agree. We have a long day ahead of us."

*   *   *

Sunday, February 17
8:07 a.m.

ATHENS WAS beautiful from the air. Jackson's view was partially obscured by low-level clouds, but they somehow added to the aura created by the jagged coastline, azure surf, and the white columns and walls and orange to red to brown clay shingles of Athens' buildings. The view compensated for the uneasy feeling that flying had created in Jackson's gut, and for the early hour. He had been up since just after five, as had the rest of the team, all so they could make the early flight to Athens so they could sit in the airport for three hours. Such was life flying in and out of small European cities like Kavala, Jackson was quickly learning.

As Team Joel filed off the plane and into the airport, no one was terribly chatty. The previous evening had remained chaotic, what with making flight, hotel, and car rental reservations, in addition to returning the rented van in Kavala and obtaining and confirming early morning transportation to the airport there. The team had also busied themselves doing more research on Masada, the Dead Sea, red and brown algae, and the possible meaning of the phrase inscribed inside Philippe's gold chest. In addition to the physical fatigue, the group was mentally worn down as well.

They ate to pass the time of their layover, and Jackson wished he hadn't. Greek fast food breakfast did not agree with him, and he wasn't looking forward to two more flights and then Middle Eastern fare for the next few days.

"You okay?" Maggie asked as she dropped into the chair beside him.

"I'll survive."

"You sure? You don't look so hot."

He made an effort to sit up. "I shouldn't have gone for the McGyro this early in the morning." He nodded at the majority of Team Joel, who sat together a row over. "What's going on?"

"Rich said he had a vision of a *Lost*-like nosedive into the ocean," Maggie answered.

"Oceanic 815 broke apart in the air; it didn't nosedive. But nice try."

"I thought it would cheer you up." She yawned. "I don't know. I think they're trying to solve the whole 'look up at the arrow's mark' or whatever."

"Without their resident genius? I'm insulted."

"Can I ask you something?"

"If you must."

She frowned at him.

"What?"

"Doesn't this bother you a little?"

"Doesn't what bother me?"

"Looking for whatever this is—treasure, a letter of the '*great deceiver*' or whatever—that could destroy the Islamic faith."

Jackson shook his head. "Not really. Should it?"

"I don't know. I get that it's not what you believe, but do you really want to take that away from all those people?"

"A, if the sky split apart and a voice from heaven thundered while blood-red clouds spelled out 'Islam is false,' I don't think most Muslims would turn away. B, you as a reporter should know there are no tears shed over exposing a lie."

"A lie? That's pretty strong."

"It's like I said, Christianity and Islam are mutually exclusive. To sincerely believe in one, you have to believe the other is a lie. Else you're being intellectually dishonest."

"Still . . ."

"I never pictured you as a bleeding heart, Maggie."

"I'm not, you know that. I just—"

"And C, and don't tell anyone this, but I don't think we're finding some sacred relic that will destroy Islam."

"You don't think it exists?"

"I don't know. I think something existed, but whether or not it could have disproven Islam is another matter. And then it still has to be in existence, in good condition a millennium later, in the same place the Crusaders left it, modern textual and linguistic and cultural experts will have to agree on its meaning . . . I'm not holding my breath."

"Wow, I thought everyone else was down this morning."

"Blame it on the meat in the gyro. Speaking of which, will you excuse me?"

Jackson made good time to the restroom, and good thing. After cleaning out, he felt better, albeit weaker. He splashed some water on his face and stared into the mirror. The glass confirmed what he felt, that he needed some sleep. But he doubted he was going to get it on some puddle-jumper propeller plane.

Flight 3603 left Athens a few minutes before eleven, by which time a granola bar from Rich had helped Jackson regain a little of his strength. The takeoff was smooth, but high winds over the Mediterranean made for a bumpy flight. By the time they landed in Larnaca, Cyprus, at a quarter after twelve, Jackson's stomach was churning. There was a delay getting off the plane, and Jackson thought he was going to have to heave over a seatback. But he made it to the restroom in the terminal in the nick of time again.

His stomach was mostly empty, resulting in several dry heaves. Jackson gave himself time. Before he got on another plane, he wanted to make sure that anything and everything his stomach might possibly reject had been examined and decided upon. As he crouched there over an airport toilet in Cyprus, Jackson couldn't help but contemplate recent events. It seemed like a whirlwind—first New York, then France, then Greece. Then all of his deductions, which had been so clinical and hypothetical at the time. And now here he was, about to board a plane for Israel. Israel—it didn't want to sink in.

Being in Cyprus was surreal too. Jackson didn't know much about it. He was pretty sure Paul had landed there on one of his missionary journeys, and he'd heard references to the island regarding the Crusades. He thought there was something with one of the World Wars as well, but he wasn't sure. And he didn't think he knew anyone from Cyprus. A Cyprot. Or was it Cypriot? Cyprussian?

He spat. It was time to get moving.

Jackson repeated the face-rinsing procedure in front of the mirror. He looked worse. Fortunately, the last leg of their journey was short. Larnaca and Tel Aviv were only a couple hundred miles apart.

There was a tennis player from Cyprus. His name sounded like "Baghdad." Marcus or Marcos Somebody. Jackson wondered if he'd ever hurled a granola bar into the toilet at Larnaca International.

Rolling his eyes at himself, Jackson exited the bathroom. He took a step in the wrong direction, righted himself, and set out after the sure-to-be-grossed out rest of his team.

He almost did a double take. Instead, he composed himself and casually strolled to a nearby drinking fountain. He took a quick sip, then stood and wiped his mouth, at the same time glancing backward.

Thirty feet behind him was a very nondescript person checking his cell phone. That was not so unusual; there were plenty like him. But they were different. They were not familiar-looking. They had not also been just a few paces behind Team Joel at the airport in Marseille a week ago.

As if nothing was wrong, Jackson wandered back to where Team Joel was preparing to board their flight after a very short layover.

"You feeling any better?" Joel asked.

"I was. Until I spotted a shadow."

"Another one?" Ian asked.

Jackson nodded. "Same guy who dogged us in Marseille."

"Are you sure?" Joel asked.

"I may be sick, but I'm sure not blind. It's him."

Joel sighed. "Well, I guess we know we have company. There's nothing we can do about it now. We'll just have to be extra careful once we land in Tel Aviv."

"That's all we need, yeah?" Ian said. "One more reason to look over our shoulders in Israel."

Chapter Twenty-Seven

1:58 p.m. (Israel Standard Time)

BEN GURION INTERNATIONAL Airport outside of Tel Aviv was, according to Aliana, the most secure airport in the world. With good reason. Several times, it had been the object of terrorist attacks and attempted hijackings, none of which had succeeded. In addition to civilian police officers, she said the team could expect to encounter the Israeli Border Police and Israel Defense Forces, both uniformed and undercover. Named after the first prime minister of Israel after the nation secured its independence in 1948, the airport would probably be the safest location the team would visit while in the Holy Land.

They touched down on schedule, then taxied and sat on the runway for almost half an hour. Fortunately, Jackson's stomach had settled on the flight, despite a windy, rocky landing. Even so, he was glad to get out of a small, cramped fuselage that had turned into an oven as it baked under the midday Israeli sun.

Finally, the team was allowed off the plane, only to be detained by long lines as they went through customs. Somehow, Jackson found himself in the front of the line and presented his passport to an angular-faced man who looked at him over wire-rim glasses.

"Mr. Douglas," he said in nearly perfect English as he studied Jackson's passport, "you have been a busy man."

Jackson decided a smart-aleck remark to an Israeli customs agent probably wasn't a good idea, and merely nodded.

"What brings you to Israel?"

"I'm part of a research team," Jackson answered, the company line Joel had given them. Unnecessary talk about treasure hunting wasn't going to help them.

"Researching what?"

"The history of Jerusalem through the Middle Ages, in particular, the siege and fall of 1187."

"Are you an author?"

"No, sir. Just working with a historian." He nodded over his shoulder at Joel. "Part of an eight-person team."

"What is your role on the team?"

"I'm an analyst."

The agent stared at him. "Do you have anything to declare?"

"No, sir."

The agent licked his lips and stared a moment longer, as if his dark brown eyes could pull the truth from Jackson. Then he violently stamped Jackson's passport. "Welcome to Israel. Enjoy your stay."

"Thank you."

Jackson took his passport and quickly walked away from the desk, feeling the eyes of not only the customs agent, but also half a dozen uniformed guards, plainclothes policemen, and security cameras. And he was a good guy.

Joel, Maggie, Ian, and Rich soon joined him, while a delay in one of the lines held up the others.

Joel checked his watch. "I booked us at the Three Kings Hotel in Jerusalem tonight. We'll journey to the Dead Sea tomorrow."

"Is it that long of a trip?" Rich asked.

"No, but it's been a long day already, and I think we could use some settling in. Besides, there's someone in Jerusalem I need to talk to."

"Who's that?" Jackson asked.

"An old friend whose name I'd rather not mention in public."

"Speaking of, any sign of our friend from Marseille?" Ian asked.

Jackson shook his head. "I didn't see him on the flight, and I checked every passenger."

"Is that what you were doing?" Rich asked. "I thought you were still sick."

"Heading to the lavatory makes for good cover," Jackson said.

"Maybe it was just a coincidence," Maggie said.

They all looked at her.

"I mean, maybe he wasn't the guy."

"He was the guy," Jackson said.

"More likely he passed us on to another handler," Ian said as he tore open a bag of M&M's. "It could be anyone, yeah?"

"We'll be extra careful," Joel said. "Another reason I'd rather not go directly to our destination tonight. And it'd be a shame to come to Israel and make Jerusalem only a whistle stop."

Aliana and Ramón finally made their way to the group. "I told you security was tight," Aliana said.

"Where's Cara?" Joel asked.

"Right behind me," Ramón said. He turned over his shoulder, and they watched as Cara pocketed her passport and came their way. She was halted by a uniformed guard with an automatic rifle slung over his shoulder.

"Please come with us," he said.

"Uh-oh," Maggie said.

Joel took a step forward, but Ian stopped him. "I'm sure it's routine."

A second guard flanked Cara, and she looked at the team with pleading eyes.

"Please," the guard said. "Now."

She hesitantly followed them, around a screen and out of sight down a hallway. Joel turned to Aliana. "Did you identify their uniforms?"

"IDF."

"Why would they want Cara?" Rich asked.

"It doesn't make sense," Joel said. "Something's up."

"But what? Cara's the least suspicious of us."

A woman suddenly appeared at Joel's arm. She was short, swarthy, dressed casually, with a shoulder bag draped around her neck. She had wavy brown hair in a braid over one shoulder and smiled as she looked at the group. "Joel Robinson?"

He turned warily. "That's me."

The woman smiled a little wider. "Can you come with me?"

Joel shook his head. "Why?"

"Please, sir."

"Not unless you give me some idea what this is about," he said as politely as possible. Jackson wasn't sure if the woman would reach for a badge or a gun, but she did neither.

"My name is Elyssa Moralto. I'm with Interpol. I have a few questions for you."

"Do you have some identification?"

"Yes, but I'd rather not flash my credentials here in public." She smiled. "There are plenty of eyes watching us."

Joel slowly nodded.

"I'll go with you," Ian said.

"It's a personal matter," Moralto said.

"Until I know you're who you say, I'm not taking any chances," Joel said. "He'll go with us, at least until we're someplace where you can show me your ID."

Moralto flashed another smile, this one plastic. "Of course. This way." She led them off, down the concourse and around a bend, also out of sight. Suddenly Team Joel was down to five.

"Well, this is good," Jackson said. "Five minutes after we land in Israel, half of us have been hauled off by the authorities. At this rate, I should be being tortured in the tunnels leading to Beirut by nightfall."

Aliana was already on her phone, announcing that she was calling Interpol to verify Elyssa Moralto's identity. She was promptly placed on hold, and while she waited, Jackson exchanged nervous glances with Maggie, Rich, and Ramón.

"You're the liaison," he finally said to Ramón. "Any idea what we should do next?"

Ramón shrugged indifferently. "It's like she said. Probably routine."

"Cara or Joel and Ian?"

He shrugged again.

"I think we should pray," Rich said.

"Not a bad idea," Jackson said, and Rich offered a quick prayer for safety and wisdom. Having experienced several of Rich's pre-meal prayers, Jackson expected a long, poetic, flowing petition. But Rich was short and to the point. When he was finished, Maggie suggested they move out of the main flow of pedestrian traffic.

"We can't be the first group who has had to wait while a member of their traveling party was detained," she said. "We'll attract more attention if we just stand here in the open."

They moved to a small seating area fifty feet down the concourse, still in plain view should Cara return. Jackson watched the flow of people coming and going, most of them Semitic in appearance. Some were dressed in traditional garb—flowing robes and garments with headdresses, scarves, and shawls—while others wore the same attire as travelers in an American airport. Jackson wondered how many were Jews, how many were Arabs, and how many cared one way or the other. Were these people living in constant fear of a terrorist attack or that the person next to them was ready to unsheathe a dagger in the name of national superiority or religious fervor? Or did the constant exposure numb them to the threat?

There were also enough Westerners that Jackson didn't feel out of place. What drove the average American or European to Israel, he wondered. Pilgrimage? Tourism? Business? For that matter, who else in the crowd was also after the Calvary Treasure?

"Nothing," Aliana reported, lowering her phone.

"She's not real?" Rich asked.

"I could not get anyone to answer my questions."

"No surprise," Jackson said. "So far, Interpol has expected this to be a one-way street."

"If she's really from Interpol," Maggie said.

"I'm hungry," Ramón said. "You guys want to grab something to eat?"

"No," Jackson said.

"I'll wait," Maggie said as Aliana shook her head.

"Not now," Rich answered.

Ramón shrugged and announced he was going to search for some falafel before shuffling off.

"He always this concerned about the other members of the team?" Maggie asked.

Aliana nodded. "I think it is a persona he plays to mask his concern."

"Like being a smart aleck," Maggie said with a glance at Jackson.

"Ha. Smart-aleck is my defining trait, not a mere persona."

"Case in point."

"Touché."

They waited another five minutes before a bedraggled looking Cara emerged from the same hallway she had been led down. A guard at her elbow accompanied her until she spotted the team, then disappeared. She hurried over to them.

"Are you all right?" Rich asked.

She sighed and blew a loose strand of hair—no longer clipped behind her head—out of her face. "I guess."

"What happened?"

"They led me down some maze of hallways and stairs to this sterile, windowless room. I about had a heart attack. Anyhow, then this lady comes in and makes me strip so they can do a full body search. Full. Then they bring in a dog and have him sniff me and my suitcase, which they then tore apart looking for something. They really did a number on all my electronic gear. Took it all apart." She sighed again. "Everything is a mess. It will take me hours to make sure everything's working properly and wasn't damaged, and to figure out who I can sue if it is. Plus I had to sit there for like fifteen minutes in my underwear, so I feel like I've been violated. And we're late." She looked around. "Where is everyone else? Eating?"

"Ramón went looking for food," Rich said. "Joel and Ian are talking with a woman who claims she's with Interpol."

"About what?"

"We don't know."

"They never said what they were looking for?" Aliana asked.

"No," Cara said. "I asked them and all they'd say was that I matched a description of a person of interest."

"They did not harass you in any way?"

"Other than mixing my underwear with my spare laptop battery, no."

Aliana nodded. "Sounds like a common ploy to . . . well . . ."

"No, nothing like that," Cara said, sighing again.

"Were they alone with your electronic gear?" Rich asked.

"No. I don't think they wanted it. I mean, maybe the lady had a scanner in her pocket or something, but I got the feeling she was really looking for something."

Jackson raised an eyebrow. "Maybe they were telling the truth. Maybe you just have a suspicious face to Israelis."

"Hey, here come Joel and Ian," Rich said. He waved as if they didn't know where to go.

"Cara," Joel said, hurrying the last few paces. "You all right?"

"I'm fine. Just a routine strip search looking for who knows what in my toothpaste."

Joel frowned.

"Where's Ramón?" Ian asked.

"I think the IDF's caning him in the preferred club," Jackson said.

"He is getting something to eat," Aliana answered. "What did that woman want?"

"I'll tell you once we're on the road," Joel said. "We're late as it is, and I don't want to hang around here any longer."

After locating Ramón, they proceeded to the rental car checkout, which did not run smoothly. It took another half hour of haggling by Joel, Ramón, and Aliana to get their vehicles, a pair of Mazdas that looked like stunt doubles from a *Bourne* movie. After going over directions, Joel and Ian split into different vehicles and briefed the rest of the team as they headed southeast out of Tel Aviv.

"Elyssa Moralto is an Interpol special agent," Joel announced to Jackson, Maggie, and Rich as he drove. "Something like their version of internal affairs. She claims that Interpol has recently become suspicious of a group working within the parameters of Interpol to locate and appropriate various stolen works of art."

"Instead of crooked cops taking coke from evidence, they're snatching Van Goghs from museums?" Jackson asked.

"Something like that. According to Special Agent Moralto, Interpol doesn't know all the details—whether there's an international ring of thieves with Interpol connections or whether the ring is made up entirely of Interpol agents. At any rate, Agents John and Fiore—who we met in New York—are on their list of suspects. Special Agent Moralto knew we'd had contact with Agents John and Fiore and wanted to question me about them."

"And she flew all the way to Israel to do so?" Jackson asked.

"She's stationed in the Middle East, out of Cairo, and figured meeting us would be the best way to conduct an investigation off the radar."

"What about the guy we saw in Kavala?" Maggie asked. "Nigel Moyers."

"She didn't recognize the name, which probably means he's not involved in this whole business. Or I should say, isn't suspected."

"So let me get this straight," Jackson said. "We have Interpol agents dogging us because they're part of a ring of thieves who want the Calvary Treasure, we have Interpol agents dogging us because we've had contact with the first group of Interpol agents, and we have a third group of Interpol agents dogging us for as of yet unknown reasons?"

"That about sums it up," Joel said.

Jackson shook his head.

"Do you believe this Special Agent Moralto?" Rich asked.

"I do," Joel said. "But I also believed Agents John and Fiore."

"Maybe Moralto's the phony," Maggie said.

"Possible. But her questions didn't suggest that she was," Joel said. "She was more interested in what John and Fiore had told us or asked us, and less interested in our progress finding the treasure."

"Isn't it true that Interpol can't arrest anyone?" Jackson asked.

"I don't know."

Jackson shrugged. "They're kind of like the French army—they dress up and act like they have power, but if you really want something done, call the Americans."

"I don't know if I'd go that far," Joel said.

"My point is, who really cares who's Interpol and who's fake Interpol. If they're legit, they can't do anything to us anyhow. We should treat them all as fakes—and threats."

Joel weighed the idea for a moment. "I suppose that's reasonable. But more because we aren't going to do anything that would permit them to arrest us anyhow."

Jackson settled back in his seat. "Right now, half a dozen countries have ICBMs pointed at us, a pregnant lady on the bus beside us at the next light might be strapped, and we're being tailed and spied on and run off the road at every turn. We really don't need any more to worry about."

"Well, isn't that encouraging," Maggie said.

Rich, from the front seat, pointed out the next turn while studying a map. Jackson was surprised—He had expected Israel to be a barren, arid wasteland. So far, it was freeways, subdivisions, and farmland. He'd thought they'd be dodging donkeys pulling carts along dusty desert roads, not four-lane rush-hour traffic.

Soon they began to climb into the hills, and before long, they were descending into Jerusalem. Once again, Jackson's expectations were blown. He was anticipating a small, walled in town like in the maps in the back of his Bible. Instead, Jerusalem's outskirts stretched toward the hills like any American city. Traffic flowed on smoothly paved roads with guard rails, streetlights, and Kelly green road signs, just like back home.

"Jerusalem's actually a city of over eight hundred thousand," Joel said in response to Jackson's astonished remarks. "The Old City covers less than a square mile, but Greater Jerusalem spans almost fifty."

"And where is our hotel?" Maggie asked.

"On the southwestern outskirts," Joel said. "Far away from anything."

"Let's hope the terrorists know that," Jackson said.

Maggie backhanded him.

"What, is it politically incorrect to admit the existence of the PLO and Hamas?"

"It's not that cut and dried."

"Why don't you cut it and dry it for me?" Jackson said.

"They're just people who want to live in their homeland too," she said. "Same as the Israelis."

"Right, because the desert twenty miles that way is so much less desirable."

"It's a holy place, Jack. You should understand that."

"Places aren't holy, Maggie. If Allah's all great and powerful, can't he be worshipped somewhere else, in the name of saving lives?"

"Can't the Hebrew God as well?"

"In the Gospel of John," Rich said, "Jesus told the Samaritan woman, in response to her question about where God was to be worshiped—either in Jerusalem or on Mount Gerizim—that *'God is Spirit, and His worshippers must worship in spirit and in truth.'*"

"Besides," Jackson said, "it's not so much about what they're fighting over as how they're fighting."

"Meaning what?"

"Meaning, one side uses fake pregnant women to blow up bus stops and hides weapons in schools and hospitals and the other side doesn't."

"It's not that simple."

"So you keep saying."

"Fight's over," Joel announced. "We're here."

They had lost the other Mazda in traffic, but as Joel pulled into the parking lot of their hotel, it appeared behind them. After sitting on three planes and in the back of the Mazda, Jackson was glad to stretch his legs and was out of the car almost before Joel had parked it. The late afternoon sun was warm and the gentle southern breeze dry, and he stood for a moment soaking it in.

"Oh, what a day," Aliana said as she got out of the other Mazda's backseat.

"Not a bad view either, yeah?" Ian said, drawing Jackson's attention to the north. Their hotel was on a hill, providing them a view of the Old City. The stone walls and Tower of David stood like sentinels on a hilltop, and the golden roof of the Dome of the Rock gleamed in the bright sunlight.

It was as if Jackson had suddenly been transported back in time a few thousand years. He was really in the place where the Crusades had been waged and where Christ had been killed and raised from the dead. He squinted at a far away hillside, imagining three crosses atop it instead of a high-rise apartment. With modern architecture and technology everywhere and with car horns and the sound of traffic in the distance, it was hard to picture Roman soldiers herding a beaten, bleeding man to His gruesome death. And yet, at the same time, it wasn't.

Despite the unseasonable warmth, Jackson felt a chill run down his spine.

Chapter Twenty-Eight

Monday, February 18
9:01 a.m.

TEAM JOEL STARTED its first full day in Israel in three camps. Joel and Ramón went to see Joel's old, unnamed friend who lived on the north side of Jerusalem. According to Joel, he was an expert on ancient Israel and possibly could provide the team with more info on Masada and goings on at the fortress from the time of Christ to the current day. Cara and Rich were staying behind to sleep, do laundry, and check out electronic equipment that had been "ransacked" in the airport the day before.

That left Jackson, Maggie, Ian, and Aliana, who headed into the Old City. Ian had a contact who might be able to provide them with some intel on the other parties involved in the search for the Calvary Treasure, as well as direct them to some resources in the Holy Land. He had agreed to meet Jackson and Ian while Maggie and Aliana did some shopping in the market. Jackson, among others, had been hesitant to let the two of them go alone, but they had both insisted they would be fine.

The morning had dawned warm and calm, and temperatures were expected to be much warmer than normal in the Israeli capital. Jackson rode shotgun with the window in the Mazda down, enjoying the flow of warm air over his bare arm. The team had done little the night before. After an early dinner, they had made a few plans for the days to come and then relaxed and turned in early. It felt like weeks since they had left Greece, not merely a day, but Jackson found himself refreshed and anxious to see a place he'd only read about in Scripture or seen on the news. Jerusalem. He couldn't believe he was really here.

It took some doing, but Ian found a parking spot within sight of the walls of the Old City. They entered through the Zion Gate in the southwestern corner—the Armenian Quarter—of the city. Bullet holes in the stones around the gates were remnants from the 1948 Palestine War, Aliana said. "*Al-Nakba*, in Arabic," she explained as they passed through the gate.

"The Catastrophe. It is known as *Milkhemet Ha'atzma'ut*—War of Independence—or *Milkhement Hashikhrur*—War of Liberation—in Hebrew."

"Are there any languages you don't speak?" Jackson asked.

She smiled. "A few."

They stopped after entering the Old City. Directly in front of them was another wall, enclosing the Armenian Monastery. The foursome circumvented it by walking along a narrow road to the east. It curved north, along a small cliff and ruins of some sort. Ian complained a minute later when they came to a large parking area with plenty of empty spots, but Aliana remarked that it was a beautiful day, and she was in a mood for a walk anyhow.

Soon they were traversing the edge of a deep ravine, at the bottom of which was the Old City wall. Beyond it, Jerusalem spread out onto the hills. Inside the walls, the Old City was a hubbub of people—mostly on foot, some on scooters and motorcycles, a few in European-model cars. Jackson saw a few cameras around necks, and a handful of people pointing their smartphones around, but the location didn't seem to be impacting everyone else the way it was him. Every bearded face was a reminder that Jesus might have walked these very streets. Never mind the knights who had hidden a priceless treasure before defending the city with their lives.

They continued to follow the curving road into the Jewish Quarter and to the entrance to the Western Wall Plaza. The massive open expanse was paved with rectangular stones and surrounded by buildings the same color as the rock into which they were built. At the northeast edge of the plaza was the Western Wall of the Temple Mount. Already, dozens and dozens of people were approaching the sixty-two-foot-high wall to offer their prayers. It was an odd spectacle, watching Jews worship and pray in the shadow of the Dome of the Rock and a Muslim minaret.

Jackson turned to Aliana, who had muttered something not in English under her breath. Then he turned to Ian, who was scanning the crowd, perhaps looking for his contact. Beside him, Maggie was reading a list of rules, written in both Hebrew and English on a placard. Among them, instructions to dress modestly, avoid panhandling, and keep cell phones off in designated prayer areas.

Next to it was a second placard, and Jackson paused to read the entirely English script:

Jewish tradition teaches that the Temple Mount is the focal point of Creation. In the center of the mountain lies the "Foundation Stone" of the world. Here Adam came into being. Here Abraham, Isaac and Jacob served God. The first and Second Temples were built upon this mountain. The Ark of the Covenant was set upon the Foundation Stone itself. Jerusalem was chosen by God as the dwelling place of the Shechinah. David longed to build the Temple, and Solomon his son built the First Temple here about 3000 years ago. It was destroyed by Nevuchadnezzar of Babylon. The Second Temple was rebuilt on its ruins seventy years later. It was razed by the Roman legions over 1900 years ago. The present Western Wall before you is a remnant of the western Temple Mount retaining walls. Jews have prayed in its shadow for hundreds of years, an expression of their faith in the rebuilding of the Temple. The Sages said about it: "The Divine Presence never moves from the Western Wall." The Temple Mount continues to be the focus of prayer for Jews from all over the world.

"Makes you feel small, doesn't it?" Maggie asked.

"Makes me feel, that's for sure."

"We'll meet you back here in an hour, yeah?" Ian said, refocusing everyone.

Aliana glanced at her watch. "It is almost nine-thirty."

"Make it ten-thirty then," Ian said.

The women agreed and started for the market.

Ian nodded toward the wall. "Eli's meeting us at the entrance to the Western Wall Tunnel, north end of the plaza."

"After you."

Ian led the way, past a long, covered, wooden ramp that led up to the top of the Western Wall, presumably an entrance to the Temple Mount. They passed a group of young students huddled together, speaking what sounded like German; several Orthodox Jews, identifiable by their black hats, suits, and long beards; a squad of uniformed soldiers, off-duty if their jovial expressions were any indication; and more than a few women whose bodies were completely covered, save for their faces. Whether they wore jeans and casual tops or skirts and dresses, all the women wore coverings on their heads. It was a long ways from a stroll along the Santa Monica Boardwalk.

As they drew closer, Jackson could hear the quiet murmurings from the worshipers at the base of the Western Wall—the "Wailing Wall." There had to be a hundred of them, some standing, some kneeling, some rocking in place. He wondered what they were praying for. Were they asking for health and safety for their families? Were they seeking a solution to a crisis? How many of them were asking for peace? Were any praying against the religion that occupied the other side of the wall?

Jackson quickened his pace to keep up with Ian, who apparently wasn't as reflective as Jackson. Directly ahead of them, six arches were carved into a stone wall beneath more buildings. From a distance, the Old City resembled one massive building, and Jackson was quickly learning the narrow streets only appeared once close up.

They stopped in front of a sign announcing the entrance to the Western Wall Tunnel. Ian squinted as he scanned the plaza before turning back to the sign. "This must be it, yeah?"

Jackson nodded. "How exactly do you know this Eli guy?"

"It's a very long story."

Jackson waited a beat, then realized Ian wasn't going to tell the story. So he merely nodded.

They waited five minutes, and Jackson observed the crowd around him. It was purely a guess, but he deduced almost half the people present were there to sightsee and maybe offer a token prayer. It was surprising. After all, how many people could go to the Wailing Wall to ask for their daily bread?

"Hi there, you boggin' doowally!"

Jackson and Ian both turned to see a short, tawny man approaching. He wore beige khakis and a black turtleneck. Several days' growth of beard masked his facial features, and aviator sunglasses hid his eyes. His black hair was short and unkempt, which matched the lopsided smile he flashed briefly at Ian.

"Eli, you old schlepper." They hugged briefly, backslaps and all. "I see you still can't work a razor, yeah?"

"And you can't find a barber in all of Scotland," Eli answered, his fake Scottish accent replaced with a very subtle inflection on otherwise perfect English. "And you've brought company."

"Jackson Douglas, an American private detective. He's working with us. Jackson, meet Eli Haddad, former Mossad agent. Eli's now a . . . freelancer."

Jackson extended a hand, then wondered if that was an appropriate greeting in the Middle East. Eli apparently thought nothing of it and gripped Jackson's firmly. "Nice to meet you." Still behind the sunglasses, his eyes turned to Ian. "Shall we walk?"

Eli led them silently to a flight of stairs that led away from the plaza. At the top of the stairs, they made a series of quick turns and entered a short passageway that led to an open street. Open being a relative term. It was at most ten feet wide, with three-story buildings on either side. Large tapestries hung over the entrance to a shop on the left while a sign on the right advertised a Moroccan restaurant. The canopy above the open door nearly touched the tapestries on the other side of the street, and it seemed to funnel the smell of some poor dead animal out to Jackson. He suddenly longed for a Greek breakfast.

A dozen steps took them past a fruit stand, a beggar with an eye patch, a small curio shop selling everything from gold crosses to Muslim prayer beads, a man in a gray rastacap playing his guitar, and a man on a small motor scooter arguing with a woman in a second-floor window. Beneath them, the street rose and fell, sometimes with a few steps built in, sometimes not. All Jackson could think of was the song *Via Dolorosa* and what the Jerusalem streets had been like two thousand years ago as Roman soldiers cleared a path for Jesus as He bore His cross to Golgotha. Had they had to shove shoppers and diners and guys arguing with second-story women out of the way?

"So, what brings you to Jerusalem?" Eli asked when the street widened slightly and they were able to walk three abreast. "Are you still working with the bombastic Frenchman?"

Ian grinned. "No. His former partner."

"Ah, so you are here seeking treasure?"

"More or less."

"Surely you do not need my expertise to find the Holy Grail?"

"More like to tell us who else is looking for it," Ian said. "You hear the chatter, yeah?"

"I hear plenty," Eli said. "The challenge is sorting the legitimate intel from the *bopkes*."

"And there's no one better."

"In my time, perhaps."

"The day time passes you by is the day a Scotsman turns down a drink."

"It is not time that is passing me by, but the establishment. They have traded me in for a younger model, someone whose political views are broad enough to encompass our 'brave new world.' But you did not come all this way to hear me *kvetch*." He pointed to a side passage off the main street. "This way. What specifically do you want?"

"We've been tracked from New York to France to Greece and then here," Ian answered.

"By whom?"

"Interpol agents, for starters."

"Interpol?"

"Aye. Including some rogue agents."

"You're after more than treasure, it sounds."

"We've also identified at least one other party tailing us," Ian said.

"You haven't been able to make an identification?"

"No."

Eli turned to Jackson. "You are not one of the hotshot American P.I.s then? A Thomas Magnum?"

"A guy can dream."

Eli grinned. "I grew up on *Magnum, P.I.* reruns."

"I knew I wasn't the only one," Jackson said.

"We don't know who's following us," Ian said, "so I thought maybe you'd know who else might be here for the same reason we are."

"The Calvary Treasure."

Jackson stopped.

"I told you there was no one better," Ian said.

"It was nothing," Eli said. "You said you were working with Joel Robinson, the former partner of Philippe LeCavalier, a distant descendant of Leon of Toulon, A.K.A. Leon LeCavalier."

Jackson stopped again. "Philippe is related to Leon of Toulon, the one-time High Commander of the Knights Calvary?"

"He's French," Eli shrugged. "All Europeans can trace their ancestors back to the Middle Ages. But that is not the point."

Jackson begged to differ. Knowing that Philippe was related, however distantly, to the former head of the Knights Calvary was indeed pertinent. He just wasn't sure how. He also wasn't sure why Joel and Ian didn't know that or, if they did, why they hadn't shared it with him. At any rate, the wheels in his head were spinning as they continued down a narrow, darkening alley of a street. He hoped he could trust Ian and thus Eli, because all his years of watching Magnum and other TV detectives told him they were headed into a trap.

"Once I knew who you were traveling and working with," Eli continued, "where you'd been in recent days, and the fact that you are now here . . . well, it wasn't much of a jump to figure out you're after the Calvary Treasure."

"There's no point in denying it," Ian said.

"And you think it's here, in Jerusalem, all this time?"

"No," Ian said, stepping aside to let a bicyclist pass. "But close."

"Any idea what it is?"

"Just theories."

"Come, my friend. There's no point lying to me."

Ian looked at Jackson.

"Hey, don't ask me. I'm just a California P.I. You're the one who knows the former Mossad agent who's leading us into the bowels of Jerusalem as we speak."

Eli placed a hand on Jackson's back, just below the neck. It was a friendly gesture, the slap of a pal. And yet, if Jackson wasn't mistaken, it carried with it the very subtle reminder that Jackson was completely at the Israeli's mercy. Eli confirmed it. "If I were up to no good, trust me, my friend, it would do you no good to worry. You would be as good as dead."

"I feel so much better."

Eli removed his hand. "Your business is yours. Buried treasure does not interest me anyhow. Too much red tape and paperwork before it becomes something I can spend."

They turned again. By now, they were in either the Muslim Quarter or Syria.

"There's a man named Sauveterre," Eli said. "He's very quietly a member of the *Chevaliers Calvaire*. You've heard of them?"

Jackson and Ian both nodded.

"He arrived in Tel Aviv last night."

"How . . ."

"I'm very well connected."

"Maybe he knows what the guards at the airport were looking for in Cara's bag," Jackson quipped.

"Sauveterre," Ian said. "Is he alone?"

"I doubt it. But none of his traveling companions raised any alarms."

"What about Interpol?"

"They don't concern me. They come and go all the time."

"You know an Agent Elyssa Moralto?" Jackson asked. "Short, good-looking in the buttoned-down 'I could kill you without touching you' sort of way?"

"I know of her. She's harmless."

"How about Duncan John, Alexandra Fiore, or Nigel Moyers?"

"You certainly have been attracting attention, haven't you?" Eli said. "I know of Moyers. Also harmless. The other two I've never heard of."

"Anyone else?" Ian asked.

"Again, no one who raises alarms. But I would not take Sauveterre lightly. The *Chevaliers Calvaire* aren't known to be ruthless, but they are determined."

"Which brings me to my second request," Ian said.

"Of course," Eli replied. "You are, no doubt, Robinson's security force."

"Aye."

"And bringing any sort of weapons into Israel would attract far too much attention at Ben Gurion."

"It would."

Eli nodded as he pointed at another passageway, this one more of a tunnel staircase leading up. "What do you need?"

"Nothing too fancy," Ian replied. "Just a handgun or two for self-defense."

"Where are you staying?"

"The Royal Palms, on the Dead Sea."

"You travel in style."

"Aye."

"You arrive tonight?"

Ian nodded.

"I'll see that there's a package waiting for you."

"*Toda.*"

"*Bevakasha.* Just keep in mind, what you do with them is out of my hands. And remember, this is Israel. Gunfire here tends to attract a big crowd in a big hurry, and not even I have enough pull to save you from that."

"I sincerely doubt that's true," Ian said.

Eli reached into his pocket and withdrew a blank card and a pen. He scratched a quick sentence and handed it to Ian. "That's the address for Asher Hillel."

"Who's he?"

"A cranky old man who lives in the desert. He knows the land, its history, and where to go to scrounge up everything from supplies to local gossip. As far as contacts go, Asher is to the Negev and Arabah what I am to Jerusalem."

Ian nodded.

"Just be sure to introduce yourself with my name, or you may not be too warmly welcomed."

They passed through one more tunnel and into bright sunlight, and much to Jackson's surprise, back into the Western Wall Plaza.

"You see, my friend, you had nothing to fear," Eli said with another clap on Jackson's back.

"Thank you again, Eli," Ian said.

"It's nothing for an old friend. If I hear anything further, I'll let you know. Douglas, nice to meet you."

"Likewise."

Eli nodded at Ian. "*Shalom*, my friend."

"*Shalom*."

Eli turned, blended into the crowd, and was gone.

"Any point in asking again how you know that guy?" Jackson asked.

"We had a mutual life-saving experience in Algiers a number of years back."

Jackson shook his head. "What I couldn't do with the L.A. version of him. It'd be like having a 1-800-Solve-the-case hotline."

"Aye, but he's expensive."

"I didn't see any cash trade hands. He owe you or something?"

"In a manner of speaking. Come on."

They crossed the plaza, which by now was much busier, and returned to the entrance where they had parted ways with Maggie and Aliana. It was twenty after ten, ten minutes before their scheduled rendezvous. Glancing around to make sure they weren't being listened to, Ian asked, "You know how to handle a weapon, yeah?"

Jackson nodded.

"Joel and Rich have never fired a gun, and between you and me, I don't trust Ramón with more than a dull fork."

"What about Aliana and Cara?"

"I'm a wee bit old fashioned, but the lovely hands of a lady are no place for a nine millimeter."

Jackson nodded. "Yeah, I know how to handle a weapon."

"Good."

"You think we'll need them?"

Ian shrugged. "I just know I'd rather be prepared than caught with my pants down, yeah?"

An elderly man limped past them, shuffling toward the Wailing Wall. Jackson watched him for a minute, then scanned the panorama. The sky was bright and clear, the day as still as it had been at dawn. Jackson still couldn't get over the fact that he had just walked the streets of Jerusalem and was within shouting distance of two of the most sacred sites in both Judaism and Islam. Surreal didn't begin to describe it.

Ian reached for his pocket. "A text from Ali," he said after pulling out his phone and consulting the screen.

"What's it s—"

A cloud came over Ian's eyes. Then, without a word, he took off running.

Chapter Twenty-Nine

10:24 a.m.

JACKSON HESITATED ONLY a second before following Ian. The Scotsman led him around a corner, up a flight of stairs, and into a narrow passageway between several buildings. Calling it an alley would have been an overstatement.

They nearly tripped over a beggar and, in the process of avoiding him, Ian knocked over a garbage can, forcing Jackson to hurdle it. He felt his ankle give slightly on the landing, but it didn't slow him.

When the passage ended, Ian made a right turn and sprinted down another narrow street. Jackson was on his heels, dodging other pedestrians, a cyclist, and vendors of every kind. Hucksters hyped their wares, everything from rugs to scarves to fruit to slabs of meat to trinkets and baubles to religious icons. Jackson ignored them all, fighting to stay with Ian, who ran like a madman.

The street turned slightly, at the same time rising three steps. Ian leaped over the span, landing in full stride. Jackson's steps didn't come out right, and he had to take the stairway in two steps. When he looked up again, he saw Maggie and Aliana by a fruit stand, with three bearded men huddled close around them. The men were dressed in beige and khakis, one wearing a turban, another a dark baseball cap.

Jackson didn't think much of the scene until he saw one of the men had a firm grip on Maggie's elbow. Then he saw the flash of a knife blade in the man's hand.

Ball Cap looked up as the sound of Ian's shoes pounding the pavement reached him, but it was too late. Never slowing, Ian threw a running haymaker that caught the man with the knife flush in the jaw. He crumpled to the ground, unconscious before he hit it.

Jackson assumed Ian had assessed the sides properly, and he joined the fray by lowering his shoulder and plowing into Turban. He had turned in anticipation of the blow but expected a punch instead of a tackle. Jackson drove him backward and they crashed into a fruit stand, sending oranges, grapefruits, and avocados tumbling onto the street.

Someone had screamed initially, and now a crowd was gathering, with the owner of the small stand shouting frantically. Ball Cap had recovered from the surprise quickly and returned Ian's punch to his comrade with a hard right hook that knocked Ian back against the wall on the opposite side of the street. Meanwhile, Turban had tried to fight Jackson off by throwing a pair of flailing punches. Jackson dodged them all and landed an uppercut that cracked his fist almost as hard as Turban's jaw. He joined his pal, out cold.

Jackson turned and saw Ian trading punches—some blocked, some not—with Ball Cap. He doubted this was a let-Riggs-have-Joshua moment and made a second tackle. This one was a flying, diving leap, shoulder to shoulder, and it rocked Ball Cap back and knocked his cap off. His head cracked on the street with a sickening thud.

Wincing, Jackson stood and massaged his sore left shoulder with his sore right hand, a mistake on both fronts. Beside him, Ian flexed his right hand and then repositioned his jaw with his left. He then felt a puffy lip as he approached Maggie and Aliana. "Are you both all right?"

Wide-eyed, Aliana nodded.

The crowd around them had grown, pressing in on all sides, and the irate owner of the stand Jackson and Turban had crashed into was unleashing a torrent of Hebrew or Arabic at them. Not knowing the language, Jackson could tell by the tone he was probably being cursed out.

Ian reached into his pocket and pulled out several American bills. He slapped them into the man's hand. "That'll more than cover it, yeah?" He turned to Jackson. "Let's get out of here. Come on," he added, extending a hand to usher the women in the right direction. They needed no encouragement.

Jackson led the way, which would work only as long as the street continued. They were headed south, he thought, and that was the general direction they wanted to go. But the rabble behind them wasn't dying down, and already the ee-aww, ee-aww, ee-aww of a police car was growing louder.

"This way!" Ian shouted from behind, and Jackson turned back and brought up the rear as the group cut through another narrow alley. They half ran, half walked until they came out into another plaza. Then they slowed to a normal pace, blending in with the crowd. When they crossed the plaza and ducked into another side street, they again hurried their steps. They made another sharp turn, then climbed a very steep, very narrow staircase. One more burst through another narrow alley and they emerged on a familiar street, right across from the parking lot just inside the Zion Gate.

Ian looked in every direction, then nodded. "Looks like we're clear. Let's keep moving."

Breathing heavily, Maggie and Aliana nodded and followed Ian. Also gasping for air, Jackson brought up the rear, glancing over his shoulder every few seconds. An incident like this would be bad enough in L.A., but in a foreign country—particularly one where the authorities had to have hair triggers—Jackson wouldn't relax until they were safely back in their hotel, if then.

They made it through the gate without any trouble, and when they were back in the Mazda and Ian had joined Jerusalem traffic, Maggie finally sighed with relief.

"What happened?" Jackson asked from his seat beside her.

"I don't know, exactly. We were buying some fruit when those three guys came up to us. I couldn't understand a thing they were saying."

"You would not want to know," Aliana said. "I was just about to text you to let you know we were on our way when they approached us," she said to Ian. "That is how I was able to send for help so quickly."

"So they were just trying to pick up some women?" Maggie asked.

"Not for themselves, no," Aliana said.

"I think what she's saying is you were almost the stars of the next *Taken*," Jackson said.

"Sex trafficking? Really?" She winced. "We're too old."

"It is not like that," Aliana said. "The one in the baseball cap. He said they wanted you for their leader."

"What else did he say?" Jackson asked.

"Nothing more, other than some vulgar suggestions."

"Why me?" Maggie asked.

"You are American, attractive. Maybe you fit a specific profile."

"I can't believe this," Maggie said. "In broad daylight?"

"It is not common, but it is also not unheard of."

"Did they say who their leader was?" Jackson asked. "Anything about him, what he was the leader of?"

"No, unfortunately."

Maggie shook her head. "I can't believe this."

"It's a good thing we were close, yeah?"

"How did you find us anyhow?"

"I assumed you were still in the market."

"That couldn't have been the only market in the Old City," Jackson said.

Ian turned to look at him. "No, but it was the closest. Cara's not the only one who looks at satellite photos before we go somewhere."

They returned to the hotel, where stories were swapped and everyone fussed over Maggie and Aliana's experience and Ian's war wounds. In addition to a split lip, his jaw was noticeably bruised, and his right eye was turning purple. When things settled down, Joel related that his friend hadn't been able to reveal much about Masada that Cara hadn't already found online. There were a few nuggets of information he'd tucked away, in case they became relevant, but the trip had largely been fruitless. Ian also recounted for the group what Eli had told him and Jackson. He didn't mention the package that would be waiting for them at the Royal Palms or the name Asher Hillel.

"Well, if you ladies are up for it, I propose we get moving," Joel said.

"I'm fine," Maggie said.

"Me too."

"Okay. Let's load up."

As they made sure everything was packed and loaded the gear, Ian pulled Jackson aside. "I had another thought. Maybe that wasn't a kidnapping of any sort. Maybe it was an attempt to intimidate us, yeah?"

"I thought the same thing," Jackson said.

"I don't suppose it matters," Ian said. "We're clearly not backing down."

"No, but it's food for thought. Too bad we couldn't get a shot of their faces or IDs or something."

"Here, let me take that for you," Maggie said, seeing Ian wince as he picked up a duffel. "The least I can do."

Jackson held out his hands, but she had already turned away. Ian winked and followed her out to the car. According to Joel, the drive to the southern shore of the Dead Sea would take about an hour. They picked up lunch on the way, passed through a checkpoint into the West Bank, and soon were cruising through the desert east of Jerusalem.

Now the terrain looked like Jackson expected it to. Barren rolling hills the color of sand stretched for miles. Occasionally, a rock outcropping or the ruins of an old building intruded on the smoothness. There were no trees. No modern buildings. Fewer and fewer cars the farther they went from Jerusalem.

Maggie was again riding in the back of one of the Mazdas with Jackson. Joel drove, and Cara rode shotgun, furiously pecking away at her computer the entire time. She couldn't possibly have an internet signal out here unless she had hacked into a satellite.

"What's our plan for the rest of the day again?" Maggie asked, taking a break from staring out her window.

"According to the inside of the chest at Philippe's," Joel said, "we need to be atop Masada at dawn. The tram to the top only runs during daylight hours, and they don't allow hikers to utilize the Snake Path at night, for obvious reasons. The site is run by UNESCO, which is a U.N. agency, so Ramón's working on greasing the wheels with them to see if they will permit us to camp out overnight."

"What are the odds of getting approval?" Maggie asked.

"If the UNESCO rep is a woman, a hundred percent," Cara muttered.

"He's usually pretty good at working out some sort of arrangement," Joel said.

"He have a lot of experience bargaining for the right to camp on millennia-old desert fortresses?" Jackson asked.

Joel winked in the rearview mirror. "You'd be surprised." He turned his eyes to Maggie. "At any rate, we lost a fair amount of time at the border crossing, and sundown in these parts is about five-thirty—"

"Five twenty-eight," Cara said.

"And the last tram to the top leaves at four?"

"Right."

"So I don't know if we'll be able to make it up yet tonight. Even if Ramón is able to work his magic in just a few more hours, we have no supplies. So I'm thinking we'll check into the hotel, and while Ramón makes his contacts, some of us can get supplies, and some of us can organize and prep. Ian also mentioned another contact who might be able to help us out with some local intelligence, so maybe he'll try to look him up yet this afternoon."

"You all sure have a lot of contacts," Maggie said.

"It comes with the territory, and with experience," Joel said. "But then I figure we'll have a nice dinner and enjoy the desert air or the spa or whatever helps you relax for tomorrow."

"Sounds good to me," Maggie said.

Rolling hills led to more rolling hills, and just when Jackson thought they had to be getting close to Iran, they crested a small rise, and a wide valley appeared in front of them. Haze obscured the other side of the valley, but not the broad swath of pale blue that lay to the south.

The Dead Sea, also known as the Salt Sea or the Sea of Death, lay over a quarter of a mile below sea level. Its shores were the lowest places on earth, and the sea itself sunk to depths of another quarter mile below sea level. The salt content of the Dead Sea was eight times that of the oceans, making it unsustainable for animal life. Fed by the Jordan River and a number of springs around its shores, the Dead Sea had no outlets. The salt water simply evaporated in the arid climate, faster than it was replenished, recently at a rate of almost three feet per year. From the mouth of the Jordan in the north to the mineral evaporation ponds in the south, the sea stretched almost sixty miles, with a width up to eleven miles. It was roughly twice the size of Lake Tahoe.

Some five miles south of Jericho, the two Team Joel Mazdas turned south on Route 90, traversing along the western shore of the sea. They passed a few resorts and small towns and also a pair of shepherds goading some fifty or sixty sheep along the side of the road. Despite the proximity to water, there wasn't much in the way of vegetation. Just more desert cliffs on the right and the salt deposits on the shore of the sea to the left.

The Royal Palms was a mostly isolated resort on the southwestern shore of the Dead Sea. Compared to the bigger resort hotels in American tourist destinations, the Royal Palms wasn't all that impressive. But standing alone over the desert and the sea at the base of the mountains, it loomed large. The main tower was eight stories tall, with two prongs extending from the base at a right angle toward the sea. Between them were pools and an outdoor spa. In total, the Royal Palms housed several hundred rooms, including suites.

Team Joel had reserved three, and the check-in couldn't have gone more smoothly. The front desk clerk spoke fluent English and listed off the amenities of the hotel, including its spa, three eateries, and discounts on various sightseeing or discovery tours in the area. She also had a package for Ian, which drew a few curious glances from some of the team and a knowing look from Joel.

Jackson shared a suite with Joel and Rich, connected via a central common area to Ian and Ramón's suite. Across the hall was the women's suite, and Jackson paused to admire their view as he set down Maggie and Aliana's bags.

On the western side of the tower, their spacious windows looked out over the same row of mountains that had flanked them on their journey south. As opposed to the clarity of the dawn in Jerusalem, the sky over the Jordan Rift Valley was hazy, and although they were no more than a couple miles away, the mountains were partially obscured. Even so, one of the promontories in the row of cliffs had a distinct look, as if it were man-made.

"Is that . . . Masada?" Maggie asked, joining Jackson at the window.

"I think so," he said. "Can you believe it?"

She shook her head.

"Good thing there's a tram," Cara said.

"What's your view like?" Maggie asked.

Jackson nodded, and she and Aliana followed him over to their suite. In the middle of the living area were three windows. In addition to overlooking the pool area below, they offered a panoramic view of the Dead Sea. Its blue waters almost appeared white, and it was hard to tell where the water ended and the salty shore began. Looking across the sea was even worse. There were supposed to be mountains on the other side, but Jackson couldn't see them as the sea and sky intersected in a haze of white.

"I hope the weather clears before we crest Masada," Aliana said. "At this rate, we will not be able to see or identify anything."

Chapter Thirty

3:44 p.m.

TEAM JOEL AGAIN split up. Ramón, who had a number of phone calls out, and Cara took one of the vehicles over to the base of Masada to the visitor center to verify some details and get as much lay of the land as possible. Meanwhile, Jackson, Joel, and Ian took the other car and headed out into the desert in search of Asher Hillel, the man recommended by Eli Haddad. Maggie, Rich, and Aliana remained behind at the hotel, either to relax and recover from their morning ordeal or to sleep perchance to have a vision. All eight members planned to meet for dinner around sunset.

The small city of Arad was located some twelve to fifteen miles southwest of the Royal Palms, in the Judean Desert. Its population was almost twenty-five thousand, and it attracted a lot of tourists due to its incredibly dry, clear air. Team Joel had no interest in the air, however, or the city's unique architecture and history. Their focus was a small earth-colored house a few miles east of town, off Highway 31. It was built on a very small rise in a valley that itself was on the side of terrain that sloped gently toward the Jordan Rift Valley. Aside from an old windmill and an outbuilding near it, there was absolutely nothing around the house but grayish tan rock and sand. The trio might as well have been in a Spaghetti Western as the Holy Land.

"How does your friend know this Asher Hillel?" Joel asked as they parked in what amounted to Asher's driveway. The house was set back from the road some fifty yards, and from the gravel drive by another fifty feet.

"He didn't exactly say," Ian answered as he closed his car door. "Just that he was a wee bit cranky."

"I can't imagine what this place must be like in the summer," Jackson said, surveying the desert in all four directions. The temperature, according to the weather on the TV at the hotel, was in the seventies, about ten above normal. But somehow being out in the open, particularly a barren, rocky open, made it feel much hotter.

"Aye, but it's a dry—"

A gunshot suddenly blasted across the desert, the bullet biting in the dirt a few feet from where Ian stood. The Scotsman looked down at the small cloud of dust rising into the air, then up toward the house. Hidden in the shadow of the front porch was a wiry man in fatigues, squinting at them over a rifle.

"Eli Haddad sent us!" Joel shouted.

"Nev'r 'eard of 'im," the man spat, then fired a shot five feet to the side of Joel.

"You sure didn't take shooting lessons from him," Jackson said.

The next bullet sailed over his head.

"See what I mean?"

Ian took a step forward. "Eli said you could help us. If you're Asher Hillel."

The man finally left the cover of the porch and slowly approached, gun still leveled at them. He was short, his skin dark and leathery. He looked almost seventy, but his hair was black as a raven, and he stood with perfect posture.

"How do you know Eli?" Asher's voice matched the terrain.

"I saved his life once," Ian said. "He was kind enough to return the favor."

"How'd you find me?"

First holding up his palm, Ian slowly reached into his jeans pocket and withdrew the card upon which Eli had written Asher's address. He extended it until the man approached and took it. Slowly, the gun lowered.

"These friends of yours?" Asher asked.

"Aye."

"Come on in."

Asher led them into a scarcely furnished one-room house. There was an unmade bed, two old armchairs, a small TV on a stand, basic kitchen appliances on either end of a short counter, a freestanding sink, and a rickety old table. No pictures on the walls, no décor of any kind, unless a floor to ceiling bookshelf—fully stocked—against one wall counted. The room was stifling, despite a ceiling fan in the center of the room that spun lazily, generating a little breeze.

Asher nodded at the table and chairs in the dining area, and the trio sat down. Asher set the rifle on the table and joined them. "Okay, what'd Eli tell you I could do for you?"

"We have some questions about Masada," Ian said.

Asher didn't react.

"Have you ever heard of a feature known as '*the arrow's mark*'?"

Asher grunted what sounded like a negative.

"How about the phrase, 'Ascend to the place from which thou canst look upon the bloody sea of death and the way of the serpent'?" Joel asked.

Asher sent him a cockeyed look. Then he turned to Ian. "He always talk like that?"

"Aye, he's stuck in the King's English."

"Bloody sea of death'd be the Dead Sea," Asher said as if it were obvious.

"Why would it be bloody?" Jackson asked, thinking the Israeli might have knowledge they didn't.

"Every hun'red years it fills with algae and turns reddish brown." He shrugged. "I don't know. You're the ones with the riddle."

"Do you know of any other fortresses around here, other than Masada?" Joel asked.

"Fortresses? Not anymore. Maybe in ol' David's time."

"What about any legends of Crusaders being present at or around Masada?"

"Crusaders?" Asher laughed. "What're you, lookin' for some treasure?"

"As a matter of fact, yes," Joel answered. On the drive over, they had all decided—on Ian's recommendation—to level with Asher. Sure, in the movies, he'd be on the take from someone like Sauveterre and call him as soon as they left, but this wasn't the movies, and they expected they'd have to give to get. Besides, it didn't look like the old man had a phone.

Asher stared at Joel for a moment. "I want twenty percent."

"It's not that kind of treasure."

"What kind is it?"

"We suspect a very old letter, journal, or book."

"And the three of you come all this way for a book?"

"That's right," Joel said.

Asher huffed. "Sorry, but I don't know nuthin' about any of all this." He scratched his jaw. " 'Cept maybe one thing."

Joel leaned forward.

"There's a legend about a Crusader castle across the river," he said. "Sort of. It was never finished. Ran out of money or somethin'. It's little more than a tower."

"Does it overlook the Dead Sea?" Jackson asked.

"Naw. Overlooks nuthin' but rock and sand."

"So it does exist, yeah?" Ian asked.

"It exists. A dozen kilometers into Jordan, a ways south of here."

"I thought you said it was a legend."

Asher glared at Jackson. "The part about the Crusaders is legend." He shook his head. "They was going to build it to honor their leader or somethin'. I don't know."

"Who might?" Joel asked.

"I don't know what Eli told you, but I'm no historian. Not when it comes to a thousand years ago. I told you what I know of the legend, such as it is." He shook his head. "You want somethin' more, you're in the wrong place."

They thanked him for his time (and poor marksmanship, Jackson added with a grin) and trudged back to the car. Twelve kilometers into Jordan was an incomplete castle that didn't overlook the Dead Sea and may or may not have been started by Crusaders, according to a crusty old man who lived in the desert and apparently did little but read and shoot at visitors. They filed the information away into Team Joel's collective memory bank, but none of the three saw how it was relevant to their current line of investigation.

As they descended into the Jordan Rift Valley, the setting sun cast long shadows over the mountain ridges. It was beautiful, and as Jackson thought about some of the history of the region—both ancient and recent—it was also eerie. Adding to the effect was an increase of haze that turned the sun and the entire western sky orange as they returned to the Royal Palms.

In addition to a poolside bar/cantina and a casual café, the hotel also boasted a five-star fine dining establishment on the third floor, high enough to have a view of the Dead Sea. Team Joel dined on a potpourri of seafood while watching the last vestiges of daylight play out over the tranquil surface of the sea. Joel reported on the meeting with Asher, and Ramón announced his and Cara's findings at Masada and updated them on his progress with UNESCO. So far, he had not yet garnered permission for Team Joel to spend the night atop the fortress, but he said it was promising. He winked, which Cara said meant he was sweet-talking some woman and it was in the bag. Even if they couldn't get permission to camp out, Joel said they would at least visit Masada the next day—weather permitting—and scope it out. Who knew, maybe they could find 'the arrow's mark' at midday. Rich's nap had been visionless, and Maggie and Aliana had relaxed in the room before taking a stroll around the pool and spa, and they dropped several hints while describing its numerous amenities. Joel said if they could squeeze in time, it was on him. After all of their work and travel and danger, they deserved it.

Speaking of danger, they had a brief discussion about safety. Whoever it was that was tailing them—Interpol, the *Chevaliers Calvaire*, anyone else— seemed to be able to find them wherever they went, and there was no good way for eight people to travel inconspicuously. In addition to being followed, they had been run off the road leaving Philippe's place and had suffered a break-in at their hotel in Kavala. Plus there was the incident at the market in Jerusalem. Regardless of the motive of the attackers, it was Team Joel's third brush with danger since embarking on the search. Short of giving up, they all agreed the best they could do was keep a watchful eye out, anticipating more trouble.

Something about the desert beckoned Jackson, and he decided to walk off his dinner by strolling down toward the shore of the Dead Sea. He'd felt the same thing in Las Vegas and out in the Mojave before things there had gone terribly wrong. Something about the openness, the dry air—it crackled with intensity that, ironically given the location, made him feel more alive. Considering the history of the area, the feeling was only magnified.

"I'm not sure this is safe, out walking in the dark alone."

He turned to see Maggie and acknowledged her with a nod and a smile. "How are you holding up?" he asked.

"I'm fine. Really."

He nodded. "Okay, good."

"I never did thank you," she said. "For coming to my rescue."

"No, but you fawned over Ian, so I just assumed vicarious thanks from that."

She punched his shoulder, and he winced. "Ah. Bad shoulder."

"Sorry."

He grinned, knowing she had known, and thus pulled the punch.

They walked in silence down to the edge of the Dead Sea. Jackson had expected a sulfur smell, but the only aroma was from the grill at the poolside cantina. Night had fallen, and a crescent moon was low on the horizon, its light reflecting off the otherwise dark water that lapped quietly against the shore. It all seemed so out of place, a tourist haven in Israel. Religious pilgrims and history seekers he could understand, but why go chillax in the Middle East when the Caribbean had all the allure, minus the potential for dirty bombs?

"But seriously, Jack, I do want to thank you. It's nice having someone you can always fall back on."

He shrugged. "I didn't do anything anybody else wouldn't have."

"I don't know about that. I don't think a lot of people would have launched themselves into a fray with three tough guys like that."

"Not for a stranger, maybe. But I didn't go through everything in Mexico and New York just to let you die in the streets of Jerusalem."

"At any rate, thank you," she said, leaning in to give him a quick kiss on the cheek.

"You're welcome, Maggie. Although, you could do your part too."

She frowned. "How do you mean?"

"I mean, the damsel in distress isn't supposed to be a capable brunette. She's supposed to have long blond hair and fluttering eyelashes."

"Oh, you mean like that lady nurse friend of yours?"

"I'm not entirely certain who you mean."

She slugged him in the shoulder again, this time not pulling her punch.

"Agh. Are you talking about Sam?"

"Is she more your type?"

"She doesn't have fluttering eyelashes."

"You didn't answer my question."

"Sam's just a friend."

Maggie nodded. "You mean like I'm just a friend?"

"Did I say that?"

She stared at him.

"Why, are you jealous?"

"Oh, like you weren't about to ask if Ian got a kiss on the cheek too?"

"In fact, I was."

"I kissed him full on the lips."

"Taste like whiskey?"

"Milk chocolate," Maggie said as if sampling an elegant dessert.

"I prefer dark. And you know, I took out two of the guys to his one."

"You want another kiss?"

He shrugged. "I'll just go to Aliana otherwise."

Maggie drew back to punch him again but stopped just short of making contact. He winced anyhow. She smiled. "You know for a conservative, Bible-believing Christian, you sure do well with the ladies."

"Not that well, apparently," he said, rubbing his cheek.

"Uh-huh. I'm going in. Good night, Jackson."

"Good night, Maggie."

Leaving him with a playful grin, she turned and headed back inside. Jackson sighed to himself as he continued strolling, wondering just how suspicious of Sam and him Maggie really was.

Chapter Thirty-One

Tuesday, February 19
10:42 a.m.

"PICTURE A DIAMOND-SHAPED cliff," Ramón said over a light brunch Tuesday. "Herod's Palace is at the northern tip of the diamond. Most of the storehouses, residences, bathhouses, and the like were in the Northern Complex. There's also a Western Palace with more of the same, about where the western point of the diamond would be, only there's no point."

"Then how is it a diamond?" Cara asked.

Ramón ignored her. "Most of the rest is just open rock, with a few cisterns, religious structures, a couple of dwellings. According to Dalia, we can make camp by the Western Palace."

"That our guide, yeah?" Ian asked.

Ramón nodded. "From UNESCO." He had spent the majority of the morning finalizing details with various contacts, and after much cajoling, favor promising and cashing in, and perhaps some money changing hands, Team Joel had been granted permission to spend the night atop Masada, with a UNESCO guide. They were meeting said guide at the Masada Visitor Center at the base of the mountain at one. There was also a museum, which Ramón and Cara both recommended after their visit the day before. If nothing else, it would provide them some context.

From there, they'd have three options for reaching the summit. From the west, a moderate climb up the same ramp the Romans had used to storm the fortress two millennia earlier was still an option, although accessing it would require a long drive around to the west side of Masada. Coming from the east, from the visitor center, they could either climb the serpentine Snake Path or ride a tramway thirteen hundred feet to the summit. Joel mused for a few moments about the authenticity and historical appreciation that could be gained by climbing the Snake Path—especially since it was apparently referenced on the gold cross piece of the "Holy Trinity." But for the sake of time and physical stamina, he settled on the tramway, which departed every half hour until four. That would give them several hours of sunlight with which to examine the surface of Masada and, hopefully, identify the spot from which to look for '*the arrow's mark*' at dawn.

Joel, Ian, and Aliana had spent the morning purchasing supplies—sleeping bags, canteens and plenty of water, non-perishable food, firewood, and assorted camping gear, all of which were currently stuffed into the back of one of the Mazdas. Cara had performed some mathematical calculations, speculating that the instructions to *"liftest thine eyes at the arrow's mark"* as "darkness begets dawn" meant that the rising sun would create a shadow or somehow illuminate a certain feature. However, given the time of year—September then to February now, the sun's azimuth could be significantly different. She assured the team over fruit and pastries that she had the geometry down so they could adjust on the fly, as need be.

Rich had taken a late-morning nap, and announced that he had experienced a cryptic vision of "trouble on the rocks." Ramón said it sounded like a cheap cocktail. Else a B-Western, Maggie said. Joel calmed the situation by promising the team would exercise caution.

Maggie had spent the morning organizing her notes, filling in some historical research and context, and catching up on news from the past week. That had left Jackson to mull and ponder and hope he could come through in the clutch for the team again. Anticipation at what they might find, excitement about the search, awe at the locale, and fear—both of failure and of potential danger from other treasure seekers—all manifested itself in silence as he ate. Aside from the businesslike reports from various team members, Jackson wasn't alone in the silence. Nor, he imagined, in the strange mix of emotions.

At a quarter after eleven, the team split into two cars and headed into the desert. The morning had dawned clear and a little cool. It had quickly warmed, but the clarity of the air had not been tainted by the previous day's haze. Across the Dead Sea, the mountains of Jordan were crisp and distinct, bland brown against a sharp blue sky. Then there was the view to the west.

Clearly visible from the highway, Masada grew massively as they drew nearer. From the desert floor, the rocky outcropping towered nearly a quarter of a mile high. As it tapered to a point at the northern end, the rock descended in several "steps," upon which Herod had built his palace. Jackson didn't have to climb the mountain to know the palace would have provided the ancient king a magnificent view. Knowing what he did of Herod, it was too bad he hadn't gotten drunk one night and fallen over the wall.

A swirl of sand swept off the desert floor by a warm breeze temporarily blocked the view of the summit as Jackson got out of the car in a parking lot lined by palm trees. They were the only vegetation in sight. The air was hot and dry, and if not for the visitor center and the wires for the tramway ascending to the top of the plateau, Jackson would have felt a thousand miles from anywhere. And about a thousand years back in time.

They had about an hour before they were to meet Dalia, so Team Joel browsed the visitor center and the museum. Jackson found a plaque giving the basic history of Masada, fleshing out the facts Aliana had first presented a few days ago in Kavala. The majority of all known history of the site came from the great Jewish historian Josephus and from archaeological discoveries made in the last sixty years. Jackson also read a few tidbits about the various discoveries and a short bio of Josephus and examined some of the pottery and textiles excavated, as well as a 3-D model of the fortress. For whatever reason, such things always fascinated him.

At one, they met their UNESCO guide, a short, olive-skinned woman named Dalia. UNESCO was a United Nations agency with employees from all over the world, and Dalia looked as much Indian or African as Middle Eastern. Her accent gave nothing away, nor did her manner of dress—a pair of khaki pants, a maroon polo with UNESCO's logo on the left breast, and a khaki UNESCO cap through which was tucked a short ponytail. Jackson decided it didn't really matter where she was from and backtracked to the parking lot to help Ian and Rich with their camping gear.

"Hard to believe this is real, yeah?" Ian said on their way back.

"Been like that for several days now."

They had a tram to themselves, given the size of their party and their extra gear. During the three-minute ride to the top, Dalia laid out some more basic facts about Masada. "The fortress covers approximately fifteen hectares atop the rhomboid-shaped plateau," she said in a voice that would have made her a natural tour guide. "The cliffs on the eastern side tower four hundred meters above the desert floor, while the western cliffs rise to over ninety meters. A casemate wall encircling the fortress stretched over a kilometer in length and was almost four meters high and wide, containing nearly seventy rooms and twenty-seven towers."

"Wow," Rich said.

"Because of its remote location and the arid environment, Masada was largely undisturbed and well-preserved for nearly two thousand years. Due to the lore surrounding the Roman siege and the demise of the Jewish rebels sheltered here, the site was long sought after. It was discovered in 1842, but it wasn't until the 1960s that Masada was excavated by an Israeli archaeologist named Yigael Yadin."

"Did anyone occupy or use the fortress after the siege up until its discovery in 1842?" Joel asked.

"There is a Byzantine church dating to the fifth or sixth century C.E.," Dalia answered. "Other than that, there isn't any evidence that the site was occupied. As you can see," she said, gesturing out the window of the tram, "it is a rather remote location."

When the tram docked at a station built (precariously, it seemed to Jackson) into the side of the cliff, Dalia led them up a covered ramp to the top of the fortress, where they stashed their camping gear. Then she gave them a few minutes to survey the scene.

Never mind the fact that it was elevated a quarter mile above the surrounding terrain, the ruins of a small community were like nothing Jackson had ever seen. Rows and rows of rock walls delineated storerooms. Beyond them, partially crumbled buildings stood where they had centuries ago. Even so, they were remarkably sound structurally, doors and windows still evident. Everything was brown—the color of the surrounding rock—and obviously old. Still, he had to marvel that people without power tools and cranes and CAD software had constructed anything more than hovels, let alone atop a mountain plateau.

Jackson turned slowly, his eyes eventually sweeping down the side of the cliff and across the desert to the Dead Sea, where he spotted the Royal Palms, and then out to the Jordanian desert beyond the sea. On a crisp, clear day, the view was breathtaking. It seemed he could see forever, and once again, he had trouble believing he was really where he was. Across the desert before him was Iraq, a land made familiar to him by its now dead dictator and the wars fought against him during Jackson's lifetime. But more than that, it was the land of the Babylonians, where Daniel and the exiles had been held in captivity, where three brave Hebrews had resisted a tyrannical king and been thrown into a fiery furnace and survived. A land from which a man named Abram had been called long before that. They were stories Jackson had heard his entire life—stories he believed were true. But somehow, being here made them suddenly a little more real.

After giving everyone a few minutes to admire the views, Dalia drew the team's attention to the Snake Path that wound up the east side of the mountain. "Prior to the Roman siege, it was one of only three paths to the top," she said. "Using these paths, an army would have had to advance so slowly that they would have met certain demise. It made Masada nearly impenetrable."

"The fortress was initially built by the Romans, wasn't it?" Cara asked.

"According to the historian Josephus, Masada was initially fortified by the Hasmoneans and then captured by Herod," Dalia answered. "He was the one who built the fortress and palace between 37 and 31 B.C.E."

Cara nodded.

"Masada was used as a Roman garrison until the Jewish rebels, known as the Sicarii, overtook it in 66 C.E.," Dalia said. "Four years later, when the Roman Emperor Titus attacked Jerusalem, he burned the Second Temple. That is when additional Jewish zealots and their families fled to Masada and took refuge here. Almost a thousand men, women, and children."

From their entrance to the fortress on the eastern side, Dalia led them south, showing them the remains of living quarters, barracks, storehouses, a synagogue, and cisterns for collecting and storing rainwater. As they walked, she gave them more history of the siege.

"Three years after the fall of Jerusalem, the Roman Governor Flavius and the Tenth Legion marched on Masada and laid siege to it. The Romans built a circumvallation wall around the fortress as well as a number of legionary camps, which you can still see down on the desert floor. Flavius used Jewish prisoners to construct the ramp against the western wall, a shrewd plan that kept the zealots in Masada from attempting to stop the work, as they didn't want to harm their own countrymen."

"How long did it take?" Joel asked.

"Several months. The Romans were finally able to assail the wall, using a battering ram to break through in the spring of 73 or 74."

"And they found everyone had committed suicide, yeah?" Ian asked.

"Technically, only one person committed suicide," Dalia replied. "Ten men were selected by lot to kill all the rest by dagger, and then one was chosen to kill all the others. That last remaining survivor then took his own life."

"How gruesome," Maggie said.

"They also burned almost everything, except the storehouses of food. They wanted it clear to the Romans that they had not killed themselves because of a lack of provisions."

"Did they record all this somehow?" Maggie asked.

"No. Josephus wrote the account as it was passed down to him by two surviving women. According to Josephus, they survived by hiding—along with five children—in a cistern while the massacre was carried out. Josephus, who had become a Roman citizen, recorded that the Roman soldiers took no pleasure in the death of the zealots and actually admired their courage."

Dalia paused in front of stairs leading down to a small cistern. She explained it was a ritual bath, known as a *mikveh*. The next stop was a partially restored thermal bath, a first-century spa. The restoration showed stages of construction, from support pillars to the stucco finishing. Once again, Jackson marveled at the building prowess of what he considered primitive people.

They continued on their tour, with Dalia highlighting some of the artifacts that had been excavated, in some instances repeating what they had already seen in the museum. In addition to shards of pottery, weapons, and textiles, Yigael Yadin's team had found foodstuffs—including a two thousand-year-old seed that was successfully germinated into a date plant—and a number of coins dating back to the first century.

"Eleven *ostraca* were also found," Dalia explained.

"A what?" Jackson asked.

"*Ostraca*. Plural of *ostracon*, which is a piece of pottery or stone with writing that helps archaeologists determine the date the piece was from. The *ostraca* each contained a single name, including one that read 'ben Ya'ir.' Eleazar ben Ya'ir was the leader of the zealots taking refuge at Masada, so it is speculated that the other ten names were the ten men elected to carry out the massacre, and ben Ya'ir was the one who executed them before committing suicide."

Even with the sun beating down on them, Jackson felt a chill in the air as he contemplated what must have gone through the minds of the Jewish men, women, and children atop the mountain as they realized the Roman army's victory was inevitable. As if she could read his mind, Dalia said, "Eleazar ben Ya'ir apparently issued several very convincing speeches to persuade his fellow countrymen to agree to the plan. He said that a glorious death was better than a life of infamy."

"Do you disagree?" Joel asked, no doubt picking up on the change in tone in Dalia's voice.

"Like many Israelis, I am conflicted."

"You're Israeli?" he asked.

"I am half Israeli, one-quarter Egyptian, and one-quarter Jordanian," she said. They were on the west side of the fortress, and they approached the wall so that she could point out the ramp of rocks and earth the Romans had built using Jewish slaves. Crude, especially after all the years, it was also effective.

"To further answer your question," Dalia said as they stood overlooking the ramp, "there are two ways to look at the zealots' decision. On one hand, they made a heroic stand against the invading Romans. But they did take their own lives—call it mass suicide or approved murder. In either case, Jewish law forbade such an action. I am only glad I am not compelled to make such a choice on my own."

Another tour group moved into their area, this one comprised of old Japanese folks all complaining about the heat. Jackson didn't speak Japanese, but some things just translated all languages. The floppy hats, umbrellas, and chugging of bottled water were also a pretty good indicator.

Dalia led Team Joel past several more dwellings to Herod's Palace. A private, elaborate residence on the northern end of Masada, the palace consisted of three terraces on three different levels, each connected by a staircase cut out of the rock. The highest terrace had been Herod's living quarters, with the lower two reserved for relaxation and entertainment. They contained a private bathhouse, covered courtyards, and stunning views in the late afternoon sun. Dalia explained that in the heyday of Herod the Great, the palace would have boasted mosaic paved floors, ornate columns, and marble frescos on the walls. Some had been restored or recreated, but most of the ruins showed their age.

"It was here that archaeologists found the skeletal remains of a man, woman, and child," Dalia explained. "It's unknown if they were Jewish zealots who died prior to Roman occupation, Romans whom the zealots captured, or Romans who took over after the death of the zealots. Twenty-five other bodies dating to the time of the revolt were found in a cave at the base of the cliff. Again, it's unknown if they were Jewish or Roman."

As they climbed back up, she informed them that the former chief of staff of the Israel Defense Forces had at one time held a swearing-in ceremony here for soldiers who had completed their basic training. They would climb the Snake Path at night for a torchlight ceremony atop the aged fortress.

"The ceremony would commence," Dalia said as they reached a large Israeli flag flying over the eastern wall of the fortress, "with them taking the oath, 'Masada shall not fall again.'"

After thanking her for the tour and all the information—as well as for accompanying them overnight—Joel asked about some of the phrases on the gold cross and gold chest. Aside from the obvious reference to the Snake Path, Dalia had never heard of a reference to the Dead Sea as bloody, nor did she know anything about "*the arrow's mark*." Seeing as how they still had a fair amount of daylight remaining, Joel suggested the team split up and search for any possible locations that could meet that qualification.

Jackson went with Rich, Cara, and Ramón, and they worked their way south from the flag, along the eastern edge of the fortress. There wasn't much to see, other than a few old dwellings and storehouses, and the old casemate wall largely blocked their view of anything that might resemble "*the arrow's mark*." While ignoring Cara's complaints about being relegated to the "B-team" and a petty argument between Rich and Ramón, Jackson pondered the words on the gold cross and inside the chest yet again.

Ascend to the place from which thou canst look upon the bloody sea of death and the way of the serpent, and from whence true understanding of the Father will serve as thy guide.

As darkness begets dawn, thou wilt findeth the light whence thou liftest thine eyes at the arrow's mark.

They were too ambiguous. Team Joel could look upon the Dead Sea and the Snake Path from almost anywhere on the eastern side of Masada. Was that it—was simply being on Masada enough, sufficient that "*true understanding of the Father*" would guide them? If so, didn't that mean the so-called "*arrow's mark*" would have to be obvious?

They paused at the southern gate, halfway between the eastern point of the "diamond" and the southern tip of Masada. It provided Jackson a view of the salt evaporation ponds, and he looked for an arrow. The shape of the Dead Sea? It had changed too much over the centuries. The mountains of Jordan? None of them resembled an arrow any more than any other mountain. Masada itself? It was shaped like an arrowhead, at least if a guy used his imagination. Did it point at something?

"Cara, can I borrow your tablet?"

"What for?"

"Just a theory."

She pulled it from a small bag over her shoulder. "Good luck seeing anything with this ridiculous glare."

There was no Wi-Fi atop the fortress, but with Cara's help, he was able to pull up satellite footage of the area she had saved on her hard drive. "What are you looking for?" she asked.

"I'll let you know if I find it."

"Whatevs."

They had reached the southern tip of the fortress, and started back as he scanned the tablet. As far as he could tell, none of the protuberances of the rock mesa on which Masada was built pointed at anything. Sure, if he tracked a line to Russia or somewhere, he'd probably hit something of note, but that couldn't have been what the Knights Calvary had in mind. And if they meant some indistinct rock formation, hidden cave, or some other feature out in the desert, identifying it would be pure luck. Oh well, it had been an—

"Look up," Ramón said, and Jackson immediately lifted his eyes from the tablet to the sky, expecting in that instant anything from an Israeli fighter jet heading out to bomb Tehran to a crow about to drop a deuce. Instead, he bumped into several members of the very hot Japanese crowd. Muttering apologies, he stumbled through them.

"Walk much?" Cara asked.

"I warned you," Ramón said.

"You did. Than . . . ks."

"What, heat stroke?" Cara asked.

"No. . . . No, I think . . . I think I may have just figured out where we're supposed to watch the sunrise."

Chapter Thirty-Two

6:40 p.m.

ALONG WITH THEIR guide from UNESCO, Dalia, the eight members of Team Joel sat around a small fire eating jerky, cheese, pita bread, and dried fruit. They had made camp on the southeast corner of the Western Palace, near the center of Masada. Darkness had fallen an hour ago, and with it, the temperatures. It would get down into the low fifties or perhaps even the forties, Dalia said. Fortunately, the team had packed warm clothes and purchased thermal sleeping bags. Joel's AmEx bill must have been huge.

Before sunset, the team had joined up, and Jackson had shared the theory he had "stumbled" upon. The message on the gold cross said to overlook the Dead Sea and the Snake Path, which didn't do much as far as narrowing down locations atop Masada. But the inscription inside the chest had said to "*liftest thine eyes*," or look up. Depending on how one interpreted eight hundred-year-old translated words, that could mean to go to where the arrow's mark pointed and look up, or to look up from below toward the arrow's mark. Or both, Jackson had said, drawing seven "get to the point" looks from Team Joel.

"Where's the one place on Masada where we could both look down at the Dead Sea and the Snake path and look up at some feature?" Jackson had asked as the sun sunk into the western sky.

"The Northern Palace," Joel said.

"I didn't see an arrow's mark when we were down there, but I have to admit I wasn't looking too thoroughly."

"Aye, and it wasn't dawn, yeah?"

"Which part of the palace?" Ramón asked. "The middle or lowest?"

"We check both," Jackson said.

"Let's do it," Joel said.

"Not to be the declarer of the obvious," Ian said, "but it's still not dawn."

"Let's check it out anyhow."

The team trekked back to the palaces, taking the staircase built into the western cliff face as the last rays of sunlight cast Masada in a brilliant orange and burgundy contrast. When they reached the middle palace, the view was breathtaking. The Dead Sea was a given, but they were also able to view significant portions of the Snake Path. With the eastern cliffs and valley floor in shadow, no geographic features stood out. The same was true at the lower palace, and Joel suggested the team head back up before it got totally dark.

"What time is sunrise again?" he asked.

"Six-sixteen," Cara answered from memory. "Civil twilight is 5:51. The sun will rise at an azimuth of 102 degrees, or twelve degrees south of due east."

"You know if it's going to be a cold winter too?" Jackson asked.

"Just watch your step, gumshoe."

Finished exploring, they had met up with Dalia, who had directed them to their "campsite." As tourists had departed on the final few trams, the loneliness of Masada had taken hold. The darkness drove it home, creating a loneliness like Jackson had never known. Well, without good reason, at least.

After discussing general plans for the morning, the group's conversation over and after dinner revolved around more details of the Roman siege of the fortress and what the mindset of the refugees must have been as they watched the Roman army get closer and closer with their ramp.

"Regardless of whether you agree with their decision or not, it certainly took courage to take lives in such a fashion," Aliana said.

"I'd argue just the opposite, yeah?" Ian said. "Courage would have been fighting back against the Romans."

"And ending up a slave?" Cara asked.

"Aye, possibly."

"And having your wife and children taken into slavery too—or worse?"

Ian shrugged.

"They certainly had conviction," Joel said. "One doesn't give one's life without a solid belief in the reason one's doing so. Whether that's a mass suicide to prevent annihilation at the hands of the Roman army or a soldier going across the globe to fight for his country or a parent sacrificing their life for a child. It takes some serious conviction."

"Or the disciples," Rich said.

Cara frowned at him. "The disciples?"

"All but John were eventually martyred for their faith," he said. "It's one of the strongest arguments for the resurrection of Christ. If it were a hoax, these men who were closest to Christ certainly would have known—would have likely been the perpetrators. And why would they die—gruesomely, one after the other—for advocating something they knew to be false?"

"Who would die for a lie?" Jackson said.

Rich nodded.

"Death brings a lot of things into clarity," Joel said. "Like what is true and what is important. History is replete with examples of just that. And we're sitting on one of them."

"This is getting morbid, yeah?" Ian said. He reached for some M&M's, but his bag was empty, and he mumbled something Gaelic under his breath. He got up and built up the fire, using wood packed in for just such a purpose.

Joel broke out some dry cookies for dessert, then sat back and smiled. "You know, this is my favorite part of the search."

"What's that?" Maggie asked.

"When we're almost to the payoff."

"Are we almost to the payoff?" Cara asked.

"Wrong word," Joel said. "Call it the climax. We've followed the clues to their extent, and tomorrow morning is the tipping point, where all of our research and hard work comes to fruition."

"Or craps out," Ian said.

"Sometimes," Joel answered. "But still, I can feel the excitement in the air. It's my thrill of the hunt."

"I prefer the thrill of spending the treasure, yeah?"

"You all are forgetting we're not seeking a typical treasure," Cara said.

"That's our assumption," Joel said, "but we don't really know what the treasure is."

As they spoke, Dalia listened intently. Ramón had had to divulge their purpose for coming to Masada in order to get permission to camp there. So she knew what they were after. Joel wasn't worried.

"Even if it is a letter or a diary," Aliana said, "it may be accompanied by other pieces. Artifacts, ornate chests or cases, etcetera and so forth. For me, that is the thrill—finally discovering exactly what it is we are discovering, if that makes sense."

"Perfect sense," Jackson said.

"What about you?" Joel asked, looking his way. "You must experience something like this when you're close to solving a case?"

He shrugged. "This is usually the part where I have to plug a guy, so I'm glad to be here munching on stale cookies."

Maggie rolled her eyes.

"How about you?" Ian asked. "Is there a thrill right before a story goes to print?"

"No. When it comes together. I have my facts, I know the direction I want to go, I may even start writing. But there's always a time when things click, when everything seems to lock into place. That's when I make hay."

"Aye, sort of like that moment when Cara hacks through a firewall and has access to all a server's files."

"I don't hack."

"Not what you told me," Jackson said.

"I never admitted to hacking anything."

"Implying you have hacked."

"What?"

"You didn't say you never hacked; you said you never admitted to hacking."

"Because you accused me of hacking."

"Maybe it's the language barrier, yeah, what with Cara being Canadian."

"Oh you should talk," she said. "'Aye, nae, bonnie, wee, havers, fankle.'"

"I've never said 'havers.'"

"The only word you can pronounce properly is M&M's. Have you ever gone a day without chugging a pack?"

"Na'er, ya crabbit lass."

Everyone laughed at Ian's over the top Scottish accent. The mood changed from the earlier somberness as the conversation turned to more of Team Joel's past exploits. Jackson was amazed at the number of places they had been and adventures they had experienced. Ian also wove in some of his tales from his time in the British Army, all told in his unique manner.

They slowly settled in, the strenuous hiking around Masada and the heat of the afternoon having sapped their strength. They also had an early wake-up call—Joel wanted to have team members on each of the lower two levels of the palace, as well as atop Masada at multiple locations by civil twilight—and Joel made sure several people had alarms set. They did not have tents and arranged their sleeping bags around the fire. Already, a chill was in the air, and Jackson doubted the fire would last all night. So too, apparently, did Rich, as he broke out a small propane heater, which he set up several feet from his head, and well away from the fire. He was mocked mercilessly but didn't back down.

Jackson couldn't sleep. Maybe it was the temperature contrast between his warm body and cool head. Maybe it was the excitement of the search at dawn. Maybe it was the history surrounding his camping site. Or maybe it was the hard rock beneath his warm but not overly comfortable sleeping bag.

He drifted in and out of consciousness a few times, usually a sign that he was about to zonk out for good. But for whatever reason, he woke alertly from a light sleep in which he'd dreamt he was a Roman soldier about to be flogged for refusing to wear the legion's absurd skirt-and-sandal uniform. Realizing he was wide awake—and coming to full realization that it had only been a horrid nightmare—Jackson decided to get up and take a walk. He had no idea what time it was, other than darkest night, and didn't have the gumption to dig for his phone to find out.

The mountaintop fortress was several hundred feet wide, and, careful not to wake anyone else, Jackson set out for the eastern wall. The moon was high in the sky—it had been just peeking over the casemate wall when they'd settled in for the night—and should provide enough light for him to take in the view of the Dead Sea.

He was right. He entered the "tunnel" through the casemate wall that constituted the Snake Path Gate, two-thirds of the way up the eastern side, and peeked out at the vista. The crescent moon was as pure white as he had ever seen, dappling the water with just enough light to add a hint of distinction to the calm, dark surface of the Dead Sea. The moon was joined by stars like Jackson had never seen, turning an otherwise flat black sky into a depthless speckled background. It was odd, he thought, standing on a place most known for its violent ending, in a part of the world known for its tumult and upheaval and war, that he felt as peaceful as he ever had.

"It is beautiful, is it not?"

He turned to see Aliana emerging from the tunnel, one arm cradling the other as she reached to tuck a loose strand of hair behind her ear.

"Hey," he said. "What are you doing up?"

"The same as you, I suspect. I could not sleep."

He nodded. "Excitement or rocks digging into your back?"

"A little of each," she said with a smile just observable in the moonlight.

"I've been thinking," Jackson said, turning his eyes back out to the horizon, "about what you said the other day, about Americans being in awe of how old other cultures and countries are." He looked back at her. "If it didn't happen after 1776, it's almost as if it didn't happen in our mindset."

"And then you come here . . ."

He nodded.

"It can be overwhelming."

"And I can't explain it," he said. "There's just something about it that's hit me."

"I understand completely. I have been there many times." A grin tugged at her mouth.

"What is it?"

"Nothing," she said looking away. She actually stifled a laugh.

"Now you have to tell me."

"I spent a year in the United States back in 2010," she said. "For a few months, I dated a law professor who had pursued his undergraduate education at Auburn University."

"That's why you have an Auburn shirt."

"He bought it for me, and I liked it," she said with a shrug. "Our relationship did not last, as we were two people drifting in too many opposite directions. But while we were dating, he took me to an Auburn football game. I have been to several soccer matches, and the fans in Europe and South America are quite . . . well, fanatical. But it was nothing like I experienced at that stadium. Before the game, they let an eagle soar over the stands and down to the field, and I looked at Michael—my boyfriend—and he had a tear in his eye. I asked him about it after the game, and his explanation and the look on his face were very similar to yours just now. And I always thought it seemed incredibly adolescent to have such an emotional reaction to a sporting event."

Jackson nodded.

Her eyes widened. "You're not an obsessive sports fan, are you?"

"Only when it comes to USC."

"I see."

"And the Dodgers."

She nodded.

"Lakers." He waved his hand back and forth. "Rams, if they ever come back to . . ."

Aliana leaned forward. "What is it?"

He blinked as he looked down. "I could swear I just saw someone walking on the path down below."

She squinted into the darkness, and he studied the terrain, looking for movement. Even in the moonlight, it was hard to see much, but the zigzagging Snake Path seemed vacant.

"Probably just my imagination," he said.

"That or an ibex. I saw one this afternoon."

He nodded. "Yeah. Anyhow, to answer your question, I am a somewhat adolescent, obsessive sports fan."

"I am sorry," she said with a sheepish smile. "I did not mean to offend you."

"Don't worry. You didn't."

"Michael said football is like religion in the South."

"That's what I've heard."

She sighed. "Sometimes I wish religion was more like football."

"How so?"

"A couple of years ago, I heard about a giant tornado that went through Alabama, very close to the University of Alabama. There was a lot of destruction, as you can imagine, and a large number of Auburn players and fans went to help the students and fans of their biggest football rival. Sports was just a side note to what really mattered."

Jackson nodded. "I get where you're coming from, but what kind of religion would we have if we set it aside for something bigger?"

"You do not believe in people coming together, in finding common ground and unifying for a greater purpose?"

"I believe in not going to war or persecuting or harassing each other because we disagree. But religion—at least, as far as I'm concerned, Christianity—isn't about getting along and not hurting feelings."

"What is it about?" she asked.

"Truth," he said. "We obviously disagree on what that truth is, but neither of us is willing to set aside our belief, even if that means offending one another."

"But we have disagreed peaceably."

He nodded. "That's the hard part. As a Christian, I can't sacrifice the truth in the name of being nice or loving others. But I also can't sacrifice love for the sake of the truth. It's not an easy balance."

"From where I stand, you walk the tightrope quite well."

He winked at her. "Thanks, Ali."

She smiled in return.

"Now, if you'd shown up wearing a UCLA shirt the other day . . ."

She smiled again, and he turned his gaze back out to the view of the Dead Sea and the distant Jordanian mountains. He took a deep breath, inhaling the incredibly fresh and dry air.

"I think I am going to head back," she said, "try to get some . . . slee—"

"What is it?" he asked.

She held a finger to her mouth, then dropped to a crouch, reaching for his shoulder. He too crouched.

"Alia—"

She extended a finger, pointing down toward the Snake Path. At first, Jackson saw nothing but rocks and crags. Then his eyes caught a flicker of movement, a person. Clad head to toe in black, he was slowly but steadily climbing the path.

Another movement drew Jackson's eyes, and he saw a second figure a dozen paces behind the first. Then a third. He turned slightly on the path, and a brief ray of moonlight reflected off something long and metallic.

Jackson turned to Aliana. "Go get Ian. Now."

She nodded and hurried back toward their camp while Jackson prostrated himself and scanned the terrain for more black-clad figures. He spotted a total of six, maybe seven, slowly working their way up the Snake Path.

Ian and Aliana were back in a few minutes, and the Scotsman was fully awake. Jackson quickly directed his eyes to the Snake Path, and Ian studied the figures in silence for several long minutes. Then he ducked back into the shadows of the wall and out of sight.

"What do you think?" Aliana asked in a whisper.

"They're not tourists getting a crack on a morning hike, yeah?"

"Then what?"

He looked at Jackson. "You see if they were carrying anything?"

"One looked like he had a rifle."

"A rifle?" Aliana asked.

"Aye, that's what I saw too."

"I can't think of too many reasons for guys in black to be climbing the Snake Path with guns in the middle of the night," Jackson said.

"Aye, especially this night."

"You think they are coming for us?" Aliana asked.

Both men nodded.

"So what do we do?"

"This is a fortress, yeah?" Ian said. "We defend it."

Chapter Thirty-Three

Wednesday, February 20
1:14 a.m.

"DEFEND THE FORTRESS?" Aliana asked, her eyes wide and brows high.

"Aye."

"Defend it how?"

"You have your gun?" Ian asked Jackson.

He shook his head. Ian had provided him with a Jericho 941 pistol, courtesy of Eli Haddad. It was currently sitting on the dresser in his room at the Royal Palms.

Ian cursed under his breath.

"I didn't want to risk it here."

"Okay. Jack, run back to the west gate, see if they're also coming at us from the siege ramp. Meet us at camp."

Jackson nodded and hurried across the open fortress to the western gate, just north of the palace outside which Team Joel was camping. An archway built into a crumbling wall was all that remained of the gate, beyond which were recent man-made steps and a railing leading to the Roman siege ramp. Jackson surveyed it for several minutes and saw nothing—not even his mind playing tricks. Convinced no attack was coming from the west, he hurried back to camp.

Ian and Aliana were just rousing the other six members of their party. In hushed tones, the former Royal Scot took control and explained the situation.

"Is there any way to signal for help?" Joel asked Dalia.

"No. We have no fixed communications."

"Anybody's cell get service?"

While they checked, Ian asked about weapons.

"No," Dalia said. "The only weapons are in the museum."

"I've got fifteen rounds in my pistol, yeah?"

"You have a gun?" she asked.

"Aye."

"Weapons aren't permitted at the site. How—"

"We can discuss that later, yeah? In the meantime, anyone have service?"

A series of negative responses followed.

"Then we're alone. We'll have to make do."

"We can run," Rich said. "Jackson said no one's coming up the west side."

"Run to where?" Ian asked. "We're in the middle of the bloody desert, yeah?"

"We can hide, until daylight."

"At which point we'd still be in the desert."

"But they might not come after us anymore," Aliana said.

"They're climbing a four hundred-meter rock face in the middle of the night," Ian said. "What's to stop them from hunting us down in a barren wasteland?"

"I'm with Ian," Jackson said. "We can either try to fight, or we can try to stall till help arrives."

"Help?" Dalia asked. "What help?"

"When's the first tram arrive?" Ian asked.

"A little after eight."

He nodded. "They'll want to avoid being seen by a crowd, yeah? That gives us . . . better than six and a half hours."

"Okay," Joel said. "What do we do?"

"I'll take up a position on the east wall. I've got fifteen bullets. I might be able to take them all out while they climb."

"In the dark?" Cara asked.

"Worth a shot. Any I kill won't keep coming. Who knows, maybe the rest will be discouraged when they realize we can mount resistance."

"What do the rest of us do?" Rich asked.

"Hide," Ian said. "When they get too close, I'll retreat to that tower, yeah?" He gestured toward the highest point in the fortress, a tower at the southern end of the Northern Complex. "I'll do what I can to take out the rest of them."

"Where would you recommend we hide?" Joel asked.

"Two options. Hardest place to find or farthest place away. Either a cistern or a well or the lower palace."

"That's a dead end," Cara said.

"It's all a dead end."

"I don't like the idea of climbing down the stairs at night," Joel said.

"You have flashlights. Shielded by the rock."

"If it was you, Ian, where would you look first?"

"Depends what I'm here for, but there's seven or eight by my count. I'd form two teams, split north and south and follow the path of least resistance."

"That makes the lower palace the best place," Joel said.

"Aye, unless you have a better idea," he said, looking at Dalia.

She shook her head.

"This is crazy," Ramón said. "Can't we just talk to them?"

"Aye, go for it," Ian said. "It's fifty-fifty you get a word out before they shoot you."

"Who are they?" Cara asked.

"I don't know, and I don't care. But you don't do what they're doing if you don't mean business, and if you don't mean for that business to be carried out without anybody knowing, yeah?"

"We hire Ian for just this sort of contingency," Joel said. "Let's follow his lead."

"Aye, thank you."

"How much time do we have?"

"Eight to ten minutes, maybe. Twelve max."

"Then let's get moving."

"You really think you can take them all out with fifteen bullets?" Jackson asked as Joel organized several members of the team to gather basic provisions.

"I'll do my best."

"Not what I asked."

Ian stared at him. "Odds are, no. Not in the dark. Not if they're skilled. I figure I can get off two shots before they return fire."

"Okay. Can you spare a bullet or two?"

Ian frowned. "You gonna throw them with your bare hands?"

"I need the powder."

"For what?"

"If we're all hiding, with the intent of stalling, and if you can't stop them, I want to slow them down a little."

"What do you have in mind?" Joel asked, drifting over.

"Technical term is booby-trap."

Joel didn't question him. "What can I do?"

"Get everybody to safety. Recess as far back as you can, and arm yourselves with rocks or whatever you can find. If Ian or I join you, we'll whistle like a bird first, so you don't smash us in the head."

"Okay. You need help?"

"I could use one more man, but I don't want to force anybody to stay."

"I'll stay," Maggie said.

"No," Jackson said. "You don't even know what you're staying for."

"You're staying, and I'm staying, and we don't have time to argue."

He sighed. "Okay. Joel, get moving. Maggie, get all our gear inside the palace. Straight in, second door on the right," he said, remembering the layout from brief exploration born of curiosity earlier. The palace was nothing more than old stone walls, partially restored, but it provided a confined space with four walls, albeit no roof. "Arrange the sleeping bags like we're there, stuff them with whatever you can to make them look full."

She didn't hesitate to begin working.

"You know what you're doing, yeah?" Ian said, ejecting the magazine from his gun and removing two bullets for Jackson.

"I know what I'm trying."

"Here," Ian said, handing him a pocketknife.

"Thanks."

"Be careful."

"You too, man. Shoot straight."

"Aye," he said, turning and hurrying toward the Snake Path Gate. Joel had herded Rich, Cara, Aliana, Ramón, and Dalia together, and they reluctantly headed for the lower terrace of the Northern Palace. Maggie was frantically dragging camping gear into the Western Palace, leaving Jackson with two bullets from Ian. He stuffed them and the pocketknife in his pocket and got to work.

He pried his right shoe off with his left, then ripped off his sock. Tearing at the hem, he began to unravel the string, continuing until he had several lengths each about six feet long. He then tied those lengths together, forming a string of some twenty to twenty-five feet. Stepping back into his shoe and quickly tightening it, he rummaged around in one of the team member's backpacks until he found a book of matches. He stuffed them in his pocket with the string, then turned off Rich's propane heater and removed the small cylinder of propane. By now, at least five minutes had elapsed, and Maggie had taken all but the last two packs inside.

"Let's go," Jackson said, following her in, each taking a pack.

"What are you doing?"

"Set those in the corner," he said as they ducked into the room he had indicated in the palace, a small, windowless room about a dozen feet by fifteen feet. Its only entrance was the narrow, low door. "Okay, good. Reorient these two bags so they can't see immediately that they're empty," he said as he dropped to the ground. He set the can of propane down on the ground next to the outside rock wall of the room, then began to dig through one of the backpacks.

"Jack, what are you doing?" Maggie asked again. "A Molotov cocktail?"

"Wrong part of the world. Around here, they call it an IED." He pulled several tin coffee mugs from the backpack. "You done with the bags?"

"Yeah."

"Go find me a heavy, flat rock."

"What?"

"Hurry."

She did, and while she was gone, he removed all the silverware and hit the motherlode—four wine glasses and four ceramic plates that had been part of a cheap picnic set someone had purchased that morning. Overdoing the one-night roughing it camping, but so be it. Jackson unwrapped the instructions and warnings that had come with Rich's heater and tore them into several pieces. He wrapped them around the nozzle end of the propane can, forming a funnel of sorts. With that facing out on the rock surface, he loosely piled the glasses, plates, mugs, and silverware on top of the can, then draped a spare T-shirt over it all.

Maggie returned, carrying several rocks. "Will these work?" she asked.

"Yeah. Still quiet out there?"

"Disturbingly so."

"I guess if Ian isn't shooting yet . . ."

"Yeah. You thi—"

Two gunshots interrupted her, followed by two more and then a staccato burst of return fire.

"Jack!"

"I know, I know." He handed her his sock and told her to tear off several more strings.

"What?"

"Just do it," he said, taking out Ian's knife and the bullets. It took him a minute to pry the bullet loose from the case, exposing the powder. Twice more a single gunshot was followed by return bursts. "Automatic weapons," Jackson said.

"Great."

He stuck a flashlight in his mouth and very carefully poured the powder from one bullet into the tip of the funnel and out onto the rock surface in a continual line. Setting the other bullet aside, he took out the matchbook and removed all the matches. He then folded the cardboard matchbook in half, with the striking surface on the inside. He inserted the matches back into it, securing it with one of the strings Maggie had torn off.

"What . . . ?"

Jackson removed his long string and tied one end to the end of the matches, making sure it was secure. He then placed his makeshift fuse an inch from the end of the powder trail and used Maggie's rock to pin the far end of the matchbook to the ground.

"You pull the string and the matches slide across the striker," Maggie said.

"In theory." He poured the powder from the second bullet around the matchbook and up to the end of the powder line.

"It ignites, hits the propane . . ."

"And shrapnel goes everywhere," he said. "Or not. I'm kind of making up the science as I go."

"Seems logical. How do you pull the string?"

"I hide in the room across the hall."

"Are you crazy?"

"Maybe. I'm going to string this out. Very carefully brush dirt over it."

"Jack, no. There has to be a better way."

"No time to argue, Mags." He unscrewed the nozzle on the propane cylinder a fraction so that a minuscule amount of the gas would continue leaking out. Next, he played out his string, careful to avoid sleeping bags and using the doorpost of the room as a "pulley" and the doorpost of the room across the hall as a second. His string was just long enough to reach to a second doorway that led out of that room to a second hall branching west, toward the cliffs.

"And where do I go?" Maggie asked.

"Down the siege ramp."

"What?"

"There are two bottles of water in that pack in there. You go now, you can make it around the southern end, get back to the visitor center and get help."

"I thought running into the desert was a bad plan."

"It is, for all of us. But you're one person. And I don't want something to happen to you."

"That's a warm sentiment, Jack, but—"

"Look, I haven't heard a gunshot in several minutes. Which means Ian has either been shot or has retreated to high ground, meaning they're almost upon us. If you don't go now, you won't make it, and if he doesn't stop them and this doesn't stop them, we've got nothing left, and we've got nowhere to hide."

"Then I had better remember my Tae Bo training, because I am not leaving you, Jack."

He sighed. "If we get out of this, Maggie . . ."

"Yeah?"

"I am never taking you overseas again."

She leaned in and kissed the side of his head.

"Get down," he said. "They could come from the south, north, or straight across. We hide here in the corner, we're as concealed as we can be."

Four more shots sounded in rapid succession, followed by another burst. Ian was down to three bullets if Jackson was counting right.

A minute passed. Then came two prolonged bursts of gunfire, separated by a pause of fewer than thirty seconds.

"They're moving," Jackson whispered. "Cover fire."

Ian was in the tower. The Snake Path Gate was east and a little south of it. Due south of the tower and due west of the gate was the barracks. Slightly southwest of it was the old Byzantine church. Southwest of it, the Western Palace. Jackson wasn't positive, but depending on where Ian was in the tower, his line of sight might be restricted, enabling the attackers to reach the church and even the palace.

Another burst a few minutes later, then a few more shots in a steady rhythm. Jackson counted ten, sounding loud and close—like at the entrance to the palace. Maggie grabbed his arm before he could grab hers. He wound the end of the string around his finger, holding it taut. A second later, he heard muffled voices and footsteps, then saw a flashlight beam reflecting off the rock walls.

Jackson exhaled quietly, forcing himself to breathe and wait, hoping his heartbeat wasn't audible.

The flashlight beam turned into their room and played off the far wall. Even though they were hidden from anyone in the hall, Jackson shrunk further into the corner, hoping that the moonlight that penetrated the roofless palace wasn't as bright to the intruders as it was to his eyes, which had grown accustomed to the darkness, and that the intruders weren't wearing night-vision goggles. If it was or if they were, he and Maggie would be spotted the instant someone stepped into the room.

But no one did, and the light turned the other way. As it did, an excited voice shouted in what sounded to Jackson like French. He heard more footsteps, more excited words. Maggie dug her fingers into his arm.

He yanked the string.

Nothing happened at first, and he feared his Mousetrap had failed. Then he heard an excited voice, almost a shout. Rushing feet. Then their weapons opened fire.

The boom was more of a really loud pop, followed by soft clinking sounds as Jackson's handmade shrapnel ricocheted off the walls.

He hadn't told Maggie about the second part of his plan. Hearing no footsteps and seeing no movement of flashlight beams, Jackson pushed himself up, clutching a rock with his right hand. Eyes wary, he hurried into the hallway and into the room.

Several small fires burned in the corner. One man in black lay against the left wall, apparently unconscious, his head sagged against his shoulder and next to the rock wall. Another was on hands and knees to Jackson's right. A rolling flashlight and flames illuminated several shards of glass and what looked like the tine of a fork sticking out of his bloody right leg. But he was clearly conscious, and when he saw Jackson, he made to raise his rifle.

Jackson didn't give him a chance. He swept his leg at the gun, kicking it aside before it could be brought to fire. He then quickly balanced himself and swung the rock in his hand down at the man's head. It was a direct hit, and the thud of rock on bone was sickening to Jackson. Immediately a stream of blood gushed out of the man's head and he slumped to the ground, unconscious if not dead.

Jackson pried the gun from his hand and examined it. Sleek, black, with a huge magazine, it was some model he had never seen. It was the sort of weapon gun control advocates feared every rifle with a scope magically became, but in reality, was a gun almost nobody outside of military or law enforcement could get their hands on. At least, not in the States.

Jackson turned to check on the other man and found that he wasn't just unconscious, but hemorrhaging blood from a gaping gash in his neck. Not a doctor by any means, Jackson could recognize a slit carotid artery and knew the man was on his way out if not already gone.

He doubted the man he'd knocked out would recover anytime soon, but he couldn't take a chance—not with Maggie still in hiding and additional attackers unaccounted for. He quickly frisked him, finding an extra magazine for the rifle, a throwaway gun, a tactical knife, and a walkie-talkie. No cuffs or zip ties. The other man—Jackson felt for a pulse this time, and got nothing—had the exact same items on him. Clearly, they hadn't come to take prisoners.

They did have black combat boots, and Jackson made haste in untying and removing them from the man he'd knocked out. His fingers flying, he yanked out the laces, themselves fairly sturdy. Then he rolled the man over onto his stomach. He pulled back his left arm and used the laces from one boot to bind the man's left wrist to his right ankle. He then repeated the procedure with his right wrist and left ankle, effectively hog-tying him. He wasn't sure how much resistance the laces could endure, but even if the man regained consciousness—he hadn't so much as stirred yet—he wasn't in a position to generate a lot of leverage. Short of mashing his head with the rock a few more times, it was all Jackson could do.

Loading up all the confiscated equipment, he returned to Maggie.

"What happened?" she asked breathlessly.

"Two down," he reported.

"What took so long?"

"I had to tie one of them up. Here." He handed her one of the pistols, some sleek little European model.

"Tie one? What about the other? Jack, I've never shot a gun."

"And you won't have to. But if you do, hold it like this," he said, wrapping her fingers in a proper grip. "Remove the safety here, then aim for center mass and don't stop squeezing. Here, come with me."

"Where . . . ?"

He took her hand and led her out into the east-west hall. Using his flashlight in intermittent bursts, he checked out several rooms until he found a small, featureless storeroom with only one entrance. It was empty and dark. "Okay, Mags, wait here."

"Wait? Wait for what?"

"There are still more of them out there, and they could be headed for the rest of the team."

"Jack . . ." She looked down at her gun.

"Don't hesitate."

She shook her head. "What if it's you . . . or Ian?"

"We'll announce ourselves."

"This is crazy."

"Yeah, kind of." He stood.

"Where are you going?"

He hefted the rifle. "Hunting."

Chapter Thirty-Four

1:47 a.m.

"ANY OF YOU Frogs speak English?" Jackson asked into the walkie-talkie several minutes later. "I have what you want. It's by the Snake Path Gate."

He heard nothing but silence in return.

His first order of business had been finding a way to signal to Ian, still presumably in the tower, that he had taken out two baddies and, more importantly, let Ian know that he was now armed and moving about the fortress. He'd hate to take friendly fire.

He could have just shouted, and his voice would have likely carried. But that would have given away his position and clued in the attackers as much as Ian. He'd hatched several ideas, none of which proved fruitful, before realizing the rifle he confiscated had a laser pointer on it. It too risked revealing his location, but not with as great of likelihood as shouting.

Leaving the palace, he'd sneaked to the ruins of the Byzantine church and waited, seeing and hearing nothing. Then he'd aimed his rifle up toward the tower where Ian had taken residence, sending the laser beam through the window and, hopefully, against an interior wall Ian could see while taking cover. After letting it play there for half a minute, he'd repeatedly passed his hand in front of the beam, signaling with Morse code. Surely a former Royal Scot would know Morse, right? He'd sent the message "JM OK. ADVANCING" three times before dropping back down and waiting to see if anyone had picked up on his activity. Then he had crept to the southeast corner of the church and taken shelter behind the ruins of a wall. Figuring he'd rather set a trap than go stalking, he'd hit upon the walkie-talkie. Now to get a response.

"I've killed two more," he said after a minute's pause. "Your numbers are dwindling. I've got enough ammo to go all night, ladies. You want an out, you got it. Take what you want and leave."

Still nothing. Jackson figured it was fifty-fifty they heard his message and took the bait or were sneaking up behind him and ready to send him to eternity.

He waited five more minutes, seeing nothing. He had a line of sight to the top window of the tower and saw nothing from Ian either.

What was going through Maggie's head? Was the rest of Team Joel safe? If so, for how long? Had Ian even survived, or had his fire died out because he'd been shot?

A distinction in the shadows caught Jackson's attention. Two—no, three—figures emerging from the barracks south of the tower. They turned east, toward the barracks' southeast corner, invisible to anyone in the tower. From the corner, however, they'd have to cover about one hundred yards of open, fairly level terrain, during which time they would be visible from the tower.

None of the three looked a hundred feet south, to where Jackson was hidden. He'd hoped to convince them that he was the man in the tower. He left to their imagination how he would have gotten one of their walkie-talkies. But the last place they had seen anyone was the tower, and he wanted their focus there as long as possible.

The trio waited for a beat, and then one of them spun around the corner of the barracks and raked the tower with a torrent of bullets. At the same time, the other two set out for the east wall and the Snake Path, guns drawn.

They never looked south, and Jackson slowly raised up and took aim. He unleashed a stream of fully automatic fire, spent shell casings plinking off the rock as he mowed down the two men. The third man, the one strafing the tower, realized his cover fire was useless and spun around. Before he did, Jackson lowered himself so that he was hidden behind crumbled ruins, and peeked through a crack in the rock.

The third man hesitated for a moment, then set out running for the east wall. Jackson almost felt bad as he rose up again, but he remembered these men had come in the middle of the night with automatic weapons with no intent of offering quarter. He felled the man with a single burst of fire. When the echo died away, the night was ominously silent.

Ian had counted eight men ascending the Snake Path. Jackson had taken out five—three now and two in the palace with his improvised bomb. So how many had Ian taken out while they climbed, or once they reached the open courtyard? The other three? None?

Jackson waited for five minutes to see if there was any additional movement. When nothing stirred, he decided to act. If there were still more attackers, every second that went by was one in which they could find Maggie or the rest of Team Joel. If they were all dead or captured, every second was a heart attack waiting to happen. Either way, Jackson wanted to bring things to a head.

He again drew a bead on the window of the tower and began signaling in Morse code: "5 DOWN. U?"

He was halfway through a second round of signaling when three shrill, distinct whistles sounded. After a pause of twenty seconds, they repeated.

Jackson signaled again: "ALL CLEAR?"

This time, Ian's whistles were a series of short and long sounds, signaling "AYE."

Jackson stood, warily, wondering if they had possibly miscounted, if a second wave had come and would gun them down. He walked slowly and kept his eyes roving until he saw Ian emerge from the Northern Complex. He kept his gun trained on Jackson, who held up both hands, one of them through a strap in the rifle, until Ian could see his face. They approached the fallen bodies of the three who had made a break across the compound. All were gruesomely dead.

"Haven't seen Morse code in decades," Ian said.

"I was afraid the Scots used a different code," Jackson said.

A flicker of a grin crossed Ian's face. "I got two on the path. A third right over there," he said, pointing at a body partially hidden behind a small pile of ruins to Jackson's right.

"You're sure they're dead?"

"Head shots. Aye, I'm sure."

Jackson explained about the two in the palace, and he and Ian went to check on them. As they entered the palace, Jackson called out for Maggie. "We're coming to you," he said.

They first peeked in the room where Jackson had set off the bomb. In the movies, the man he'd tied up would be gone, the shoelaces ominously left behind in a trail of dripping blood. In reality, the man was still there, still bound, still unconscious.

"Fancy yourself a wee bit of a cowboy, yeah?"

"I just kept thinking, 'Masada shall not fall again.'"

Ian grinned. "Aye."

"This way."

They continued to where Jackson had left Maggie. "It's Jackson and Ian. Maggie, set the gun down on the floor."

"Okay," she called a second later, and Jackson aimed the flashlight into the room.

"Are we clear?" Maggie asked, standing with hands twisted in front of her.

"We are," Jackson said, barely getting the words out before she rushed him and nearly knocked him over with a hug. She buried her head into his shoulder, then extended an arm to include Ian as well.

"This is lovely, yeah, but we should get the others."

*   *   *

2:37 a.m.

SHAKEN BUT unhurt, Team Joel congregated in the upper palace, overlooking the lights of the Royal Palms and other resorts along the Dead Sea—so close yet so far away.

While Ian had gone to get Joel, Rich, Cara, Ramón, Aliana, and Dalia, Jackson and Maggie had transported all the camping gear, which was now stacked in a huge pile. Ian had suggested burning it, as a signal fire of sorts, in the hopes that someone would spot it and call for help. Worth a try, and they didn't need it.

All things considered, the team had come through the ordeal well. Maggie, far from a wimp, showed no ill effects of the ordeal. The five members of Team Joel and their guide who had sheltered in the lower palace showed various degrees of shock and relief, but as far as Cara—the resident "medic" could discern—no serious repercussions. The former Royal Scot had never wavered. And Jackson, now an old pro at taking lives to protect the innocent, was processing his most recent killings with something akin to detachment. Maybe it was just too surreal to fully comprehend, or maybe the adrenaline rush out of his body had left him numb.

"You okay?" Cara asked, passing Jackson a water bottle.

"Something like it at least. Thanks." He took several swigs.

"Ian has advised we touch nothing," Joel said. He was visibly shaken, but also composed and in charge. "Once we get the fire going," he said as Rich and Ramón finished arranging the pieces, "we'll shelter until morning or until help arrives. Then, we'll clearly have some explaining to do to the authorities.

What that means for our search for the Calvary Treasure is to be determined, but clearly not the priority right now."

"Are Jack and Ian going to end up in some Mossad black-site prison?" Cara asked.

"No," Joel said. "My first call will be to Rachelle. Our lawyer," he added in Jackson's direction.

"If she needs a co-counsel, I know who to have her call," he said.

"We've been in some sticky situations before. She's worked with Ramón, and I'm confident she can work out any trouble that might arise with the authorities."

"You will also have my testimony," Dalia said. She had been silent up to that point. "You clearly acted to defend us all."

Jackson nodded, hoping whoever in Israel could make his life miserable would see it that way. His experience was a few thousand years old and secondhand, but Jewish authorities didn't always exercise the utmost discretion and judicial prudence.

"Ready to light this?" Rich asked.

"Where's Ian?" Joel asked.

"Getting the prisoner still alive," Ramón said.

"What?"

"He said he'd rather have him here where we can keep an eye on him."

"By us?" Dalia asked.

"We'll keep him elsewhere," Joel said.

"How about just over that railing," Maggie said, nodding at the glass and steel barrier between them and the cliffs.

"Go ahead and light it," Joel said to a waiting Rich.

Using a pack of matches Jackson hadn't used to set off his bomb, he ignited their collection of sleeping bags, backpacks, extra clothes, miscellaneous camping gear, and remaining firewood. In a matter of minutes, it was a raging—if not small and likely short-lived—fire. Whether anyone down below would spot it, recognize it as out of place, and report it was to be determined.

The group sat and watched the fire. If they were like Jackson, they were wondering—as it seemed he had so often in recent months—how all that had transpired had actually transpired. Was he really sitting atop a two millennia-old fortress in the Israel desert, having just dispatched five black-clad assassins who had ascended the cliff face?

Scuffling steps on dirty rock and heavy breathing turned the group's attention to the right, where Ian emerged from the darkness, carrying an unconscious man in a fireman's carry. He dropped him unceremoniously on the smooth stone floor.

"What are you doing?" Rich asked.

Ian took a few deep breaths before answering. "He's the sole survivor, and I think he owes us some answers, yeah?"

"He is unconscious," Aliana said as Ian propped him against a palace wall.

"Aye. But that can be altered." He grabbed a bottle of water, twisted off the cap, and flung the contents at the man's face. He stirred slightly, and Ian dumped the rest of the bottle over his head.

The man's eyes came open, taking a moment to focus. When they did, they settled on Ian's Jericho 941 pistol. "Three bullets left," Ian said. "In case you have any imaginative ideas."

The man looked left and right, his eyes narrow as he tried to make sense of what was going on. Ian had obviously untied Jackson's makeshift restraints but had rebound the man's ankles and wrists with the shoelaces. They looked tight to Jackson, and the man didn't bother to test them.

"Your mates are dead, yeah? All of them. The only thing keeping me from throwing you over that wee railing there is that you know things I don't. Like who are you?"

The man's eyes widened, studying Ian, then looking to the other members.

Ian jabbed the gun into his neck, just beside the dried blood from where Jackson had bashed him with the rock. It had left a noticeable gash in his forehead, one that clearly needed medical attention.

"Answer!" Ian said, pushing with the gun.

"Ian," Joel said calmly.

"A little busy, yeah?"

"Let's not do this."

"You want answers or not?"

"Not like this."

Ian pulled back the gun.

"I think he's in shock," Cara said, bending over Ian's shoulder. "Rapid breathing, perspiration, pale skin. Concussed at the least."

"We should let the authorities question him," Rich said.

"We're not privy to their answers, yeah? You want to know who he is, who sent him, we ask him now."

Joel pursed his lips as they gathered out of earshot of the man.

"Well?"

"Not in front of everyone."

"Aye. Jackson."

"Wait," Aliana said. "Joel, you cannot be serious? You are going to let them torture him?"

"I'm not going to torture anyone," Ian said.

"Then what?"

"I'm going to ask him some questions. And he's going to answer them."

"Or else you will torture him?"

"Enhanced interrogation," Cara said.

"What's the difference?" Rich asked.

"Torture is pain for pain's sake," Ian answered. "It's the purpose, not the means."

"That is a fine distinction," Aliana said.

"Aye, maybe, but a distinction nonetheless."

"Joel?" she protested.

He exhaled. "Ian's right. We do need to get answers." He turned to look at Ian. "But don't hurt him."

Ian stood and approached Joel. Jackson drifted over.

"I can't guarantee answers if I don't have any leverage, yeah?" Ian said quietly. "If I don't have a way to motivate him."

"Joel, you can't allow this," Rich said.

"It is a line you cannot uncross." Aliana turned to Jackson, her eyes pleading.

"They're both right," Jackson said as Joel too looked to him. "I've been there. He's not going to volunteer info. But that doesn't justify what we'd have to do to get info, either."

"We're wasting time," Ian said.

"Talk to him," Joel said. "But no torture."

"Then how—"

"Be creative."

Ian sighed, and Jackson tapped his shoulder. "He doesn't have to know Joel said no torture."

"Aye," Ian said without conviction.

Someone—it sounded like Dalia—suddenly screamed. It was echoed by a shrieking gasp from Aliana. Even before Jackson could turn around, he saw Ian break from their group. Jackson's eyes followed him, and his peripheral vision caught movement to the right. He turned farther to see the man they had captured running at Cara.

She screamed and ducked down and to the side. The man only brushed her, continuing straight ahead. Past the fire. Just out of the reach of a diving Ian. Jackson's eyes widened and his mouth opened to emit something, only his brain didn't know what to say.

The man jumped, using his hands to propel him up and over the railing, and disappeared without a sound.

Chapter Thirty-Five

"I HAVE TO say, this isn't how I pictured it," Jackson said, looking out at the sea.

"What," Maggie asked, "you thought maybe it'd part for you?"

"Well, that would be ridiculous. It's just weird seeing modern high-rises, neon Coca-Cola signs, and cheap T-shirt vendors at a place of biblical significance."

"Time moves on, Jack."

"So it does." He turned his gaze back to the sparkling blue water in front of them. First Jerusalem and its ancient streets mixed with modern structures, then the resorts lining the Dead Sea, and now this.

It had been an incredibly long day, one that had started for most of Team Joel with a rude awakening atop Masada. It made the current tranquility that much more surreal.

After the man they had captured had somehow unbound his ankles without being noticed and summoned the strength to jump up, run, and hurl himself over the side of the ancient fortress, Team Joel had stood around in shock. Ian and Jackson had both peered over the edge, unable to see anything in the darkness but a sheer rock drop-off. There was no doubt the man had committed suicide rather than face interrogation and possible punishment. And so answers had had to wait.

That hadn't stopped the questions. Who were these guys? Where had they come from? Why? Why now? Without answers, the eight members of Team Joel and their UNESCO guide had passed the time muttering questions and staring at a dwindling fire. No one felt like sleeping, nor likely could have had they felt like it. Jackson kept replaying the brief "battle" he and Ian had waged. Jackson had taken, directly and indirectly, four more lives. He had to be continually setting some single-year P.I. record. It helped—albeit only marginally—knowing the souls whose bodies he'd exterminated had been bent on evil.

Just as the first hint of lightening appeared in the eastern sky, a distant drone slowly morphed into a steady beating sound.

"What's that?" Ramón asked.

"Chopper," Ian said, immediately on high alert. "Sounds like a Black Hawk."

Jackson's gut fell. His experience with Black Hawks was less than stellar.

"You think it's a second wave of attackers?" Maggie asked. Everyone was now tense and focused.

"No. Black Hawk is American built, a standard aircraft used by the Israeli Air Force."

"The Air Force?" Ramón asked.

"Aye. Jack, remove your weapons and throw them aside," Ian said, already doing so. "The rest of you, onto your knees, hands on your heads."

"Why?" Cara asked.

"So they know you're not a threat, yeah?"

"Everyone, do it," Joel said, having to shout over the thunderous buzz of the approaching helicopter. No sooner had they all taken the position than a beam of light stabbed out of the air, quickly honing in on the ashes of their fire and the nine people kneeling around it. The light was followed by a voice over a speaker that was louder than the pulsing blades. It issued a command first in what sounded to Jackson's ears like Hebrew, followed by English.

"Israeli Defense Forces. Do not move."

The chopper descended and hovered mere yards overhead, its blades deafening and sweeping the dirt and sand and ashes into a blinding cloud. Squinting against the onslaught, Jackson saw a rope drop from the open door of the dark helicopter. Two men in olive green descended, each holding a tactical rifle and clad in combat gear.

The chopper veered off as the men approached the group, weapons drawn. "Down on the ground," one of them said, first in Hebrew, then in English. Team Joel complied. In the distance, but still close—likely in the open expanse of the fortress—the Black Hawk's rotors began to decrease.

The two soldiers frisked everyone, then instructed them to stand. As they did, the soldiers' radios squawked, followed by an incomprehensible but urgent sounding voice. When it was finished, both men raised their weapons again. Apparently, the others in the chopper had found the carnage Jackson and Ian had left behind.

"My name is Joel Robinson, and I'm the leader of this group. We're historians and archaeologists."

A sergeant, judging by his stripes, and thus the leader of the two, looked at him. Team Joel and Dalia had lined up near the palace wall, per instructions, enabling the two men to cover them easily.

"Do you understand me?" Joel asked.

"Yes, I understand."

"We camped here overnight with our UNESCO guide, Dalia."

She raised a hand.

"We were attacked by eight men. Several of our members have military training and were able to repel the attack. We have every intention of complying. We want no trouble."

"We'll need to secure the area," the man said. "Hold tight."

The next few hours were a whirlwind.

Joel—with some help from Jackson, Ian, and Dalia—provided the IDF sergeant a thorough explanation of what had happened. Meanwhile, other IDF soldiers canvassed the fortress, ultimately reporting back in person. There were at least six of them.

Team Joel was marched, still at gunpoint, back to where the Israeli flag fluttered in the early morning breeze. The Black Hawk was parked a hundred feet away, its camo green paint showing in the dawn's light. While the IDF sergeant made several radio calls, a few other soldiers provided Team Joel with water and blankets. Not that they needed them once the sun peeked over the Jordanian mountains and bathed Masada in an otherworldly orange glow.

Team Joel and Dalia were then escorted—via the tram, under guard—down to the visitor center, where they were allowed to use proper restrooms and freshen up. They were permitted to dine on snacks from a vending machine while being questioned further by an IDF colonel, two Shin Bet (the Israeli equivalent of the FBI) agents, and a UNESCO rep. Jackson drew a no-nonsense but seemingly fair male Shin Bet agent. He'd been hoping for Shin Bet's version of Ziva David, but it could have been worse. He told the truth, albeit without unnecessary mention of the particulars of the treasure Team Joel was seeking or the clues that had led them to Masada. He then repeated his story to the IDF colonel.

By late morning, the various authorities seemed satisfied that Team Joel—particularly Jackson and Ian—had acted in self-defense and weren't guilty of any crimes. However, they asked them not to leave the area while they conducted their investigation. Joel as the leader and Ramón with his numerous contacts remained at the visitor center, along with Dalia, while the rest of Team Joel returned to the Royal Palms to sleep, eat, and wait (and, in Ian's case, contact Eli Haddad to see if he had any intel to contribute to their quest for explanation). So far, they'd been given no answers. But at least they weren't in the Mossad black-site prison like Cara had feared.

Joel and Ramón returned in the early afternoon. He reported that he, Ramón, and the team's attorney Rachelle Bentley had provided numerous reassurances and given the authorities multiple references who could vouch for them and their activities. Jackson and Ian's forthright and coherent testimony also had helped, he said. Ian's possession of the Jericho 941 pistol could prove to be a problem, but Rachelle was working on it, and, given the circumstances, the possession charge wasn't of high concern to the Israelis. They had asked the team to remain in Israel for several days, but Joel had, after providing contact information and an itinerary, been given permission for his team to leave the immediate vicinity.

"Why?" Cara asked.

"Couple of reasons. One, we can't do anything right now. Masada is closed for at least today, so we can't do what we came to do. Two, I think we could use a break, some relaxation if possible under the circumstances. Three, if whoever sent those guys is still out there, I'd rather they not know where to look. And four, the media has caught word of what went on and has descended on Masada. We had to fight through a gaggle of reporters leaving, and if they haven't already tracked us here, it won't be long. I'd rather avoid all that, if possible. Rachelle and the Shin Bet agent in charge agreed."

"Did they give you any answers about who this was?" Maggie asked.

"Not as of yet. No IDs on any of the bodies, and they don't have facial rec or fingerprint technology that works in the middle of the desert."

"Joel, are we safe?" Aliana asked.

He pursed his lips. "I don't know. One of the things we need to think about is whether we want to continue or not. We've had a few scares, but this was different. This was a hit squad. They were coming to take us out, by all appearances."

"Aye," Ian said as Joel looked at him.

"I'm not going to force anyone to continue. And I don't want anyone faking bravado. If you want out, raise your hand, and I'll put you on the first flight back."

"And let these turds win," Cara said. She harrumphed.

"I'm with the Canuck, yeah?"

Joel looked around the room.

"We have been in danger before," Aliana said. "And frankly, if Jackson and Ian could protect us from a 'hit squad' with one pistol and a bomb rigged from camping gear, I actually feel quite secure."

"You ain't seen nothing yet," Maggie said, clapping Jackson's shoulder. "I'm staying."

Rich nodded.

Ramón shrugged.

"Jackson?" Joel asked.

"I'd hate to bow out if the danger's over," he said. "I'd hate even more to leave you all if it's not. I'm in."

Joel nodded. "Okay. I've booked two suites at the Queen of Sheba Hotel in Eilat, a couple hundred kilometers south of here on the Gulf of Aqaba. Aliana, if you don't mind, I'd like you and Ramón to hang back with me for a few hours. I promised the Shin Bet agents a few more answers, and your knowledge of Hebrew, reputation in the world of antiquities, and demeanor can help assuage any concerns they still have."

She nodded.

"The rest of you, take one of the cars and head south, and we'll meet up with you later."

After briefly packing, Jackson, Maggie, Rich, Cara, and Ian had crammed into one of the Mazdas and made the two and a half-hour drive through the Negev Desert to the port city of Eilat. Situated on a wedge of land between Jordan and Egypt, it was Israel's southernmost city and a growing resort destination. Joel had figured it was about as far off the map as his team could get, within reasonable distance, and more relaxing than some small town in the middle of the desert. It had also satisfied the Shin Bet agents, who were the only ones who knew where they were going since Joel had used an alias to book the rooms.

After checking into adjoining suites at the Queen of Sheba Hotel, the group had set out to walk the promenade along the Gulf of Aqaba. One of two "fingers" extending from the Red Sea, the Gulf of Aqaba separated the Sinai Peninsula from Saudi Arabia. The gulf tapered to only a few miles across at the northern end, where Egypt, the southern tip of Israel, and the southwestern corner of Jordan all came together. Or would have, had it not been for the Gulf.

The five had perused a few shops but had been largely uninterested in trinkets and baubles. Eilat was a long way—literally and figuratively—from Masada, and yet the events of the night before were still present in their minds. So while Ian accompanied Cara in search of a cell phone retailer so she could purchase a new cover for her phone, Jackson, Maggie, and Rich stared out at the Gulf and mused.

"Is there any chance they let us back up there?" Maggie asked.

"I don't know," Jackson said.

"And if not, what do we do? Just give up?"

"Don't underestimate Ramón and Rachelle," Rich said. "They've negotiated us out of some pretty sticky situations before."

"Not underestimating them," Maggie said. "Just not overestimating Shin Bet and Mossad and the IDF either."

"They seemed to believe us," Jackson said.

"Sure, or we wouldn't be here. But those guys, Jack, were white. Meaning probably not Israelis or Palestinians. Meaning this is an international incident at a World Heritage Site, in a nation that lives on edge."

He shrugged.

"What's eating at you?" she said.

"Nothing."

"You're acting weird."

"What do you mean?"

"You just keep staring out at the water."

"Desert air is oddly invigorating."

"Uh-huh."

He shrugged again. "I'm just picturing these waters being parted so a million Israelites could walk through."

"Their likely crossing point wasn't actually in the gulf," Rich said.

"I know. I actually read a book a few years back, proposing a southern Red Sea crossing. They found chariot wheels on this sort of land bridge and everything. Still, this is just kind of . . . weird being here."

Maggie stared at him until he looked her way. "What?" he asked. "Now you're acting weird."

"It's nothing."

"Desert air?"

"You really don't seem like the type to believe all these Old Testament stories—parting seas, fish eating people, shepherds with slingshots."

He didn't answer.

"You're just not the stereotypical Christian."

"Maybe not."

"That's a good thing. The stereotype's a little stale. You don't fit that mold."

Ian and Cara returned and reported that Joel had texted. They had just set out and wouldn't be arriving for several hours. "He said we should go ahead and grab something to eat, yeah?"

"I'm game," Jackson said.

"I also heard back from Eli."

"Anything?" Maggie asked.

"Not a word. Whoever this was, they entered Israel without tipping off Eli's sources, which is practically miraculous."

"Wonderful."

"Aye. Wine with dinner then?"

There were numerous eateries to choose from in the vicinity, a complex of hotels, shops, and attractions situated on the coast and around a lagoon and marina. Once again, Jackson found Israel not what he expected. They passed on sushi, a burger joint named Moses, a noodle bar tabbed Giraffe, and a place called Whale, and settled upon Chicago Grill Bar in their hotel. After all their experiences, they were ready for something a little less cultural.

Over steaks and burgers, they talked about anything to take their minds off what had happened the night before. Maggie filled Rich, Cara, and Ian in on her Mexican exposé that had made her semi-famous, providing details that hadn't made her *Los Angeles Times* story. Ian and Cara shared several humorous "ladykiller" stories about Joel and various women with whom he had failed miserably and comically—at least to the rest of the team. Rich provided a history of Eilat, linking it to the Exodus and Solomon's mines and the Queen of Sheba. And Jackson provided his geographical insight.

"A drowning man signaling for a boat?" Maggie asked.

He nodded. "If you look at a map, the Med looks like a boat. The Nile delta looks like a net. And the Red Sea is a man holding up two fingers to signal to it."

"Signaling what?"

"That he's drowning," Jackson said with a shrug.

"In what, the Indian Ocean?"

"Sounds more like he's ordering beers, yeah?"

"Where did you hear this?" Cara asked.

"My dad taught me when I was a kid. He drew a rough map on a piece of paper. It's how he taught me to remember the geography."

"Your dad wanted you to remember Middle East geography as a kid?"

"Well, he didn't want me to grow up just to be good looking."

"And this is relevant to our discussion how?" Maggie asked.

"Have you followed this discussion? Nothing's relevant."

"Aye, he's right about that," Ian said, reaching for the check. "This one's on me."

"I saw Joel give you a credit card," Cara said. "But nice try."

Eilat's nightlife had awakened while they'd eaten, and the cityscape was lit up in a blend of colors now that the sun was down. The group wandered for a few minutes but were all feeling the exhaustion of the day. So they returned to their hotel and suites on the seventh floor, overlooking the lagoon below and the city to the west. Shortly before eight, Joel called from the lobby and said he, Aliana, and Ramón had arrived. Five minutes later, the team reunited in the women's suite.

"Any updates?" Ian asked just before Jackson could.

"Shin Bet, working with Mossad, identified one of the men Jackson shot as Hugo LaPierre, a member of a French separatist group called *Liberté ou Mort*. Another is a former French Navy quarter-master believed to be part of the same movement."

"Some French militia did this?" Cara asked.

"That's what it looks like."

"Why?"

"I don't know. Mossad is researching any connections LaPierre might have, and also looping in Interpol since they're tied into this. Ramón has several discreet feelers out, and Rachelle is checking with a few legal contacts in Europe. Hopefully, one of them will turn something up. But for now, we're still in the dark."

"Awesome," Cara muttered.

"A French army," Jackson said. "It explains why they went down so easy."

"Any word on when Masada might open again?" Maggie asked.

"No, not as of yet. I was advised to check back tomorrow."

"So that's it, yeah?"

Joel nodded.

"So what do we do?" Cara asked. "Hit the ice skating mall tomorrow?"

"We could probably use some down time, mindless escape," Joel said. "But right now, I'm starved. You all happen to know where I can get a good burger?"

Chapter Thirty-Six

"I DIDN'T MEAN it in a bad way," Maggie said.

"Didn't mean what?" Jackson asked.

"The other night, when I said you weren't the stereotypical Christian, that you didn't fit the mold."

From the driver's seat of the Mazda, Jackson turned to look at Maggie. The team had left the Queen of Sheba Hotel shortly before two a.m., "under the cover of darkness." Joel had been only half-joking when he'd said it. They had spent the better part of Thursday relaxing—catching up on sleep, touring Eilat, taking a dolphin cruise in the Gulf of Aqaba, or viewing endangered and unique animals at the Yotvata Hai-Bar Nature Reserve. Then, at an early dinner, Joel had updated them on where their search for the Calvary Treasure stood.

"I heard from the head Shin Bet agent earlier this afternoon," he said. "Hugo LaPierre, the French separatist who led the attack, is a direct descendant of a man named Clément d'Bordeaux."

"*The* Clément d'Bordeaux?" Aliana asked.

"You know him, yeah?"

"So to speak. When Leon of Toulon died in 1194, the Knights Calvary endured a power struggle between Tristan II of Béziers—the eventual successor to Leon—and Clément d'Bordeaux, who was a twelfth-century 'war hawk.' His movement ultimately dwindled and died out, and he became a footnote in history."

"Until eight hundred years later when his great-great-lotta-greats-grandson decides to play *Call of Duty: Masada*," Jackson said.

"For what it's worth," Joel said, "Rachelle checked up on the ancestry, and it seems legit."

"So we have the CC after us," Maggie said, "the descendants of the Knights Calvary, and also the descendants of a failed Knights Calvary coup?"

"Something like that," Joel said. "But the good news is, Mossad has heard no chatter about any further activity from this separatist group, nor have several other governments and agencies, supposedly."

"Whoop-de-doo," Cara said.

"There's more," Joel said.

"Goodie."

"For real. Ramón spoke to Dalia a few minutes ago, and she has agreed—and UNESCO has agreed—to let us go back up to the top of Masada."

"When?" Aliana asked.

"In . . . about twelve hours."

"Tomorrow morning?"

Joel nodded. "Instead of camping again, Dalia will take us up in a tram about an hour before dawn."

"Seriously?" Cara asked.

Another nod.

"Well, why didn't we think of that the first time?"

"We did, but UNESCO wouldn't go for it," Ramón said. "I had to pull serious strings to let us camp out there."

"But now they're willing?" Jackson asked.

Joel nodded again. "Apparently Dalia was quite impressed and lobbied on our behalf."

"Impressed with us or with Ramón?" Cara asked, eliciting a grin from the Spaniard.

"She helped sell them on us going again, and taking a tram was the obvious choice for several reasons," Joel said.

"So when do we leave?" Ian asked.

"By two. We didn't leave anything at the Royal Palms, so we should be set. I'm not enforcing curfew, but considering where we'll be hiking and what we'll be doing, choose your own level of alertness."

Jackson had been in bed by eight, asleep by nine, and up at one-thirty. He'd felt reasonably awake and offered to drive. Maggie had opted to ride shotgun, and Rich and Cara had taken the backseat of their Mazda. They had both been asleep since the outskirts of Eilat, whereas Maggie had dozed briefly while Jackson spent the better part of ninety minutes following the other car's taillights and looking out for jackals or hyenas or whatever manner of accursed animal occupied this wasteland.

Now Maggie was awake and apparently feeling apologetic.

"How do you mean it that I'm not a stereotypical Christian?" he asked her.

"So many Christians seem like they're cut from a cloth. They use the right buzzwords, always have a trite Bible verse on standby. They line up for the same causes, do ridiculous things like have 'harvest festivals' so they can get away with celebrating Halloween without celebrating Halloween."

"Whereas I just ignore the day entirely."

"But you know what I mean? Too many Christians come across as . . ." She looked over her shoulder at Rich. "Him," she whispered.

"What's wrong with him?" Jackson whispered back.

"Nothing. And yet . . . I don't know, there's just a vibe about people like that that's a turnoff."

"I'll bring it up at the next elder meeting."

She smacked his shoulder.

"You're going to leave a mark pretty soon."

"I'm serious, Jack."

"I know, Mags. I'm just not sure why this is our conversation right now."

"What would you like to talk about?"

"Hmm. Good question." He looked her way. "I get you, Maggie, I do. I see it too. But I think it's like with a lot of things, the stereotype exists for a reason, but it gets largely overblown and a lot of people who shouldn't be get lumped into it."

"Like Muslim terrorists?"

"Yeah. Quite a bit like that." He checked his rearview mirror, as he had sporadically, just to make sure no one was following them. No one was. "Good thing you have me and Ali to break all those stereotypes."

She turned in her seat. "Speaking of Aliana, what were the two of you doing over by the Snake Path Gate to see LaPierre's people coming anyhow?"

"Which is more believable, making an interfaith blood pact or making out by moonlight?"

She rolled her eyes. "You are so juvenile."

The two vehicles arrived at the Masada visitor center shortly before five o'clock. Black was just turning to dark blue on the eastern horizon, with sunrise more than an hour away. Dalia, dressed as she had been three days before, but with a zip-up jacket over her UNESCO polo shirt, greeted them in the parking lot. Team Joel commended her bravery and thanked her for her help as they walked toward the tram.

As they made the ride to the top of the fortress, Jackson couldn't help but scour the Snake Path that wound up the cliff beneath them. He did not see any black-clad Frenchmen.

Dalia used the time to announce that the fortress had opened again the previous day, returning to business as usual. When asked how she was dealing with what had happened personally, she forced a smile that spoke volumes more than her hesitant, "Okay."

Using flashlights, they made their way from the tram station to the Snake Path Gate entrance and up and through the courtyard to the Northern Complex. Then they journeyed through it to the stairs and walkway that led down to the lower levels of Herod's Palace.

"All right, the original plan, which is still in place," Joel said, halting the group, "is to split into four different groups. I'd like one at the lower palace, one at the middle palace, and two up top, maybe one group at the northern end and then one at the easternmost point."

"Who would you like where?" Aliana asked.

"Your druthers."

"I would love to walk down a staircase on the side of a cliff in pitch-black conditions," Cara said.

"Okay, you can stay up here. Ian, stay with her?"

"Aye."

"Dalia, any thoughts?"

"I will accompany the team to the lower palace, if that is okay, to help as a guide."

"That works. Any other preferences?"

Joel was answered with shrugs.

"Okay. Jackson, I want you and Rich to accompany Dalia. Ali and I will take the upper palace, and Maggie and Ramón, I'll let you sort out with Ian and Cara who goes to the northern tip and who goes to the eastern end."

They nodded.

"Keep your eyes peeled, and remember the inscription inside the chest: 'As darkness begets dawn, thou wilt findeth the light whence thou liftest thine eyes at the arrow's mark.'"

"Also watch out for French ninjas," Cara muttered.

"If you do see anything suspicious, shout a warning. We have a tram this time."

"Aye, and Jackson's packing."

Joel looked at him, and he nodded.

"I don't think we'll have to worry about it," Joel said. "So let's focus on what we came here for."

"Agreed," Aliana said, and with that, the group split up. Dalia led Jackson, Joel, Rich, and Aliana to the narrow cliffside staircase leading down, urging them to watch their steps. Proceeding by flashlight, they went slowly, stopping at the middle palace.

"Please be careful," Dalia said to Joel and Aliana.

"We will," Joel said, shining his flashlight on the ruins.

With a nod, Dalia continued down to the lower level, where she, Jackson, and Rich took up positions at the western wall of the ancient palace. Dawn was now a faint orange glow that drew a distinction between the night sky and the Jordanian mountains. Even so, and even with the light from a reasonably bright night sky, the Snake Path was indiscernible in the cliff face.

None of the trio said much. That was fine, as far as Jackson was concerned. He didn't have to answer the questions he was sure Dalia had and for which he didn't likely have answers, and Rich didn't confess to any more nightmarish "visions." His last had been of trouble on the rocks, before a team of commandos had tried to kill them all atop Masada. Jackson didn't buy his visions any more than he believed TV psychics were anything more than con artists, but he couldn't deny that, at least this time, the vision had been somewhat specific and accurate.

Gradually, the sky began to brighten, and the darkness shrouding the desert floor dissipated. Rocks and striations and swirls began to take shape, and as Jackson craned his neck to study the side of the fortress, he could make out a slightly lighter color in the rock and sand where the Snake Path made its hairpin climb.

"You are looking for an arrow?" Dalia asked.

"Something like that."

"After eight hundred years? Is not erosion likely to have changed the features of the terrain substantially?"

"Very possibly."

"Then what do you do?"

"Go back to the proverbial drawing board."

She frowned, perhaps not getting the American idiom, but it didn't matter. The sky directly above the mountains was glowing; the sun was moments from rising.

It was hard for Jackson to keep his eyes on the side of the cliffs, brilliant as they looked at sunrise, and not at the sun itself as it crested the mountains and beat down on the Dead Sea and the desert, signaling yet another day of life in the wilderness. As it rose, it painted sharp contrasts in the cliffs, basking rock faces in magnificent shades of red and orange while coloring the crevices dark purples and browns. Jackson ran his eyes over the entire cliff several times, paying particular attention to areas around the Snake Path. Even using his imagination and accounting for erosion, he didn't spot anything he would categorize as an arrow.

He peeked to the east, where the sun had fully emerged from behind the mountains. Already its light had overcome the night, and its warmth was evident. Jackson would have loved to sit back and watch the morning unfold, cherishing the beauty and celebrating the rebirth it represented, especially given what had transpired here forty-eight hours ago. But he couldn't. The higher the sun rose, the less likely it was to provide the answer the team desperately sought.

From above them, Aliana shrieked.

Jackson couldn't tell if it was in glee or alarm, and a look into Rich's eyes confirmed neither could he. Jackson stepped back, craning his eyes to the middle palace. He couldn't help but also run them over the cliff face to see if Cara's French ninjas had made an appearance.

A minute passed. Then Joel appeared, waving his hands. He then gave a giant come-here motion with his right arm. It didn't look like a signal of duress.

"Let's go," Jackson said.

It took them just a couple minutes to climb to the middle palace, where Aliana was exuberantly staring at her smartphone.

"She take a killer sunrise selfie, or you find something?" Jackson asked.

"See for yourselves," Aliana said, turning her phone to them. She swiped through several hastily taken and less than high-quality images. Even so, they clearly showed a shadow on the side of the cliffs that resembled an arrow. A squished, squiggly arrow, but an arrow.

"Did you see anything?" Joel asked.

"Not from our vantage point."

"Is it above the Snake Path?" Rich asked.

"It appears to be a little bit off to the side," Aliana said. "But the sun was coming from a southern trajectory, more so than it would have in September of 1187."

"Let's see if anybody saw anything from up top."

They began the arduous climb back to the top of the fortress. Aliana showed her pictures to Ramón and Maggie, then the seven headed to find Ian and Cara. They were sitting inside the tunnel to the Snake Path. Ian popped to his feet as soon as he saw the rest of the team.

"Did you see it?"

"You saw an arrow?" Joel asked.

"Aye. Cara has pictures."

She had remained seated, studying her tablet. "It's upside down," she said as they crowded around her, "and a little off to the side, but tell me that isn't an arrow." Aliana handed Cara her phone, and she studied the two images for a moment. "That's the same place."

"We found it," Joel said beaming. "We found *'the arrow's mark.'*"

Chapter Thirty-Seven

6:49 a.m.

"IT LOOKS LIKE a blank rock face," Ramón said, studying blow-ups of Cara and Aliana's photos.

"This isn't exactly a Canon," Cara said, holding up her tablet. "And the sun's at the wrong angle, meaning the arrow's pointing to the wrong place."

"How much of a wrong angle?" Maggie asked.

"Given the approximate date range in September of 1187, about fifteen degrees."

"How much would that matter?" Ramón asked.

"Roughly one foot for every four of distance. And we're looking at what, thirty feet?"

"Fair guess, yeah."

"So seven and a half feet over," Ramón said with a shrug.

"Unless we have an exact measurement, that's imprecise."

"But gives us a ballpark," Joel said.

Cara shrugged.

"How long would it take you to make a 3-D model of the cliff and recalculate the angle of the sun?" Rich asked.

"Forever."

"I thought you had this all down," Ramón said.

Cara sighed. "The sun's a piece of cake, but the cliff is where it gets tricky. I could probably do it in a few hours, given the various images I've found of the cliffs."

"Might could do you one better," Jackson said.

"How's that?" Joel asked.

"There's a pretty good-sized 3-D model up by the palace, or else down at the visitor center, and we've got flashlights to replicate the sun."

"That would still be inexact, and I'm not sure the model's big enough. But nice thought."

"What then?" Ian asked.

314

"We do it the hard way," Joel said. "We go examine the area, imprecise as it is, and see what we can find."

"That area is very treacherous," Dalia said. "One wrong step could create a rockslide, and you will not stop falling until you reach the desert floor."

"Super," Cara said.

"I thought people climbed the Snake Path all the time," Rich said. "Those French guys did it at night without flashlights, yeah?"

"The path, yes," Dalia said. "But if you stray off the path . . ."

"We'll exercise great caution," Joel said. "But we'd better get going before the tourists start arriving en masse."

With Dalia again in the lead, Team Joel began the slow climb down the Snake Path. It was steeper than it looked and just as narrow as it looked, and Jackson hoped the Calvary Treasure—and his cut in particular—was worth all this.

Repeatedly consulting photos, Joel and Cara estimated the approximate location of the shadow arrow and called a halt to the group. "Right about there," Joel said, pointing to a slightly lighter section of rock ten feet above them and some dozen feet north of the path's hairpin turn.

"Okay, if we're looking at thirty feet, and from here that seems about right . . ." Cara said, pausing to let several agree to her estimate, "we need to factor in fifteen degrees in the change of sunlight, which would shift the arrow approximately seven to eight feet north."

"South," Joel said.

"Right, duh, sorry. South."

"Lovely," Ian said. "A blank rock face."

"You expected a big X?" Jackson asked.

"Aye, that would have been nice."

"This is an approximate location," Joel said. "Could be a few feet left or right, could be a few feet higher or lower."

Jackson turned to look at the outcropping of rock that had created the early morning arrow-like shadow. His untrained eye was unable to detect any obvious signs that the outcropping had been altered in any way over the years. He wasn't sure if the trained eye of a geologist could even pick up signs of such change, so he concentrated on studying the face of the cliff.

The morning sun was now hot, shining on them in full force. As it reflected off the stone face, it was almost blinding, and Jackson questioned why he didn't wear sunglasses. He'd never done so, largely because he didn't like having things on his face. But squinting had its limitations.

315

"There," Rich said. "What's that?"

"That is a crack, yeah?"

"It looks like writing, right there."

Joel and Aliana looked at where he was pointing.

"I do not see anything," Aliana said.

Joel only shook his head.

"What exactly are we looking for?" Maggie asked. "You think knights wrote something on the face of the cliff?"

"It's possible."

"And it survived the centuries of wind, sand, rain . . . ?"

"And wasn't observed by the thousands of people climbing this path and excavating the site?" Ramón asked.

"For that matter, do we have any reason to believe it's still here?" Cara asked.

"The knights clearly believed this treasure or the next clue could be found at some point in the future."

"But not eight centuries."

"Probably not. But we have to give them the benefit of the doubt."

Jackson kept his eyes roving, and they kept coming back to a crevice in the rock about ten feet above the hairpin corner. A very small shelf, less than half a foot deep, ran at an angle above the path before eventually blending into the face of the cliff farther south. At the northern end, just north of the hairpin, it stopped suddenly, the rock beneath it creating a very thin north-facing cliff before it blended into the overall east-facing wall of rock. At the base of that shelf, just before it stopped, was a small crack, only a few inches in height, one of thousands of such openings that existed in cliffs that had been exposed to the elements for centuries. But this one just happened to be in the rough area where a September sunrise would cast the shadow of an arrow-like rock formation.

Jackson tapped Ian's shoulder as the Scot took a drink of water. "Can you get me up there?" he asked.

"Balance you on my shoulders while balancing on the path at the edge of a cliff?" He took another swig. "Aye, I can do that."

Recruiting Rich to help, Jackson and Ian approached the edge of the path. Just a few feet to their right, the terrain began to drop off more and more steadily. Jackson ignored it as he climbed, with Rich's help, onto Ian's shoulders. Bracing himself against the rock, he extended himself until he was standing, with Ian's hands clasped around his calves.

"So this is what a cheerleader feels like," he said.

"You have some heavy cheerleaders, yeah?"

Song Girls, actually, at USC, and they had the good sense not to stand on other people. But since he was here . . .

"A little left," Jackson said, holding the wall as Ian sidestepped a foot left. "Good." With the others all watching, Jackson reached his hand up, feeling over the ledge and toward the crack. "Dalia?"

"Yes?"

"Please tell me you don't have scorpions in Israel."

"Yes, the Israeli or Palestinian yellow scorpion. Also known as the deathstalker."

"Great."

"Also rattlesnakes, vipers, tarantulas."

His fingers suddenly hypersensitive, Jackson extended his hand into the crack. At first, he felt nothing but various edges of the rock. But then one of them moved. He thought it was just a loose pebble or stone until he tried to ease it out of the crack. He clasped all his fingers around it, lifting it so as not to scrape it, then extracted a piece of something smooth, at least several inches wide and long. Holding onto the wall with one hand to steady himself, he raised the object up so he could look at it.

Shaped not dissimilarly to a Native American arrowhead, it appeared to be a large shard of pottery about the size of his hand.

"You found something!" Aliana said.

"Might just be kosher recipes, but it's an odd storage place if so."

"Bring him down," she said.

"Aye," Ian grunted, then slowly lowered himself to a knee so Jackson could slide/jump/fall down. He did so without damaging the shard in his hand.

The rest of Team Joel and Dalia rallied around Jackson to examine the object. Aliana extended her hands and asked them to back away and give her some room while she retrieved a pair of gloves from her bag, then asked with near-pleading eyes if she could hold the shard. Jackson handed it to her.

"It is clearly ancient," she said. "I cannot be sure without running some tests, but the color, texture, and style all suggest it is consistent with the other pieces found here."

"What is it?" Cara asked.

"A shard of pottery."

"An *ostracon*, was it?" Rich asked.

"Yes."

"Is that writing?" Joel asked.

The group crowded in again to see what was etched on the piece of pottery:

et vocavit nomen illius Ioseph dicens addat mihi Dominus filium alterum
et surrexerunt inde nocte et ibant usque ad munitionem
turris fortissima nomen Domini ad ipsum currit iustus et exaltabitur

"Bible verses?" Ramón asked.

"They are very hard to make out," Aliana said. "And so small." She rotated the piece to reveal even more writing on the opposite side:

quis enim ex vobis volens turrem aedificare non prius sedens conputat sumptus qui
necessarii sunt si habet ad perficiendum
bibe aquam de cisterna tua et fluenta putei tui
columba mea in foraminibus petrae in caverna maceriae ostende mihi faciem tuam
sonet vox tua in auribus meis vox enim tua dulcis et facies tua decora

"At least it does not appear any letters are missing," Aliana said.

"How can you tell?" Ian asked

"None of the words approach the edges, at least not very close. I cannot be sure, but if I had to guess, I would say this piece was broken off or found, and then used as a tablet of sorts."

"You said it was consistent with other pieces here," Rich said. "So does that mean it wasn't written by the Knights Calvary?"

"I said my initial observations suggest it is consistent with other pieces. But assuming the Knights Calvary wrote this, it is perfectly reasonable to believe they used a shard of pottery that was here instead of bringing their own."

"Jackson, any chance there was anything else in that crack?" Joel asked.

"If there is, someone's going to have to stand on my shoulders to see it."

"Take a picture with your phone," Cara said.

Maggie chuckled.

"Right. With my phone."

Jackson looked to Ian. "Your shoulders up for it?"

"Aye."

They repeated their climbing procedure, and Jackson took a dozen photos with Cara's phone's camera. Ian lowered Jackson again without accident, and he returned Cara's phone. The pictures were less than perfect but seemed to reveal an empty crack.

"All right," Joel said, taking a deep breath. "I think we've found what we came for. Let's get going."

"Where to, exactly?" Ian asked.

"We still have the rooms at the Royal Palms. Let's go there and see if we can figure out what we found."

*   *   *

12:19 p.m.

TEAM JOEL had walked back up the Snake Path to the tram station, ridden down to the visitor center, profusely thanked Dalia for her help, and set out before too many tourists arrived at Masada. They'd returned to their suites at the Royal Palms, where they had refreshed and changed and then met up over room service sandwiches and fruit to contemplate the meaning of the message(s) on the *ostracon*.

Cara and Aliana had again done the work of translating, this time made much more difficult because of the indistinct letters that, in places, were almost indecipherable. They'd done a little guessing, some deductions based on the surrounding verbiage, and eventually agreed that the shard of pottery contained five more Bible verses and one verse from the Apocrypha: Genesis 30:24, I Maccabees 5:29, Proverbs 18:10, Luke 14:28, Proverbs 5:15, and Song of Solomon 2:14. Once again, the verses initially told them a lot but ultimately told them little.

Now, munching on leftover sandwiches, they continued to contemplate.

"Why aren't they in order?" Rich asked.

"Huh?" Ramón asked.

"The Proverbs verses should go before Song of Solomon and the Luke verse should be at the end."

"And what is Maccabees and why is it in there?" Cara asked.

"It is part of the so-called Apocrypha," Aliana answered. "Books considered by some denominations—Catholics and Orthodox Christians, primarily—to be biblical, but not in the 'canon' of Protestant Bibles. If I remember correctly, I Maccabees recounts the Jewish revolt against Greek ruler Antiochus Epiphanes."

"You said Catholics and Orthodox Christians consider it part of the Bible?" Maggie asked, eliciting a nod from Aliana. "So what about the Knights Calvary?"

"It is part of the Latin Vulgate, so very likely so. The fact that a verse from it was included on this shard would indicate that as well."

"Even so, it's out of order," Rich said.

"Maybe the verses mean something in particular order," Cara said. "Joel, can you read them again?"

He reached for his tablet, on which he had been studying English translations of the verses. Swallowing a bite of roast beef and cheese on rye first, he read:

"Genesis 30:24: '*And she called his name Joseph, saying: The Lord give me also another son.*'

"First Maccabees 5:29: '*And they removed from thence by night, and went till they came to the fortress.*'

"Proverbs 18:10: '*The name of the Lord is a strong tower: the just runneth to it, and shall be exalted.*'

"Luke 14:28: '*For which of you, having a mind to build a tower, doth not first sit down and reckon the charges that are necessary, whether he have wherewithal to finish it?*'

"Proverbs 5:15: '*Drink water out of thy own cistern, and the streams of thy own well.*'

"Song of Solomon 2:14: '*My dove in the clefts of the rock, in the hollow places of the wall, shew me thy face, let thy voice sound in my ears: for thy voice is sweet, and thy face comely.*'"

He set down the tablet.

"Back looking for a fortress again, yeah?" Ian said.

"Where'd you come from?" Cara asked. "I thought you were taking an important call, again."

"I was." He grinned. "With the lovely Monica."

Cara rolled her eyes at the mention of what she had earlier tabbed "one of his old girlfriends."

Ian shrugged with a "what can I say?" look on his face.

"Not just a fortress," Rich said. "But a tower. The keep, perhaps?"

"Or a cistern," Maggie said. "Could this be referring to Masada again?"

"A clue at Masada to go to Masada?" Joel asked.

She shrugged.

"I suppose it could be."

They continued to toss out ideas, wondering what Joseph had to do with anything, why the Knights Calvary had suddenly included the Apocrypha and what the context of I Maccabees 5 was, how Solomon's description of his bride factored in, and how they were supposed to conclude which tower of which fortress was next on the trail of the Calvary Treasure.

"Last time, we had external evidence to point us to the fortress," Joel said. "In this case, all we have is these verses."

"Aye, unless we're missing another shard of pottery tucked into another crevice somewhere in this massive desert, yeah?"

"Let's work on the theory that this is the only clue, because otherwise we're lost since we have no idea where to look for another piece."

"Fair enough."

"That leaves us with these six verses to determine which fortress or tower is the right one."

"What about that one we found?" Maggie asked. "Kerak, was it?"

Jackson nodded.

"It was somewhat close to Masada."

"But in Jordan," Cara said. "Didn't Joel say the Muslims already controlled it by the time the knights hid the treasure?"

Joel nodded.

"Who's Joseph?" Jackson asked.

"In that passage, it's the eleventh son of Jaco—"

"I mean why are we told about Joseph?" Jackson said before Rich could finish his lecture. "Are we supposed to clue in on the particulars of his birth or his life, or is there another Joseph we should know?"

"Probably a few Joes over the years," Cara said.

"But we have to consider the Crusader era," Joel said. A light bulb suddenly appeared over his head. "Where's the journal?"

"In my bag," Aliana said. She retreated across the hall to the women's room and returned a moment later. "Here."

"What's in the journal?" Ian asked.

"Leon of Toulon was the Knights Calvary's High Commander in 1187, and Jacques IV of Aragon was the leader of the KC in Jerusalem, the city. But he makes reference . . ." He flipped through the pages, taking several minutes. "Here, yes, that's it. At the time, the Crusaders controlled the Kingdom of Jerusalem, or at least had until recently, an area comprised of modern-day Israel as well as parts of Egypt, Jordan, and Beirut. And Jacques mentions a Knights Calvary general, a man by the name of Joseph le Saint."

"General?" Maggie asked.

"Not dissimilar from today's vernacular. He was in charge of the order in a particular geographic region, in this case, the Kingdom of Jerusalem, subject only to the High Commander."

"What does it say about him?" Jackson asked.

"Nothing. He's merely listing the command structure," Joel said, closing the journal.

"Do we know anything else about him?"

"The name is familiar now, but no. Ali?"

She shook her head.

"Okay, let's dig into that. Also, any thoughts on the Song of Solomon verses?"

"Aye," Ian said. "The Crusaders were lonely."

"Let's see if we can find something more pertinent than that."

The group split up for a while, conducting research in various methods. Cara attacked the internet. Joel made phone calls. Aliana thumbed through a mental Rolodex of historical knowledge. Rich napped. Jackson went for a walk, letting his brain ruminate on the six verses found on the *ostracon*. As he strolled along the coast of the Dead Sea, ignoring the tourists and mud-bathers, he kept coming back to the verse from Luke: *For which of you, having a mind to build a tower, doth not first sit down and reckon the charges that are necessary, whether he have wherewithal to finish it.* It had originally been given by Jesus as an example of the cost of being a disciple, but had the Knights Calvary meant it literally?

And what about the references to cisterns and wells? Maybe a cistern dug beneath a tower—or keep—of a castle? Joel really needed a medieval architectural expert on his crew, somebody who knew the ins and outs of castle plumbing.

When Jackson returned to the suite twenty minutes later, Joel was just finishing an animated phone conversation. He ended the call and called the group together. Only Ramón was absent—"Washing his drawers, yeah?" Ian said—and Rich was awake and without premonition.

"That was Dr. Etienne D'Alembert, a colleague of mine from Paris," Joel said. "He's an expert on dates, names, and places related to the Crusades. Much of what I've learned, I've learned from him."

"What'd he have to say?" Rich asked.

"He gave me a rundown of Joseph le Saint's history. Jacques' journal didn't note it, but according to Dr. D'Alembert, he died at the Horns of Hattin on July 4, 1187."

"Remind me again," Cara said.

"One of the major battles of the era in which Saladin's forces routed those of Raynald of Châtillon and Guy of Lusignan, bringing about the ultimate downfall of the Kingdom of Jerusalem. Prior to that, however, Joseph le Saint was a huge proponent of trying to spread the kingdom and, in particular, the Knights Calvary's place in it. He was responsible for organizing several raids on Muslim settlements—"

"And caravans?" Maggie asked.

"Possibly. He also established several cities and fortresses in the decade preceding the fall of the Kingdom of Jerusalem, when the Knights Calvary were at their strongest."

"Any of them happen to be a castle bearing his name?" Rich asked.

"No. A couple of outposts near the Jordan River, a small castle near Nazareth, and a second closest to the current Jordanian city of Al-Hussayniyah that was never finished due to Joseph and the Knights Calvary running out of money and needing to concentrate on other tasks, namely rebuffing Saladin's growing empire."

Jackson stepped away from the wall he'd been leaning against. "A partially finished castle?"

Joel nodded.

"'For which of you, having a mind to build a tower, doth not first sit down and reckon the charges that are necessary, whether he have wherewithal to finish it.'"

Joel's eyes widened. "Of course."

"Where specifically was this partially finished castle?"

Joel retrieved a map off the dresser. "According to Dr. D'Alembert, right around here," he said, pointing to a location not all that far from Masada, some ten or twelve miles southeast across the Dead Sea, into the Kingdom of Jordan.

"In the middle of the desert," Maggie said.

"Aye, just like Asher mentioned the other day."

Joel snapped his fingers. "That's right. What did he say?"

"Hard to remember, what with him taking potshots at us most of the afternoon," Jackson said.

"Something about a legend of a Crusader castle across the Jordan that was never finished," Ian said. "'Little more than a tower,' as I recall, yeah?"

"So we have a verse giving us the name Joseph," Jackson said, "a verse mentioning a fortress, another talking about running to a tower, and a verse warning against starting a tower but not completing it."

"That has to be it, yeah?"

"It's a good candidate," Joel said.

"Is it still there?" Maggie asked.

"Dr. D'Alembert didn't know."

"Sounded like it, according to Asher," Ian said.

"I know someone who might be able to confirm it," Aliana said. "An expert in Jordanian ruins and historic places. Let me make a phone call."

"Ramón, might want to start putting out some feelers about us getting access to the Kingdom of Jordan," Joel said.

"On it."

"What about the other two verses?" Rich asked, consulting Cara's tablet screen. "'*Drink water out of thy own cistern, and the streams of thy own well.*' and '*My dove in the clefts of the rock, in the hollow places of the wall, shew me thy face, let thy voice sound in my ears: for thy voice is sweet, and thy face comely*'?"

"Perhaps there's a cistern by or inside the tower," Joel said.

"That was my thought too," Jackson said.

"Or they hid another shard of pottery in the cleft of the rock, yeah?"

"It fits a pattern," Joel said. "They tell us where to look, generally, with the reference to a partially finished castle built by Joseph le Saint, then tell us where to look specifically—in a cistern, the cleft of a rock, or a hollow wall."

"I still don't get all the complexity," Maggie said. "Why make it so confusing and hard to find?"

"They didn't want the wrong people finding the treasure," Rich said.

"Right, but did they want the right people to?"

"They no doubt figured a Christian would be able to discern their meaning in these verses whereas a Muslim would not," Joel said. "Another layer of security, but I get your point. A little straightforwardness would have helped."

"Where's the fun in that?" Jackson asked.

Aliana was off the phone in mere minutes. She beamed. "According to Dr. Basil, the ruins of Sanctifié Castle still exist. The castle was set on a hilltop far off any current beaten paths, so it isn't much of a tourist spot."

"Not to mention it's in Jordan," Jackson said.

"But we can get there?" Rich asked.

She nodded. "If Ramón can get us into the country and secure permission to excavate and retrieve any findings, according to Dr. Basil, we should have no trouble."

Jackson chortled. "That would be a first."

Chapter Thirty-Eight

Saturday, February 23
5:03 a.m.

AN EERIE CALM hovered over the pre-dawn Dead Sea as Team Joel loaded themselves and their gear into their two Mazdas. Armed with coffee, tea, energy drinks, and a cooler full of sandwiches for later, they left their hotel before sunrise for the second straight day, again with no one seemingly noticing their departure. Vehicular access to Jordan was extremely limited, and the nearest border crossing was some twenty miles to the south. Joel split up Ramón and Aliana. She ended up in Joel's vehicle with Jackson and Rich. Ramón joined Maggie and Cara with Ian in his car.

The previous afternoon, Aliana's colleague Dr. Basil had confirmed that Sanctifié Castle—translated to "Hallowed" Castle, a reference to its visionary, Joseph "the Saint"—was still in existence in the western mountains of Jordan. Ramón had gotten seriously busy greasing the wheels for Team Joel to cross into Jordan and conduct their search at the castle, and to remove the Calvary Treasure if they found it. By the time the team had gathered for dinner Friday night, he'd reported that everything was in place. Ramón had been murky on the details, leaving Jackson with the impression that their permission from the Jordanian government was more of a back-alley handshake and less of an official green light from the prime minister. He had also speculated that the Jordanian government had a different understanding of Team Joel's proposed activity in their country than the team did. But if Joel was good with it, so was Jackson—or so he'd tried to convince himself while staring at the ceiling trying to fall asleep.

Masada was just another shadow of auburn against a dark sky as the group headed south on Route 90. The Dead Sea flowed into the evaporation ponds that made up the southern end of the body of water. Like mirages, more resorts appeared out of the desert in Ein Bokek and Neve Zohar. Then they were past the sea entirely, in rocky wilderness more barren than anything Jackson had ever seen before coming to Israel.

No one spoke in Jackson's vehicle until Aliana pointed out the colors in the eastern sky. A thin haze hovered over the valley, capturing the first light of dawn and reflecting it back into the sky, a magnificent pink that began to turn to orange and then yellow as Joel turned off Route 90 onto the road leading to the border.

"Here we go," Rich said as Joel, in the lead vehicle, coasted toward the border checkpoint.

"This is the easy one," Joel said. "It's getting out that has me anxious."

Joel lowered his window and a fatigue-clad guard with a machine gun strapped to his back bent over and said something in Arabic.

Aliana leaned over and said something back. All Jackson caught was what sounded like, "English."

The guard nodded. "Papers for everyone."

Joel handed four passports out the window, and the guard turned and walked back to a small guard station a couple dozen feet away. He was there almost five minutes, during which time Joel reported the guard was on the phone at least twice. Finally, he slipped out of the booth and walked back toward the car.

"Should I tell him the car behind us is with us?" Joel asked.

"Let me," Aliana said. "I do not think his English is too good."

The guard nodded as he handed the passports back to Joel. "All set."

Aliana again leaned over and spoke more Arabic, a fast flurry that caused the guard to nod and issue a staccato burst of his own. Then he looked at Joel again and said in English, "Go."

The gate rose, and Joel needed no further encouragement to drive his vehicle into the Kingdom of Jordan. Safely past the checkpoint, he pulled over to wait for Ian's car. They were stopped for only a minute at the checkpoint before being admitted into Jordan. "Whatever you said must have worked," Joel said to Aliana as he pulled back onto the road.

A mile into Jordan, Joel turned north on Highway 65, an ancient road that had at one time been the King's Highway (referenced in the biblical book of Numbers) and the *Via Traiana Nova* in Roman times. Now it was called the Dead Sea Highway, running some 370 kilometers from Aqaba at the mouth of the Red Sea (just across the border from Eilat) to the northwestern corner of Jordan.

They drove past the southern end of the Dead Sea again, minus all the resorts and hotels that had lined the Israeli side. They were replaced by small huts and tents. The sun had yet to rise over the mountains, and the trip was uneventful except for one occasion when Joel had to stomp on the brakes to avoid hitting a dog that had run into the road.

"A jackal," Aliana explained.

"How's that for an omen," Jackson said.

A little bit south of due east of Masada, Joel turned onto a road that wound through a mountain pass and slowly climbed out of the Jordan Rift Valley. Morning had broken by the time they reached the city of Kerak, famous for the Kerak Castle, a Crusader structure erected in the middle of the twelfth century. It was an impressive fortress, even today, sitting high on a hilltop to look over the city of Kerak and the panoramic, albeit sparse, landscape in every direction.

Called *Crac des Moabites* by the Crusaders, the castle had enabled them to manage trade routes between Damascus and Egypt as well as provide a southern bastion against Muslim encroachment. Saladin had besieged Kerak Castle in 1183 in retaliation for attacks on Muslim caravans and Mecca by Raynald of Châtillon. Baldwin IV of Jerusalem had come to the Crusaders' rescue, but Saladin, after his victory at the Horns of Hattin, had again laid siege to Kerak. It had ultimately fallen in 1189. The Mamluks had added onto the castle, and it had been fought over and used by the Egyptians and Ottomans up until the late nineteenth century.

Aliana related the history while Joel navigated the switchbacks leading into and out of the town of Kerak. From there, they headed south through several towns of various size, including Mu'tah, which Aliana reported was the scene of the first battle between Muhammad's forces and those of the Eastern Roman Empire. Jackson thought said empire had fallen long before that and was amazed at how many cities and villages existed in western Jordan. He'd believed there was nothing but sand and goat-herders from here to the Far East.

They gradually left civilization behind, then paved roads. A few miles from the border between two of Jordan's twelve governorates—or states—they began a measured climb up and around a knoll overlooking a dry riverbed to the north, a gentle valley to the west, and a wide, deep basin south and east. If not for a faint haze on the horizon, Jackson was sure he could see to the Persian Gulf.

The road had become rough and uneven, not so much a road as a dirt and crushed-rock path. The Mazdas scraped bumpers and undercarriages several times but made it to an informal parking area on the west edge of the hillock. The eight members of Team Joel got out, immediately hit by the dry heat of the desert. As far as the eye could see, there was no sign of another person or human development.

As stunning as the barren vista was, their attention quickly turned to the top of the knoll. The centuries and the elements had not been kind to Sanctifié Castle. Its main tower stood some thirty feet above the ground, with a rock wall extending west and another headed southeast. A dozen yards down the slope, a second partial wall appeared to have been swallowed up by the ground, hardly discernable from a natural rock ledge except for its straight lines. Two more towers—or rather, what would have been towers—were crumbling and decaying. Sanctifié Castle looked as if it had melted in the desert heat. It was understandable.

"Let's start by taking a look around," Joel said. "Get the lay of the land."

"This is not a preserved tourist site," Aliana said, "so be careful."

Mulling over the six verses found on the *ostracon*, Jackson went with Maggie, Joel, Aliana, and Ian as they surveyed the castle. It was small compared to others in the area and followed the Crusader architectural patterns. Inner and outer walls had been completed, it appeared, along with the keep and at least parts of several buildings. It would have functioned as at least a rudimentary stronghold, Ian said, wondering aloud why it hadn't been finished after being constructed to this extent. "Surely Joseph le Saint could have scraped together the necessary funds, yeah?"

"I'm guessing it had less to do with money and more to do with the political climate," Joel said.

"It would explain why it was a safe hiding spot but Kerak wasn't," Jackson said. "Why would Saladin waste time besieging this?"

After an hour of looking around, the eight reassembled "inside" the castle. The south and east walls were completely in shambles, and the north wall was half eroded. Even the tower, from the inside of the castle, was less a tower and more a pile of rocks.

"What are the odds whatever we're supposed to find is buried under the rubble?" Rich asked.

"Good," Cara said.

"How do we search then?" Maggie asked. "Can you get permission to get a backhoe in here?"

Ramón smirked.

"Let's eliminate any other possibility first," Joel said.

"So where do we start?" Ian asked. "Cisterns, desert wells, clefts in the rock?"

"'*He hideth my soul in the cleft of the rock*,'" Jackson sang out in a rich baritone.

They all stopped and looked at him.

"What, you have no appreciation for the sacred hymns of the faith?"

"Is that what that was?" Maggie asked.

"This is sure a '*dry, thirsty land*,'" Jackson said. "It fits."

"Save it for Sunday," Cara said. "And your church back home."

"Tough crowd."

"Meanwhile, back at the archaeological survey . . ." Ian said.

Joel smiled thinly. "In answer to your question, Ian, all of the above. Look anywhere that might possibly be referenced by the verses on the *ostracon*."

"And no singing," Cara muttered.

The group split into foursomes, Jackson going with Maggie, Ian, and Aliana. They were tasked with scouring every inch of the tower while the others went to examine the rest of the castle for possible cisterns, hollow places in the wall, or other features that might somehow relate to the verses found at Masada.

"So with all these references to towers and cisterns," Ian said, "we're not really sure if we're supposed to look for a tower or a cistern or a cistern in a tower, yeah?"

"Or supposed to pick something else obscure out of those verses," Maggie said.

"Or if that *ostracon* was some Hebrew scribe's favorite verses he tucked away one day," Jackson said.

Before entering the tower through a stone archway, Aliana spent several minutes studying it and shining her flashlight into the opening.

"Are you worried it isn't stable?" Maggie asked.

Aliana nodded. "We had a bad experience in Morocco once."

"I'm not an architect, yeah, but I doubt it's going to choose today to crumble."

"Unless we disturb something that is hanging precariously," Aliana said.

"We'll be careful."

The tower was approximately thirty feet in diameter. Upon entering through the archway, they found themselves in a narrow corridor between concentric circles. Openings led right or left, with stairs leading up to the right and down to the left. A third opening went straight ahead, and Jackson shone his light at walls fifteen to eighteen feet away. His light went up to the ceiling, a mere seven feet above. It showed rotted and worn timber planks, as did the floor, and he reached out a hand to stop Maggie before she could venture into the chamber.

"What?"

"After eight hundred years, I think there might be some termite damage. Wouldn't want you to plummet into the *oubliette*."

"I am impressed," Aliana said.

"I had a thing for castles when I was a kid."

"Where'd they find wood around here?" Ian asked.

"I do not know."

"Why do you think there're no trees?" Jackson asked him.

"So where do we look first?" Maggie asked.

"Cistern's down, yeah?"

"Jackson?" Aliana asked.

"Yeah. Sort of. Think about this a minute. We have six verses on the shard of pottery, right?"

She nodded.

"Each seems to have a meaning. Genesis 30:24 gives us the clue of Joseph, the one from Maccabees mentions a fortress, and the verse in Luke suggests the fortress or tower isn't completed. That all leads us to this castle, right?"

She nodded again.

"Proverbs 18 tells us the righteous run into the tower, which puts us here, in the tower. Proverbs 5 directs us to the cistern, which is down, like Ian said. Then the Song of Solomon verse mentions *'the clefts of the rock, in the hollow places of the wall.'* So I'm guessing what we're looking for is in the walls of the cistern."

Aliana's eyebrows rose. "That makes sense. And explains why the verses were in the order they were in."

"I agree," Maggie said.

"Aye, we trust the detective."

"Does that earn me any M&M's?"

"I'm all out, yeah? Going through withdrawal myself."

"Well, let us get started," Aliana said. "And be careful on the steps."

Flashlight beams leading the way, the foursome began descending the circular staircase that wound around the outside of the tower, boring down into the earth. Despite the location in the desert, the air quickly grew cool and a little damp. Spider webs stretched across the narrow corridor, some of them intricate and fully spun webs, others remnants of old webs hanging in strings.

They moved methodically and slowly, shining their light on all the stones that made up the walls and the stairs, paying particular attention to the cracks and crevices or any "markings" on the stones. When they had made approximately half a revolution, they came to another doorway leading to the interior of the tower, whereas the stairs stopped, butting up against a solid wall.

"The dungeon," Jackson said, shining his light into the interior. It was nothing but blackness.

"No," Aliana said, aiming hers down. "I think this is the cistern." Her light revealed a flat, relatively smooth floor some seven or eight feet down. "This looks like water storage."

Ian clicked off his light. "Lower me down."

"Not without some sort of rigging or harness," Aliana said. "And we have no idea what condition the floor is in."

"Aye. There's rope in the cars. I'll be back."

He was back in five minutes, and it took another ten to rig a crude rope ladder they attached to pitons driven into the stone walls.

"Ladies first?" Ian asked.

"Age before beauty," Maggie replied.

"Aye, touché." With a wide grin, he lowered himself onto the ladder and climbed down. His beam flashed around for a moment before shining up. "Floor's secure, yeah? Come on down."

One by one, they followed him down the ladder until they were all standing in the large cistern. Four flashlight beams played around the dark, dank room, looking for anything out of the ordinary. When nothing jumped out at them, they split the cistern into quarters and repeated their methodical search. It turned up nothing, and they were just assembling to reassess when a head peeked through the opening from which they had descended.

"How's it going?" Joel asked.

"Short of feeling every stone to see if it's loose . . ." Ian said.

Jackson shone his light up, at the underside of the stairs. The cistern was not a perfect circle but resembled a spiral, its arc growing ever wider to incorporate the expanse beneath the stair corridor into its area.

"You see something?" Maggie asked.

"'. . . *in the hollow places of the wall*,'" Jackson quoted. "What are hollow places in these walls?"

"There aren't any."

"Because it's a solid wall, so you'd have to create a cavity for the purpose of creating a cavity."

She nodded.

"But what about under the stairs?" Jackson said, aiming his beam at the underside of the stairway.

"It's a smooth surface," Maggie said.

"Aye, but what about under the risers?" Ian asked, coming over. "Inside the stairs, yeah?"

"That's what I was thinking," Jackson said.

"You see anything?" Joel asked. "Any reason to think something's there?"

"No."

"Well, we found nothing. You guys ready for a lunch break?"

"Aye," Ian said. "There's nothing here."

"Wait," Jackson said. "Shine your light over here."

"What is it?"

"On that stone, right there, what do you see?"

Ian focused his beam on a stone about six inches square, built into the back of the staircase, roughly ten feet above the cistern floor. In addition to having no noticeable mortar on its right side, there appeared to be very faint etchings in its otherwise smooth, dark surface.

"Is that . . ."

"What?" Aliana asked, coming closer and aiming her light up at it.

"If I'm not mistaken," Jackson said. "It's a figure holding a sword."

"A knight?"

"Or an angel."

"An angel?"

He moved his beam a foot to the right, where another six-inch-square stone had crude etchings, these resembling a leaping animal.

"A lion," she breathed.

"The symbols of the Knights Calvary, on either side of a foot-square stone with no mortar on either side," Jackson said.

"We're going to be a while on lunch, yeah?"

Chapter Thirty-Nine

4:40 p.m.

"HOW CAN IT be empty?" Cara said, picking at a weed and flinging it toward the outer wall of Sanctifié Castle. She sat next to Jackson, Maggie, Rich, Ian, and Ramón, looking north across the dry riverbed at hundreds of miles of nothing. The late afternoon sun was low enough that the terrain had taken on an amber glow where dark shadows didn't knife into ravines and gullies.

"Someone beat us to it," Rich said.

Cara snorted. "Who?"

"The *Chevaliers Calvaire*."

"Interpol," Ramón suggested.

"And how'd they do that, yeah? We had all the clues."

Cara shook her head and thudded a small rock into the dirt. "How can it be empty?"

Contrary to Ian's comments, the team had taken a break for lunch after Jackson had discovered the two Knights Calvary markings on the underside of the cistern's staircase. The tricky part had been accessing them, their being ten feet above the cistern floor, and Team Joel had muted its excitement with a discussion on how to get up to the stones in question while they ate a lunch of day-old sandwiches purchased from one of the restaurants at the Royal Palms the night before.

Rich proposed standing on shoulders like Jackson had done the day before at Masada. Ian proposed Rich be the one to lend his shoulders.

Ramón suggested rigging some sort of harness, but they weren't sure what to anchor it to.

Cara said they should emulate the Romans at Masada and build an earthen ramp up to it, but that would have taken too long and would have also stressed a floor they weren't sure was solid.

Ultimately, they chose to knock out several planks in the floor of the ground level chamber, which also served as the ceiling of the cistern. Then, using every last foot of rope—including the crude ladder that had let the team down into the cistern to begin with—they rigged a harness and man-powered pulley system by which to dangle one of the team members under the stairs to access the stones.

Aliana was chosen because she was the lightest and also the archeologist of the group. After lowering Joel and Maggie into the cistern to shine lights for Aliana, Jackson, Ian, and Rich went to man the rope, with Ramón and Cara as messengers and lookouts. "Watch out for booby-traps, yeah?" Ian said with a wink at Aliana before lowering her through the opening in the chamber floor.

"Thank you."

"Spinning blades, false floors," Jackson said. "And don't pick up any gold idols."

"You two are wonderful, you know that?"

Aliana was trim and light, but still, the trio had their work cut out keeping her level and steady. After several minutes, she announced that she was in place, and they steadied themselves. Time passed in increments as Jackson couldn't see what she was doing. Aliana did pass word through Ramón, who was stationed on a sturdy section of planks, prostrate to spread his weight and to look down into the cistern.

"The stone is loose," he reported. "And heavy."

"Can she manage it?" Ian asked.

Ramón lowered his head. When he raised it a moment later, he nodded.

The next voice was Aliana's, asking a question Jackson couldn't hear. Then a huge thud sounded.

"What was that?" Rich asked.

"She just dropped the stone," Ramón said.

"On purpose?"

He nodded.

Aliana's next words were audible to everyone. "It is empty."

"Empty?" Ian asked first.

She spoke to the group down in the cistern, then raised her eyes up to communicate to the others. "There is a cavity about a foot wide and deep, but there is nothing inside of it. No markings or writing. Nothing."

"Lovely."

Aliana was passed Cara's camera to take more pictures, then was drawn back up to the chamber. Jackson and Ian then lifted the others out of the cistern, and the entire team assembled outside the tower.

"A decoy?" Ian asked.

"Did we read the clues wrong?" Maggie asked.

"Does it go deeper or something?" Ramón asked.

Aliana shook her head. "Hard rock on all five sides—top, bottom, left, right, and back."

"The etchings," Cara said. "Are you sure they're the Knights Calvary marks?"

"They certainly look like them. Very similar to the ones in the church on Thasos."

Weary from their work, they'd sat down and had some water and leftover fruit. Then Joel had rallied the team to search the rest of the tower—going up—and the ruins of the other started towers. Maybe there was a second hidden compartment. Maybe the cavity they had searched wasn't the place referred to by the *ostracon*, but a hiding place formed by the members of the Knights Calvary who had built the castle, even though it fit all the criteria on the pottery shard. Maybe . . . Joel didn't know what other maybes, but they had come this far, and he wasn't ready to quit.

Without much enthusiasm, Team Joel had scoured the castle, covering every inch of it. Dejected, six of the team members had dropped onto the ground by the northern wall while Joel and Aliana had checked out one final idea, the half column of the gate, on the southwest corner.

"*How* can it be empty?"

"How many times are you going to ask that question?" Ian asked.

"Until it makes sense."

"Could be a while," Jackson said.

Maggie sighed and flopped back onto the ground, hair splaying in various directions. "This has to be the right place. Everything fits." She turned her head to look at Jackson. "You interpreted those verses down to the precise location."

He shrugged. "I read a hunch into a set of data. That doesn't mean it's the only possible conclusion."

"Then where else?"

"This could be the wrong tower," Ian said. "They could have meant one of these fine remnants." He nodded at the northwest tower, little more than a pile of rock.

"You think there's a secret compartment under the stairs leading to a cistern in that tower too?"

He shrugged.

"This might not even be the right castle," Ramón said. "Face it, we're back to square one."

A few minutes later, Joel and Aliana returned and reported finding nothing. Exhausted, with nothing further to do at the moment, and with daylight waning, Joel called an end to the search. Wordlessly, Team Joel loaded into two Mazdas and began the two-hour drive back through Mu'tah, Kerak, and the border checkpoint to Israel. By the time they reached the Jordan Rift Valley and drove south along the Dead Sea, the shadows were long and pointed, and nothing had erased the dejection blanketing the team.

They made it through the checkpoint without harassment and returned to the Royal Palms, where they showered and ordered room service to the common area between the guys' rooms. As they ate, they contemplated their failure.

"Let's back up," Joel said. "All the evidence seems to point to Sanctifié Castle and that compartment. But assuming we weren't scooped, that means we went wrong somewhere. So where? Wrong part of the castle? Wrong castle? Wrong interpretation of the *ostracon*? Was that not the clue we were supposed to find at Masada? Was Masada not the correct place to search?"

"If that wasn't the right castle," Cara said, "how in the Sam Hill do you explain it matching every single clue on the *ostracon*?"

"If the *ostracon* wasn't the right piece of evidence, then how did it come to be hidden at the arrow's mark?" Ian asked.

"If Masada wasn't right, how do you explain the arrow?" Maggie asked. "It all seems to fit."

"Aye."

"So then what?" Joel asked.

"I think somebody beat us to it," Ramón said.

"Aye, they interpreted clues they didn't have, removed the stone and the treasure, placed the stone back so Ali could detect no evidence of it, and did so without leaving any trace of evidence behind."

"What trace would they leave?"

"Footprints."

"In the scrub and rocks?"

"Tire tracks?"

"We never looked for tire tracks," Joel said.

"The ground was hard," Cara muttered.

"I'm with Ian," Maggie said. "There's no way somebody else found that. When would they have?"

"You are assuming it was recently," Aliana said. "The treasure could have been found years, decades, or centuries ago. Maybe someone stumbled into the ruins. Shepherds, Bedouins." She shrugged. "Maybe someone followed the knights who hid it there."

"Or maybe it was never there in the first place, yeah?" Ian said.

Cara shook her head. "What, this is all a cruel hoax perpetrated a thousand years ago so a few knights could have their jollies thinking about the saps who would one day come along and look for a treasure that wasn't there?"

Joel sighed. "We're clearly at a dead end. Let's sleep on it and see where we are in the morning before we make any drastic decisions."

"Aye," Ian said. "Sleep and drink on it."

*   *   *

Sunday, February 24
6:57 a.m.

FOR WHATEVER reason, Jackson woke up early. He'd gone to bed around nine, somewhere in the middle of the pack after a long day with an early start. Team Joel had been disconsolate—some of them ready to throw in the towel; others determined to figure out where they'd gone wrong. Jackson had hoped Joel was right, and a good night's sleep would cause the missing piece to click in his brain. It hadn't, and he felt groggy as he peeked out the window at a hazy morning over the Dead Sea.

Joel and Rich were still asleep, so as quietly as possible, Jackson took a shower. The warm water woke him up. It did not bring any novel ideas to his mind. Maybe that was because there wasn't a missing piece to the puzzle, just a puzzle that when fully complete was less than satisfying or that, like the ones he did at his grandparents' house as a kid, didn't have all the pieces. The more he thought about it, the more he was convinced they had followed the clues correctly. They just hadn't found the Calvary Treasure.

Rich was reading his Bible when Jackson came out of the bathroom, only to be replaced by Joel. Not until the second glance did Jackson realize Rich's hands were trembling.

"Hey, man, you okay?"

Rich looked up. "I . . . I had a vision last night."

Jackson just nodded. Rich's visions were batting about .500 if his tally was correct, or about the same as Dodgers' opponents the previous season.

"We're in big trouble," Rich said.

"How so?"

He shook his head. "I don't . . . I don't know. I just saw very bad things happening."

Jackson nodded again. "You tell Joel?"

"He said he'd pray in the shower."

"No specifics in the vision?"

"No."

With a final nod, Jackson tossed his dirty clothes toward his duffel bag. He was due for another few loads of laundry. "We set a breakfast time last night?"

"What? Uh, no, I don't think so."

Jackson looked at the clock—not quite seven-thirty—and flipped on Israeli TV. The only thing he knew about world events was that Syria was a mess and Russia was posturing—in other words, the usual. He found no news on but did find an update on the weather. The warmth was expected to continue for at least a few more days. It was already the last week of February. Hadn't this whole venture started at the beginning of February? Where had the month gone?

Rich closed his Bible and ostensibly began to pray. Jackson did him the service of muting the TV. He didn't understand Hebrew anyhow. When Joel came out, Jackson asked if it was too early to call the rest of the team.

"No, we need to figure out what we're going to do."

"No clarity for you this morning either?"

Joel shook his head, and Jackson reached for the phone. He tried Maggie, Cara, and Aliana's room first, hoping Maggie would answer just awoken from slumber. He'd called her in similar situations before, and liked her top-of-the-morning (or middle-of-the-night) husky voice and temporary confusion.

Nobody answered.

"Seven-fourteen, right?" he asked.

"The girls? Yeah."

"No answer."

Joel frowned.

Jackson dialed again, letting it ring ten times. "Still nothing."

"Maybe they went down to breakfast."

"I'll try Ian and Ramón," Jackson said. His brow furrowed as their extension rang and rang with no answer. At eleven, he hung up.

"Nothing?"

Jackson shook his head.

Rich's eyes were wide with fear as he stood up. "What's going on?"

"I think we woke up in *The Twilight Zone*," Jackson replied.

"I'll try Cara and Ali's cells," Joel said, retrieving his phone.

"Meanwhile, maybe you'd better go back to sleep and see if you get any more details," Jackson said to Rich.

Joel dialed Aliana first and reported getting only her voicemail. While he called Cara, Jackson pulled out his cell and dialed Maggie's number, suddenly getting that sick feeling in his stomach.

"Hi, this is Maggie. Leave me a message."

He closed his phone.

Joel lowered his at the same time. "Let's try doors."

Jackson and Joel headed out into the hall, where Joel banged on the ladies' door. Twice. Nobody answered. Normally calm, Joel's eyes were wide as they returned to their suite, where Rich had roused Ramón. He'd thrown on jeans and a T-shirt, but the shirt was backward and his hair looked like he'd rubbed a balloon over it while sticking his finger in an electrical socket. "Hey, man," he said, squinting and blinking. "What's going on?"

"The girls are missing," Joel said. "Why didn't you answer the phone?"

"I was sleeping. What time is it?"

"Seven-forty. You hear anything from Cara, Ali, or Maggie?"

"No. What's going on?"

"They're not answering their phones, their cells, or their door."

"Maybe they're sleeping."

"We're going to go check restaurants and the grounds, make sure the cars are here. Get Ian, and we'll split up."

Ramón yawned and turned back into the room.

Joel was back in control. "Rich, you wait in the room in case they call. We'll check in if we find them. Jackson, you hit the lobby and the pool. I'll take the restaurants and have Ian and Ramón split up to take the rest of the grounds and check the garage."

Jackson nodded as Joel turned back to Ian and Ramón's room. Ramón met him at the door.

"Uh, Ian's not here."

"What?"

"He's not here."

"Was he last night?" Joel asked.

"Yeah. We hit the rack like eleven or something. Maybe eleven-thirty. Before midnight."

"You didn't hear anything? See anything?"

"No, man. I was out till Rich banged down my door."

Joel looked at Jackson, his eyes wide again. Jackson looked from him to Ramón to Rich. His eyes made Joel's look like slits by comparison, and his jaw was visibly quivering. "My . . . my . . . my vision. It's happening!"

Chapter Forty

JACKSON, JOEL, AND Ramón made a sweep of the hotel and grounds but found no signs of the missing half of their team. They returned to find Rich alternating between praying and hyperventilating. "You didn't find them?" he asked.

Joel shook his head.

"What are we going to do?"

Joel ran his hand through his hair. "I don't know. Ramón, you're sure Ian didn't say anything about where he might have gone?"

"No, man."

"Was he acting weird last night?" Jackson asked. "Did he say or do anything unusual?"

Ramón scrunched his shoulders. "No. He was typical Ian."

"We should call the police," Rich said.

"Not yet," Jackson said.

"Why not?"

"Because this isn't an L.A. missing person's case. We call the Israeli authorities and tell them an American, a Canadian, a Scot, and a French Muslim are all missing—especially on top of what happened a few days ago—we'll cause an international disaster."

"I don't know, Jackson," Joel said. "I think Rich is right."

"We can't just do nothing," Rich said.

"No. We won't. Ramón, look through Ian's stuff. See if his phone's here, see if any clothes are missing or if anything looks out of place."

"Yeah, sure."

"Shouldn't the private investigator do that?" Rich asked.

"The private investigator's going to be looking at the girls' room."

"Can you pick the lock?"

"It's electronic. But I have another plan." He turned toward the elevator.

"What should we do?" Rich called after him.

341

"Try their cells again. Ian's too if Ramón doesn't find it."

Alone in the elevator, Jackson had a few moments to think and pray. He was getting pretty good at operating in these high-stress, desperate situations. So good, in fact, that he could push aside the gut-wrenching fear that otherwise would paralyze him. That is until he was alone in an elevator with nothing to do but think. If something happened to Maggie . . .

When the elevator dinged at the lobby, he untucked his shirt, mussed his hair even worse than it was, and punched himself in the nose hard enough to make his eyes water. He wiped them as he shuffled over to the counter, reaching in and feeling various pockets.

"Can I help you, sir?" a young woman asked.

"I, uh . . . I must have left my key in the room last night. It's uh . . . seven-fourteen."

"Of course. Do you have any identification?"

Jackson smiled sheepishly. "I left that too. My name's Ali Naceri. It should be on the reservation."

The woman touched her monitor a few times. "We have an Aliana Naceri."

Jackson sighed. "Sounds like a woman's name, I know. Old family tradition. I tried going by Al for a while, but Dad disapproved."

"You're an American?"

"Third generation."

"What brings you to Israel?" she asked as she swiped a keycard through a groove on the side of her monitor.

"Sort of a pre-spring break," Jackson answered.

"A little old for that, aren't you?" she asked with a smile.

He winked. "Never."

"Well, here you go, Mr. Naceri."

"Thank you," he said, saluting with the card.

"Enjoy your stay at the Royal Palms."

Jackson returned to the elevator, resisting the urge to look over his shoulder to see if the woman was calling security. She seemed to buy his story but could have been snowing him right back. He also vowed to find a new way to give himself a bleary-eyed look—he'd almost broken his nose.

Joel and Rich reported getting no answers when he returned to their room, and Ramón announced matter-of-factly that Ian's stuff was gone.

"What? All of it?"

He nodded.

Jackson was reeling, but pieces were starting to fit together too. "Okay," he said, "let's check the girls' room."

Using the newly acquired keycard, Jackson opened the door, and he, Joel, Rich, and Ramón stepped inside. The first thing they noticed was some sort of ethnic music coming from the clock radio between two queen beds.

"Alarm clock," Jackson said, walking over to shut it off. He stood there for a moment, surveying the room. Both beds were empty, and both unmade. The covers were half on the floor of one bed, while the other bed was a disaster, as if it had been jumped on by a couple of rowdy kids. Two duffel bags and a suitcase sat on the floor in the corner, all open. Two of the dresser drawers under the television were also ajar.

"Look," Ramón said, pointing at a gray V-neck draped over the edge of one suitcase. He was about to pick it up when Jackson warned him to stop.

"Don't touch anything," he said. "We're just looking."

"Well, wasn't that the shirt Maggie was wearing last night?"

"Why does that matter?" Rich asked.

Ramón shrugged.

"If the clothes they wore last night are here, it means they changed, which means they at least went to bed," Jackson said.

"You think they didn't?" Joel asked.

"Right now, we're looking for any facts. The beds are unmade, but that could be from the previous day."

"Not likely. Cara and Ali are both pretty good at keeping things tidy."

"Should we be looking for pajamas?" Ramón asked.

"If you know what to look for."

"Cara wears typical pajama pants," Joel said. "Usually with a Maple Leafs tee. Ali I don't think I've ever seen in pajamas, and I don't know about Maggie."

"I think she wears a Mark Messier jersey," Jackson said. "Shorts and a tank top likely. Don't ask how I know." He took a few steps away from the nightstand. "Okay, Ramón, see if you can find pajamas, but don't touch anything. Rich, check out the bathroom and see if it looks like they got ready this morning. Same deal. Touch nothing. Joel, do you see anything else that looks amiss?"

"I don't see Cara's laptop or tablet," he answered. "I doubt she'd put them away overnight."

"How can I look through luggage if I can't touch anything?" Ramón asked.

"Use a Kleenex," Jackson said, nodding at a box of tissues on the table.

"The door didn't show any signs of being jimmied or picked, did it?" Joel asked.

Jackson shook his head. "Window either."

"Meaning they weren't kidnapped, right?"

"Unless they knew the kidnapper," Jackson said. "Or he had a key."

Joel frowned.

"I don't see any jammies," Ramón said as Rich emerged from the bathroom.

"Nothing looks touched," Rich reported. "Their toothbrushes looked dry, there's no water around the sink, no makeup out or anything. And the bottom of the tub is dry."

"That's good work," Jackson said, turning his attention to the beds.

"Jackson?"

"Yeah. I'm just trying to figure this out."

"Figure what out?"

"How they were sleeping, who was where, how they got up."

"How?"

"Well, I'm guessing Maggie had her own bed, which puts her here, where only one pillow is depressed."

"That's Cara's glasses case," Joel said, pointing to a nightstand beside the other bed. The case was closed, and Jackson eased it open without leaving a print. The glasses were still inside.

"Oh no," Rich said.

"How well can she see without them?" Jackson asked.

"She can function," Joel said. "But unless she was just going down the hall to get ice or something, she would have had them."

"Meaning she left against her will, right?" Rich asked. "That's what we're dealing with?"

"Maybe," Jackson answered.

"Where's the maybe?"

"Probably, but let's not rush to conclusions. We know they came back to their room, changed into pajamas, set the alarm, and went to bed. They got up, didn't change, didn't shower or primp or anything, and left, Cara without her glasses."

"Plus Ian's gone," Joel said.

"Right. So what's the connection there?"

"You're the P.I.," Ramón said.

"Joel, give one of the girls a call."

He frowned but obeyed. A few seconds later, a chirp erupted from the far bed. Jackson turned and lifted up the pillow, revealing three cell phones.

"What does that mean?" Rich asked.

Jackson shook his head. "It confirms they didn't leave on their own."

"What are we going to do?"

"Just give me a minute."

"We should call the cops, man," Ramón said.

"I'm leaning that way too," Joel said.

"Hold on."

"What is it?"

"Hold on . . ." Jackson said, putting his hands on his head. The tumblers were falling into place.

"You got something?" Rich said.

"Maybe. Just go with me. Maggie, Aliana, and Cara all went to bed last night and left, undressed, unprepared, no phones. Ian's bed is slept in too, but he's gone. Packed. Cleared out."

"What are you getting at?" Joel asked.

"Remember what I told you, that the girls' room wasn't broken into?"

"You think Ian had something to do with their disappearances?"

"I think it's time to ask the question."

Joel shook his head. "No. I don't buy it. That's coincidence, nothing more."

"Why?" Rich asked. "Why would he do it?"

"Because he's working for someone else," Jackson said.

"Who?" Joel asked.

"Philippe."

"What?"

"Ramón, when you guys got to Kavala, Cara texted Joel. Do you remember that?"

"Um . . ."

"Right before you went to dinner."

"Yeah."

"What was Ian doing?"

"What?"

"What was Ian doing while she texted?"

"I don't . . ." He shrugged, then frowned. "I think he said he had a phone call to make. I don't remember."

Jackson turned to Joel. "That's when Philippe excused himself to take a call, right before dinner."

"That doesn't prove anything."

"Ian was also texting on the balcony of the Lucy Hotel, shortly after we decided our next move was to Israel."

"A lot of us were texting and calling then," Joel objected.

"And his calls to and from some girl named Monica day before yesterday? Cara said it was just an old girlfriend, and he gave some dumb excuse. But we don't *know* who he was talking to. Three calls after we find the clue at Masada and as we're figuring out we need to go to Sanctifié Castle in Jordan, where we find nothing after deducing all the clues perfectly?"

"Jackson . . ."

"That's awfully thin," Rich said.

"Okay. How about when he and I met his friend Eli in Jerusalem, Eli asked if Ian was still working for the 'bombastic Frenchman,' and Ian brushed it off and said he was working for his former partner. I thought nothing of it at the time, just semantics, but maybe Eli let slip something more incriminating."

"This is still all conjecture," Joel said. "Circumstantial is an overstatement."

"Ian's been with you since you were with Philippe. What if your split wasn't as amicable as you claim? What if Philippe has been paying Ian all along to be his mole? He lets you do the hard work of finding the Calvary Treasure and then swoops in to take it, thanks to his mole?"

"You really think someone else beat us to the treasure?" Rich asked.

"How?" Ramón said.

"Anybody with a basic knowledge of the Knights Calvary could have made the search we did and found what we did."

"If they had our clues," Ramón said.

"Which Ian could have supplied. The same guy who several times made a stink that nobody could have had them when the theory was suggested and who was most adamant that nobody else could have possibly beaten us to the castle. Methinks he doth protest too much."

Joel shook his head.

"It would explain why he has so much cash, man," Ramón said. "He's always flush."

"I can't believe this," Joel said, turning and pacing. He shook his head again. "No. I refuse to believe Ian's up to something like this."

"He also told me he'd never been to Jerusalem," Jackson said. "And yet he knew exactly which streets and alleys to take to rescue Maggie and Aliana."

"He could have looked at a map," Rich said.

"Yeah, that's basically what he said. But unless he memorized every avenue and alley . . ." Jackson shook his head. "The more I think about it, the more examples I keep coming up with of him being duplicitous."

"Duplicitous is a long ways from kidnapping members of our team," Joel said. "And even if you're right—and I don't think you are—what's his motivation? Why do anything to the girls? If your theory is right, he and Philippe have the treasure. Why not just disappear?"

"I don't know," Jackson said. "This is all tumbling out at once, and I'm trying to organize it the same as you are. All I know is something about Ian doesn't smell right, and I don't like coincidences."

Rich shook his head. "So what do we do?"

"I tell you what I'm doing, man," Ramón said, turning for the door. "I'm splitting."

"What?" Joel asked.

"Treasure's gone," Ramón said. Jackson, Joel, and Rich followed him back across the hall, into their suite, and into his and Ian's room. "Half our crew's missing," he said as he ducked into the bathroom and scraped several items off the counter. "We don't know who's in on it. I'm out."

"You can't just leave," Rich said.

"Watch me, choir boy," he said, dumping the items into his duffel. He grabbed a few loose pieces of clothing, stuffed them in as well, and zipped it shut.

"How are you getting home?" Rich asked.

"I'll figure something out. My advice to you guys, do the same."

"Ramón, wait," Joel said, reaching out to take hold of his arm.

Ramón stopped. "I hope they're all right, man, I really do. But I gotta do what's good for Ramón, man. And that means getting out of this country while I still can." He broke free and stepped through the doorway. "Let the cops handle it, man," he called, and then was gone.

Rich sat down, eyes closed, lips moving.

Joel looked at Jackson. His eyes revealed the weight upon his shoulders. "I'm calling the police, Jackson. I don't know what else to do."

Jackson nodded slowly. "At this point, I think you're right."

Chapter Forty-One

THE LOCAL AUTHORITIES consisted of a hotel detective, a pair of uniformed policemen, and finally an inspector. No Shin Bet, Mossad, or IDF forces, but then again, they didn't likely respond to missing person cases. Jackson, Joel, and Rich told their story multiple times, leaving out some of the minor details, but not holding back anything relevant. The inspector took the trio's statements as well as descriptions of Maggie, Cara, and Aliana—and Ian—while the police searched their rooms.

Shortly after eleven o'clock, the inspector took down Joel's contact information and promised to be in touch. He was not overly optimistic about the disappearance of three women, and Jackson wanted to puke when his mind recalled horror stories he'd heard from this part of the world.

Joel then made calls to various embassies (American, Canadian, and French) in Israel, alerting them of the situation and asking them for any possible help. As expected, there was little they could do in such a situation. He also called his contact with the Israeli Shin Bet, just in case anything in their investigation of the French separatist group responsible for the attack on Masada was relevant to the women's disappearance. There had been nothing credible to suggest the French group was in any way still active in Israel or had any further intentions of harming Team Joel, but he wanted to cover all bases.

The trio also debated trying to get in touch with Eli Haddad. But if there was any accuracy to Jackson's theory that Ian was involved in Maggie, Cara, and Aliana's disappearance, then Eli fell under suspicion by association. Besides, they had no clue how to get in touch with him anyhow.

So they were left to wait, eating an early lunch of sandwiches that had no taste. Joel paced. Rich prayed and repeated his earlier warning of doom. Jackson sorted through all the facts at his disposal again and again, trying to find something to prove or disprove his suspicions of Ian and shed some light on where the women were.

When Joel's phone rang, all three of them jumped. Joel quickly looked at the display. "Unknown number," he said.

"Put it on speaker," Jackson said just before Joel answered.

"Joel Robinson."

The voice on the other end was muffled and sounded manually distorted. Even so, Jackson thought he picked up a faint Middle Eastern accent.

"We have your women. We will kill them if you do not do what we say."

"We're listening."

"Come to Jerusalem. Enter the Old City on foot through the Jaffa Gate. Walk along the east side of the Tower of David. Look for a man in a blue hat. Follow him until you come to a white van. Bring all of your research and evidence on the Calvary Treasure and leave it in the back of the van."

"If we do this, will you give us the women back?" Joel asked.

"The van will drive away. If you do as you are told, a second van will arrive with the women. You will then leave Israel immediately and never come back."

"We'll do exactly what you say," Joel said.

"If you don't, the women will die. If you try to find us, the women will die. If you contact the police, the women will die."

"We'll do exactly what you say," Joel repeated.

"You have two hours. Do not be late."

The phone clicked off, and the three men looked at each other.

"What do we do?" Rich asked for what seemed like the thousandth time.

"Exactly what they say," Joel said.

Jackson nodded.

"I can back up everything to a cloud drive in ten minutes," Joel said.

"Can they track that somehow?"

"Only if they were hacked into my computer or my cloud drive, and if they were, they'd know what we know already."

"Go. Rich, get everything of ours packed that you can. I'll pack the girls' stuff."

Rich nodded and departed. Jackson quickly packed as much of Maggie, Cara, and Aliana's stuff as he could. He lugged their bags over to his room, where Joel was working feverishly. A million thoughts went through Jackson's head. Who had the girls, and why? Was Ian involved? Would the kidnappers carry out the exchange as promised? Would that be the end of it? He tried to prepare for every contingency, but it was hard when he had no idea what the contingencies might be.

"All set," Rich said.

"One minute . . ." Joel said, tapping away at his computer. "Okay, everything's backed up. The hardware is expendable."

"The gold cross and the *ostracon*?"

"In my bag, here."

"I hope the tower collapses on them when they search. Let's go." Jackson stopped before opening the door. "Keep in mind, they might be watching us from the moment we step into the hallway. Just get to the cars. Joel, are you up to driving?"

He nodded.

"Okay. Rich, you're in front."

Without another word, the trio headed downstairs. Joel checked out of all three rooms while Jackson and Rich carried the luggage to the garage and to one of their two Mazdas. Not surprisingly, the other was gone, likely taken by Ian or Ramón. Joel joined them, and at five before noon, the trio was on the road, headed for Jerusalem.

Hazy sunshine was blinding, turning the ribbon of highway in front of them into a shimmering mirage. To the right, the Dead Sea appeared to be evaporating by the moment. The dry and barren wasteland was a fitting locale for the unfolding nightmare.

In the backseat, Jackson rifled through the various bags. He had made sure to place his, Joel, and Rich's bags in the trunk, so he was sitting with the three women's. Now he searched for tennis shoes, socks, underwear—despite his own objections—a loose shirt and pair of pants from each bag, and some basic toiletries. It took him three tries, but he managed to cram everything into Rich's backpack, the contents of which he had emptied into Maggie's duffel.

"What are you doing back there?" Rich asked.

"Prepping a crash kit," Jackson said. He reached into his back pocket and withdrew the women's passports, which he stuffed into a side pocket of the backpack. "In case we have to make a run for it."

"You think that's possible?" Joel asked.

"Just preparing for any situation."

"To that end, do you have your gun yet?"

"I do."

"You're not going to carry it, are you?" Rich asked.

"Why not?"

"What if they frisk us?"

"Who? Blue Hat?"

"I don't know. I just don't want to endanger the girls."

"They never said no weapons," Jackson said. "If they frisk us, I'll divulge I have it and get rid of it."

"What about the security checkpoint?" Rich asked.

"They didn't search the car last time. I'll hide it."

Joel seemed satisfied. "Do we need any other plans?"

"I don't know. But I've got an hour to figure it out."

*   *   *

1:15 p.m.

JOEL PARKED in a lot several hundred feet south of the Jaffa Gate on the western side of the Old City of Jerusalem. Rich had suggested one of them stay with the car so they could make a quick getaway, but Jackson argued that would involve eventually driving into the Old City—which he doubted was a good idea—and Joel didn't want to split the team up any more than it already was. So they left the Mazda and struck out on foot.

The midday heat was oppressive as the trio walked along Omar Ben el-Hatab Street. Rich carried Joel's backpack with the cross, *ostracon*, copy of the journal, computer equipment, and various printouts and notes—his insistence—since Jackson had one of the nine millimeters Eli had procured for them stuck into the back of his pants. Joel led the way, checking his watch every few paces. They were on schedule, but if he was like Jackson, he was counting the hours the three women had been missing. They were going on six, and that was just since their disappearance had been noticed.

Jackson was also tortured by the thought that they were being misled. There was no guarantee Maggie, Cara, and Aliana would be exchanged according to the deal. For that matter, there was no guarantee they were in Jerusalem or even alive. Equally bad, Jackson had no knowledge of the area, no frame of reference to act upon if things went south. Even if he did, opening fire in the Old City of Jerusalem wasn't a strategy likely to end well. So he did the only thing he could do: he prayed.

Jackson had been in tough jams before—arguably tougher than this. But there was something to the environment, to the unknown enemy, to the stakes that apparently were the foundation for the crisis in which they now found themselves, that made this one seem worse. And there was also something to being in Jerusalem. Jackson knew that no location on earth made him any closer to God, and yet this was a place where so much biblical history had happened. It didn't affect his current situation one way or the other, but it sure felt like it did.

Vehicular traffic entered the Old City just south of the actual Jaffa Gate, and the trio could have walked along the stone-paved street into the Old City. But because the man on the phone had said to use the Jaffa Gate, that's what they did. Once inside the walls of the Old City, they were immediately amongst a throng of mismatched people. Male and female. Young and old. Jew and Arab. Well-dressed and poverty-stricken. Coming and going. On their left were shops and stores. On the right, the walls of the old Tower of David, a citadel that had been destroyed and rebuilt several times since it was originally erected in the second century B.C.

"Blue cap, right?" Rich asked.

Jackson and Joel both nodded, their eyes scanning the masses. They followed the road as it curved along the old fortress for some hundred yards, then appeared to come to an end at what looked like a barracks. As they approached the two-story building, Jackson saw a narrow street running alongside the building. A moment later, as he swept his eyes over the people milling about, he spotted a blue hat.

It was a baseball cap—a Dodgers cap, for a twist of irony. The wearer was short and swarthy, also wearing a brown leather jacket and khaki pants. He stood in the shadows, reading a newspaper. His face was totally obscured.

"Ten o'clock," Jackson said.

"I see him," Joel answered.

Almost immediately, the man turned, folding his newspaper and striking off down the street in one motion. Not breaking stride, Jackson, Joel, and Rich followed the man into an alley no more than a dozen feet wide, with walls on either side. There was the occasional store entrance, but otherwise stone walls several stories high closed them in. It was a perfect place for an ambush, Jackson noticed as they continued a dozen paces behind the man in the blue hat.

The alley opened into another street, not much wider than itself, and void of people. They followed the man to the right, toward a white van parked facing away from them. It was a European model, something between a minivan and a crossover. The man walked up to it, opened the back door, and climbed through it to the driver's seat.

"Stick to what they told us," Jackson said as they neared the van. They stopped, and Joel lifted the backpack from Rich's back and set it on the bumper of the van. While he unloaded his laptop, tablet, Rich's laptop, stacks of paper, the journal, the carefully wrapped *ostracon*, and the gold cross, Jackson surveyed the street. Nothing looked out of place, but there were a lot of little doorways and windows and grottos where someone could hide to observe or ambush. The hair on his neck standing up, Jackson looked into the van. Except for the blue-hatted driver, it was empty. The rearview mirror was angled down, and Jackson couldn't make out anything about the driver's features.

"That's everything," Joel said, placing the empty backpack in the back of the van as well. "Once the women are returned, we will proceed directly to Tel Aviv for a flight out of Israel."

"Shut the door," the man said, and Joel obliged. As soon as the door latched, the van drove away.

"Now what?" Rich asked.

Joel nearly shook as he wiped his hands against each other. "Now we wait for another . . ."

Jackson turned as Joel drifted off. Behind them, a replica of the first van was slowly coming toward them, waiting for a couple of pedestrians to clear out of the way.

"Lord, please . . ." Joel breathed.

The van slowly coasted to a stop, moving just above an idle until it was in front of the three men. The driver's side door opened and a man got out. Dressed head to toe in flowing white robes, he wore a turban around his head. His face was covered by a bushy black beard, and sunglasses blocked his eyes.

"Get in," he said.

"Where are the women?" Joel asked.

"I will take you to them."

"That wasn't the plan," Joel said.

"If you want to see them again, get in."

Jackson wasn't sure, but he thought the voice matched the one on the phone. He looked at Joel and Rich, the fear obvious in their eyes. Both of them silently asked, "What should we do?"

Jackson nodded slowly. "We're getting in," he said.

They had no choice. Their bargaining chip, such as it was, was gone. Their only hope was that they would indeed be taken to Maggie, Cara, and

Aliana. Yes, this put their lives in grave danger. But as far as Jackson was concerned, if he couldn't bring Maggie home with him, his life wasn't worth sustaining.

The trio walked around to the back of the van, where another man dressed in white opened the back door. "Stop," he said as Joel began to climb into the back of the van. Joel obeyed, and the man quickly frisked him.

As Rich stepped forward to be frisked, Jackson deftly reached for the gun tucked into the back of his pants. While the man wasn't looking, he pushed it past the waistband so it fell into his pants. Straightening his leg, he was able to pin it at the bottom of his pants, resting against the denim and the top of his shoe.

The man took a moment longer with Rich, examining the contents of the backpack. He confiscated the phones, but otherwise, let Rich pass.

Jackson limped forward, trying to keep his leg straight. He raised his arms, and the man frisked his side, waist, and down the side of his leg to the ankles. He was forceful and clumsy, and the weight of his hand as it raked Jackson's leg caused his knee to buckle and the gun to slip and clank against the pavement. The man reached for the exposed snout and ripped the handle from Jackson's pant leg. He looked up with a sneer before tucking the gun into a fold of his robe.

"Get in," was all he said, and as the trio climbed into the back of the van, Jackson hid a sigh of relief that he hadn't gotten them into any more trouble. There were no seats, just two benches, one on either side. The man laughed as he swung the door shut, leaving Jackson, Joel, and Rich temporarily in the dark. With the driver watching them through the mirror, they sat down, the fear almost palpable.

The other man got in the side door and withdrew a small handgun—not the Jericho 941—from somewhere in his robe. "Over there," he motioned to Joel, who switched sides to sit between Jackson and Rich. The man then took the opposite bench, gun brandished and ready. "Okay, go."

Before trying anything desperate, Jackson wanted to see where they were being taken. Maybe they were really being driven to Maggie, Cara, and Aliana. If that were the case, it would be a shame to get all shot up.

They continued south, making slow progress as they dodged pedestrians. Eventually, they turned left, to the east, driving on a similarly narrow street between two stone walls devoid of any doors or recesses. After a quick S curve, the street widened, and Jackson recognized the Zion Gate from his first trip to the Old City.

"Where are you taking us?" Joel asked.

"Silence."

They continued on, following the same path that Jackson, Maggie, Ian, and Aliana had traversed nearly a week ago. The road led them to the entrance to the Western Wall Plaza, where the driver turned toward the Dung Gate.

Once out of the Old City, they navigated to one of the main roads. Jackson found it odd at first that they were being transported down the highway. But he reasoned it made sense. There was nothing to identify the van as being part of something underhanded, and if they ever wanted to see the women again, Jackson, Joel, and Rich wouldn't try to signal passing motorists for rescue. It continued to sink in to Jackson that they had no leverage whatsoever.

No one spoke as they passed through a checkpoint into the West Bank and then continued cruising on the highway. Jackson spent his time paying attention—as best he could—to where they were headed while also studying the man holding the gun on him. He was thin, particularly in the face, where no beard hid his features. Unlike his partner, he didn't wear sunglasses, revealing bluish green eyes that were squinted and focused on the targets at the end of his gun.

Jackson tried to pick up the guy's mood. His face was taut, the lines around his mouth hard. His jaw was slightly discolored on the left side, bruised perhaps. He blinked steadily, and never moved except to wipe sweat from his forehead with his off-hand sleeve once or twice. That, and the occasional flexing of his fingers around the gun. Almost once a minute, he straightened one or two of them, then firmly grasped the gun again.

Jackson added the driver to his rotation of observances. He kept his eyes on the road, never checking the mirror. He trusted his partner to guard the trio. Without discernable movement, Jackson flexed the muscles in his legs and arms, making sure they remained limber.

"How much farther?" Joel asked.

"Silence."

"Is that all you say?" Jackson asked.

The man shot him a glare.

"Why are you doing this?"

"Silence."

"Allah is a swine."

The man clenched the gun tighter. "Shut up. One more word and I will put a hole in you."

Jackson sat back, getting a warning look from Joel. The van continued for another five minutes, leaving Jerusalem behind and heading out into the desert. Another sinking feeling began to wash over Jackson. He checked the guard again, watched him flex his hand on the gun, his eyes focused mainly on Jackson.

He flexed again, thirty-eight seconds after the previous flex. Jackson counted again. Thirty-six seconds. Then thirty-four. Then twenty-nine. He continued counting, watching the driver, checking out the terrain.

Forty seconds passed. Jackson tensed and relaxed his right leg.

Thirty-five seconds. The man glanced to Joel and Rich and back to Jackson.

Thirty-two seconds. The van hit a small bump.

Thirty-six seconds, and three of the man's fingers momentarily came off the gun. Jackson swung his leg up, the toes of his shoe hitting the side of the barrel and jarring it to the side. It was far from a perfect strike, not even knocking the gun loose. But it was the only chance Jackson had.

He lunged forward, swinging his arms like windmills, chopping at the gun and the man's wrist. Although he hadn't knocked the gun loose with his kick, he had shaken the man's grip. He fought to regain it, but before he could get his fingers around the trigger, Jackson chopped on his wrist, and the gun fell to the van floor.

Immediately, Jackson changed his tactics. Closing his hands into fists, he launched a series of uppercuts that caught the stunned guard on the jaw, toppling him back to the side of the van. He had no chance to put up a fight. The blows had dazed him, and seconds after kicking the gun, Jackson stooped to pick it up.

The driver saw the fight and swerved to the side of the road. Before he could get out of his seat, Jackson had the gun trained on him. "Move and you're Swiss cheese," he said. "Or maybe I should say Camembert."

Chapter Forty-Two

1:38 p.m.

"BOTH HANDS ON the ceiling," Jackson said to the driver, who obeyed. Jackson turned an eye to the guard, who was still slumped on the bench. He walked to him and, staying in the driver's sight via the rearview mirror and keeping the driver in his, stuck the gun to the guard's temple. "Joel, he has my gun, pocket or fold on the right side, waist high. Stay low and come grab it."

Trembling, Joel followed Jackson's instructions and quickly found the gun.

"Safety's on the left side by the thumb. Down is off. Turn the safety off, aim at the guard, and if he moves, squeeze until the mag is empty. Got it?"

"Got it," Joel said with reasonable conviction.

Jackson waited until Joel held the gun on the guard, then deftly stepped around him and took a few steps forward. The driver hadn't moved, his hands still on the van's ceiling. Jackson slipped into the passenger seat. He chanced another look back and saw that Joel was back on the bench, his gun leveled at the guard. Jackson nodded at the driver. "Right hand, slowly unbuckle your seatbelt."

He obeyed.

"Hand back on the ceiling."

He obeyed again.

"Last September, I killed twenty paramilitary mercenaries in the Nevada desert," Jackson said. "A few nights ago, I mowed down four of your buddies atop Masada," he said, checking the man's eyes at that last remark. They flashed confusion. "Point is," Jackson continued, "I know how to handle a weapon, and I have the guts to use it. You don't do exactly what I say, you die. Understand?"

The driver nodded. The guard, now sitting and holding his head, made a slight bob to show he comprehended as well.

"Joel, keep your gun on the guard and slowly move to open the back door. Then step down, keeping your gun on him."

Joel did as he was told, and Jackson kept his eyes roving back and forth between the driver and the guard. Neither made a move.

"Okay, Rich, stay out of Joel's line of fire and get out behind him."

When he had taken his position, Jackson addressed the guard. "Slowly, get out, lie down on the ground. Joel, keep your gun on him."

Once more, everyone followed his instructions. Jackson then opened the passenger door of the van and exited. "Okay, now very slowly follow me out," he said to the driver. Moving cautiously, he crossed the passenger seat and stepped down onto the shoulder of the road. "Sunglasses off. . . . Toss them. . . . Now lay down." The man obeyed every instruction.

Jackson backed up to where he could keep an eye on both men. They were on a dusty, barren road in the middle of nowhere, with no sign of civilization, people, or other drivers. And yet, they couldn't be more than ten miles from the outskirts of Jerusalem. They must have turned off the highway when Jackson was counting the guard's finger reflexes.

His pulse pounding, Jackson instructed the guard to get up and move around to the side of the van and lie down beside the driver. He obeyed.

While not paying specific attention to the weather, Jackson felt the sun beating down on him and the dry desert breeze whipping sand around the van. He nearly succumbed to a flashback of the carnage he had caused in Nevada several months prior but managed to stay in the present.

"Rich, see if you can find anything in the van to tie these guys up with. Joel, step over to the side of the van."

Both obeyed, and Jackson walked around the two men to Joel, looking him in the eye for the first time since the takeover. "You okay?"

"I . . . I think so," he said, and Jackson noticed his hands were trembling. Neither the guard nor the driver was looking, so Jackson reached over and turned the safety on Joel's gun back on. He winked at him.

"If either of them move, shoot them in the butt."

Joel nodded that he understood the bluff.

Rich returned with a roll of duct tape.

"Both hands behind your backs," Jackson said to the men. He turned to Rich. "Bind their wrists. Tight. Use plenty of tape. Then their ankles."

While Rich worked, Jackson moved around the men and aimed his gun at their heads, lest they get the idea to try anything. When Rich was finished, Jackson instructed him to turn them both over, onto their backs. He frisked both men and found a knife and another gun and two cell phones, all of which he gave to Rich. "Now, get in the van," he said. "Both of you."

"What?" Joel asked.

"Get in the van."

"What are you going to do, Jackson?"

"Now," Jackson said, calmly but firmly. "I'm going to get the girls back."

"How?"

He only nodded at the van, and the duo hesitantly climbed in. Jackson glanced left and right, up and down the road. There was nothing. He turned his attention toward his two captives, swallowing the bile that tried to rise in his throat.

"Okay, one chance. Where are the women?"

Neither man spoke, and Jackson looked them both in the eye. The driver seemed defiant. The guard a little less so. So Jackson approached the driver and placed his gun on the man's shoulder joint. "Where are they?"

"You won't shoot me. Not in cold blood."

Jackson squeezed the trigger, and the man howled as the bullet tore through his flesh and destroyed his shoulder. The report of the gun echoed across the desert and disappeared, while the man continued to holler. Leaving him to writhe in pain, Jackson turned casually toward the guard. His blue-green eyes were now wide with fear, and Jackson placed the gun on his shoulder. "Where are they?"

"I don't know."

Jackson pushed the gun barrel hard into his shoulder.

"I—I—I d-d-don't kn-know."

"Where were you taking us?"

"In-into the d-desert. We were g-g-going to d-dr-drop you."

"Where are the women?"

The man shook his head, biting his lip. "I don't know," he said in anguish.

Jackson looked at the driver, who had rolled halfway onto his good shoulder. "Does he?"

"No. W-w-we were just told to take you into the desert and let you go."

"By whom?"

"A man named Petra."

"The guy in the blue hat?"

He nodded.

"Where do I find him?"

"I don't know. We . . . we had a rendezvous point. In Jerusalem."

"Where?"

"Take *D-D-D-D—*"

"Slow down."

The man took a breath. "Take *Derech HaShiloah* past the Gihon Spring, just south of the Old City. Just before the P-P-Poo-Pool of S-Siloam, there's a left turn. I don't know the road name. Turn left and go about a hundred m-meters. There's a t-t-two-story house on the left with a Palestinian flag over the door."

"Guards?"

"No."

"How many men are there?"

"Two, maybe three. I don't know."

"Armed?"

He nodded. "P-Probably."

"And Petra's there?"

"I don't know," the man said, almost crying.

Jackson jammed the gun even harder into his shoulder. "If you're lying to me . . ."

"N-N-No, I s-s-sw-swear!"

Jackson nodded. "Were you supposed to call or check in after dumping us?"

"No. Just ret-t-turn to the house."

Jackson nodded again as he lifted the pistol. "Just in case you are lying," he said, swinging it down and cracking the man on the head. Then he clicked the safety on, stuck the gun back into his pants, and walked around to the driver's side of the van. His stomach tried to heave, and Jackson spat violently into the dirt, quelling the urge to vomit. Taking a deep breath, he opened the door and climbed into the driver's seat.

"What happened?" Joel asked from the back bench. Rich sat right beside him.

"I got a location," Jackson said. "Their rally point. Hopefully, someone there knows where the girls are."

"Did you shoot one of them?" Rich asked.

Jackson nodded as he put the van in gear and made a Y-turn on the dusty highway.

"You shot a man?" Rich asked.

Jackson ignored him. "Their HQ is a house in Jerusalem, south of the Old City. For what it's worth, I think the intel is trustworthy but shaky. Several hostiles, likely armed."

"What do we do?" Joel asked.

"We should call the police," Rich said.

"And tell them what exactly?" Jackson asked.

"The truth."

"Three women were kidnapped, and we overpowered the kidnappers and tortured them into telling us where their hideout is?"

"Yes."

Jackson shook his head. "I don't know how warrants work in Israel, but if the cops don't find the girls at this house, they probably get moved and disappear for good. We have the element of surprise. We go in now."

"Go in?" Rich asked.

Jackson nodded with grim determination on his face.

Chapter Forty-Three

1:49 p.m.

"JACKSON," JOEL SAID, "we're not soldiers."

"I meant me," he said. "I'll go in."

"Jackson." This time it was Rich. "I really—"

"Look, I know you guys aren't used to this sort of thing, and I won't ask you to do something you're not comfortable with. When we get there, you want to call the cops, then call them. But these guys have Maggie, and I don't trust foreign cops to get her back. I'm going in. Once I'm in, do what you have to do."

Joel and Rich were both silent.

"I don't think these guys were Arabs," Jackson said a moment later.

"What?" Joel asked.

"The guard had bluish eyes. And they didn't speak to each other in Arabic. The only reason I can think of for them using English is because they didn't want us to know which language they really spoke. And then when I blasphemed Allah, the guy—already on edge—doesn't pistol-whip me. He just tells me to shut up. That sound like a jihadist to you?"

"Not all Arabs are jih—"

Jackson cut Rich off with a glance. "They were dressed like Arabs, the one had the beard. He had an accent on the phone. They wanted this to look like another instance of Islamic extremists doing something terrible to Westerners, but it wasn't."

"Okay, so if not Islamists trying to get the treasure, who then?" Joel asked.

"Who do we know who wants the Calvary Treasure—or who doesn't want us to have it?"

"Interpol," Rich said.

"This isn't Interpol's style. Even rogue agents."

"What about *Liberté ou Mort*, that French separatist group?"

362

"The Masada attackers?" He shook his head. "When I mentioned that, the driver either had no idea what I was talking about or else deserves an Oscar."

"The leaves the CC," Joel said. "The *Chevaliers Calvaire.*"

"Right."

"You think these guys were French?"

"*Oui.*"

Joel shook his head.

"Look, Eli mentioned a guy named Sauveterre, a member of the CC who was in Israel. He also said they weren't ruthless but very determined. So far, that matches what we've seen from them. Toughness and bravado, but no violence."

Joel's eyes narrowed as he pondered.

"And did you see the guard's bruise? Consistent with the punch Ian threw that cold-cocked one of the guys harassing Maggie and Ali in the market. I didn't get a good enough look at that guy that day to know for sure, but it could be him. The CC, dressed like Arabs, one of them in a ball cap, trying to scare us off and cause trouble . . ."

"So what's Ian's connection then? You still think he's involved?"

"I don't know. I still think the evidence suggests he's in cahoots with Philippe. Philippe's surname is LeCavalier, same as Leon of Toulon, the original leader of the Knights Calvary, from which the CC originated. It all fits. Sort of."

"I just can't believe he'd be part of kidnapping the girls," Joel said.

"You wouldn't have believed he'd sell you out, either."

"I still don't," Joel said. "Not fully."

Jackson didn't tell them that his theory was, hypothetically, good news. If the CC was behind the kidnapping, it was less likely that Maggie, Cara, and Aliana would be killed. Not certain, but less likely. At any rate, he didn't want to give Joel and Rich false hope, nor do anything to dull the rage-like determination coursing through him.

He turned back onto the highway and soon they were in Jerusalem. Traffic was thin on a Sunday afternoon, and Jackson called Joel to come up front and help him navigate. There was a map in the glove compartment that showed the major streets, but not the Gihon Spring, Pool of Siloam, or *Derech HaShiloah*. Skirting the eastern side of the Old City, still in the West Bank, Jackson finally stumbled upon the narrow city street. A sign indicated the spring was just ahead, and he pulled over to the side of the road.

He repeated the guard's directions for finding the headquarters house. "If you both want to wait in the van, fine. If you want to call the cops, go for it."

"You can't go in alone," Joel said.

Rich nodded. "We'll go with you."

Jackson shook his head. "I can't put you in danger."

"We have three guns," Joel said.

"Have you ever fired a gun?"

"At a range, once. Years ago."

Rich shook his head.

"I go alone."

"As strongly as you feel about Maggie, we feel the same about Cara and Ali," Joel said. "If you're going in after them, then we're going to do everything we can to help you."

Jackson sighed. He was very hesitant to put weapons in the hands of untrained users, but they weren't giving him a choice. So he joined them in the back of the van and gave them a crash course on using the handguns they had lifted from the driver and guard.

First thing, he made sure the safeties were on. "You click the safety off, be ready to fire. Hold it like this," he said, demonstrating with his weapon. "Left hand underneath, right hand on the handle. Hold it like you're shaking your future father-in-law's hand. Finger over the trigger guard unless you are ready to fire. I do not need a bullet in the back."

They both nodded.

"If you have to shoot, aim for central body mass, take a deep breath, and gently squeeze the trigger. It's going to kick a little. Don't worry about getting your gun off. Just make sure you get one good shot. Even if they're wearing a vest, it will slow them down."

"What about squeezing until the mag is empty?"

"Theatrics to scare baddies."

They nodded again.

Jackson looked both of them in the eye. "This is for real. We have one objective, and that is to get Maggie, Aliana, and Cara out safely. Anybody who gets in our way or tries to stop us gets shot. It's them, or it's the girls. That has to be your mindset. And if you can't get to that place, then stay in the van. Are we clear?"

Solemnly, Joel and Rich nodded again.

"I've taken lives before," Jackson said. "It changes you. Forever." He made eye contact. "I won't think any less of either of you if you want out. It doesn't mean you care any less about finding the girls. It—"

"We're in," Rich said.

Joel nodded.

"Okay. I'll lead. Joel, you're next. Rich, bring up the rear. Keep your eyes and ears open. Guns down, safeties on, until I say so. You hear shots, get down and protect yourself. Closed fist means stop. You need my attention, don't talk; grab my shoulder. Got it?"

More nods.

"Questions?"

They shook their heads.

"Okay, let's do this."

Jackson returned to the driver's seat and guided the van south, looking for the road the guard had indicated. It was little more than an alley, leading east toward a hillside covered with houses. Fifty yards in, it curved to the south. Another fifty yards along, Jackson spotted a house on the left with a red, white, green, and black flag hanging over the doorway. He kept going another hundred yards before he turned around in a driveway and returned north.

"Okay, get out the back and come around to the street side," Jackson said as he pulled over in front of the door.

Joel and Rich both nodded and Jackson put the van in park. He killed the engine, pocketed the keys, and got out. Joel and Rich met him on the driver's side of the van.

"Guns ready?"

"Ready."

"Safeties on?"

"Yes."

"Yes."

"Okay. Let's go."

Jackson peeked around the front windshield of the van, surveying the house. One door, a window on either side. Both dark. Two upstairs windows, equally dark. Flat roof with a satellite dish. The building itself looked old and rickety, as did the rest in the neighborhood. They all merged together, sharing walls, with no yards. An occasional alley or sidewalk cut between the buildings, but from Jackson's vantage point, it looked like one huge building stretched along the hillside. Graffiti covered everything—walls, doors, boarded windows. The siding and roofing was different on every house, sometimes on the same house. Living room furniture sat on the sidewalk in front of the house two doors down. A basketball hoop was mounted over a garage a few houses in the other direction. The only constant was a dirty tan color that seemed to pervade everything. That, and an abandoned feel. As Jackson led the way to the front door, he saw no other humans. Less collateral. And likely no neighborhood watch captain to stir up trouble.

The front door was solid, no windows. Jackson held up a fist and took a few steps over to the window. Putting his face right up to it, he still couldn't make out anything in what appeared to be a darkened room. So he moved back to his place in front of Joel and Rich. The doorknob didn't turn. So much for a soft entrance.

In that moment, just before he kicked in the door, Jackson realized how ridiculous this was. Three Americans, only one of whom had any sort of tactical training or experience, about to storm a house in the West Bank to rescue three kidnapped women. He was pretty sure this was how international incidents got started, if not outright wars. For the tenth time, he questioned his refusal to call the police. But for the tenth time, he found himself convinced that if they paused for even a minute, the trail would go permanently cold. Besides, whoever was waiting to rendezvous with their captors would be expecting them back from the desert drop-off soon.

Pausing only long enough to offer a one-word prayer for help, Jackson stepped back, then kicked the door, just beside the knob. It swung in and slammed off a wall, almost closing again. Jackson pushed it open and took two steps forward so that he was all the way inside the darkened room. Gun in front of him, he turned left and right, spotting nothing.

The room was completely empty. No furniture. No shelves. No boxes. Nothing. Directly ahead from the front door was a stairway, and on either side of the stairs, doors. Jackson held a fist to halt Joel and Rich, then pointed to Joel. Jackson motioned toward his own eyes and then to the stairs, instructing Joel to watch them. He nodded that he understood. Jackson gave Rich the same visual instructions about the door on the left while he moved over and checked the one on the right. It was a bathroom, toilet and sink only. No personal items. No sign of recent use.

Jackson switched places with Rich and found that the left door led to a hallway that ran under the stairs with empty rooms—bedrooms, likely—on either side and another door at the end of the hallway. Rear entrance? Garage? Storage closet? He decided to check the upstairs first.

Returning to the main room, Jackson motioned again, this time for Rich to guard their rear as they climbed the stairs. So far, all was quiet, which meant the place was deserted, the occupants were deaf, or they were lying in wait.

The stairs creaked, and halfway up, Jackson gave up on stealth and hurried to the top. A hallway branched left and right, with doors opening on both sides. Jackson pointed for Rich to guard the stairs and Joel to guard the hall to the right. He moved down the hall to the left, clearing two empty rooms—more bedrooms, he guessed—and a bathroom. Then they switched sides, and Jackson cleared a kitchen and dining area and another living room. Both were completely void of furniture, utensils, or decorations. This place was either a decoy or a meeting place, nothing more.

Jackson rejoined Joel and Rich at the top of the stairs. "Empty," he said quietly.

"So where is everyone?" Joel asked.

"Where are the girls?" Rich asked.

"There's still the back door," Jackson said. "You guys good?"

They both nodded.

"Come on."

Jackson led the way down the stairs and through the main room into the back hallway. The door looked sturdier than the front door, with hinges on their side of it. Jackson nodded back out of the hallway.

"I'm going to check the van for something I can use as a pick," he said when they were assembled in the main room. "Joel, keep an eye on that door. Anyone comes through, shoot. Rich, watch the front door. If it isn't me . . ."

Rich nodded.

"If it is, don't shoot," he said with a wink. "I'll knock four times, bap-bap-bap-bap, like that."

"Got it."

The street was still deserted, and Jackson quickly ransacked the van. He found a simple toolkit that would work, he thought, as well as a flashlight. He returned to Joel and Rich and gave Joel the flashlight while he picked the lock. Then he stood and took the flashlight again, holding it backhanded in his left hand and balancing the gun across it with his right, just like they did on TV. With a nod, he opened the door.

He shined the light down a stone stairway, hand-hewn out of the rock. His light barely reached the bottom, revealing a tunnel boring into the hill, only a few feet wide and just high enough for him to stand upright. Carefully, he led the way down the stairs. The tunnel extended maybe twenty-five feet before stopping at a T intersection. The age-old dilemma—left or right?

For whatever reason, Jackson turned to the right, and they proceeded along a tunnel twice as wide and similarly high as the one leading to the house. The tunnel was uneven, cracked, and dripping water. The floor was wet, with a few trickles of water running the same direction Jackson was walking. Fifty feet along, his light reflected off iron, and he stopped the convoy at a metal gate.

"What is this?" Rich asked quietly.

"The Gihon Spring on the other side of the road is the start of Hezekiah's Tunnel," Joel said. "I'm betting this is another subterranean aqueduct. Or at least it was at one time."

"Why the gate?"

"I don't know," Jackson said, grabbing hold of the iron barricade. It rattled slightly, but was secured with a padlock and firmly anchored to the sides of the tunnel.

"Can you shoot it?" Rich asked.

"Last resort. Let's try the other direction."

They turned around, Jackson again in the lead, and made their way up the tunnel, past the entrance to the house. The tunnel began to twist to their right and ascend. The floor was covered in a thin sheen of water that made the footing slippery and the going slow. Jackson felt as if he was miles away from civilization, burrowing deep into the heart of the earth to find unknown enemies. Jules Verne meets Frank Peretti sort of stuff.

Suddenly Jackson stopped and doused his flashlight. He'd heard a noise ahead of him, and as he strained to see in the darkness, he thought he spied a dim light reflecting off the walls of the tunnel. Waiting a minute to let his eyes adjust, he was able to make out a recess in the tunnel to his right, some thirty feet ahead. Another offshoot.

His eyes weren't playing tricks—light was definitely flickering from the new branch. Waving his finger forward, he led Joel and Rich, tiptoeing toward the opening. Just before it, he stopped, holding up his fist again. The light had stopped flickering and was now a steady but very faint glow.

Jackson took a deep breath. In one motion, he whipped around the corner, flicked on his light, and leveled his gun. "Don't move!" he shouted.

He nearly dropped his gun when he spotted the man standing fifteen feet into the tunnel, a small penlight strapped above his ear, and a gun in his hand aimed at Jackson.

"Aye, you either."

Chapter Forty-Four

2:31 p.m.

"IAN?" JACKSON ASKED, not believing his eyes.

"Aye," Ian said, looking down the barrel of his pistol. "Looks like you and I have a wee predicament, yeah?"

"Not so much," Joel said, stepping beside Jackson, his gun also raised. "It's two to one."

Ian actually grinned. "I think you'd better count again, yeah?"

The words were still on his lips when Jackson felt cold steel pressed against the back of his neck. Immediately, he tensed. Beside him, Joel actually dropped his gun, the clank echoing throughout the tunnel.

Jackson's first thought was that Rich had double-crossed them. He had been playing them all along. He was actually a Green Beret or a ninja or something, faking to be a vision-receiving Pentecostal. But before his mind could begin to round off the edges on this new piece of the puzzle, Rich wedged his way between Joel and the wall, his hands up. The cold steel pressed against Jackson's neck didn't waver.

"I believe the odds have changed, yeah?" Ian said.

Jackson was about to drop his gun when the pressure in his neck relented and a man stepped forward between him and Joel. He held two guns, one in each hand, both held up in a defenseless posture. He spun the guns, handing the one in his right hand to Jackson.

Slowly, skeptically, he took the gun, then raised his flashlight to reveal the surrendering gunman.

"Eli?"

"Nice to see you again."

Jackson looked back to Ian. "What are you doing here?"

"I'd bet the same as you. Looking for the girls."

Now the pieces in Jackson's head were from several different puzzles, and nothing fit together. "How'd you know?"

"I called Ali this morning, she didn't answer, no one answered the door, and I started to worry. So I conned a key from the guy at the front desk and found them gone. That's when I called Eli."

"Why didn't you tell us?" Joel asked. "We thought something had happened to you too."

"I didn't know who I could trust, yeah? I thought it might be an inside job."

"Yeah, the feeling was mutual," Jackson muttered.

"So I gathered."

"How did you find this place?" Joel asked.

"Eli and I spent the morning working sources and following leads. We came in from the north end of the tunnel."

"What kind of sources?"

"Remember I told you about a member of the CC named Sauveterre?" Eli asked.

"Is it him?"

"We think so."

"So where are the girls?" Joel asked.

Ian turned. "Behind that door, yeah?"

"Then what are we waiting for?" Rich asked.

"Hold on," Eli said. "We can't all just storm through there."

"Aye, especially those who've never fired a gun." He looked at Jackson. "What were you thinking?"

"I was thinking it was me against the world, seeing as how our munitions man had run out on us. Besides, they wouldn't take no for an answer."

"Where'd you get the extra guns?"

"Off a crippled phony Arab."

Ian frowned but didn't ask further questions. They spent a few seconds forming a plan, in which Eli, the former Mossad agent, took the lead. Jackson and Ian were next, with Joel and Rich—safeties on—guarding the rear.

As Ian finished picking the lock and led the way into another narrow tunnel, only wide enough for them to advance single file, several questions nagged at Jackson. Why had Ian called Aliana early in the morning? If he had conned a keycard from the guy at the front desk, why hadn't the woman been more suspicious when Jackson did the same thing later on? Did the Royal Palms not have any sort of notification built into their computer system to log such things? If Ian was on Team Joel's side, what did that mean for all of Jackson's earlier questions? Did Ramón play some role in all this?

He didn't have time to get to the rest of the questions because they came to a stairway that climbed steadily upward, through a tunnel so low they had to stoop at times. The stairway curved back around itself, and Jackson started flashing back to a Hardy Boys novel . . . something about smugglers and a stairway through the cliffs down to the bay.

At the sixty-fifth step, they reached a landing and another door. Eli pulled a small device from his pocket and held it to the door. It was attached to a wire clipped to his back and ending at an earpiece in his left ear. He stepped back. "Hot."

Ian nodded. "On three."

Eli counted with fingers. After two, Ian crashed his shoulder into the door. It gave way, and he tumbled into a hallway, followed immediately by Eli. By the time Jackson followed, Eli had already fired two silenced shots to the left, and Ian was crouching and facing right. Jackson moved straight ahead, into another hallway. He cleared a bathroom on the left, then kicked in a door on the right. A bullet spat into the wood beside him, and he dropped, at the same time leveling his gun.

More bullets bit into the door, and he somersaulted forward, into the darkened room. As he came to his feet, he swung the gun around and saw a burly figure moving toward the door. The shape was too big to be any of the girls, so Jackson plugged four slugs into him, felling him in the doorway.

Jackson jumped up, sweeping the darkened room with his eyes. Empty. He found a light switch and flicked it on as he kicked the gun away from the fallen man with his foot. The light revealed he was wearing robed garments, similar to those worn by the driver and the guard Jackson had taken out earlier.

Jackson turned back into the room, a bedroom with no windows and sparse furniture. He checked a closet, found it completely empty, and stepped back into the hall over the dead man.

"Clear!" Eli hollered back from the original hall. Jackson turned down his hallway and found another bedroom and a linen closet, both empty.

"Clear," he announced as he returned to the main hallway. "One down."

"Two," Eli said, meeting him from the right.

"None," Ian said. "Clear."

Joel and Rich were still huddled in the doorway. "Where are the girls?" Joel asked.

"Not here," Ian said. "I had a living room and kitchen."

"Bed and bath," Eli said.

"So where are they?"

"Yours dead?" Eli asked Jackson.

He nodded.

"Mine too. Let's search the place."

They spent five minutes combing the house, which actually opened from the living room onto a street at the top of a cliff above the original building Jackson, Joel, and Rich had entered earlier. There were no vehicles parked out front and no signs of activity. And there was nothing in the house to suggest where Maggie, Cara, and Aliana were being kept.

"Cell phones?" Ian asked.

"One," Eli said, "on the first guy I shot."

"Can you do anything with it?" Rich asked.

"I might know a guy."

"Were there any other side tunnels?" Jackson asked Ian.

"Dead ends."

"What about the gate?" Rich asked.

Eli looked at him. "What gate?"

"South in the main tunnel," Jackson answered. "An iron gate blocked the entire tunnel."

"What kind of lock?"

"Padlock."

"Let's try it," Eli said. "It's all we've got left."

"No," Jackson said. "Something still isn't right here."

"What do you mean?"

"I mean, what is this place? Who has a house connected by a winding staircase to an underground aqueduct that connects to another house on another street?"

"Probably some rather unsavory characters, yeah?"

"Right."

Joel shook his head. "What are you getting at?"

"Both of these houses have been just that. I haven't seen any gun racks, ammo stockpiles, hiding places."

"You think there's a secret door or something?"

"Maybe. Before we clear out, I think we should check it out again, with that specifically in mind."

They nodded and split up into two groups, checking over the house again. Jackson thought he was onto something when he kicked a rug aside in front of the kitchen sink, but there was no trap door as he'd hoped. But a few moments later, Ian's shout rang out from the bedroom he had originally cleared. The others quickly joined him.

The flimsy mattress and box springs from one of two twin beds had been tossed aside, leaving just a frame a few inches off the floor. Cut into the tiled floor was a wooden panel two feet square. One bang with the butt of Ian's gun caused a metal latch to loosen, and he grabbed the handle of the door. "Ready?"

Jackson and Eli both nodded, their guns trained on the opening.

Ian heaved it open, revealing a dark, steep set of stairs. Jackson handed Ian his flashlight, and he led the way down, the flashlight and the light strapped to his head providing ample light. Jackson was right on his tail, his finger over the trigger as Ian's lights revealed a twelve-by-twelve fieldstone cellar. The wall directly ahead was lined with shelves, but they were all empty. Ian rotated his light back along the staircase, and immediately he stopped.

Maggie, Cara, and Aliana sat on the floor, gagged and bound hand and foot. Aside from their restraints, they appeared unhurt, and as they recognized Jackson and Ian, their eyes went from wide with fright to tearful with relief.

Jackson actually tossed his gun to the side, then dropped down in front of Maggie. He removed her gag, a ragged strip of cloth. "Are you all right?"

She tried to speak, but only nodded instead as he reached around her to unbind her wrists. They too were tied with strips of cloth, and in a moment, he had undone her bonds. Immediately, Maggie wrapped her arms around his neck.

He held her for a moment and then pulled back, sweeping sweaty, tangled hair out of her face. "Are you okay? Did they hurt you?"

"No," she said. "I'm . . . thirsty."

"I'll get some water," Rich said.

"I don't know if I trust the water in this place," Jackson said. "We'll get something as soon as we can." He reached to untie Maggie's ankles while Eli and Ian untied Cara and Aliana. They were all wearing pajamas, all thirsty and weak, and all—save for some bruises and raw skin where their wrists and ankles had been trussed—uninjured.

"Let's get out of here," Jackson said.

"Yes," Aliana said. "The sooner, the better."

Eli led the way, and the other guys helped the women up the stairs and into the bedroom. Eli immediately went to the window and checked the street. "Clear."

"What do you have as far as transportation?" Jackson asked.

"A pair of motor bikes," Eli answered.

"We can all fit in the van," Rich said.

Jackson paused, not knowing how to split the group since he still wasn't sure who he could trust. Eli solved the dilemma.

"I'll go get the van," he said.

Jackson nodded as he reached for the keys. "Rich, you can show him where it is. While he drives, do what you can to make the back comfortable."

With a puzzled look on his face, Rich followed Eli back into the tunnel system.

Jackson turned to Ian. "You've got some explaining to do."

"How's that?"

"I think it can wait until we get out of here," Joel said.

"Where are we going?" Cara asked.

"Home," Joel answered.

"Really?"

"To get you back, we had to agree to leave Israel."

"Back from who?" Cara asked. "Who took us?"

"A Frenchman named Sauveterre," Ian said. "A member of the CC."

"Why?" Aliana asked.

"Ransom," Jackson said. "Our research and evidence for you. Only they double-crossed us."

"Then how did you find us?" Maggie asked.

"By hook or by crook."

"What's that supposed to mean?" Cara asked.

"I'll explain when we're clear."

"Are we still in danger?"

Jackson shrugged. "I'll be comfortable when we're at thirty thousand over the Mediterranean."

"Um, I don't think we can fly in these clothes," Maggie said. "And we don't have our passports."

"All in the van," Jackson said, peeking out the window. It would take Rich and Eli a couple of minutes to get down through the tunnel, then a couple more to drive around the block.

"How did they capture you?" Rich asked.

"I do not know," Aliana said. "They just showed up in our room. I woke up, and someone was standing over the bed. I tried to scream, but . . . They put something over my face, and I passed out."

"They had guns too," Maggie said. "I tried to elbow one of them and get away, but he grabbed my hair and pulled me back, and then gassed me."

"I never woke up until we were in the van," Cara said. "We were blindfolded until we were stashed in here."

"Inside man," Jackson said, glancing at Ian.

"Bribed somebody at the hotel, yeah? Else conned a key like we did."

"The Royal Palms needs to beef up their security," Joel said.

"We'll fill out an online comment card."

"So we're just flying home?" Cara asked. "Giving up?"

Joel nodded. "We're at a dead end anyway, and I don't feel like testing this Sauveterre character right now. It isn't worth losing lives over, at any rate."

Jackson heard a vehicle and glanced out the window again. It was the van, and he nodded. "Okay, gang, after me. Ian, guard our tail."

"Aye."

They all nodded, and Jackson led the way to the front door. He started to survey the surrounding block before opening the door, but Rich was already getting out the side door of the van. So Jackson yanked open the front door and darted outside. He swept his eyes and the gun right, up across the street, and left. Everything was dead except for two boys kicking a soccer ball at the end of the block. Jackson turned and watched Aliana, Cara, Joel, Maggie, and then Rich climb past him into the van.

"Where's Ian?" he asked.

Rich turned. "I don't know."

Jackson looked back at the house, then ducked his head into the van. "Maggie, was Ian on your six?"

"Yeah."

"He didn't come out?" Joel asked.

"No." Jackson turned to the driver's seat, which was also vacant. "Where's Eli?"

Rich paled. "I . . . I don't know. I got out and . . ."

"What's going on?" Cara asked.

"I don't know," Jackson said, pulling the door shut behind him. "Joel, you drive."

"We cannot leave Ian," Aliana said.

"He left us," Jackson answered. "And there's more to this than you know."

"Jackson?" Maggie asked.

"I'll explain once we're out of the West Bank, okay?" He turned to Joel and Rich. "Safeties on?"

They both checked and nodded.

"Okay, Joel, take her easy. Rich, find the passports in the backpack."

Eli had parked the van facing south, and Joel easily navigated back to *Derech HaShiloah*. From there, it was a short jaunt to the main drive that led along the southern edge of the Old City and back into the State of Israel. When they crossed the border, Jackson took a deep breath. But his relief was short-lived. They were still driving a van that had been commandeered from kidnappers. It could have been stolen or reported as stolen by the kidnappers, or merely suspicious to the already suspicious authorities. He spent a few minutes debating swapping the vehicle for the hour-long trip to Tel Aviv but decided against it.

They did stop at a modern gas station with a small convenience store near the outskirts of Jerusalem. With Jackson acting as a guard, his gun tucked into his pants, the women used the restroom to change and freshen up a little. Joel, meanwhile, called the airport and arranged flights. When Jackson, Maggie, Cara, and Aliana returned, he announced they were booked on a five-thirty flight to Rome.

"What times is it now?" Cara asked.

"Three-forty."

"Where to after Rome?" Aliana asked.

"We'll figure that out then. Jackson suggested getting the quickest flights out of the country."

The rest of the trip to Ben Gurion Airport was uninteresting, although Jackson kept a wary eye on their surroundings and the side-view mirror. They received some odd looks going through security, but there were no holds on their passports or last-minute calls to the guards to detain them. At a quarter after five, they boarded an Airbus A310 bound for Rome. Fifteen minutes later, it was screaming down the runway.

Sitting beside Maggie, Jackson closed his eyes as the wheels finally lifted, and the jet soared over the Israeli coast and out over the Mediterranean Sea.

Chapter Forty-Five

7:24 p.m. (Central European Time)

JACKSON SPENT THE flight watching the sea darken beneath them. His mind was on the events of the day, which felt like three days. It had started with Maggie, Cara, and Aliana missing from their hotel room, and now Maggie was sleeping beside him while Cara and Aliana dozed in the row in front of them. In between, terror so real it had been like a constant knife in Jackson's gut, even though he'd seldom taken the time to think about it. He once again realized he'd prayed for help too little, acted too much, and somehow—by the grace of God—still come out of another scrape. He'd killed another man—the total count was now thirty-five if Jackson was doing the math properly—and seriously wounded another. As was always the case, it was for a good cause, saving the lives of innocent women. But the number was taking its toll.

He glanced at Maggie, now in jeans and a blue T-shirt. Her hair was a little unkempt, and her head was resting at an awkward angle, likely giving her a stiff neck. She was still beautiful in that natural, no-effort way that she always was, and seeing her sleeping peacefully eased a little of Jackson's guilt and agony.

Behind them, Joel and Rich were both napping too. They had come through the entire ordeal admirably. It was bad enough for a civilian like Jackson to be thrust into a life-or-death, guns blazing chase through the West Bank. But neither of them had ever fired a weapon, and he had essentially required them to play SWAT with him. To their credit, neither of them had wilted. Or shot him in the *tookus* by accident.

Ian and Eli were still a mystery—one that had been steeping in Jackson's head all evening. Just when he was starting to consider the possibility that he had misjudged Ian, the Scotsman had disappeared. There were some serious loose ends to be tied up, along with unreturned rental cars, unclosed missing person reports, and unknown—as of yet—by the authorities collateral damage done by Jackson and Eli. He hoped Joel's connections and his lawyer Rachelle—and his liaison Ramón, if he was still part of Team Joel—could smooth that all out. For now, Jackson was happy to be headed home in one piece.

Maggie stirred, and Jackson gave up on watching the sea.

"Hey," he said.

She stretched as much as she could in coach. "Hey. Where are we?"

"Should be making our descent pretty soon. How you feeling?"

"Worse. Ugh. I feel like I've been sitting here for three days."

"A good night's sleep and you'll be as good as new."

Maggie sat up slightly. "Do you have a minute?"

"Well, I was thinking of parachuting into Rome, but . . ."

"A serious minute."

"Okay."

"I need to tell you something."

He sat up slightly too. "I'm listening."

"I had a lot of time to think while I was tied up in that basement, not knowing where I was, what was going to happen, if I'd live to see another day. I was terrified, and I started to think seriously about dying. It hit me . . . They could storm down those stairs at any minute and slit our throats. You and I faced death on that plane in Mexico, but this was different. This . . . I had time to sit there and think about it. In Mexico, at the Vasquez estate, I had hope that you would come and save me, but here . . . it was a wish at best."

He nodded.

"And I thought about everything you've said over the last couple of weeks. And years for that matter. And . . . I don't know, it all sort of suddenly seemed relevant. I've always resisted because I didn't think a religion based on something two thousand years old could matter now. But there I was, sitting in some cellar in Israel, where you turn a city block and turn back the centuries. I don't know how else to explain it other than it dawned on me that I wasn't ready to die. I mean, no one's ready to die, but more than that."

Maggie looked up, her blue-gray eyes connecting with Jackson. "I prayed, Jackson. I asked God to have mercy on my soul on the day I died—be it today or sixty years down the road. I don't know if I believe everything I'm supposed to—I don't even know exactly what I'm supposed to believe. I certainly don't understand it all. But I know what I've heard from you so many times, that Jesus walked the streets we walked just last week—that He died on a Roman cross—barbarism that seems suddenly more relevant after a night atop Masada, looking at the siege ramp and Roman camps on the desert floor. I know what the Bible says, that He died for me, shedding his blood to pardon the wrong I've done. All I can say is that's a concept that suddenly doesn't seem so far-fetched to me anymore."

"Maggie—"

"No, let me finish."

He nodded.

"I can't describe it, Jackson. I was still terrified. I shake now when I think about what . . . what could have happened. But there was also—while I was terrified, a part of me wasn't afraid anymore. I don't know, it's weird. Anyhow . . ." She fiddled with the hem of her shirt before looking back up. "I wanted you to be the first to know."

Jackson nodded again. "I'm glad, Maggie. Very glad."

"Me too."

He leaned over and kissed her cheek. "Welcome to the family." He sat back. "Sorry, that sounded corny. Like you just married into the mafia or something."

"Yeah, you sound like a mold-fitting, stereotypical Christian."

"Ouch."

"I was actually expecting some line about 'finding the true Calvary Treasure' or something."

"Hmm. Yeah, that would have worked. But seriously, Mags, don't feel bad about not understanding everything. I sure don't. You certainly have the basics, the important stuff. The Bible says the Holy Spirit will teach you what else you need to know."

She shook her head. "This still seems a little hokey to me. A Holy Spirit leading and guiding me. It just doesn't fit anything I know."

"Well, it's not some ethereal manifestation, at least not in my experience. There are days where I find Christianity and faith in God a little strange myself. I think that's all part of the journey. The important thing is you've started on it."

She leaned her head on his shoulder. "Thank you for not giving up on me, Jack. I gave you a lot of grief."

"What are friends for?"

"And thanks for saving me today. I can tell by the look on your face it wasn't pleasant."

"You're welcome, Maggie." He laid his head back and closed his eyes. "Just make sure I get good press this time."

*   *   *

Monday, February 25
11:06 a.m.

"ARE YOU sure about this?" Joel asked Jackson.

"Reasonably."

"You don't think we're in any danger?"

Jackson shook his head. "You know him better than anyone, but no."

Joel nodded. "Okay." He turned to the remaining four members of Team Joel. "Let's go."

Jackson, Maggie, Joel, Rich, Cara, and Aliana took their place in line, waiting to board a Douglas DC-9. After arriving in Rome the night before, they had decided to stay the night, giving everyone a chance to rest and sleep. They'd checked into a hotel near the airport and, before falling asleep, recapped the events of the past day while eating authentic pizza. The guys had filled in a few of the details, such as Ian's defection, Ramón's bailout, the ransom call, turning over the team's research, and the trail they had followed to find the women in the cellar. In turn, the women had recounted bits and pieces of conversations they had heard while being transported, including a slipped exchange between two of the men in French. But otherwise, the kidnappers had done a good job disguising their identities, saying little. Most importantly, Maggie, Cara, and Aliana all seemed to have come through the ordeal unscarred.

In the morning, Jackson had pitched his plan first to Joel, then to each of the other members of the team. It was a no-go, he had said, unless each one of them agreed. One after the other, and without much persuasion, they all had. Joel had then called the airport and booked six tickets to Paris with a stopover in Marseille.

The flight went quickly, touching down in France shortly before noon. Joel had also made arrangements to rent a van, and after grabbing some sandwiches to go for lunch, the team made its second journey in as many weeks toward Château LeCavalier high in the Alps. Along the way, Jackson outlined his reasoning to everyone again.

"First of all, we know that Philippe's ancestry points back to Leon of Toulon, A.K.A. Leon LeCavalier, the High Commander of the Knights Calvary back in 1187. Out of the Knights Calvary grew the *Chevaliers Calvaire*, the CC, who we have it from several sources are after the treasure or don't want the treasure found or whatever. Those sources include Ian's friend Eli who stated that a man named Sauveterre, a member of the CC, was in Israel. And he's the one Ian blamed for the kidnapping."

"Which would be based on Eli's intel," Joel said. "But do you trust Eli?"

"Yes and no. I'm just laying it all on the table here."

"Fair enough."

"Except for the slip into French Cara mentioned, the kidnappers spoke in English with a Middle Eastern accent. They were also dressed like Middle Easterners, which I'm guessing was to throw us off into thinking this was some form of treasure-hunting jihad. However, the guy I got the location from yesterday sort of lost his accent when I put a gun into his shoulder, they weren't offended when I insulted Allah—sorry, Ali—and I don't think many Arabs have blue eyes. That all points away from them being Muslim, and the slip into French would suggest it is their native tongue. That leaves us with two groups of people, *Liberté ou Mort* or the CC. As far as we know, *Liberté ou Mort* only came after us once, at Masada, and they came with lethal intent. On the other hand, we've been told the CC isn't big on violence, which seems to fit with what happened. The girls weren't harmed physically, and the guy guarding us seemed pretty nervous with the gun. I think they were first-timers too, which explains how any of us escaped."

"I'll buy the CC," Joel said. "It makes perfect sense, actually."

"All to keep us from finding the treasure?" Maggie asked.

"Or to find it themselves," Jackson said. "They're our Brotherhood of the Cruciform Sword."

"Okay," Aliana said. "But how does all this tie to Ian?"

"One, he knew you were kidnapped."

"Didn't he say he tried to call Ali yesterday morning?" Rich asked.

"He said that. But he didn't say why. Or why he split with all his bags and didn't come to any of us."

"He said he couldn't trust us," Rich said. "Or didn't know who he could. Same as us with him."

"Okay, I'll give you that one. But he also said he conned the front desk out of a keycard, which was the same trick I used. I seriously doubt they'd fall for the same room twice."

"I checked, and I do not have a call from Ian yesterday morning," Aliana said. "So how did he know we were missing?"

"Working theory . . . The CC took you, Philippe found out, and he informed Ian."

"How would Philippe find out?"

"Because I'm betting he's part of the CC, if not the head of it."

"So the CC kidnaps us against his will and then Philippe sends Ian to rescue us?" Cara asked.

"Something like that."

"So Ian isn't a bad guy?"

"Not in terms of kidnapping you, no. But as far as finding the treasure, I think he's working against the interests of Team Joel." He went on to give his reasons, from Ian's long-standing relationship with Philippe to being flush with cash presumably from being on the take, to the way Ian knew his way around Jerusalem despite never having "had the pleasure" of visiting Israel. Then there was Ian and Philippe both being on the phone at the same time Cara was texting Joel that half of the team had arrived in Kavala, Ian's texting after they decided to go to Israel, and his phone calls to and from "Monica" as the team was deducing the treasure was in Sanctifié Castle in Jordan.

"I admit, none of it's concrete," Jackson said. "But it definitely bears further investigation."

"And you think Philippe has answers to your questions?" Aliana asked.

"Yeah. Because the more I've thought about it—and I've thought a lot over the last day and a half—I think we nailed our interpretation perfectly. I think the Calvary Treasure was hidden in that cavity under the stairs in the tower at Sanctifié Castle. And I think somebody beat us to it. Not the CC, because they wouldn't have bothered kidnapping you three if they had. Which means someone else found it. And the only person who could have had the whole riddle—let alone the answer—is one of us. I think Ian relayed our findings to Philippe, who sent in another crew to retrieve it and cover their tracks."

"But I thought you said Philippe was part of the CC," Rich said.

"Yep. And I think he's playing both sides against the middle. Not being a murderer, when he found out his cronies had the women abducted, he sent Ian to the rescue."

"So isn't this dangerous?" Rich asked. "Going to him now and accusing him of taking the treasure?"

"Philippe's not a killer," Joel said.

"You also trusted Ian," Cara said.

"We all did," Jackson said. "And Ian isn't a killer either."

"So what are we getting out of this visit?" Maggie asked. "You surely don't think Philippe will hand over the treasure, do you?"

Jackson shook his head. "No. But he might let us see it. And if it's the object we all think it is, that's good enough."

"I still don't know about all this," Cara said.

"I'm not convinced either," Rich said.

"I gave you a chance to back out."

"Nobody's backing out," Cara said.

"Then we'll know soon enough," Joel said.

Château LeCavalier was still blanketed in snow when they arrived, but it lacked the cozy, romantic feel of the fresh-fallen powder from last time. They had not contacted Philippe, so Jackson hadn't been sure if they would be admitted past the gate. But the same austere feminine voice admitted them—albeit after a lengthy pause—and they parked and made the trek across the stone walkway to the massive front doors. Dufort, in another pantsuit, again greeted them and showed them into the same den where they had met Philippe last time. The room was brighter than before, and absent the host of the castle.

"Master LeCavalier will be with you shortly," Dufort announced, then stepped backward, closing the double doors behind her.

"You ready for this?" Jackson asked.

Joel nodded. "I think so."

They waited almost ten minutes, during which time Aliana remarked that the den seemed colder than last time. No fire, Rich observed.

At the stroke of three on the grandfather clock, the doors opened, and Philippe LeCavalier stepped through them. He wore a white sweater over a navy collared shirt, slacks to match the shirt, and loafers. In his left hand, he cupped a snifter of cognac, from which he took a sip before acknowledging his guests.

"Jo-el, what a pleasant surprise. To what do I owe the pleasure of another visit from you and your team?"

"Then you haven't heard?"

Philippe's brow furrowed. "Heard what?"

"Cara, Aliana, and Maggie were kidnapped from our hotel on the shore of the Dead Sea."

"My goodness," he said, setting down his cognac. "Are you ladies all right?"

They nodded.

"What ever happened?"

Jackson took his cue. "Your cronies grabbed them in the hopes of getting us off the hunt for the Calvary Treasure."

"My cronies?"

"The *Chevaliers Calvaire*," Jackson said.

If Philippe faltered, it was only for an instant. "Joel, what is he speaking about?"

"Some things don't add up, Philippe."

"And so you have come here to accuse me? I am wounded."

"If wishing made it so," Jackson muttered.

"Joel, our friendship goes back a long way. Please do not trespass upon my goodwill by allowing this comrade of yours to fling his accusations."

"Forgive him, please, Philippe, but there are several points we're hoping you can clarify for us."

After raking Jackson with a stern look, Philippe softened. "Of course, Joel. Anything."

He invited them to sit down, and Joel—with a few interruptions from Jackson—ran through a more detailed version of events since they had left Philippe two weeks ago. He also laid out the evidence that Jackson believed indicated Ian had been working for Philippe as a mole within Team Joel.

"That's preposterous," Philippe said when he was finished.

"That was bad enough, but then you had the girls kidnapped," Jackson said.

"I did no such thing!"

Jackson stood. "Then explain how Ian knew they were missing. Explain why their kidnappers spoke French. Explain why everything keeps tracing back to you."

"I have to explain nothing to you," Philippe said. "But I assure you, Joel, I had no part in any underhanded scheme—"

"Are you going to take any more of this pompous, self-righteous, faux indignation?" Jackson asked.

"Now just a minute," Philippe said, pushing himself up. "You come into my home and accuse me of all manner of nefarious activities, and I put up with it well enough. But when you insult me by suggesting I had anything to do with a heinous kidnapping, it is too much. My hands are clean in this matter, and I refuse to lis—"

Jackson lunged forward, grabbing Philippe by the collar and pushing him back onto his couch. "You lying sack of—"

He was cut off as Maggie, Joel, and Rich all pulled him back, forcibly sitting him down on another couch. He struggled against them, and Maggie and Rich practically had to sit on him to hold him in place.

"This is outrageous!" Philippe blustered, straightening his shirt. "I should call the authorities."

"You do that," Jackson said around Maggie's head. "Ask them to bring Interpol and the Israeli Police and the CIA for that matter. Your butt's going to end up in a sling, if they can find one big enough."

"Leave!" Philippe shouted. "I will not take this anymore!"

"I'm sorry, Philippe," Joel said. "But I'm afraid it's not that simple."

"What do you mean?"

"He means your little minion came clean," Jackson said. "Ian. He spilled his guts and told us everything. We also have phone records, showing his calls and texts to you at very incriminating moments."

Philippe whitened.

Jackson suddenly relaxed. "And the Oscar goes to . . ."

Philippe stared at him, his face slowly but surely narrowing into a frown. "What?"

"Your eyes just gave you away," Aliana said.

"N-no," he said. "I assure you, I had nothing to do with your kidnapping. In fact . . . I—I even . . ."

"You even what?" Joel asked.

"I called Ian," he said, his shoulders slumping. "When I found out you had been taken."

"So he was working for you?"

"Yes."

"For how long?"

"Always," Philippe answered. "He has been on my payroll since before the two of us parted ways."

"Why?"

"For the Calvary Treasure. Please, let me explain."

"Sure thing," Jackson said, unwrinkling his pants as Maggie and Rich retook their seats. "But first, do you think you could have your cute French server get us something to drink? I'm parched from playing Bad Cop."

Chapter Forty-Six

3:12 p.m.

PHILIPPE HAD CHRISTELLE bring in an assortment of beverages, and when everyone had something to drink, he stood, cognac in hand, and paced. "I am a direct descendant of Leon of Toulon, the legendary High Commander of the Poor Soldiers of Christ and the Cross of Calvary. I have never made it public, but I am also a member of the *Chevaliers Calvaire*, what remains of the order to this day."

He took a sip with a look on his face as if he had just admitted to capital murder.

"Although I am a member, our motives could not be more different. The *Chevaliers Calvaire* seek to stamp out Islam from the modern world, just as the original order sought Christendom's victory over the Muslim world."

"And you?" Jackson asked.

"Eliminating one world religion or another won't solve our problems. If anything, it will only add to them by inflaming the devout. But if we can look at history, truly study and understand it, perhaps we can resolve our conflicts differently here and now."

"And then we can all frolic in a field of flowers like little bunnies," Jackson said.

"Your attitude is quite insulting," Philippe said.

"So's being run off the road, shot at, and kidnapped."

"I told you, I had no part in the kidnapping, nor in running you off the road or any shooting. Joel, please let me finish."

"Go ahead, Philippe."

"I've long had 'the Father' and the journal, but they in themselves could never lead me to the Calvary Treasure. My body is not what it once was, and I've lost both the ability and the inclination to travel the world looking for artifacts and clues. When I realized several years ago that Joel had a similar interest in the Calvary Treasure, I realized I had my chance. He could be my legs."

"But when we split . . ."

"I knew you would find it one day. Ian was my way of keeping tabs on you. But I do not believe he would ever harm you, and he certainly never received any instructions from me toward that end."

"How did you find out about the kidnapping?" Joel asked.

"As I mentioned, I am a member of the *Chevaliers Calvaire*. They do not know of my personal pursuit of the Calvary Treasure, and in fact, I've given them my word that no one else would ever see 'the Father.'"

"Are they looking for it too?" Aliana asked.

"Indeed. They are probably the ones who have caused you grief. I know for a fact they have been keeping very close watch on your search. In addition to getting reports from Ian, I have also been well informed by my contact with the *Chevaliers Calvaire*."

"Not a guy named Sauveterre by any chance?" Jackson asked.

Philippe sat back down. "Yes. It was he who phoned me yesterday morning, letting me know that members of the *Chevaliers Calvaire*, without his approval, had taken three members of your team hostage. I immediately called Ian with the news. You must believe me, Joel. If you cannot forgive me for what I've done, I understand, but you mustn't hold against me this thing which I did not have a part in."

Joel turned to Jackson and the rest of the team.

"Do you or your pal Sauveterre have any connection to a Hugo LaPierre and his separatist movement?" Jackson asked.

Philippe frowned and shook his head. "I've never heard of him."

It fit, given the story from Shin Bet and Mossad that *Liberté ou Mort* had originated from a split amongst the Knights Calvary, but Jackson had wanted to be sure the rotund Frenchman had nothing to do with the attack on Masada.

"I guess that only leaves one more question," Joel said. "Did your people find the Calvary Treasure?"

Philippe nodded. "Ian kept me abreast of your deductive progress. Friday afternoon, he alerted me that you had a possible location."

"'Monica again, yeah?'" Jackson mimicked.

"I had a recovery team on standby," Philippe continued. "Ian said he could stall you for the rest of the day and night."

"He never said anything," Aliana said with a frown.

"He didn't have to," Joel said. "It took until the next day for Ramón to get us access and permission and for us to be ready to go anyhow."

Philippe resumed. "I sent them to Sanctifié Castle that night with orders to recover the treasure and bring it back to me, leaving no trace behind."

"Well, they certainly did a good job of that," Cara said.

"It was not easy."

"So you have it here?" Joel said. "The Calvary Treasure is in this castle right now?"

"No," Philippe answered, slowly shaking his head.

"Then where?" Aliana asked.

Philippe took a swallow of cognac before answering. "I destroyed it."

"You what?" Aliana spluttered.

"I destroyed it."

"Why?"

"Because I thought it would destroy us. It would only lead to more hate and dissension."

Joel shook his head for several seconds before managing to ask, "What was it?"

"A simple brown box, no larger than a shoebox, locked and sealed. Inside was a fragment of parchment, clearly aged, half rotted away, crumbling to dust." He paused for a sip and, likely, dramatic effect. "Only a handful of the words on the parchment were legible, written in Arabic."

"So you don't even know what it said?" Joel asked.

"Not true. I have studied Arabic for years. I'm quite fluent." To prove it, he turned to Aliana and spoke a short sentence.

"What did he say?" Rich asked.

"He said, 'I speak Arabic fluently. Please hear me out before you judge me.'"

Philippe bowed slightly.

"Go ahead," Joel said.

"The words and few sentences I could read were very fragmented, obviously, but they read like a *mea culpa*."

"How so?"

"Admitting to discrepancies, to deceit, to misleading. It also referenced gross misinterpretations of original intent. At the same time, it was an angry, passionate script, like that of a man possessed. Or terrified. The author several times expressed concern about his death, which he felt was drawing near."

"Who was the author?"

Philippe shook his head. "I do not know. That part was missing from the parchment. But it was addressed to Abu Bakr, dated in the year 632."

Aliana shook her head as he finished. "You allow no one else to read it? You allow no one to test it? To verify what you say?"

"Who's Abu Bakr?" Maggie asked.

"He was the father-in-law of Muhammad and the first Muslim caliph after Muhammad's death," Aliana answered. She then turned to Philippe. "Why? How could you so wantonly destroy something you spent years pursuing?"

"Because I know what people would have claimed the letter was. There is no proof it was written or dictated by Muhammad, nor enough in the words that remained to conclusively show he was attempting to counter his previous writings. But that is what people would claim. They would twist and distort the parts they could make out and use them as another Crusade against Islam." He shook his head. "For all we know, it was a hoax perpetrated by the Crusaders themselves to further their cause, with just such intent in mind."

"It could have been tested," Joel said. "The date could have been verified. Linguists could have compared it to Muhammad's other works."

"Joel, you yourself should know that skeptics and agitators will always find a way to use something like this against those they wish to assail. Imagine what this letter could have done to an already fragmented and fragile world, a world that is growingly hostile to Islam."

"Yes, but what if it was real and spoke the truth?" Jackson asked.

"What would truth matter?"

"Where have I heard that before?"

"Truth is in the eye of the beholder," Philippe said. "As long as we keep quibbling over matters of politics and religion, we can never achieve harmony."

"Unless your truth is wrong," Rich said.

"I have no truth."

"Here, here," Jackson said.

"Is nothing left?" Aliana asked. "No copies? Photographs? The box you found it in?"

"All destroyed, my dear. As far as the world knows, the treasure was never found, and I will deny any reports to the contrary to my grave."

"What about your other team?" Cara asked.

"The box was still sealed when it came to me, so none of them know what it contained. Even so, their loyalty has been purchased."

"Ian's too?"

Philippe nodded and drained his snifter of cognac.

"Speaking of the devil, where is he?" Jackson asked.

"You don't know?"

"All bluffing. We haven't seen him since he hightailed it out of the house in the West Bank."

"I haven't heard from him, other than a brief call to let me know you three ladies were safe." Philippe shrugged. "He's in the wind."

Joel and Aliana both appeared too stunned to speak. So Jackson stood. "Well, unless you've got any more duck for us, I think we got what we came for. Metaphorically, of course."

The rest of Team Joel stood.

So did Philippe. "Do you know how it pained me to destroy such a historical artifact? What I did, I did for the cause of humanity."

"Famous last words," Jackson said.

Joel shook his head. "I'm sorry, Philippe. I'm afraid . . . this cannot be forgiven."

Without another word, Joel led what remained of his team out of Château LeCavalier.

*   *   *

Tuesday, February 26
11:21 a.m.

TEAM JOEL arrived in Paris late morning. There had been no word from Ian, and none was expected. Ramón would turn up in time, Joel said. Just in time for the next hunt.

Joel had arranged for the team to have one final meal together, at a bistro inside Paris Charles De Gaulle Airport, before they split and went their separate ways. Joel, Rich, and Cara were headed to New York. From there, Rich and Cara would return to their respective homes, whereas Joel would meet with a few people on various matters unrelated to the Calvary Treasure before heading home himself to "put a bow" on their recent search. Aliana was on her way to London, via train, to consult on another matter. That left Jackson and Maggie waiting for a nighttime flight to Los Angeles. The jet lag would be brutal, but Jackson had nothing scheduled for the rest of the week other than sleep.

While they ate, Joel electronically transferred the appropriate payment to everyone's bank accounts. Though they hadn't found a treasure, he had agreed to pay each of them a flat fee in addition to any potential finders' fees. Jackson's total, for nineteen days of work, came to a tidy $9,500. Not a bad haul.

"I guess that's about it," Joel said as the meal was winding down. "I want to thank you all for everything. Although we came up empty, we did follow the clues to the end. I appreciate the hard work, long hours, and personal sacrifice each of you put in. I also want to apologize for subjecting you to the deceit and danger. Especially you three ladies. Believe me, if I'd had any idea that our search would lead to your kidnappings, I never would have left the States."

"We all knew what we were signing up for," Aliana said. "And everything turned out all right."

"Yeah, except that Philippe burned the Calvary Treasure," Cara said. "But he forgets we had a journalist along."

"Are you going to expose him?" Rich asked.

"That's up to Joel," Maggie said.

"No. I hired you to chronicle our journey and search, not to dictate what you wrote."

"If you claim Philippe found the treasure, what good will it do?" Aliana asked. "He will deny it, and there is no evidence to the contrary."

"But it's the truth," Maggie said. "If Joel has no qualms, that's what I'm going to write."

"You think your editor will run it?" Aliana asked.

Maggie shrugged. "If he doesn't, I'm sure I can find a buyer somewhere. A story like this . . ."

"Only without the happy ending," Joel said. He slapped both of his thighs. "But, that's the way it goes sometimes."

"What if he's bluffing?" Cara asked.

"Philippe?"

She nodded. "Maybe he just told us that to get us to leave. He could have it stashed in that high-tech tower vault."

"If so, it's as good as lost," Joel said. "No one will ever see it. Philippe wasn't lying about not wanting to make it public, and I seriously doubt he plans to sell it."

"Well, then," Jackson said, "until his estate sale . . ."

"What frustrates me is that he shouldn't be the one to make that decision. We can't rewrite history. Whatever the letter stated, whoever wrote it . . . It deserves to come out. Let the world reach their own conclusions."

"I agree," Aliana said. "Islam does not need protection. It has stood the test of time."

Jackson shrugged. "I don't think it would have mattered anyway."

"What?" Cara asked.

"Philippe was right about one thing. If the letter was what he stated, it would have just caused more hostility and friction."

"I didn't picture you for the 'coexist' type," Rich said.

"I'm not. But it's like Jesus said, '*they will not be convinced even if someone rises from the dead.*' Some thousand-year-old, half-missing letter with no signature and no means of confirmation certainly wouldn't shake the faith of anyone."

There were still plenty of loose ends: Who had run them off the road after leaving Philippe's the first time? Who had broken into their hotel in Kavala? What was Interpol's connection to the treasure and who within the agency was good or bad? What was the true nature of Philippe's relationship with the CC and with Sauveterre in particular? And how had the French separatist group come to track Team Joel and attack them on Masada, and what remained of the group? Those questions might never be answered. But it didn't really matter, they concluded. The treasure was gone, and they were all safe.

After everyone had finished eating and Joel had paid one final bill, the group said their goodbyes. Aliana's train departed before their flights, so they saw her off to a shuttle that would take her to the railway station. She hugged each of the members of the team, saving Jackson for next to last, right before Joel.

"Goodbye, Jackson. I will miss our conversations."

He grinned. "I'm not sure if that makes me Tom Cruise or Ken Watanabe."

Aliana frowned.

"I will too," he said. "Goodbye."

She said her goodbye to Joel and turned for the shuttle.

Joel, Rich, and Cara's flight departed some forty-five minutes later, and by the time the group reached their gate, it was in the early stages of boarding.

Jackson offered Rich a hand. "It was nice working with you," he said sincerely.

"You too, Jackson."

"No visions about our flight home, I hope?"

"None."

Jackson nodded with a smile, still unsure what to make of Rich's "visions." Not that he didn't believe God could do such a thing; he just didn't believe God did. Yet, Rich was seeing something. God? The devil? Heartburn? Random dreams? Another unsolved mystery.

"Goodbye, Jackson," Cara said, reaching up to give him a hug. "We couldn't have done it without you."

"I was going to say the same thing," he said. "And for the record, I like you a lot better than the last Canadian I met."

"I guess I'll take that as a compliment."

He winked at her as Joel offered him a handshake that turned into a bro hug that turned into backslapping, at least on Joel's part. "Thank you, Jackson. I'm with Cara. I don't know if we would have made it out of Israel without you. I'm forever indebted."

"I couldn't have done it alone."

"You take care of yourself."

Jackson nodded. "If you ever decide to track down the Ark of the Covenant or the lost city of Atlantis or something . . ."

"You're my first call," Joel said.

The goodbyes said, the trio got in line. Jackson and Maggie waited until they had entered the Jetway before taking a leisurely stroll down to their gate. Their flight didn't leave until six-twenty, touching down in Los Angeles twelve hours later, at quarter after nine local time.

They sat down at their gate, which wasn't even boarding the flight ahead of theirs yet. After watching airport scenery out the window for a little while, Jackson went in search of something to eat. He returned with a vending machine bag of M&M's.

"We just ate," Maggie said. "How can you eat those?"

"My mouth's bored," he said through several pieces of candy. "Besides, I'm not going to let one traitorous Scotsman steal my milk chocolatey joy." He held the bag to her, but she declined.

"Can I ask you something?" she said as he popped a few more M&M's.

"Yup."

"Remember how I used to pester you—"

"Yes."

She gave him the evil eye. "How I used to pester you about sex?"

"Yeah."

"And you told me that sex was something you were saving for marriage?"

He nodded.

"And how marriage was the culmination of a relationship built on the foundation of a shared faith in Jesus?"

"I don't think I ever put it that eloquently."

"You didn't."

"Yeah, I remember."

"Well . . ."

Jackson turned to face her, lowering the bag of M&M's to his lap. "Are you proposing to me now that you're a Christian?"

"No." She rolled her eyes.

"Because, I mean, we are in Paris, and the crowded-airport-drop-to-one-knee is sort of romantic, I guess."

"Like I'd want to share that moment with a bunch of strangers."

He nodded. "So me someday having the Trojan Marching Band spell out 'Marry me, Maggie?' at halftime of a USC game is out then? Noted."

"Can you be serious with me for a minute?"

He smiled and focused on her blue-gray eyes.

She took a breath. "The basis you had for not entering a quote-unquote relationship with me was that I wasn't a Christian."

"That wasn't the only reason."

Maggie's eyes narrowed and turned a little more gray than blue. "What else?"

"I wasn't sure either of us was ready for a quote-unquote relationship. It seemed we were both good with it being casual."

"I see."

"Are you saying you're ready for a relationship?"

Maggie shrugged. "There aren't any barriers in the way."

"No. No, there aren't."

Her turn to look him in the eyes. "I guess . . . I'm game if you are."

Jackson smiled.

"What?"

"I think that was actually how my dad proposed to my mom."

She whacked his shoulder.

He chugged some M&M's.

"Now you're stalling."

He shook his head and swallowed. "I'm trying to figure out how to say this."

"Just say it, Jackson. If you're not ready, that's fine. We can keep it casual. I just won't pester you about sex."

"It's not a no, Maggie. It's a not right now."

She nodded. "That's okay."

"Let me finish. You just made the most important decision of your life. I don't think this is the time to rush into a relationship."

"You think I did this so you and I could go steady?"

"No. I think that we're coming off a huge emotional roller coaster, at the bottom of which you made a very significant personal decision. And a relationship—of any sort—is another emotional roller coaster, especially at the beginning. I just think it makes sense to get the wobbles out of your knees between rides."

"I think I follow."

"Besides, coming to faith in Christ isn't the end. It's the beginning, like we talked about yesterday."

"That was two days ago."

"Whenever. Time has lost all meaning to me. But the point is, now you get the ups and downs and twists and turns of the Christian life. Talk about a roller coaster. I think maybe for a little while, that should be preeminent in your life."

"Isn't there room for both?"

"I don't know," he said. "I suppose there is. I just think we'd be better off if we waited a few weeks, maybe a month, before we make any relationship decisions."

"You're not making an excuse?"

"No. Scout's honor."

"You weren't a Scout."

"Honest, Mags. No excuses. I meant what I said. Every word."

She nodded. "Okay. That works for me."

He had some more candy.

"So for now, does that still leave us in our casual whatever-we-call-it?" she asked.

"Yeah, I guess." He shrugged as Sam briefly flashed through his mind. "It's worked pretty well so far."

"It has," she agreed. Then she dropped her head onto Jackson's shoulder. "Got any casual plans for this weekend?"

"No, and I should be awake by then. What'd you have in mind?"

Author's Note

I HAVE TRAVELED extensively in France, Greece, and the Middle East—all via Google. I did my best, considering the limitations of the internet and my abhorrence of research, to depict these places accurately. That said, I utilized artistic interpretation to drop castles onto barren mountaintops, erect border crossings where they don't exist, and dig tunnels only Hezekiah could confirm or deny. Many of the places, people, and events referenced in *Blood and Treasure* are real. Many more are the product of my imagination. Some are a combination of the two. To those who have visited these actual locales or more thoroughly researched world history and can spot my errors, my apologies. (To those who haven't and can't, disregard this paragraph.) It was never my intent to misrepresent anyone or anything or to blur history; just the opposite. I tried to use real events and places as much as the plot would allow.

That being said, Masada is real, and was depicted in this novel as accurately as possible. Like my protagonist, I have long been fascinated by this fortress in the desert and the blood-chilling history surrounding it. Someday, I'd like to see it in person.

There is, to my knowledge, nothing to suggest Muhammad ever dictated or wrote a letter invalidating Islam. It was not my intent to suggest there was, but merely to drive a novel's plot. Hence the ending. It was my intent, however, to show the differences between Islam and Christianity. They are distinct and carry monumental consequences, and ultimately come back to the centuries old question, who is Jesus? The Christian answer—the biblical answer—is quite clear, as are the implications. And I believe the Christian/biblical answer stands up to scrutiny and warrants a response of faith. That was what I tried to convey, using the vehicle of a novel. Some of you may not like being "preached at" while reading, and I get that. I hope it didn't come across as a sermon, but I do hope it compelled you to ask the question, if you haven't previously, "Who is Jesus?"

As usual, I had a great deal of support while writing and editing this book. Much thanks to my wife, Sierra; my parents, Doug and Jean Birr; my sister and brother-in-law, Tiffani and Mark Robinson; and my wife's aunt, Chris Hembel, for proofing and listening to numerous ideas. Thanks also to all who have added their encouragement and provided feedback for my writing.

It has been quite an adventure with Jackson Douglas, and there's a lot more in store! I hope you'll keep reading.

www.ingramcontent.com/pod-product-compliance
Lightning Source LLC
Chambersburg PA
CBHW020929020726
47495CB00002B/421

* 9 780099 818135 6 *